PRAISE FOR

THE CITY OF
LOST FORTUNES

A *LIBRARY JOURNAL* BEST BOOK OF 2018

"A masterly game played by gods and monsters, a devastated city trying to rebuild, and compelling characters struggling to find their place in a strange world are all pieces of this fantastic and enthralling puzzle of a story . . . Camp's thoroughly engaging debut is reminiscent of Neil Gaiman's *American Gods,* with the added spirit of the vibrant Big Easy."

—*Library Journal,* starred review, Science fiction/
Fantasy debut of the month

"A phantasmagoric murder mystery that wails, chants, laments, and changes shape as audaciously as the mythical beings populating its narrative . . . boisterously ingenious debut novel . . . For a first-time novelist, Camp shows adroitness in weaving the real-life exoticism of present-day New Orleans with his macabre alternate universe that's almost—what's the word—supernatural. (Among the unique characters attending a burial service for one of the murder victims: a centaur, a hairy giant, and 'a fat brown-skinned man with the head of an elephant.') Things only get weirder and more intense from there, but the engaging style, facility with folklore, and, above all, impassioned love for the city its characters call home keeps you enraptured by the book's most chilling and outrageous plot twists. One hopes for more of Camp's dangerous visions to spring from a city that, as he writes, 'is a great place to find yourself, and a terrible place to get lost.'"

—*Kirkus Reviews,* starred review

"There isn't a dull page as Jude determines who his real friends are. Anne Rice fans will enjoy this fresh view of supernatural life in New Orleans, while fans of Kim Harrison's urban fantasy will have a new author to watch." —*Booklist*, starred review

"A deft and expansive fantasy imbued with real magic and wild plot turns." —Kelly Link, author of
Pulitzer Prize finalist *Get in Trouble*

"Camp's fantasy reads like jazz, with multiple chaotic-seeming threads of deities, mortals, and destiny playing in harmony. This game of souls and fate is full of snarky dialogue, taut suspense, and characters whose glitter hides sharp fangs . . . Any reader who likes fantasy with a dash of the bizarre will enjoy this trip to the Crescent City." —*Publishers Weekly*

"A complex story that seduces the reader into a Crescent City filled with beauty and danger, loss and hope . . . seeking New Orleans and finding his own secret city . . . is Camp's true magic as a writer." —*New Orleans Advocate*

"Camp clearly cares for the Crescent City's soul, and he brings its scenes to sweltering life: the cafés, cemeteries, flood-damaged ruins, low-life bars, botanicas, pelican-skimmed causeways, diners, guard dogs, festivals—a phantasmagoric panorama of a true urban fantasy." —*Seattle Review of Books*

"With mysticism emanating from every page, Bryan Camp paints a stunningly deceptive post-Katrina New Orleans in his debut, *The City of Lost Fortunes* . . . Camp succeeds in creating an alluringly magical fantasy realm, and he also knits it seamlessly into the reality of a vibrant New Orleans. *The City of Lost Fortunes* is a composition as stunning as the music that springs from its Louisiana setting. Play on, Bryan Camp, play on." —*Shelf Awareness*

"Take a walk down wild card shark streets into a world of gods, lost souls, murder, and deep, dark magic. You might not come back from *The City of Lost Fortunes*, but you'll enjoy the trip."

—Richard Kadrey, best-selling author of
the Sandman Slim series

"In *The City of Lost Fortunes*, Bryan Camp delivers a high-octane tale of myth and magic, serving up the best of Neil Gaiman and Richard Kadrey. Here is New Orleans in all its gritty, grudging glory, the haunt of sinners and saints, gods and mischief-makers. Once you pay a visit, you won't want to leave!"

— Helen Marshall, World Fantasy Award–winning
author of *Gifts for the One Who Comes After*

"Bryan Camp's debut novel, *The City of Lost Fortunes,* is like a blessed stay in a city both distinctly familiar and wonderfully strange, with an old friend who knows just the right spots to take you to — not too touristy, and imbued with the weight of history and myth, populated by local characters you'll never forget. You'll leave sated with the sights and sounds of a New Orleans that is not quite the real city, but breathes like the real thing, a beautiful mimicry in prose that becomes its own version of reality in a way only a good story — or magic — can. You won't regret the visit."

— Indra Das, author of *The Devourers*

"With sharp prose and serious literary chops, Bryan Camp delivers a masterful work of contemporary fantasy in *The City of Lost Fortunes*. It reads like the New Orleans–born love child of Raymond Chandler and Neil Gaiman, featuring a roguish hero you can't help but root for. It's funny, harrowing, thrilling — the pages keep turning. *The City of Lost Fortunes* establishes Bryan Camp as the best and brightest new voice on fantasy literature's top shelf."

— Nicholas Mainieri, author of
The Infinite

THE CITY OF
LOST FORTUNES

THE CITY OF
LOST FORTUNES

BRYAN CAMP

A John Joseph Adams Book
Mariner Books
HOUGHTON MIFFLIN HARCOURT
Boston   New York

First Mariner Books edition 2019
Copyright © 2018 by Bryan Camp

For information about permission to reproduce selections from this book,
write to trade.permissions@hmhco.com or to Permissions,
Houghton Mifflin Harcourt Publishing Company,
3 Park Avenue, 19th Floor, New York, New York 10016.

hmhco.com

Library of Congress Cataloging-in-Publication Data
Names: Camp, Bryan, author.
Title: The city of lost fortunes / Bryan Camp.
Description: Boston : John Joseph Adams/Houghton Mifflin Harcourt, 2018. |
Series: A Crescent City novel
Identifiers: LCCN 2017054025 (print) | LCCN 2017045346 (ebook) |
ISBN 9781328810816 (ebook) | ISBN 9781328810793 (hardcover) |
ISBN 9781328589828 (paperback)
Subjects: LCSH: New Orleans (La.)—Fiction. | Psychic ability—Fiction. |
Magic—Fiction. | BISAC: FICTION / Fantasy / Contemporary. | FICTION /
Fantasy / Urban Life. | FICTION / Fairy Tales, Folk Tales, Legends &
Mythology. | FICTION / Fantasy / General. | GSAFD: Fantasy fiction.
Classification: LCC PS3603.A4557 (print) |
LCC PS3603.A4557 C58 2018 (ebook) | DDC 813/.6—dc23
LC record available at https://lccn.loc.gov/2017054025

Book design by David Futato

Printed in the United States of America
DOC 10 9 8 7 6 5 4 3 2 1

Illustrations: *The Magician* licensed from Jeffrey Thompson/Shutterstock.
The Hermit, *Wheel of Fortune*, *The Hanged Man*, *The Fool*, and *Judgment* licensed
from Jeffrey Thompson/Cutcaster.

To New Orleans, my city; and to Beth Anne, my home

PART ONE

IN THE BEGINNING, there was the Word, and the Void, and Ice in the North and Fire in the South, and the Great Waters. A universe created in a day and a night, or billions of years, or seven days, or a cycle of creations and destructions. The waters were made to recede to reveal the land, or the land was formed from the coils of a serpent, or half of a slain ocean goddess, or the flesh and bones and skull of a giant, or a broken egg. Or an island of curdled salt appeared when the sea was churned by a spear. Or the land was carried up to the surface of the waters by a water beetle, or a muskrat, or a turtle, or two water loons. However the world was made, it teemed with life; populated by beings who evolved from a single cell, or who were molded from clay or carved out of wood or found trapped in a clam shell. They wandered up from their underworld of seven caves, or fell through a hole in the sky, or they crawled out of the insect world that lies below. All of these stories, these beginnings, are true, and yet none of them are the absolute truth; they are simultaneous in spite of paradox. The world is a house built from contradictory blueprints, less a story than it is a conversation. But it is not a world without complications. Not without conflicts. Not without seams.

One of those complications was a man named Jude Dubuisson, flesh and blood and divine all at once, who stared out at Jackson Square, at the broad white expanse of St. Louis Cathedral, at the plump, fluttering mass of pigeons, at the tidal ebb and flow of tourists on the cobblestones, and saw none of it. He was likewise deaf to his surroundings: the constant mutter of the crowd, the hooves clopping on pavement, and the hooting echo of the steamboat's calliope coming from the river. His attention was fixed inward, on thoughts of the old life he'd done his best to forget. All those years of standing between the worlds of gods and men, of the living and the dead.

For his entire adult life, he'd straddled the seam between two worlds and brought trouble to both: a walking, breathing conflict with a fuck-you grin. That had been before the storm, though. Those memories belonged to a different man. In the six years since those fateful days in 2005, he'd tried to put it all behind him. Tried to ignore all the impossible things he knew. But the last few days, the past was like a storm cloud on the horizon, a rumble of thunder that refused to stay silent, a gloom that refused to disperse.

The past just refused to stay dead.

Jude was what the more liberal-minded in the city these days —those for whom the term "mixed race" sounded somehow offensive—would call "Creole," and what older black folks referred to as "red-boned," some indeterminate mix of white and African heritages along with whatever else had made it into the gumbo. All Jude knew was that he had light brown skin, a white mother, and a father he'd never met. The rest of the world always seemed more concerned about defining his ethnicity than he was.

He kept his hair shaved close to his scalp and a scruff of beard that was more stubble than style. He wore jeans and a long-sleeved dress shirt despite the cloying wet shroud that clung to New Orleans in the summer, the heat that made any act an effort, even breathing. The damp shirt pressed tight against his skin, the sweat tickling down the small of his back. Jude reached up, absently, to wipe off his face with the handkerchief his mother had taught him a gentleman always carries, but stopped himself, pulled from his introspection by the self-conscious awareness of the leather gloves he had on. He tucked his hand back into his lap, out of sight.

Not that anyone paid him any attention. He'd been out on the corner right across from Muriel's since early that morning, had set up folding chairs and his rickety-ass table, laid out a chalkboard sign, a cash box, and a battered paperback atlas the same as he did most days, but in all the hours he'd been in the Square, only a few people had bothered to ask what the sign meant. None sat down. His services, unlike the tarot card readers and the brass bands and the art dealers, weren't part of the cliché of the Quarter, and thus flew under the average tourist's radar.

But today the lack of clients suited his mood. He'd have found it hard to feign interest in anyone's problems with the way his thoughts had been circling nonstop. Pacing back and forth, as tense and feckless as an expectant father. Or a criminal awaiting execution.

A young street performer—Timmy? Tommy? Jude could never remember—stopped in front of Jude's table, casting a long shadow. Jude frowned at the intrusion into his thoughts, even as he appreciated the shade. The white kid's face, streaked with the sweaty remnants of clown paint, was split by an unguarded grin. He wore a golf cap and a tweed vest with no shirt on underneath. Less than ten years separated the two men, maybe as little as five, but to Jude's eyes he was just a boy.

Grown more used to silence than speech, Jude had to search for his voice before he could speak. "You need something?" he asked, the words scratchy.

"About to ask you the same thing," the boy said, pulling off the cap and swiping sweat from his forehead. "Headed to the grocery 'round the corner." He gestured with the limp hat in the store's direction before slipping it back onto his head.

Jude shook his head. "Thanks anyway."

"Ain't nothin'," he said. He turned to go, then looked back. "You coming tomorrow night?" Jude shrugged and raised his eyebrows. The boy threw his hands into the air. "I only told you, like, twelve times already. My band finally got that gig? At the Circle Bar?"

"Oh, right," Jude said. He imagined being crammed into a tight space with a crowd of strangers and lied to the kid. "Yeah, I'll try to make it."

The boy's grin widened into a smile that took another five years off his age and made Jude feel like an older, more cynical version of himself. Tommy moved on to the next table, the sole of one of his shoes flapping, pitiful, on the street.

Jude sighed, inhaling the rich odor of the Quarter: stale beer and musky humanity and the moist, dark scent of the river. It was hard to live as he did, hidden in the seams between the life he had known and this new life he wore like a mask, but—because of those things he tried not to think about—Jude belonged there.

Or so he believed.

A short while later, Jude got his first and only customers of the day, a couple of out-of-towners. College kids, judging by the Greek letters on their T-shirts and the bright green plastic drink cups in their hands. She was a white girl who had spent hours in the sun darkening her skin, and he was vaguely West Asian, but spoke with a tap-water American accent. Lovers, Jude guessed, from the way the boy rested his hand on her shoulder, and the way the girl introduced the both of them—Mandy and Dave—like the conjunction made them a single unit. The girl seemed by far the more eager of the two. When she asked Jude what his sign meant, Dave looked toward the other side of the Square, as if searching for an escape.

"It means what it says," Jude said. "If you've lost something, I can tell you where it is."

"Like, anything?" Mandy asked, glancing at Dave to see if he was listening.

"Yeah," Jude said, "like, anything." She seemed not to notice the droll mockery in his voice, but Dave turned and frowned at her.

"It's a scam," Dave said.

"First try is free if you're not satisfied," Jude said. "Ten bucks if you are."

Dave's frown deepened, but Mandy lowered herself into one of the aluminum chairs across from Jude. "Come on, sweetie, let me at least try it. Mom'll kill me if she finds out—" She turned a sly glance in Jude's direction. "If she finds out I lost what I lost." Dave made an incredulous sound in the back of his throat and checked the time on his phone, doing everything but tapping his foot to signal his impatience. His every gesture told Jude he'd been hustled before.

But Jude was no hustler, at least not today. He'd always had an affinity for lost things. Even as a child, he could point out that a friend had left a toy beneath a sofa cushion, could lead a neighbor to where her cat had stranded itself too high in a tree.

This magic was the one true gift Jude had ever gotten from the father he'd never known. As he aged, or with practice—Jude wasn't sure which—this affinity strengthened, grew more nuanced. A brush of his fingertips against a hair left on a pillow and he knew the lost child's name, knew that she was hungry and cold and alone, knew that she was locked in a basement in Ohio, even though she'd only vanished from her room a few days before.

The more complex the loss, though, the more cryptic his gift became. Sometimes deciphering the sensations and visions was impossible. Some things *wanted* to stay lost. But far more often than not, his magic worked. This power had lived at the core of him, became the foundation he'd built his life upon. He'd always been the man who could find things.

Then came the hurricane, and a rip at the seams.

The seam split between a government and its citizens when the levees that were built to protect . . . didn't. It split between the people of New Orleans and their lives, the lucky ones cast out like dandelion seeds thrown by a fierce wind. The stitches that held together communities and families and homes strained in that wind. Some frayed, some tore. In the flood of lost things that followed, the space inside of Jude where his magic lived ripped open wide.

In the aftermath, Jude found his power had become a raw, unhealing wound. Something fundamental about his gift had changed, had turned on him. Before, he'd had to focus, to reach for the knowledge his magic could give him. After, he could barely hold it at bay. Like many after the storm, he'd done what he could to numb his senses to all the loss around him. Booze, sex, any number of bad decisions. It worked, but only for a while. His power was too much a part of him to be denied. Eventually, he'd figured out that if he didn't touch anything or anyone — hence the gloves — and if he released a trickle of his magic every few days, he could manage, just barely, to stay sane. For six years he'd survived, though he couldn't really call it living, not going back to his old life, unable to move on to anything new, each day nearly identical to the one before. He'd tucked himself quietly away in the seams, like a coin lost beneath the sofa cushions. Being nowhere and nothing, he'd decided, was better than feeling all that loss.

Jude slipped off his glove beneath the table and a rush of sensation flickered along his naked skin, like the pins and needles of returning circulation. He reached out and took the girl's slender hand in his own, focusing on the single item she sought. If he had merely touched her, he would have seen and felt everything she'd lost in her young life. Even a seemingly happy and pampered girl like her would have lost enough to exhaust him.

"Your mother's earrings are in your hotel room," Jude said.

Dave let out a sharp, bitter laugh. "Good guess, Sherlock," he said. "Real big leap to see that we're tourists. Do people really fall for this?"

Jude's first instinct was to tell Dave just how far up his patronizing ass he could put his attitude, but he held his tongue for Mandy's sake. She was a good kid. That wasn't just a first impression; Jude *knew* she was, could feel it through her skin. "Not where you're staying in New Orleans," Jude said. He flipped through the atlas with his free hand, opening it to the Louisiana section, flipping to the map of Baton Rouge, and dropping his finger onto a street intersection without looking. "Were you here at any point in the last few days?" Mandy gasped and pulled her hand away. Jude fought the urge to smile. He'd phrased the last part as a question, but he'd known he was right. He knew more, the name of the hotel, the room number, that the two of them had snuck away from a church youth group–sponsored protest at the Capitol Building for a day of sin in the Crescent City, but he'd learned that if he got too specific, people went from intrigued to scared. Dave took a ten out of his wallet and sat down.

"The next one is twenty," Jude said.

Fifteen minutes and fifty dollars later, Jude said something dubious and vague enough that Dave's cynicism returned, and they left. Jude could have kept them there all night, parceling out the answers to the little mysteries of their little lives until their cash ran out, but the money meant nothing to him. This petty game with the tourists was all about the release valve for his gift.

He'd been so much more than this, once.

Later, as he started to pack up his belongings, he saw that Mandy had left her phone behind. It looked more like a child's toy than a piece of technology: a pink flip phone covered in rhinestones. *If only she knew someone who could find lost things,* he thought, smiling for what felt like the first time in days. As soon as he picked it up, as if bidden by his touch, the phone jumped and buzzed. Jude snatched it open, startled. An incoming text from an unknown number.

Meet me for a drink in an hour, the message said. *The usual place, very important. Have something for you.* Then, as he read, the phone twitched with another message. It read, *This is Regal.*

Jude started to type a reply, but sighed and snapped it closed instead. Regal wouldn't take no for an answer.

An hour to make it Uptown. He could get there easily if he had a car—or a driver's license, for that matter—but he didn't. He dismissed the idea of a cab, as well. If the streetcar didn't get him there in time, Regal could wait. Or she wouldn't, and that would be fine, too. It wasn't like he actually *wanted* to see her.

On his way out of the Quarter, he dropped the fifty dollars he'd skimmed from Mandy and Dave into the upturned hat of three kids tap-dancing on the corner. He could tell himself that meeting Regal was only professional curiosity, that he was only going to find out what magic she'd used to find him through a stranger's phone, but he knew the truth. What gnawed at him was the more basic question of her reaching out to him at all. What could be so important that she'd track him down? What could she have for him that she wouldn't have given him years ago? Was this why the past had been churning around in his mind lately?

Of all the things that had been lost in this city, why had she bothered to find *him?*

Walking into St. Joe's bar was like descending into a cave and discovering a chapel. The shock of the colder air made Jude's skin prickle and every hair stand on end. Dozens of crosses hung from the ceiling, not one of them resembling the next, one simple and carved out of wood, another an ornate twisting of wrought iron. The dusty scent of years of cigarette smoke and the sweet, green odor of fresh-cut mint leaves filled the tight space, coating the worn church pews and the high bar and the mirrors on the walls, dull in the dim light. Across the pool table in the back of the room, a dark hallway led past an ancient, churning ice machine and the toilets and out to a small patio. Speakers in high corners played a Rebirth song, sharp bursts of brass instruments at a frantic, exuberant beat. The whole front of the bar had been a plate-glass window once, but plywood covered it now. Boarded up since the storm.

Jude squinted against the sudden darkness, saw that he'd gotten there before Regal. The bar had only three other customers this early in the afternoon, a Vietnamese man playing a touchscreen game on the bar and a young, blond white woman talking to the scruffy Latino guy behind the counter. The bartender's hands were busy chopping mint for the mojitos St. Joe's was known for, but his eyes remained fixed on the girl, a slight smile on his thin lips. She stretched, her shirt pulling up and revealing the dimple of flesh where her lower back met the curve of her buttocks. Jude pushed down a sudden surge of lust. He looked away and leaned against the bar, trying to keep his distance from all of them.

The man playing the video game was middle-aged but prematurely toughened by years of smoking and hard drinking. He stared, vacant, tapping the screen and feeding it dollar bills and taking long drags off his cigarette without ever changing his expression. Jude's fingertips tingled. Right beneath his sternum something sharp and insistent, like a fishhook piercing the core of him, yanked taut and yearned toward the man, toward his sense of loss. The man called himself Lee—the latter half of "Willy," not Bruce—even though his parents had named him William, after his father. Lee hated William Sr. and wanted no connection to him. But he'd always felt like he'd lost something, in not having a father he could admire.

Jude cursed silently and clenched his hands into fists. Sometimes things leaked in even with the gloves, especially around strangers. This was a mistake. He shouldn't have come here. To hell with Regal and whatever she had for him. Just as Jude decided to leave, the bartender noticed his presence and slouched over, with a curt nod and a "Whatcha need?" Jude ordered an Abita and eased onto the stool, keeping his gloved hands out of sight below the counter.

Regal's got until I finish this beer, he told himself, and then, like she'd timed it that way, the door opened and there she was, framed by the fading sunlight.

She'd cut her hair. What he remembered as an auburn silky drape down to her shoulders was now clipped short and spiky. The rest of her hadn't changed, though. Her deep-set eyes remained that clear, molten brown, like honey. The grin that slanted across her full lips still straddled the line between amused and mocking. She was a small white woman, both short and petite, who moved across the room with the confident glide of someone twice her size and the grace of a woman who knew how to handle herself.

"Dubuisson," she said. "It's been too long." Despite everything — the sleepless nights, his unease at being out in the world, this life colliding once again with his own, the tendrils of loss twisting and curling into the cracks in his resolve, despite it all — the sound of her voice made him smile. Regal Sloan. His partner and closest friend in a life he'd left behind. Or tried to.

"Hey, Queens," he said, the old nickname slipping unexpectedly out of his mouth. She smirked and started to speak, but the bartender interrupted with Jude's beer. Regal ordered one for herself, and they said nothing while they waited. When the bartender returned, Regal, still standing behind him, reached over Jude's shoulder, close enough that he could feel the warmth of her, the brush of her breath against his neck. Jude forced himself not to flinch away from her invasion of his personal space, knowing it wasn't true flirtation so much as an attempt to make him uncomfortable, to keep him off his game. She folded a napkin in half and traced a two and a zero across it with her fingertip. Regal pushed the napkin to the bartender, who scooped it up as payment without questioning it.

"Keep the change, boo," she said.

Jude took a sip of his Abita, savoring the crisp sharpness on his tongue. *Same old Regal,* he thought. He didn't realize he'd said it out loud until she laughed.

"Way I remember it," she said, "you taught me that particular trick."

"Taught you all the tricks you know, rook."

"Memory slipping in your old age?" She picked up both glasses. "Let's talk in back."

Jude dug a twenty out of his pocket and dropped it on the other side of the counter between a couple of bottles where the bartender would find it later, and then followed her, discomfort roiling in his gut like water about to boil. As he slid past the blonde at the other end of the bar, whose thumbs were now dancing across her cell phone, the bitter taste of blood filled his mouth. *Great,* he thought. *Just great.*

The next room seemed like a different bar, with patio tables spread across the bare concrete floor and bright paper lanterns strung above. The lanterns rustled in the breeze from the large box fan rattling in the corner, stirring the soupy air around more than providing any relief from the heat. Regal set Jude's beer in front of him, slurping the foam off the top of her own. He wondered if she had seen his gloves yet and if the glass was safe to touch without them. He thought about taking one off under the table, unsure if he could do it without her noticing.

"So," Regal said, after licking her lips, "you got your shit together, or you still hiding from the storm?"

Some would call Regal blunt or tactless. Some had harsher names for it. Once, a middle-aged hausfrau had called her "a gash-mouthed cunt" in front of her two young daughters. Jude knew, though, how carefully Regal chose those barbs of hers. It was how she kept people back on their heels. That same housewife had been selling the virginal menstrual blood of her eldest to a voodoo woman.

Still, it hurt that she'd jabbed at Jude's weak spot like that, like he was just another prick in the way of her doing the job. Made him a little angry, too. But mostly it proved that she had more on her mind than a drink with an old friend.

"That guy's gonna catch hell when his till comes up twenty bucks short," he said. "I only ever used that trick to fuck with the kind of assholes who have it coming. Broke-ass bartenders trying to make rent money don't exactly qualify." He worked at keeping his voice level. It wouldn't help anything to lose control here. His temper was something else — or so Jude's mother had always said — that he'd gotten from his absent father.

She cocked that same grin at him, only this time it seemed insulting. "You're a real ray of sunshine, you know that?"

"First," Jude said, raising a finger as he counted, "I know the blonde out front will be dead sooner than not, sucked dry by the vampire that's got her enthralled. Second, you've got a bit of magic hidden on you, a weapon by the feel of it, something sharp and nasty. Third? There's a change coming, something that's got even the boss man rattled. And fourth, you're stalling. That's what I know."

She turned her head back the way they had come, squinting as if she could see through the wall that separated them. "Does it bother you?"

"What, the girl? Of course it does."

She shook her head. "Actually, I was asking if it bothered you to be such a know-it-all prick all the time, but let's talk about the girl. Bet you wanna go rescue her, don't you? Gonna swoop in and save the day?" She made a disgusted noise in the back of her throat. "Not every woman is lost without her big, strong man, you know. That hero complex of yours is gonna get you in deep shit one day, bucko."

"Thanks for the advice," he said, taking a swallow of his beer. "Timing could be better, though." This wasn't the way he'd hoped this conversation was going to go. Regal seemed tense. Unsure, even. She mocked him for wanting to save the girl, but she hadn't stopped staring in her direction, either.

"How did you know all of that?" she asked.

"Because whoever dear old dad was, I'm my father's son," he

said. "Some things I just know." Which was bullshit, of course. The taste-of-blood vampire warning was just a residual thing, an unintended side effect from a protection spell he'd done years ago. Everything else he'd said had been presumptions and educated guesswork, his tongue moving faster than his brain and hoping to get lucky. Regal knew a little about his father, though, so convincing her he knew a bunch of stuff he didn't know—couldn't know—wasn't much of a gamble.

Tell someone you're the bastard child of a god, and they'll believe you're capable of just about anything.

"So, quit with the foreplay," Jude said. He leaned forward, the chair creaking under his weight. "Mourning sent you to talk me into coming back, didn't he?"

"No."

Jude raised an eyebrow. "So you just thought you'd look your old buddy Jude up after six years and knock back a few?"

"Okay, yes, Mourning sent me." She bit her lip, uncertain. "But it's not what you think."

"Fuck Mourning." Jude felt his control slipping, anger and magic threatening to wriggle free, to take shape as fire and storm. He shouldn't have come. This was the last thing he needed.

"It's not what you think," she repeated. Regal stuck two fingers into her back pocket and took out an envelope sealed with red wax. The paper looked thick and old, like parchment. She glanced up, then her eyes darted away, unable to meet his. "You're pissed, I get it. I didn't want to get involved, but you know how it is. Mourning wants something, he doesn't exactly ask, you know? But this message isn't from Mourning. We were just hired to find you and deliver it."

Jude wanted to say that he didn't care. That he didn't want any part in any of this, just wanted to go home and drink until he forgot all the impossible things he knew. Things that had been a part of that other life, like magicians who called things up out of the darkness to do their bidding, or hoodoo women who cast curses for a fee and then charged double for the cure, or monsters that walked the daylight pretending to be human and hunted in the night. Things that were only partly human, or not human at all. Things that even the gods had abandoned.

Instead of saying any of that, though, his curiosity won out. "That envelope isn't ticking, is it?"

She laughed, but it was an unconvincing, desperate sound. She said nothing else, just held the message out to him, shaking it a little when he didn't take it.

"Who sent it?" he asked.

"No idea. All I know is I'm supposed to give you this," she said, sliding the parchment across the table, "and tell you that the favor's being called in."

Jude cursed under his breath. He owed a lot of debts, to more people than he'd ever be able to pay back. But only one of them would refer to his debt as a favor: Dodge Renaud, the fortune god of New Orleans. Sure enough, when he picked it up, the envelope was sealed with red wax impressed with an ornate *R*.

Fucking perfect, Jude thought. He started to take a sip of his beer and instead tilted it up, gulping, draining the glass, no longer concerned with whether she saw his gloves or not. He found, to his surprise, that his hands didn't shake.

Six years. That was a decent span of time for normal human problems, hangovers and avoiding exes and pretending you were happy with your shitty pay at your shitty job. Six long years away from dancing to the whim of gods and all the nasty bullshit that came with it. For six years he'd stayed low, stayed quiet, tucked down in a seam of a life so boring, he'd convinced himself that he'd vanished entirely, that petty problems would be all he'd have to deal with for the rest of his life. He should have known better.

Six years went like the blink of an eye if you lived forever.

CHAPTER TWO

THE ENVELOPE HELD exactly the sort of simple, cryptic message Jude had always gotten from the fortune god: a sketched map of the edge of the Garden District closest to the Quarter, specifically the nine streets named after the Muses of Greek myth. Instead of names, though, the streets on the map were labeled with the symbols of each Muse's domain—a scroll, a frowning mask, a smiling one, a flute—with a bright red X halfway down the block between Clio and Calliope. That told him the place, and a Polaroid of the clock on the central spire of St. Louis Cathedral told him the time: midnight.

As for Jude's other questions—the who, what, and why—he'd have to show up to find out for sure. That was Dodge's way.

The mention of his debt, though, first sent Jude back to his apartment—once he had endured a few barrages of Regal's vulgarity-strewn interrogation and made a strategic retreat, leaving her at St. Joe's—so he could collect the satchel Dodge had given him long ago. Whirls and angles of protective charms were cut into the faded brown leather, and the dozens of pockets inside bulged with magics both potent and petty: amulets and gris-gris pouches, vials of milky liquid and stones etched with ancient writing, and only a god knew what else, since it had already been full when Jude got it from Dodge. Back then, he'd thought that the satchel's contents had been worth owing a god a favor. He'd craved the control over his own fate he'd believed it promised. Now, his only real hope was that Dodge would take the bag back —along with the odds and ends Jude had added to it while it was his—and call it square.

As plans went, it was a pretty shitty one. Power always had a cost, and the fine print never included a generous return policy. But it was all he had.

Twenty minutes or so of wandering around the Garden District while he consulted the crudely drawn map led Jude to a spot where no one else would stop: a cracked stretch of sidewalk and a fence overgrown with thick, clinging vines. On the other side of the fence, accumulated junk rose in a mound of mattress springs and broken chairs, half burying the sharp fins and graceful curves of an old car frame. The detritus and the overhanging foliage nearly hid the decrepit building lurking there. It was a shotgun house like most of the old homes in this part of the city, only one room wide but stretching four rooms back, the porch leading to the living room to the bedroom to the kitchen and then out again. This one was more ruin than structure.

After giving Jude only a brief glimpse into the yard, the street-light overhead buzzed like a huge hornet and went out, plunging everything into darkness. Jude stepped toward the fence, and a crawling sensation along his skin told him that he'd just crossed over the threshold of a magical ward. There was a shimmer in the air, and where a moment before there had been only unbroken chain-link fence, he now saw a rusted gate swinging open. Jude couldn't help but appreciate the craftsmanship of the spell. It was similar to the shroud he'd pulled over his own apartment, but where Jude's magic merely kept the building out of public notice, this actively pushed people away. Any random passerby would cross the street to avoid this place, without noticing that they'd done so. Even with an invitation, it had been hard to find.

As Jude entered the yard, a shape moved in the shadows, quick and low to the ground, bursting forward in a blur of wet fangs and fierce barking.

Jude spoke a single word in a language whose name he didn't know, and the dog's mouth snapped shut. It slumped to the ground, lowering its muzzle to the dirt. The dog whined once, let out a deep sigh, then lay still. It was large and shaggy, with the high, pointed ears of a German shepherd. Jude grinned and shook his head. Anyone or anything powerful enough to see through Dodge's magic would be able to handle the dog—if it was only a dog—as easily as Jude had. Which meant it was really only there to jump out and scare guests as they arrived.

Because on top of everything else, Dodge was kind of a dick.

Jude dropped to one knee and scratched the beast between its ears, hoping there were no hard feelings. Even through the gloves he could sense a deep, aching loss from the creature, so he pulled away before he could feel anything more distinct. Definitely not just a dog, then.

Jude rose to his feet and stepped onto the rot-wood porch, hesitating for only a moment before reaching for the knob. The handle turned, but the door, swollen into its frame, refused to budge. Jude put his shoulder into it and went sprawling into a dark, cramped space filled with cobwebs and the musty, nose-tickling stink of mold. Inside, entropy had long been at work, leaving behind crumbling Sheetrock and exposed brick, years of grime and dust. Jude stood in a long hallway, barely able to make out the outline of a door at the far end. When he reached it, doing his best to ignore the scuttling shapes amid the debris on the floor, he saw that it had been painted, recently, with bright red paint. He pulled it open, his pulse thundering in his ears. Light spilled out into the hallway, and Jude heard the snap and rustle of cards being shuffled, the clink of ice against glass. He smelled tobacco smoke tinged with a faint hint of cinnamon.

Inside, floral wallpaper covered the walls, faded and curling at the seams. The air in the windowless room sat thick and heavy, saturated with a haze of cigar smoke. On the wall, a clock in the shape of a cat kept time, its bulging eyes and curled tail moving in sync, a motion made somehow eerie by its wide, toothy leer.

In the center of the room, a single light bulb dangled over the green felt of a poker table. Dodge sat at the far side, fat and bald and ever smiling, his spray-tanned white face flushed with too much drink. He looked every inch a New Orleans god of fortune, his twinkling eyes the crisp green of fresh-printed hundred-dollar bills, his grin fluorescent bright.

Against his better judgment, Jude stepped inside. The door closed behind him without anyone touching it. He studied the players as Dodge dealt the next hand: a fat man with long, gaunt fingers and skin the purple bruised color of a corpse; an angel, wings soft and white as powdered sugar, eyes as blank and cold as frozen milk; a middle-aged black woman wearing a straw hat tipped at a jaunty angle, a pipe clamped between her teeth; and a brown-skinned man with the head of a bird, his beak curved and cruel as the blade of a scythe.

All this, and yet what inspired the most fear in Jude were the cards left face-down on the table. The empty seat at the game.

Waiting, it seemed, for him.

Jude dropped into the empty chair, leaving his cards face-down in front of him. It wasn't like he didn't have a choice. He could run. He could beg. He could demand to know what was happening. But none of those choices felt worth a damn. One god he could handle. Well, *maybe*—and probably not even then—but if it had only been Dodge, he could at least lie to himself that he had a chance. But a room full of gods?

"Fucked" didn't begin to describe it.

Whatever Dodge had planned was going to play out the way the fortune god wanted it to play out, yet Jude felt oddly, impossibly, calm. There was peace, he realized, in surrender.

He looked around the table, at the inhuman, immortal eyes watching him. Waiting. Expectant. Anticipating his reaction like five cats with a new mouse. Would he cower? Murmur some polite obsequy? Prostrate himself in prayer?

Fuck that.

"Who you gotta worship around here to get a drink?" Jude asked.

Laughter came from all around the table: a thumping bass drum from the fortune god; a throaty chuckle from the woman with the pipe; a dry rasp from the bird-headed god; and from the corpse-skinned god, a high, tittering squeal like a car engine on its last gasp. The angel's silence was equally unnerving.

Dodge pulled a flask from nowhere and poured some of its contents into his own cupped palm, then made a "there you go" gesture in Jude's direction. Jude took a sip from the glass that appeared in his hand. Rum and Coke and a hint of lime, just what he'd have chosen if he'd been asked. The other gods, Jude saw, already had their various libations to hand. *How long have they been waiting on me,* he wondered.

"Anybody else got a last request?" Dodge asked, his voice deep and booming, excessively cheerful. He looked from face to face, his eyes sharp and shrewd. "Splendid," he said, when no one answered. "Let's begin."

He set the deck down and swept up his own hand, fanning the five cards out and rearranging them as he spoke. "The game tonight is Fortunes. Nothin's wild, everything's open. Prosperity trumps calamity. Side bets are binding, so tally 'em up before the next hand. Last one standing takes home the big prize. Big and little blinds vary every hand, dealer's choice." He nodded to the god to his left, the one with the corpse's skin. "Scarpelli, first bet's to you."

Scarpelli inclined his head, baring his teeth in an approximation of a smile. His yellowed incisors stretched long and sharp. Jude took another sip of his drink, to try to wash the sudden taste of blood out of his mouth. *Vampire. This gets better and better.* Emaciated fingers scooped bits of what looked to Jude like chips of broken china from the pile in front of him, tossed them onto the center of the table. Each had a single, stylized image carved into it. They clacked against one another like dice until they came to rest. They were teeth, Jude saw. *Human* teeth.

Then it was *his* turn.

The regard of the room full of deities fell on Jude, as implacable and severe as the Mississippi's current. He had a pile of coins in front of him, big and colorful and stamped with a variety of images: Mardi Gras doubloons.

Jude did the only thing he could; he slid his cards forward, understanding enough of what Dodge had said to know that he didn't know nearly enough about the game to play. "Fold," he said. With all those godly eyes on him, the word came out strained, like the last breath squeezed from the lungs of a dying man. After what felt like hours, their heavy stares fell away from him.

"You got balls, little one," Dodge said, chuckling and puffing on his cigar. "You ain't even gonna look at your cards?"

Jude shrugged, tried to look like he had any damn idea what he was doing. He took another drink of his Cuba libre, a long swallow that slid down sweet and hot, a burning blossom in his stomach. They were playing some kind of poker, which meant Jude only had two hands to learn what was going on before he had to put some skin in the game. He regretted that phrase as soon as it occurred to him. In this game, it might be far too literal.

Dodge cleared his throat. "You're up, Wings," he said, that bright, sharp grin splitting his wide face. "You're always up, though, ain'tcha?" The angel frowned and the vampire laughed, and the sound was like dirty nails scraping across Jude's skin. The angel somehow managed to make pushing cards half an inch across a table look haughty.

"Wings *folded!*" Scarpelli said, his voice high and tremulous. He chuckled at his own joke.

"Why can't you ever play nice?" the woman next to the angel asked. She had a heavy Caribbean accent, stretching "can't" out so that it sounded like "haunt."

"What's it to you?" Scarpelli's voice stayed soft, but there was no hiding the menace in his tone. "You think those pure hands would ever get dirty for you, Pops?"

Jude looked at the woman next to the angel and, instead of a human woman sitting before him, saw the god who rode within her: a slim, wizened old man, with furrows of smile lines crinkling his ochre skin. *Pops,* he thought. *As in, Papa Legba, loa of the cross-roads? Has to be. Wouldn't be a party without a little voodoo.*

"It seems to me all our hands are a little dirty, no?" Legba said, grinning around the pipe clenched in his teeth. Jude blinked and saw the woman once more. She traded two of her cards, seemed to like what she saw, and placed a small leather pouch among Scarpelli's wagered teeth.

The last god Jude recognized, as any New Orleanian would have, from the Mardi Gras parade that used his name and image: Thoth, the ancient Egyptian god of scribes. He wore a Jazz Fest T-shirt, its open collar showing where his thin, feathered ibis neck tapered to human skin at the shoulders. He held his cards cupped in thick, meaty hands, his bird's eyes moving in quick twitches behind a pair of round spectacles. He folded, as well.

Dodge flicked his own cards to the table as soon as Thoth laid down his. "Always deal myself rags," Dodge said, chuckling.

As the gods showed their hands, Jude raised his glass to his lips, surprised to find himself holding it, his glass refilled, his face hot and numb. How much had he had already? Clever trick, that.

He stretched and set the drink down an arm's length away, so he couldn't pick it up without meaning to. This game would be hard enough to survive with his wits intact.

He studied the cards flipped over on the table, only vaguely understanding the rules of the game. They used a tarot deck: swords and wands instead of spades and clubs, coins and cups instead of diamonds and hearts. The shapes, he had learned from listening to the card readers in the Quarter, were meant to be male and female, each suit one of the four elements. The rest of it lost him, though. He'd never paid enough attention to know what the other cards meant, what combinations would constitute a good fate or a bad one.

Legba won the first hand, the vampire won the second, and Jude kept folding, kept finding his drink in his hand. The cards were dealt a third time, and once again the gods turned their eyes to Jude, their attention like six feet of earth pressing down on him.

His bet.

Jude spread the doubloons out in a fan in front of him, certain that they represented more than just money. The gods played for the highest stakes. Each one he touched sent a shock along his fingertips despite his gloves, like the snap of static electricity. He still had no idea what the cards meant, didn't even know what he'd be wagering. *Fuck it,* he thought. *Dodge is probably stacking the deck anyway.*

He chose the coin stamped with a stylized heart and tossed it to the center of the table.

"I'm in," he said. Then the gods were laughing, all of them, laughing. At him.

Shame and the trembling suspicion that he wasn't as sober as he'd thought burned like ice water in his veins. Dodge rolled his cigar between his fingertips, staring at the smoldering tip, the only god not laughing.

"You made too small a wager, sweetmeats," Scarpelli said, sadistic glee in his voice. "A heart. What would we want with a broken little thing like that?" His bloodshot gaze went from Jude to Dodge, and after a moment, he clicked his tongue. "If you don't tell him, I'll be delighted to."

Dodge spoke without looking up from the contemplation of his cigar. "Too small a wager means you forfeit the choice. That's the rule."

The vampire tittered, something dark and violent in the sound. He splayed his gaunt fingers across the skin of his dark, blotchy face, a haunting parody of reflection. "I want your blood, of course. Every last drop." A doubloon stamped with a raindrop of crimson rose up onto its side and rolled next to the one Jude had thrown forward.

Dodge said something that sounded like "hey," but shorter, a mere huff of breath, and the angel's eyes closed in contemplation. When the angel's lips moved, the words sounded to Jude like his own voice, a shout echoing back through an empty cathedral. "The Lord demands his faith," the angel said. Another coin made its wobbling journey across the table to join the first two.

Jude glanced down at the cards he'd left face-down on the table. Part of him wanted to laugh. The whole thing was too surreal. Everything riding on a hand of poker that didn't make a damn bit of sense. It had to be a joke. He just couldn't figure out whether he was the audience or the punch line.

"I'll have his speech," Legba said. Jude saw the loa again and not the woman he rode, his kind smile twisted and hungry. Another coin.

Thoth turned one glassy bird's eye toward Jude, a cawing gull's screech coming from his beak. It didn't seem to matter that Jude didn't know what Thoth demanded, because the table did. Jude's final coin rolled away from him.

Dodge toyed with his cards, considering, his gaze distant. The moment drew out, and Jude no longer felt like laughing. His limbs were numb, leaden; his lungs refused to fill, like he drew breath through a straw. Sweat squeezed from every pore. He couldn't stand to look at the gods anymore, their teeth and eyes too bright, something dark and nasty slithering in the shadows, or maybe it was the shadows themselves, shifting and pregnant with something he was unable to face.

"The first wager was enough for me," Dodge said at last. One by one the gods put their markers on the pile of coins, covering it with a burial mound of their own wagers, teeth and feathers and scraps of paper and serpent's scales. It felt like a hole opened in Jude's stomach. Of course they wanted to play. He had skin in the game now, and everyone wanted a taste.

Legba laid his cards down, a nonsense poker hand of jumbled suits and tarot symbols. The other gods followed, amid appreciative murmurs or sighs of disappointment. Some of the images seemed familiar, the faces of people Jude had seen before — the cashier at the place where he made groceries, a former pro athlete who sold used cars now, the local weather guy who'd lost his shit after the storm. Dodge turned his cards over one at a time: THE QUEEN OF COINS, THE QUEEN OF SWORDS, THE HIGH PRIESTESS, THE QUEEN OF WANDS, and THE QUEEN OF CUPS — each of them wearing Regal Sloan's face.

The vampire made a noise of disgust and flicked his own cards to the center of the table without turning them over. Between that and the fortune god's smug grin, Jude guessed that whatever Regal's fate was, it was a winning hand for Dodge.

Jude ran his thumb along the edge of one of his cards. He still hadn't looked at them. What did they matter? All that mattered was what was going to happen to him next. He doubted it would be as simple as debt. Whatever these cards showed, they would decide his fate. The gods had demanded pieces of him. If they split the pot, they'd tear him apart. The best-case scenario was that one of these deities was about to own him, asshole to appetite.

Jude leaned forward, reached over his cards, and picked up his drink. "Like the song says," he muttered, "'drink a little poison 'fore you die.'" He drained the glass in one raw, burning swallow, let out a ragged sigh of mingled pleasure and pain, and—with a wink in Dodge's direction—showed his hand. For a moment, he thought his vision had failed him.

They were blank.

The angel hissed like a cornered cat; Legba cursed in a language Jude didn't know; the vampire laughed and laughed and laughed. Jude had no idea what empty cards meant, but whatever it was, it was a dead man's hand.

He stood, staggering, fear and liquor robbing him of balance. He yanked up his satchel off the back of his chair, knocking it over onto its side, nearly followed it to the floor. The gods only watched him, waiting. He backed away, reaching for the door. They still hadn't moved. His hand found the doorknob and twisted, felt it opening behind him, and finally he did fall, the bottom dropping out of the world.

He fell and fell into a shifting, profound darkness, a shadow that swallowed him whole.

Awareness and light came abruptly, found him tangled in sweat-heavy sheets, his muscles aching, breath coming in quick gasps. His heart pounded, and he tried to calm himself, tried to tell himself that it had only been a nightmare, even though he knew that he was lying to himself. He lay there, watching the ceiling fan as it swayed with each spin, as the predawn light revealed the room around him bit by bit, thinking about Dodge, and Regal, and Mourning, and the seams where worlds collide. He lay there, trying to divide the impossible from reality: meeting Regal in the bar, the card game, those wagers each of the gods had demanded of him circling his mind. Trying—and failing—to convince himself that it had all been just a bad dream.

He lay there until his phone rang long enough that he had no choice but to answer it, and Regal told him that Dodge had been murdered.

CHAPTER THREE

WHEN THEY ARE the giants who are the children of the angelic sons of God and the earthbound daughters of Men, we call them Nephilim. When they are the result of a vampire's lust for a human woman, we call them dhampir. Ancient Egypt had Imhotep, son of a mortal and the architect god Ptah. India had Arjuna, son of the human Queen Kunti and Indra, the god of lightning and thunder. The Welsh had Cú Chulainn, the Hound of Culann. Phaethon wrecked the chariot of his father, Helios. Gilgamesh built the walls around Uruk. Theseus and the Minotaur fought in the Labyrinth, one fathered by the sea and the other descended from the sun. They are heroes and monsters; the products of lust or accident, grace or fate. They are demigods: the power of a deity bound in the fragile clay of a mortal. Always greater than those around them; always weaker than what they might become.

❧

Even after a long, hot shower and half a pot of coffee, Jude stumbled around his apartment in the grip of the kind of hangover that would have driven him to prayer, if the only god he knew on a first-name basis wasn't already dead. As he dressed—jeans and a worn Saints T-shirt and a thrift store suit jacket—it occurred to him that he had no memory of getting home the night before, that there was just an empty space between fleeing Dodge's game room and waking in his own bed. Blank like the cards he'd turned over. What kind of a fate was he supposed to make with empty cards? Limitless potential, or no future at all? A winning hand or a losing one? Where would he even start to figure out something like that?

Mourning might know, he thought.

Images from the night before came back to him, like single frames snipped out of a film. Vampire. Cards. Doubloons. Angels and voodoo loa and gods. All of them hungry. He began to seriously consider the many benefits of the coward's path: wholehearted, self-preserving flight.

He could pack a few things, magic the nearest ATM into giving up all its cash, and just go. Fuck Dodge, fuck Regal and Mourning, fuck this whole lost and ruined city. Break whatever hold New Orleans had on him and get the hell out, like he should have six years ago when it all went to shit. He'd walked away once. He should have kept walking. Should have run. He might have made it. But this wasn't six years ago. Running from murder, from a *god's* murder, would look all kinds of wrong to all the wrong sorts of people.

He found the magician's bag buried under his crumpled clothes from the night before and was about to rummage through it for a hangover cure or an escape plan, whichever magic his fingers discovered first, when the pretty pink phone that belonged to Mandy the tourist buzzed with a text. He knew what it said before he read it. Regal, parked downstairs and waiting for him.

Somewhere in the Caribbean, that's where he'd go. Blue water and hot white sand. Rum and native girls and a long, slow slide into oblivion. *Go to Zihuatanejo,* he thought, *like Andy Dufresne in* The Shawshank Redemption. Except not even an empty beach in the middle of nowhere would be far enough to escape Mourning's reach. Jude couldn't hide anywhere this side of the grave.

Maybe nowhere on the other side, either.

Regal said nothing when Jude slid into the passenger seat, barely even waited for him to close the door before she stomped on the gas and headed downtown. He tried to think of something clever to say, but he needed a few more hours of sleep before he could manage anything approaching wit. She didn't seem to be in the mood for it either, worrying at a thumbnail with her teeth, cursing under her breath at the slightest delay.

Jude stared out the window, a hand across his brow shading his eyes from the too-bright morning, trying to remember something — anything — that had happened after he'd turned over those blank cards. The absence was maddening.

Regal turned off Canal and onto North Peters, easing over to the curb. She threw the car into park, then popped her door open and burst out of the car in one continuous motion, practically humming with nervous energy. Jude followed her out into the oven's blast of heat and the rushing, blaring noise of traffic.

Canal Place towered overhead, thirty-two stories of concrete and glass, an upscale mall with a movie theater on the first few floors, a plush hotel higher up. And something else, something almost no one, not even those who walked on the supernatural side of the street, knew about. Something old and sly, something that wore a man's shape and called itself Mr. Mourning. Jude had an idea who — and what — Mourning was, but it was a thought he'd never shared with anyone.

This close to the Mississippi, Jude imagined he could catch the river's rich, brackish scent floating along on the hot summer breeze. A few minutes of walking would bring him to the Quarter, a few minutes more and he'd be back in the Square, at St. Louis Cathedral, Jackson rearing back on his horse, pointed spires and roosting pigeons and crowds of tourists. He pictured himself hiding there, claiming sanctuary, wondered if any ground was sacred enough to protect him.

Frowning, Regal led Jude up the steps to the glass doors and into the cool quiet of the shopping center. Everything about this space said wealth. Smooth marble floors swept up into massive columns; polished brass and gleaming mirrored reflections. Hushed whispers of conversation, like in church. The chilly air, the silence, the scent of bleach and air freshener—all of it made Jude feel somehow crude and soiled.

Maybe that was just the hangover.

Jude wiped his forehead with the back of his sleeve and turned to the elevators tucked away in a corner, the doors sliding open as he approached.

Regal stuck a foot against the door so it would stay open. "Here," she said, holding out a small medallion about the size of a quarter. It had a stylized sunburst engraved on one side, and reminded Jude of the doubloons he'd used as poker chips the night before. The metal felt cool and smooth against his fingertips. "You remember how it works?"

"Yeah," Jude said. He pressed it into a depression on the elevator panel beneath the other buttons. All the numbers lit up when he snapped the medallion into place.

Regal started to say something but seemed to reconsider. "Good luck," she said, instead.

"You know me. Better lucky than good."

Regal stepped back and smiled for the first time that morning before giving him the finger with both hands. The doors closed with a soft chime.

Jude widened his stance and braced himself. He'd been on a ride at Jazzland once that felt like the elevator to Mourning's office, a slow incremental climb and a sudden, jaw-clenching drop, followed by a minute or so of doing an excellent impression of a yo-yo. At least at amusement parks, they strapped you in. This time, thankfully, he managed to keep his feet. Another soft chime sounded, and the car jerked to a stop. He pried the sunburst free and dropped it into his bag. His ears popped, and the doors slid open with a gritty, aged rumble.

Everything in the waiting room was an anachronism, from the thick brown carpet that covered the floors and the wood paneling on the walls to the scent of lemon wood polish in the air. The desk was covered in antiques: a rotary phone, a bright green secretary's lamp, a monster of a typewriter. The door on the far wall had ACQUISITIONS AND INVESTMENTS painted on the frosted glass. Jude had the urge to look down at himself, to make sure he hadn't shifted into the black and white of an old noir film.

Even the tweed vest and coat of the little man sitting behind the desk seemed yanked from the past. He clacked away at his typewriter, absorbed in some task. The only thing odder than the room's quaint antiquity were the segmented ram's horns that curled up from the secretary's forehead, thick where they burst from the skin and tapering into points above his thinning hair.

When Jude stepped out of the elevator, the doors closed behind him and vanished. Mourning's office was like Dodge's card room—like any number of places in this city, not one where the entrances and the exits stayed put. Jude found himself settling into his old role easier than he would have expected, taking things like disappearing doors and men with horns for granted—as if magic and all its implications were a pair of worn, comfortable jeans, loose and familiar.

The horned man, as much a fixture of the waiting room as the carpet and the stenciled lettering on the glass, didn't seem small at first due to a trick of perspective. Everything around him—his desk, his lamp, even the potted plant behind him—had been shrunk down to his size. In truth, the secretary stood no higher than Jude's waist. Since Jude had never learned the creature's name, and since only one expression ever crossed his face, Jude had always just thought of Mourning's secretary as Scowl.

Jude waited for a moment and then cleared his throat. Scowl turned at the sound, appeared to recognize Jude, and, true to form, puckered his face into a grimace of disapproval. He nodded toward the bench across from him, a curt, dismissive gesture, then returned to his slow, intermittent typing. Jude sat, his knees popping as he settled on the uncomfortable seat. Getting old or, at the least, out of shape. Just one of the perils of mortality.

Jude waited with growing impatience while Scowl removed one page from his typewriter and added another, seemed to take a full minute adjusting its placement, and went back to work, never once acknowledging him. Jude's nerves, already frayed, seemed to twinge and strain with every hesitant clack of the typewriter's keys. Considering the sort of people that came to see Mourning — powerful, dangerous beings — Jude found it surprising that Scowl hadn't long ago had his officious little spine ripped out for offending the wrong deity. He took a deep breath, trying to rein in his anger.

"I'm here to see Mourning."

The typing stopped. Scowl clasped his hands together over the keys and turned moist, almost tearful eyes toward Jude. "I see. And you are expected?" he asked. He spoke with a slow, rhetorical-question sort of cadence, as though speaking to a stupid person who had asked an extraordinarily stupid question.

"I am," Jude said. "He sent for me."

Scowl nodded, tracing a finger down a yellow legal pad to his right. "Name?" he asked. *First name Eat, last name Shit,* Jude thought, but said only his name. Scowl made a brief clucking noise with his tongue, turned a page. "I am showing no appointments under that name. Are you certain you have the correct establishment?" Without waiting for a response, he returned his stubby, hairy-wristed hands to the typewriter.

Jude clenched his jaw, swallowing down a sliver of anger. He could point a finger and set the asshole's grease-slicked hair on fire. He could speak just one word, and those curlicue horns would twist and grow until Scowl's scrawny neck snapped from the weight.

Most of the contents of his magician's bag were benign—potions and amulets and protective charms—but he was sure he'd find a weapon in there if he looked hard enough. He had a thunderbolt that would leave nothing of Scowl behind but a snide little smear of a memory.

Coils of magic twisted in Jude's gut, begging to be released. He could do it. It would be easy. Instead, he took another deep breath. He forced himself to stay calm, partly because he needed a clear head when he went into the next room, partly because he knew most of his anger was only frustration at Dodge's murder searching for an outlet.

But mostly because as easily as he could snuff out Scowl's mean, petty life, Mourning could do the same to him.

"He sent for me," Jude repeated. "Why don't you check with him?"

"Mr. Mourning prefers not to be interrupted."

Unbelievable. Jude opened his mouth to say something else, but the phone on Scowl's desk let out a soft buzz. The secretary held up a sharp-nailed finger, shushing Jude, and answered it. "Yes, sir," he said, into the receiver. "I believe so, sir." He held the phone away from his ear. "Mr. Dubbysin?"

Jude managed, barely, to resist the bait of the mispronounced name. "That's me."

"Yes, sir, he has arrived. Yes, straightaway, sir." He hung up the phone and turned that suffering gaze back to Jude. "Mr. Mourning does not appreciate tardiness. He will see you now." Jude's anger drained away into the urge to laugh; Scowl's contempt was so complete it went past infuriating and entered the realm of the sublime.

On the way to the door, Jude twitched a finger and muttered a curse. When it took hold, Scowl's typewriter would type increasingly vulgar obscenities, no matter what keys he punched, for about an hour. Childish, sure, but a little justified, too. The small release of magic itself felt better than Jude wanted to admit, an itch scratched, a muscle stretched. The knack came back easily. It felt natural, felt right, like an athlete finding the groove.

Or an alcoholic falling off the wagon.

He opened the door and stepped into Mourning's office, squinting as his eyes struggled with the radiance that poured in through the floor-to-ceiling windows. Jude tried to keep his breathing even, nervous as he always was in Mourning's presence. For one thing, the man was simply too bright; the sunlight seemed to refract around him, prismatic, shifting, brilliant, making Jude's vision swim. Then, like a switch had been thrown, it dimmed, and he could see again. Nothing about Mourning's blue eyes dimmed, though; if anything, they burned brighter than ever. Jude couldn't meet that gaze for more than an instant—the eyes were too sharp, too knowing.

Mourning's skin was the color of burnt umber, burnished with the patina of old bronze. He wore his dark hair long and swept back behind his ears, and day or night his cheeks were as clean as if he'd just left the barber's chair. Mourning tapped his full lips with two of his fingers, a smile curling behind his hand. There had been rumors when Jude still worked for him about that blinding radiance, that overpowering presence. Some said Mourning had a faerie glamour he cast when people came into the room—magic designed to make him appear beautiful, powerful. Others thought he might be Apollo or Ra, or some other sun god in disguise. Whispered rumors, of course. Jude believed the truth to be something more complicated, more sinister, but had always kept his thoughts to himself. The one thing everyone who had ever met him agreed on was that Mourning's beauty was the shimmer on the edge of a wickedly sharp knife.

Mourning sat at a desk made entirely of glass, which added to his ethereal appearance, bare except for a nameplate, which simply said s. MOURNING, MANAGEMENT. His silver watch flared as he gestured for Jude to take one of the black leather armchairs. Aside from Mourning himself, the most striking thing about the room was its uniformity, everything either transparent or black or white, the floor covered in a checkerboard of jet and slate, the nameplate dark walnut etched with pale letters. A small end table of carved ivory and glass in between the armchairs held a porcelain mug, steam wafting above it. Jude sat and picked up the cup, inhaled the scent of chicory coffee, grateful for some sort of normalcy in the room. Mourning himself wore a suit black and shiny as fresh poured tar, a tie the color of bleached bone. That unsettling smile still stretched across his face.

Jude tried to speak, found his throat dry, and sipped at his coffee instead. Mourning steepled his hands in front of his lips and waited.

"You wanted to see me?" Jude asked when he found his voice.

"Yes, Mr. Dubuisson," Mourning said. "I certainly did. You might say I felt seeing you was of the utmost importance." He had a soft, buttery purr of a voice, a hissing lisp on each sibilant consonant that Jude found entrancing. It crept into his thoughts and made it hard to concentrate, like television static, in the background at first but growing louder and louder. His heart was beating so hard, he thought it might burst.

He said nothing. Mourning looked down at a black file folder on his desk that hadn't been there a moment before. No flourish, no word of command, just magic, used with the offhand, natural ease of a god. Jude put his coffee mug down, sure that any second now his trembling hands would betray him and spill it everywhere.

Mourning spoke, not looking up from the folder. "It says here you have, of late, resisted any involvement with those concerns that fall under the auspices of this office, so far as we are able to ascertain." Behind him, downtown New Orleans stretched gleaming to the cloudless, empty sky, the summer heat blanching the blue from the air.

"Yes. That's right."

Mourning looked up, cocking his head to the side like a curious bird, his smile vanishing. "Which aspect? We are accurate in our understanding that you have sequestered yourself? Or are we correct to doubt the veracity of this presumption?"

"Um." Shit. Not the tone Jude wanted these questions to have. He fought the urge to squirm, tried to remain still despite his discomfort. "I've been laying low," he managed to say. "Haven't used magic in six years."

Mourning held up an index finger. "Aside from this very moment, when you profaned my affiliate's Underwood."

Jude paused. "Right."

"Might you be so kind as to elaborate as to your rationale behind this?"

The words were out of Jude's mouth before he could stop them. "Because your secretary is a rude little prick who had it coming."

Mourning smiled, a brief flash of white so keen it could leave a blister. "He does have the tendency to undertake his role as sentinel with undue diligence," he said. "My inquiry, however, was in regard to your argument for complete withdrawal from our coterie."

Jude thought of numbers and *X*'s spray-painted on doors, of water stains on walls higher than his head, of the city crying out for all that it had lost. "Just don't have the stomach for it anymore," he said.

"Ah." Mourning pursed his lips and nodded. "Indeed. For an individual of your particular appetence, these environs must have become quite, hmm, harrowing, of late. Yes?"

Jude agreed, waiting for the ax to drop.

"And yet."

There it was. Even though he expected it, Jude flinched from the blow.

Mourning leaned forward, the leather of his chair creaking. "As a former member of my employ, you are no doubt aware that I take a certain pride in my apprehension of the occurrences here.

The who, what, where, when, and whys, as it were. Here is what I know. Last night, you engaged in a speculative enterprise with some rather potent opponents, the outcome of which is both significant and—for at least one of its participants—most unfortunate, yes?"

Jude nodded, certain that if he opened his mouth he'd only make things worse.

"So you will forgive me if I am thus puzzled, as I am, that current events do not conform to the narrative of non-involvement with which you persist."

Jude started to nod, but froze when he realized exactly what Mourning was implying. He opened his mouth, closed it again. There were two men in Jude's head. One of them was the Jude who had hidden for six years, a gibbering, reeling, panicked voice desperate to give Mourning whatever information he asked for, to agree to whatever demands he made, anything to get out of this room as quickly and as intact as possible. The other one was the old Jude, who wouldn't know how to bow even if he wanted to, who spit in the eye of authority on principle, sometimes just for the hell of it. That one wanted to tell Mourning exactly where he could shove his insinuations, his intimidations, and his ornate lexicon, too. In their brief struggle for Jude's voice, Mourning spoke again.

"Usually, Mr. Dubuisson, this is the point where you would attempt to clarify any of my misconceptions before my suspicions solidify into, well, let's call them motivations."

Here, beneath Mourning's glare, the broken Jude won.

Words rushed out of him in a torrent, like water through a broken levee, assurances that Dodge's summons had come as a complete surprise, a list of the game's participants and their interactions, confusion about his own cards being empty, fleeing the game and waking up in his own bed. Through it all Mourning said nothing, his only motion the tap of his fingers against his lips. When Jude finished, he was filled with the embarrassing conviction that he'd started to babble. His throat had gone dry. He sipped from his coffee, which had grown tepid, hoping he'd given Mourning what he wanted.

After a silence that dragged on from awkward into full-on un-comfortable, Mourning spoke. "Quite the aberrant turn of events," he said. "I must admit an inordinate level of curiosity as to the ra-tionale behind *your* inclusion among so puissant an entourage. Per-haps the connection is hereditary?"

Mourning's words cut through Jude's anxiety. He'd wondered himself why he'd been invited to the game but hadn't considered this possibility. His thoughts whirled. Was that why Dodge had been willing to give him the satchel? Had he finally found his fa-ther, only to lose him again?

Before Jude could try to get him to say more, Mourning glanced at his watch — the face turned to the inside of his wrist — and sighed. "Brevity it is, then," he said. Mourning put his hand down on his desk on top of a small pile of folders that, once again, simply appeared. He flipped through them, absently, as he spoke. Jude had the impression of someone who had already moved on to other business. "Mr. Dubuisson, in your previous occupation with us, you conducted various inquiries, yes? In similar fashion, would you be so kind as to dedicate your eminently suitable abilities to this particular problem?"

Jude realized what the bright god was asking him and fought down a quiver of panic. He'd told himself that if anyone in this city would know where to start looking for a god's murderer, it would be Mourning, and here he was, handing Jude this assignment like this was still his job, like the storm and the past six years hadn't happened. But Jude wasn't that man anymore. "No," he said. "I can't."

Mourning kept talking, as though he hadn't heard, and for a brief, terrible moment, Jude thought he was going to have to re-peat himself, but then Mourning stopped mid-sentence. "Beg pardon, but perhaps you have misapprehended me." Those eyes, a blue so deep they were nearly purple, bored into Jude, robbing him of speech. "Do not mistake courteous wording as denoting the presence of a request, Mr. Dubuisson. You were one of the last people to see this city's fortune god still alive. You may either choose to assist this inquiry, or you implicate yourself as its potential target. I advise careful consideration of these two options."

Jude bit down on the smartass response that leapt to his tongue. Not here, not with Mourning. "I want to help," Jude said. "I do. But the truth is, this, uh, inquiry is way out of my depth. Whatever you're looking for killed a god, Mr. Mourning. I'm so low on the totem pole, I've gotta take shit from your secretary out there. I'm not saying no because I won't. I'm saying no because I *can't,* much as I hate to admit it. But I really like breathing and having a heartbeat, and I'd like to keep doing both as long as possible."

Something passed across Mourning's face that Jude had never seen before, an odd twist of his lips, a widening of those unearthly eyes. After a moment, Jude realized Mourning was surprised. "How disappointing," he said. He closed the file on his desk and shook his head. "I must confess myself unimpressed with your lack of ambition, Mr. Dubuisson, as well as disdainful of the fervor with which you cling to your mediocrity. Rest assured, however, that my offer stands as only a brief opportunity, after which you will firmly enter the categories of 'witness' and 'suspect,' rather than the much more preferable status of 'ally,' which you might otherwise enjoy." He turned his wrist up to check the time again. "I have, however, neither the time nor the inclination to compel your cooperation at present. Now, if you will be so kind, I have another engagement."

Jude stood, dismissed, dizzy at the sudden rush of blood to his head. He picked up his bag, swung it across his shoulder, mumbled some parting words. Mourning nodded and waved him off, already turning to other papers on his desk.

It wasn't until later, after he'd stepped out of Mourning's office and into the bathroom of a bar in the Quarter, after he'd texted Regal from the tourist's phone to tell her that his meeting was done, after he ventured out into the street, that Jude realized that he hadn't felt the tug of a single lost thing all morning.

That he had, in fact, forgotten his gloves at home.

CHAPTER FOUR

JUDE SAT at an otherwise empty table at the Clover Grill, staring at the coffee cup in his hands. The hot, thick smells of bacon grease and syrup mingled with the sting of bleach. A rush of noise filled the air, the clink and splash of washing dishes, the hiss and crackle and clank of the open grill, the plaintive croon of an '80s pop hit from the jukebox, the murmur and chuckle and outbursts of conversation, of food being ordered. Like most diners open around the clock, the lights shone full blast, an aid to bleary-eyed insomniacs perhaps, or a reminder to the drunks that they'd finally left the bar.

Jude had always liked this place. He found an odd comfort in its tenuous cleanliness, its blatant disregard for health-conscious eating, its raunchy joke-filled menus. It also, like Jude himself, existed within the seams, tucked onto the corner of Bourbon and Dumaine where the tourist traps and college kid–catering bars and the gay clubs and the quiet residential section of the Quarter all collided.

Its patrons matched its eclectic location. Tonight, bright-cheeked twenty-year-olds drinking milkshakes sat on stools next to middle-aged women trying to keep their tattered feather boas out of their eggs and grits, while a pair of tight-muscled, soft-voiced men exchanged pleasantries with a man who might be homeless, considering his worn jeans and his gnarled beard, each of them at varying levels of sobriety and hunger.

All this surrounded Jude, and yet, to his surprise and delight, he found himself—for the first time in a long time—comfortably numb. He sat with a slight smile on his face, staring at the chipped ceramic mug in his hands.

In his *hands*.

Without gloves to block out his magic, he should be getting images of the waiter who brought it to him, of the person who had washed it, of the dozen or so people who used it that night and the day before. He should know their regretted angry words, the choices they wished they could take back, the things they had lost in the storm. He should be drowning in a well as black and as bitter as the coffee in the cup.

Instead, for the first time in years, his head felt clear and whole and empty of anything but his own thoughts. He'd wagered away parts of himself in that card game. His passion, his blood, his devotion. He didn't know which represented his magic, didn't know which god had snatched the affinity for lost things out of him, but it was the only explanation that made sense. Inviting him to the game wasn't just a trap.

It was a robbery.

Regal rapped her knuckles on the table. "Yoo-hoo, anybody home?" she asked, singing the words at him. Jude blinked and looked up. She grinned her lopsided smile and eased into the chair across from him. "Jesus. I must've said your name, like, ten times. You okay?"

"I'm good. Really good."

Her eyes searched his for a moment. "Know what? You look it.

Couple of hours ago, you looked like a prolapsed asshole. Mourning cure your hangover for you?"

Jude spun his cup on its saucer, trying to decide how much to tell her. Mourning would probably send Regal hunting after Dodge's killer, now that Jude had turned him down. She had a right to know what she was getting into.

Before he had a chance to answer her, a waiter stopped at the table to take their order. Regal got biscuits, a double order of hash browns, and a vanilla milkshake. Jude got a club sandwich and asked for more coffee. After getting the specifics, butter or gravy, fries or tots, his questions punctuated by "hon" and "sugar," the waiter left, and Regal turned her attention back to Jude. She looked at his hands, then back at him.

"No creepy germaphobe gloves today?"

"Don't need them anymore," he said, and then, when he realized he'd have to explain what that meant, decided to tell her everything. "How much do you know about what I can do?"

Regal reached across the table and picked up Jude's coffee, taking a sip while she watched him over the rim of the mug. "You find things, right? All you need to do is—oh, touch. I get it."

"Right. Since the storm, it's been out of control. I don't know if it had to do with how much got lost, or if it was me, or what. But I felt *everything*. You can't imagine what it was like. I couldn't stand being around people without a way to shut it out. The gloves worked sometimes, but never for long enough. Last night at the card game, something happened. I'm not sure what, but it's gone now. The power, the curse, whatever you want to call it. I'm free. I feel like me again for the first time in, hell, I don't know how long."

Regal went still and silent. Only her eyes moved, flicking back and forth, looking at the tabletop but focused on something beyond it. Then she shook her head. "That is the biggest crock of shit I have ever heard," she said.

Though part of him knew it was exactly the wrong reaction, Jude let out a sharp bark of a laugh.

"Things get fucked up and you hide until it gets better?" She leaned in close to the table and spoke in a furious whisper, as though she wanted to avoid drawing attention. "People needed you, Jude. *I* needed you. What you can do. The good you could have done." Jude opened his mouth to say something, but she kept going. "And you expect me to be happy? That you're back, just in time to be caught up in all this shit? To get me caught up in it? Fuck that. Fuck you, too."

"Regal, stop." She quieted, but leaned back, folding her arms across her chest. "Fine," he said, her anger awakening his own. "Be pissed if you want. But stop making it sound like I'm some kind of savior."

"And you stop talking like you're some kind of goddamn victim. What about that girl you found, the one in Ohio? You telling me you didn't save her?"

"That was one time," Jude said, low and growling. Rage and magic roiled in his gut. He breathed in through his nose, concentrated on letting it out slow. *She's provoking you, like she always does,* he thought. "That was one time," he said again, more calmly. "People get snatched from their lives every day. You know what I usually see? Nothing. No lost person at the end of my magic trick. No trail of cryptic bread crumbs to follow. A shallow grave? The morgue? Skipped town? Who knows. The point is they're not lost. Just gone to where they're supposed to be. It's shitty and it's not fair, but that's the end of the stick some people get. Don't come looking to me for happy endings, Queens. If I ever was that guy, I'm sure as hell not him anymore."

She clenched her jaw. He watched as she chose her words. She pulled her phone out of her pocket, a slender thing that looked like a solid piece of glass, glanced at the screen, and set it on the table. "That's exactly the point," she said. "When you're losing is when you're supposed to fight the hardest, moron. Didn't anybody ever teach you anything?" Jude had to fight back a smile. Even directed at him, her anger felt comforting, familiar. He'd almost forgotten how stubborn she could be.

The waiter returned, slapping plates of food in front of them, seemingly oblivious to the tension in the air. He filled the silence with his own chatter, polite nothings and questions he didn't wait for them to answer. After a moment, he was gone again. Regal stabbed a fork into her hash browns with one hand, drowned them in Tabasco with the other. Jude sipped at his coffee, his hunger driven away by the tightness in his belly.

The longer his ex-partner ate without speaking, the more uncertain he became. How much of his reaction to the storm had been the twisting of his magic and how much his own frailty? Could he have withstood it if he'd been stronger? Could he have been healed sooner if he'd forced himself to face it head-on? "Look," he said, dreading the admission even as it came out, "maybe you're right. Maybe I took the easy way out."

"Maybe?" Even with her mouth full of food, her disdain was evident. She swallowed and pointed her fork at him. "Only maybe here is maybe you once had balls. Sure don't now." Regal dropped her fork, pushed her plate away, and wiped her hands together. "I don't want to talk about that anymore," she said. "I'm too pissed to make any sense. No more about your damn gift, or the storm, or anything further back than two days ago. All I want to talk about is what's next." Regal checked her phone again, compulsively, then met his eyes. "Mourning got me up to speed before he sent me to get you. What kind of spell you got for getting in touch with this fortune god?"

"For—wait. You mean *Dodge?*"

"Duh. You were always good at that spooky hoodoo, that calling-up-spirits shit. Don't tell me you lost *all* your skills last night."

Jude hesitated a moment before answering. There was a kind of elegant directness to the idea that was so perfectly Regal. Looking for a murderer? Summon the victim's ghost and ask. Problem was, it was also five kinds of crazy. "Don't take this the wrong way," he said, "but this is way out of your depth."

She let out a burst of sarcastic laughter, abrupt, like a slap in the face. "Fuck you again. Sideways. Maybe you were my teacher once, but those days are long ago. You have no idea what I've dealt with since you've been gone. You think I don't know how serious this is? You think I'm playing games here?"

He ran a hand over his face, across his scruff of beard, and sighed. "It *is* a game, Queens. That's what you don't understand. To them, it *is* a game. All of it. And there's no way for us to win."

She scowled, that stubborn clench of her jaw that said he needed to come at her from another direction.

"Besides, have you considered what happens if you actually figure out who killed Dodge? What the final solution is? Because I promise you, Mourning isn't planning on putting anybody in jail. We're talking about gods, here. Capital punishment is the only kind they believe in."

"Don't think I didn't notice that you avoided my question, dick. Don't give me any bullshit about whether you should or what the consequences will be, just tell the truth." Her voice got uncomfortably loud. "Can you summon the dead god or not?"

The customer behind Regal turned around, slow and wide-eyed, as if unsure he had heard what he thought he'd heard. Beneath the table, Jude's fingers started twitching through the motions of a "nothing to see here" charm—his version of a Jedi mind trick—but stopped midway through when it occurred to him that he might not have much magic left at all. Instead, Jude grinned at him. "D and D," he said. The man nodded but didn't seem entirely convinced. To Regal, Jude said, "I honestly don't know. Let's say I give it a try. First things first. If I'm going to rip a hole in reality and reach into the afterlife, I've got to know which direction to reach."

Regal lifted an eyebrow.

"In other words, did Dodge go to Heaven or to Hell?" She started to answer, but Jude spoke over her. "Last I saw him, he wasn't repenting any sins, so let's presume it's a bad place. The next question is which one? Do you know where his people stay? Because all I know about him is 'fortune god.' Is he Norse? Because the punishment afterlife for them is a freezing wasteland beneath the roots of the World Tree. If he's more Old Testament–inclined, then I should be looking around Gehenna, a burning valley of torment. Shit, I'd be lucky if he's in one of the hundreds of underworlds I even know about, and not some weird god Hell that I've never heard of." Jude picked up his coffee, felt through the mug that it was cold, and set it back down.

"I just told Mourning I wasn't good enough to play at this level, and that was before I knew about this." He held his palms up to her and wiggled his fingers, showing the lack of gloves, the lack of magic. "I don't know how much juice I've got left. If any. Frankly, I hope it's all gone. I'm out, Queens. And that's right where I want to be." He knew, of course, that he had to have at least a little magic left, since he'd cursed Scowl's typewriter, but Regal didn't need to know that.

Regal poked at the remains of her meal with her fork. Her jaw tightened and unclenched. "I get what you're saying, I do. And I sympathize. But I got bad news for you. Orders have come down from on high. You think I'm here for the company? You're not out. You can't even see the exit from where you are. You know Mourning doesn't take no for an answer. You help me with this, maybe it leads me somewhere that takes the attention away from you. You don't? He sends somebody less pretty."

Jude toyed with his coffee cup, swirling the brew around like his thoughts, wondering how he'd gotten here, what he could have done differently in the past few days, what words he could have chosen in Mourning's office to avoid this.

He couldn't come up with anything.

There were no favors to call in, no one left to ask for help. Nowhere to run, nowhere to hide, no option but to walk right into what felt more and more like a trap. With that realization, something shifted inside of Jude. A decision made. He knew he should be afraid, knew most people would hate feeling goaded and led and caged like this, but Jude had to fight the urge to grin.

Fucking up other people's plans was his specialty.

"You have to understand, you're asking me to do something that can't be done. It's not just a matter of whether I should — though it does break just about every rule I ever learned — it simply isn't possible."

She sighed. "So you're not even going to try." It wasn't a question.

The corner of his mouth quirked up. "Oh, I'm gonna do it. Shouldn't take more than a couple of hours. I just want you to fully appreciate how badass I am when I deliver the impossible."

PART TWO

A YANTRA WOVEN, thread by thread, image by image, into a fine carpet. Chalk on a gravestone sketching out a shaky veve that won't last through the next rain. A temenos built of marble that survives for centuries longer than the forgotten deity who made it sacred. A mandala sculpted out of colorful sand, poured with the grace of deep meditation. A Solomonic circle, drawn according to precise formula. Ancient as the kivas of the Anasazi, modern as the copper mesh of a Faraday cage. Arcane symbols and geometries, ritual and craft and symmetry. Sacred spaces, messages, prayers, boundaries, traps. The universe made small, the soul writ large. Circles within circles, all with one purpose: to let the magic in and keep the darkness out.

It had been difficult for Jude to let Regal into his apartment. It wasn't much, as magicians' lairs went — bedroom, kitchen, and living room a version of any college dropout's bachelor pad in the country — but he'd gone through a lot of effort to maintain his anonymity and privacy. The building was empty except for his apartment on the third floor, an abandoned carpentry shop taking up the first two. A handful of pretty clever magics had kept the building off any redevelopment maps in the wake of the storm—one spell added the address to the list of properties condemned and scheduled for demolition for anyone wanting to buy it, while another named it a historic site for anyone in the municipal government— and he'd worked a few charms to ensure that the bills for his power and the water came out of a couple of rich assholes' discretionary funds, the cards they kept under aliases for various debaucheries and, thus, never questioned when they ran unusual charges. From the street, it either looked like a warehouse for a thriving construction company or a derelict housing complex, depending on who was watching. It might be a little shithole that some condo association would love to tear down and replace with one of the million-dollar units that were popping up all over the Warehouse District, but it was private and quiet, and it was *his* little shithole.

Aside from a couple of very drunken one-night stands, Regal was the only person aside from Jude to see his apartment in six years. She hadn't been impressed, just went straight to his fridge, got herself a beer, and asked when he'd be ready to get started. Even after a few hours of research and spellwork, it still felt strange for Jude to see someone else in his place.

"Most magic," he said to Regal while they worked, "is bullshit." She made a noise to show that she'd heard but didn't look up. She knelt on the hardwood floor hunched over a chalk ideogram, which she was copying from an open book with geometrical precision. "All the fasting," he continued, "the detailed inscriptions, the exotic ingredients, the archaic languages. It's just ritual. You do it to convince yourself that the spell will work when your every instinct, your every experience, says that it won't."

Regal sat back on her heels and stretched, a couple of vertebra popping audibly. She rolled the chalk in her fingers but didn't put it down. "So you're saying I just wasted an hour of my life bumble-fucking around on my hands and knees," she said.

Jude hesitated before answering. "Look at it this way. Doing magic is, in essence, defying the laws of nature, right?"

Regal nodded, conceding the point.

"Something is one way," he continued, "is *supposed* to be that way, but you speak the right words with just the right cadence and you make it be some other way. You mix a bunch of oils and com-pounds together that, chemically, shouldn't do anything except give you the runs, but when you drink it, you're five years younger or you can see things you could never see before. You put a pic-ture and some bones and some herbs in a little bag, and the object of your affection falls in love with you. Imposing your will on the world around you like that only comes from true conviction. From faith. Most people have to look outside themselves for that level of belief. They need the ritual, but only because they *think* they need it."

Jude stopped talking, realizing that he'd given very nearly the same speech to his former teacher—a powerful magician named Eli Constant—years before. Eli hadn't appreciated Jude's thoughts on the matter, which was a nice way of saying they'd never spoken again.

Regal smirked and shook her head.

"What?" he asked.

"You, that's what. You're just such a *man* sometimes." There was a weariness in her voice that made it clear she didn't mean it as a compliment. "Things are easier for you, so it must mean that you're enlightened and the rest of us are just wandering around with our eyes closed, right? You ever think that it's not *who you are* but *what you are* that makes magic such a cakewalk for you?" She held up a hand when Jude tried to speak. "I know, I know, we're not supposed to talk about it because you're such a sensitive little pussy willow about it, but you gotta face facts, my friend. Your daddy was a god. You don't need all this shit like the rest of us because you've got liquid faith running through your veins."

The old Jude would have held his ground, would have grinned his most disarming smile and said something clever about godhood and being hood rich. If he'd learned anything in the years since his gift had turned on him, though, it was that he didn't understand himself as well as he'd once thought. He'd contemplated the many ways his unusual upbringing might have impacted him, of course, but had come to the conclusion that his facility with magic came from a childhood free of adults convincing him that magic wasn't real. He'd always thought of himself as merely a man who saw the world differently than everyone else. Maybe it was more fundamental than that. Maybe he wasn't merely a man, at all.

If his magic lived not in his mind but in his *bones*, it might explain how his affinity for lost things could be taken from him, or why its absence was a persistent ache, like a phantom limb.

"Might be you're right," Jude said, breaking a silence that was just starting to become uncomfortable. "Maybe there is something different about the way I do magic. In fact, I hope you're right, because I'll be honest, all this shit?" He waved a hand at the circle they'd constructed. "I'm making this up as I go." They had spent hours studying the files from Mourning and rifling through most of Jude's books on the occult, but the results hadn't been promising. There were whole books devoted to the diagrams meant to invoke the supernatural, and a half-dozen ways to call up the dead. When it came to dead gods, though, they'd found nothing. If it had ever been tried before, no one had bothered to write about it. Probably because they hadn't survived the experiment.

Regal rose to her feet, careful not to disturb any of the letters she'd written on the floor. "On that less-than-comforting note," she said, brushing chalk dust onto the leg of her jeans, "walk me through this spell step by step. Because I'm starting to think you'll shit the bed and get us sucked down into the Ninth Circle of Hell."

"You planning on betraying somebody?" Jude asked.

Regal whipped her head around, her face a mask of fury. "The fuck you just say?"

Jude held up his hands. "Take it easy. I'm fucking with you. You screwed up your Dante is all. Sorcerers like us end up in the Eighth Circle, not the Ninth. Number nine is for betrayers."

It took a couple of deep breaths for her rage to smooth into a frown. "So you read a fucking book. Congratulations."

Jude managed to bite back a reply, but only because he wasn't sure how she'd react. Her sudden intensity had startled him. Had she thought he'd said something else, something offensive? Or was mentioning betrayal the nerve he'd struck? *It's been six years,* he reminded himself. *Maybe she's not the same old Regal after all.*

Whatever the reason for her outburst, she slid right past it. She'd already turned back to the spell, tracing designs in the air and muttering to herself. When she spoke, she didn't look at him, instead pointing to the three concentric circles that made up the bulk of the diagram: a white, powdery line of salt, a gleaming ring of chain, and thick gray ash. "So these inner circles hold whatever you summoned here and keep it from doing anything nasty, right?"

"Right," Jude said, "salt for purity and cold iron for binding and ash because we're dealing with the dead."

"And this writing in the outer circle is what does the summoning?"

"No, the actual call comes from the magician. Your will. That writing's what forces whatever you summoned to go back to wherever it came from."

She studied the spellwork a moment more. "There's nothing specific, though. How do you know you're willing the right thing here?"

"For that, you need a focus. Something that represents what you're seeking. It varies. If we were trying to call one of the loa, it's basically a bribe: food and rum and a good cigar. For the dead, you need a part of their once-living body: a lock of hair, a splash of blood, a shard of bone. In order to bind a demon, you'd have to know its true name. For Dodge?" Jude shrugged. "I improvised." He reached into his satchel and—couldn't find what he was looking for. He paused, puzzled. It occurred to him only now, in the ability's absence, that he'd never had to actually search for anything in the bag, just stuck his hand in and found it. Now, for some reason, he had to sift through the satchel's contents until he found what he sought: a pewter statue of a bald, smiling fat man covered in shiny gold paint. One of the statue's hands gripped a cloth sack tossed over his shoulder; the other was outstretched and had a small hole drilled through it to hold incense sticks.

Regal lifted an eyebrow. "You're gonna summon Buddha?"

"This is Budai, not Buddha," he said, digging through his satchel once more, frustrated and distracted by the need to search.

"This is fun for you, correcting people like an asshole instead of answering their questions?"

Jude chuckled. "It is a little fun, honestly. Budai is a Chinese fortune deity. Ah, here we go. Remember this?" His fingers finally closed on the envelope that held his invitation to the card game. He peeled the red seal off the parchment, careful not to crack the ornate *R*, then licked the wax and pressed it to the statue's bald head, holding it until he was sure it would stick. "There, see? A bald, fat fortune god with Dodge's name on it." The expression on Regal's face said she was unconvinced. "It's symbolic. Gods love symbolism."

Jude put the fortune god statue in the center circle and stepped back, reaching down deep for the magic, the part of his mind he'd strained to keep closed for the past six years. More to prove to himself that he could than anything else, he pointed one by one at the candles they'd placed at five points on the innermost circle and, with a wave of his hand, lit them. It was a simple, basic magic, but relief flooded him when it worked. His gift might be gone, but not his magic. Not all of it.

With the candles burning, the shape of the summoning spell

clicked into place for Jude, like a puzzle's image becoming clear. He reached out, with his hand and his intent both, toward the statue. At the barest touch of his will, it twitched, as though it had been anticipating this moment. He pushed harder, and it moved, rocking back and forth at first, like a fat man getting the momentum to stand, and then it spun, whirling, balanced on the tip of one foot. The wax burst into bright red flame, hissing like a road flare. Jude ignored it, picturing the fortune god's money-colored eyes, imagining his booming laugh. He clenched his jaw and willed Dodge to appear, straining a part of himself that had no name, like willing his eyes to adjust more quickly when the lights went out. He felt the reverberation of a reply. The statue melted, oozing across the wooden floor in a dark red stain, the color of movie theater blood. It soaked into the floor, and everything went still, even Jude's breath.

This was wrong. Whatever was coming, it wasn't Dodge.

With a splintering groan, the floor bowed up, as if something huge shifted beneath it. There was a crack—a sound in the air, a sensation in Jude's mind, a hole in the world—and then a shape rushed up, stretching and growing and creaking in jerky, halting movements. Between one moment and the next, the floor in the center of the summoning circle thrust up into three straight edges and an ornate, antique twist of metal. A door. A *red* door.

The Red Door to Dodge's card room.

"Well," Regal said, "how do you want to do this? Rock-paper-scissors, or age before beauty?"

"As in, who opens the door? That's a bad idea. Most magic might be unnecessary ritual, but the protection stuff is *really* fucking necessary. Circles keep nasty shit in, so long as *you* stay *out*. You break the circle? All bets are off. I've had spirits take the shape of weeping children, dying friends, anything to try to get me to enter. Demons usually go for impossibly sexy and very naked, promising to do anything you can imagine. The point is, you never, *ever* break the line of a summoning circle."

"Sure, I get it. Don't cross the streams."

"I'm sensing a 'but,' here."

"But we're not going to get a whole lot of information questioning a door, are we?"

"No, we won't." Jude studied the door, considering his options. When Dodge had given him the satchel, the fortune god had also taught him a couple of words in a magically potent language. One of them meant *open*, the other meant *close*, and without them, the satchel would be useless. The words worked on pretty much everything, though, not just magic bags. Back when he'd been a full-time magician, Jude had whispered open password-locked computer files and had commanded wounds to close. He hesitated now, though, because using the word could unseal the protective circles of the summoning spell along with the door, a door he wasn't even sure he wanted to open.

He explained this option and his reticence to use it to Regal, who shrugged.

"This magic word of yours that'll open any door, is it 'friend' in Elvish, by any chance?"

Jude laughed. "First *Ghostbusters* and now Tolkien? You might be a little bit of a nerd, Queens."

She grinned. "How else do you think a good little Catholic girl gets mixed up in all this occult shit? Little Regal Sloan wanted dragons and fairies to be real so bad, she went a little nuts trying to find them. We can't all be miraculous bastards like you. Some of us had to break some rules to get here." Her grin faded, and she was suddenly very far away. It occurred to Jude that in all the time he'd known her, they'd always been in the moment. Some lesson about magic or some problem Mourning had been hired to fix. He felt like he knew her well, but didn't actually know very much about her.

He knew her well enough that he saw her face shift when she

came to a decision, when she hissed, "Fuck it," and—too quick for Jude to stop her—reached across the summoning circles. Jude felt the tense knot of the spell's protection loosen and unravel and braced himself for a reaction that didn't come.

Regal looked almost disappointed when nothing happened, even more so when she jiggled the knob and found it locked. She managed to look sheepish when she looked over her shoulder at him. "Little help?" she asked.

When Jude tried, it turned easily and the door creaked open onto darkness. He shot Regal a look. He wanted to scold her, but with all the shit he'd pulled in the past, anything he said would be nine kinds of hypocrisy. "Let's get this done," he said, and stepped inside.

He breathed into his cupped palm, igniting a trickle of flame he could use as a lantern, relieved to find that this magic remained potent, too. *So magic is like sex and air,* he thought, *don't matter until you ain't gettin' any.* The room revealed itself to be just as he remembered it, faded wallpaper, the card table, the creepy cat clock, but he and Regal were the only ones there. It was more than just empty; their presence felt somehow *transgressive,* like rifling through someone's possessions when they weren't home. The clock was still and silent.

As he walked farther into the room, a shudder ran through him, a flicker of ghostly figures, a flash of sound and scent. He leaned back and encountered it again, laughter and ice tinkling in a glass and cigar smoke and cinnamon. After shifting back and forth, he caught just the right angle, found that if he held himself just so, he saw shapes at the card table, Thoth and the angel immediately recognizable by their unique silhouettes and, strangely, a shape sitting in the chair he'd occupied. After a second, Jude realized that the shape in his chair was his own.

"How the hell are you doing that?" Regal asked.

"I really don't know. It's not on purpose. You can see it? From where you're standing?"

"Yeah. It's like it's dark in here, but for just a second, the light comes on, and it's full of people. Well, *sort of* people, anyway. Only they're all frozen in place." She pulled out her phone and, by the sound of it, took a few pictures.

"Let's look around some more," Jude said. "Maybe the room is—this sounds stupid—but maybe it's trying to show us something."

Jude moved slowly around the room, stopping every time he encountered a shiver of a moment, then shifting around until it came into focus. The first four slices of time were during the card game. He could tell that time was passing because the cat clock's hands kept jumping ahead. In each moment, Jude waited for the artificial shutter noises of the camera on Regal's phone to stop before moving on to the next. The fifth came when Jude was almost to the other side of the card table, and it captured the instant when he'd been forced to show his hand, the laughter among the gods, the fear on his own face. Jude didn't linger.

"Here's what I don't get," Regal said.

"Yeah?" Jude could tell by the tone of her voice that the unnatural quiet of the room was getting to her, so he let her talk, even though he didn't really think this was a good time to get distracted. In all honesty, he was glad she'd broken the silence.

"We keep calling them gods, but they're not. Not all of them, I mean. Sure, Thoth is a god. Legba is too, I guess. But an angel? Christ on a bender, a vampire? He's not a god. He's a goddamn *monster.*"

"Look at it this way: you've got this . . . being, right? It's got the power to change the world around it. Not like other people; this guy can change the rules. What do you call that?"

She made a noncommittal grunt. "Neo? Superman?"

"Sure. If he's a good guy, he's a hero. If he's a bad guy, he's a monster. That's a little morally relativistic for my tastes, but just for the sake of argument."

"I know you're talking bullshit when you start pulling out the ACT vocabulary."

"Not bullshit," he said. "Bastard son of a god, remember? I've done my homework." Jude stopped talking for a second, shifting around, thinking he'd seen a flicker of the card game. After a few tries, he moved on and picked up where he left off. "Okay, so take Hercules. He ends up on Olympus with the other gods, but he wasn't born one. Just the power to be a hero. That's the only real difference between your average person on the street and a hero or a monster: power. And if a hero or a monster's got the stones to proclaim, 'I'm a god' —"

Regal chuckled and muttered the "Ray, if someone asks you if you're a god" quote, which Jude pretended not to hear.

"—and not get smacked down, and he's got the juice to live longer than anyone who remembered him when he *wasn't* a god . . . well, guess what? That's the recipe for godhood, at least as far as gods with the little 'g' are concerned. Vampires just happen to be monstrous, shithead death gods, that's all."

"That's really all it takes to be divine?"

Jude shrugged.

"Well, goddamn, sign me up. I can be the goddess of drunk texts and regrettable hookups."

"You're skipping the fine print. Being a god means becoming the personification of an idea, but it also means that's all you'll ever be. Like an actor getting typecast, only it goes on for centuries."

"Spooky. But don't you mean it goes on forever?"

Jude pressed his lips together. "Everything dies eventually, Queens," he said. He'd nearly reached the other side of the room, stood next to Dodge's chair, now. "Even gods."

When the final moment came into focus, the stink of blood filled the room in a wave so sudden and powerful that Jude whirled around, certain they'd been ambushed by the vampire Scarpelli. When he moved, though, the smell vanished along with the rest of the scene. Dread climbed up his spine. He eased back into the right position, and the stench returned, along with its source, Dodge, slumped face-first onto the table, a dark, sticky stain spreading across the green felt.

"Christ," Regal muttered. "Don't get any deader'n that."

Jude didn't answer, just let her take her grisly pictures, and then he moved back toward the door, back through time: Dodge murdered; Dodge still alive and Jude's blank cards on the table; the game rewinding until he stood back in that first moment, with Dodge still shuffling the first hand. Something about the whole situation tugged at him, like a word on the tip of his tongue.

"What a waste," Regal said.

"How do you mean?"

"We've got everything we need right here. If we could see the seconds we wanted instead of these random ones, we'd have the murder happening right in front of us."

And there it was. Not what she'd said about the moments being random; the longer he spent in Dodge's place, the more he felt that the seconds had been deliberately chosen to show him something specific. No, what sparked a connection in Jude's mind was her comment about everything being in this room.

Or more accurately: every*one*.

"You look like you've thought of something," Regal said. When he started to explain, she held up a hand and talked over him. "Can you explain it back in the real world, please? This place gives me the heebie-goddamn-jeebies."

They left the card room, the door slamming shut behind them. The frame tipped backward as the door swung closed, and so with a single, solid bang, the Red Door became ordinary floorboards once more. Regal made a little grunt of surprise at the noise, her hand darting to the small of her back, as if she were reaching for a gun tucked away in the back of her jeans. Jude pretended he hadn't noticed. Instead of mentioning it, he busied himself making a pot of coffee, trying to put the idea he'd had in the card room into words. By the time he filled two mugs with steaming chicory—black for Regal, lots of cream and sugar for himself—he knew what he wanted to say, and where they had to go next.

"I've been coming at this all wrong," he began. "My thinking was that we had to figure out who could kill a god. As in, who had the juice, right?"

Regal made an affirmative noise, sipping at her coffee.

"But really, I should have been thinking about who had access. The game was invite only. I had trouble finding the way in, and I had *directions*. You had the door right in front of you, and it wouldn't open when you tried. Don't you see? If Dodge was killed in that room—"

"Then the killer has to be one of the players at the game," she finished. "Not bad, Dubuisson." She set her phone on the kitchen counter and scrolled through the pictures she'd taken of the card game. "You just narrowed the suspect list down to five."

"Four," Jude said. "The vampire, the angel, Legba, and Thoth. That's four."

She spun her phone around, showing Jude a picture she'd taken of him at the table. "And the bastard named Jude," she said. "That's five."

"Seriously?"

Regal pulled a face that said she wasn't entirely joking, took another slurp of her coffee. She looked back down at her phone. "Thought you said your cards were blank."

Jude's breath caught in his chest. "They were; they are. What did you see?"

Regal did something with her fingers and enlarged the image she'd taken, focusing in on the spread of cards on the table in front of Jude. Most of them were blank, but one of them had a stick figure sketched on it, one arm up and the other down like some sort of yoga pose. Jude studied it for a long time, and then pushed it away.

"Well?" Regal asked.

Jude could only shrug, staring into his coffee. He'd felt like he was getting a handle on things, figuring out where he stood, and now this. Another mystery knot without a thread to pull on. Regal cleared her throat. "Didn't mean to piss on your parade, sorry. You were saying? We've got our list, but as far as I can see, we're back to square one. Got any ideas on how we find these shit-weasels?"

Jude took the phone from her and scrolled through until he got to the picture of the woman in the straw hat, smoking a pipe. "Him," Jude said. "We start with him."

Regal smirked. "Hate to bust your balls when you're getting your detective on, but that there is a woman, Columbo."

"That's Legba. He's a voodoo god, a loa. The rules are a little different for them. Most gods let the prayers come to them. When a voodoo priest calls on the loa, he — or she, in this case — opens herself up to be possessed by the god." He tapped the phone. "That makes her a mamba. We find her, we'll get her to get Legba to come down and have a little chat." He swallowed down half of his coffee, poured his cup full again. "Problem is, you and me? We're what she would call bokor, sorcerers. Means we're about the last people in the world she's going to want to discuss her faith with. We'll have to arrange an introduction. Luckily Leon Carter still owes me a favor."

"Leon — you mean *Sweetwater* Carter? The musician? He's a voodoo priest? Or a — what — a bokor, like us?"

Jude laughed. "No, not even close."

"Thank Christ," Regal muttered, putting her coffee mug into the sink.

"He's a zombie."

CHAPTER SIX

EVERY CULTURE in the world has its theories about what happens to a person on the other side of death. For many, crossing the threshold between life and that other realm is not a thing to be feared; rather, it is a natural, even sacred step that should be embraced. What almost all cultures agree on, though, is that one should be very afraid of anyone who finds the way back. They are spoken of throughout human history, even as far back as *The Epic of Gilgamesh*. The Germanic peoples of the far north call them afturganga, the "after-walkers." In the mountains of Tibet, doors are built with low lintels, in the belief that the Ro-lang, the risen, cannot bend at the waist. Whether they are shambling, ravenous beasts or reanimated bodies devoid of a soul, they are known throughout the modern world by the name given to them by the practitioners of Haitian voodoo: zombie.

Jude and Regal hurried to the Lee Circle stop and caught the street-car down St. Charles, riding it all the way Uptown to Carrollton.

They got off at Oak and walked the few blocks down to the Maple Leaf, where the crowd spilled out the door and onto the sidewalk. The ground throbbed with the music coming from the bar. There was a short line to get in, but it wasn't moving. The Asian girl in front of Jude turned around as they approached. She wore a black Voodoo Fest T-shirt with the sleeves cut off and her tight midriff bare. She shrugged, waving her hand in the direction of the bouncer at the door. "They won't let more people in unless somebody leaves," she said. "Sucks for us."

"Yeah," Jude said, rummaging around in the magician's bag hanging at his hip. "We'll see." Since the card game, it seemed like the bag was fighting him, hiding what he was looking for; after a couple of wrong guesses, he took out a small dark bottle and unscrewed the top, letting out the acidic stink of crushed insect. The slim glass rod of an antique medicine dropper extended from the bottle's lid, a single liquid bead glistening on its tip.

Regal wrinkled her nose. "Dude, that stuff is *noxious*."

"You remember how it works?"

"I remember ruining two marriages and getting a lifetime ban from the Tulane library. Shouldn't it be your turn?"

Jude grinned and tipped his head toward the bouncer. "He look like he swings my way?"

Regal didn't answer, just smirked and licked the potion off the dropper. She shuddered.

Jude had used the philtre before; when it hit your tongue, it felt like you'd stuck a live wire in your mouth. Regal's shoulders drooped, and a sleepy smile spread across her face. She ran the tip of her tongue along her lips. Jude made sure he looked away before she opened her eyes. Using magic to make someone love you was pretty much impossible, but sex magic was almost comically easy. The philtre made whoever drank it irresistible to anyone who locked eyes with them, so long as they were into your particular flavor. Jude had found that being the sexiest guy in the room for a few hours could open up a lot of doors. He tried not to use it on himself, though; the magic made you desirable, but it also made you horny as a fallen priest and more than a little stoned. Jude slipped the bottle into his bag and led Regal toward the door.

The bouncer held up a meaty hand as they approached. "Whoa there," he said. "You don't see the line? We're full up tonight. Pushing fire code as it is."

Regal slinked forward, her voice somehow husky and pouty at the same time. "Don't tell me you forgot me already," she said. "You said we could get back in if we went to pay for parking. You're not really gonna make me wait, are you?"

He looked down her body and then back up, flinching when his eyes met hers as if she'd slapped him. A flush rose into his cheeks and across his bald head. "Damn," the bouncer said, drawing the word out, probably not realizing he said it out loud. "No, you're good. Go on in."

As they walked through the door into moist, hot darkness and noise, Jude leaned in and shouted into her ear so he could be sure she heard. "Meet me after the show," he yelled. "Don't do anything I wouldn't!" She nodded and went straight for the bar. *God bless whatever handsome bastard she picks to get that potion out of her system,* he thought. Normally Jude would want her watching his back, but one look in her eyes and he'd forget all about why he was here. Besides, he shouldn't need backup for this. Leon Carter had been a friend, once.

Jude fought his way through the crowd, crammed in tight between the bar and the stamped-tin-sheet-covered wall. Above the roar of too many people in too small a space, the room shook with the fast, deep pulse of a tuba, slapping drums, the throaty warbles of trumpets and trombones. A voice sang out, as thick and smoky as the air it drawled its woes into. Up on stage, past the rows of outstretched hands and upheld drinks, Leon "Sweetwater" Carter leaned on a stool in the center of a hazy spotlight. There was a drummer and a couple of other horn players, but the light and the crowd's focus were only on him.

Sweat beaded on the dark skin of Leon's forehead and fell from the tips of his dreadlocks, black hair streaked through with coarse wires of gray. Thin-framed spectacles hung low on his nose. The fervor and strain that he blew through the mouthpiece of his saxophone gave him the appearance of a revivalist preacher. His fingers stabbed up and down the neck of his instrument with the precision of a sewing machine's needle, weaving a tapestry of sound. A battered black case, too small to hold a guitar, rested at the foot of the stool he sat on.

Jude stood in the middle of the crowd, a lone, still figure among a seething, writhing dance. It took four songs for Leon to notice him, impatience beginning to clench the muscles of Jude's neck and shoulders. When Leon recognized Jude, his hands faltered on the keys. Though he recovered, turning it into a sliding moan from the sax that seemed deliberate, the other musicians noticed, exchanging a glance behind him. Jude caught the reaction, too, pointed to the side door, and mouthed, "After." Leon nodded and turned that into part of the act as well, shouting, "Yeah, yeah, yeah," and getting an echo from his audience.

Relaxing a little, Jude made his way to the bar. Leon would play for another hour at least. Might as well get a drink and enjoy the show.

Jude watched as Leon rose to his feet, pulling the sax's strap from his shoulders. He leaned the instrument against one of the speakers, which let out a shrill burst of feedback until he cut it off. Behind him, the drummer and the tuba player kept a beat going. Slow, tired, the musician eased back down, then leaned in close to the microphone. "If y'all don't mind," he said, his speech thick and heavy with an old Ninth Ward accent, "I got a real special tune I wanna play tonight." Leon reached beneath his feet and picked up the small case, a bunch of his fans cheering the gesture, knowing what it contained. Jude finished his drink and threw the plastic cup away, rolling his shoulders. Surely Leon wouldn't try something here, in front of all these people. But if he did, Jude wanted to be prepared. Not that he had anything in his bag of tricks that would help him if Leon really cut loose. Nothing he was willing to use on Leon, anyway.

The musician opened his case and pulled out an old trumpet, the tarnished brass gleaming in the light of the stage. An audible hush moved through the crowd like the sound of a wave retreating from the shore. For a moment, the room was silent save for the *thump-thump-thump* of the bass drum, like the beating of a huge, patient heart. Leon looked straight at Jude and smiled. "Listen now," he said. "Listen close and listen good. You give ol' Sweets just a couple three minutes of your time, I got a story might save you a whole world of trouble. You see, I had this here horn a long, long time." He toyed with the trumpet's slides as he spoke, as if out of his hands it might have gotten just slightly out of true. "Means a lot to me, this horn. More than any hunk of brass and spit ought to mean to a man, 'cause one hot summer night just like this one, at midnight, I went down to the corner of—well, I ain't gonna tell you where." His sly wink elicited laughter from the crowd. "I ain't tellin', 'cause there at the crossroads I met the devil." Cheers went up at this, a few at first, then more and more, as people caught on. He pressed the mouthpiece to his lips and blew one clear, trembling note. "I sold that ol' devil my soul, and this is what I got," he said. "Y'all tell me if I made a good deal."

What came from his trumpet then was far more than music. It was more, even, than magic. It sounded like the sweet love child of blues and jazz, but it was more haunting, more evocative than mere sound. Music could be ignored, magic could be fought, but what came out of Leon "Sweetwater" Carter's horn slipped past the skin as gentle as a lover's sigh, seeping down into the meat and marrow of you. He could open a door into the soul in a way that was beyond any power Jude had ever commanded. Truth was, Leon's story was more history than fiction. All those years ago, Leon had met someone at midnight, but not the devil; it had been Legba, the voodoo loa of the crossroads. Legba had shaken Leon's soul loose from his body, leaving him a zombie, a creature not alive and not dead, existing in the seam between this world and the world to come. This music, this power, was what he'd gotten in return.

Jude slipped through the crowd and out the side door into a small alley, where he waited for Leon to finish weaving his spell, whatever it might be, on his unsuspecting audience. A shallow drainage ditch, still slick from a recent rain, ran down the center of the cobblestones and disappeared beneath the locked iron gate that blocked the way out into the street. A high wooden fence separated the bar from the restaurant next door whose dumpster filled the alley with the pungent, moist odor of deep-fryer oil and seafood shells spoiling in the heat. Jude's ears still rang with the insistent whine of speakers turned up high and loud. Between the heat and the stink and the past two days, his skin felt like it had a coating of grime. The beginning of a headache tightened at his temples. He wanted, badly, to get what he needed out of Leon and get home to a long, hot shower.

A while later, the music gone quiet and the crowd dispersed, the metal door opened with a hollow bang and out stepped Leon, looking back and forth as the door swung shut behind him. Jude had instinctively put his back to the wall, half-hidden by shadow. "You sounded great, Sweets," Jude said.

Leon squinted into the darkness and, when he recognized Jude, nodded. He held his trumpet case in a loose-fingered grip at his side. "'preciate that, Jude," he said, falling silent for a moment. He shook a cigarette loose from a pack, lit it with a plastic lighter. "Ain't seen you for a minute. Not since the storm. Figured you was gone."

"I was. I'm back."

The musician nodded again, looking up and away into the night sky, where thin wisps of clouds obscured a sliver of moon. He sucked his upper lip between his teeth, making a hissing sound. "So we just shootin' the shit, or is there somethin' you need?"

"I could use a little help, now that you mention it."

Leon blew twin plumes of smoke from his nostrils. "Yeah, Jude Dubuisson is back all right."

"You hear about Dodge?"

Leon's head dropped down, staring at his feet. His grip tightened on the trumpet case's handle, his shoulders stretching taut. His whole body seemed to clench. "Got nothin' to do with that," he said.

"Never said you did. I just need to know—"

"No, you ain't heard me. *Got* nothin' to do with it, don't *want* nothin' to do with it, neither. You'd stay clear yourself if you had the sense you was born with."

"I need a name, Leon."

Leon shook his head, his dreads fluttering at his shoulders. "Boy, how many different ways I gotta tell you 'no'? Only name I got for you is Puddin' Tain. Ask me 'gain and I'll tell you the same." He flicked his half-smoked cigarette away into the darkness and turned to the door, but at a whisper from Jude the lock clicked shut with an audible snap. Leon looked back over his shoulder, the small disks of his glasses glowing in the moonlight. He shook the trumpet case meaningfully. "I ain't gonna ask twice," he said, his hand still on the knob.

"Me either." Jude took a glass bottle from his bag and uncorked it, pouring a fine white sand into the palm of his hand. Part of him, the old Jude from before the storm, the part of him that had played with fire wearing a fuck-you grin, that part of him was thrilled that Leon wasn't making this easy. That part of him had been waiting to get let off the leash for a while. "You know what a pain in the ass it is to make zombie powder?"

The musician's mouth hung open. Then he closed it and swallowed. "Bullshit," he said. "You ain't got none."

Jude curled his hand into a fist. "I mean, making it isn't so hard. I imagine the ingredients were harder to track down before the Internet. It's the precautions you gotta take that are the real pain in

the ass. One good sneeze while you're grinding this up and *poof*."
With his other hand, Jude made an explosive motion. "Knocks the
soul right out of you. Nasty shit." Jude felt a smile that held no
warmth split his face, the kind of smile Mourning or Dodge might
wear. "Honestly, I don't know what it'll do to someone who's already a zombie. Maybe it'll rip the rest of your soul loose, knock
you all the way dead. Maybe it'll yank your soul back from wherever it's hiding. Can't imagine it would be real pleasant either way.
Maybe it won't do anything at all. Now, you can either tell me the
name of the mamba Legba rode to the game, or we can find out
what a face full of this does to you. Your call."

He raised his hand to his lips, his fist becoming a makeshift
blowgun. He inhaled, deeply, through his nose.

"Dorcet," Leon said, pronouncing it "door-say." "Celeste
Dorcet. Used to stay out in the east, 'fore the storm. Think she got
a shop off Rampart now." He shuddered, turning his head away.
"Now put your damn hand down." Jude swallowed and lowered
his fist, spoke the door unlocked. The old Jude wanted to gloat, but
then again, the old Jude had been a real bastard, even to his friends.

The zombie snatched the door open but paused in his flight to
look at Jude. His eyes were dark pools above the shimmer of his
spectacles. "Y'know, the difference between a bokor and a priest
ain't just the kind of magic you do. It's who you are. That darkness you got? That shit come from the heart." Then he closed the
door and was gone.

Jude waited until he was sure the musician was gone before he
wiped the salt from his palm. Part of him wished Leon had called
his bluff, so his old friend would know he hadn't made something
as nasty as zombie powder. He'd never messed with that kind of
magic, that bokor shit, the necromancy. That hadn't been the kind
of magician, the kind of *man* he was.

The question was, what was he now?

CHAPTER SEVEN

WHEN SHE picked him up at his apartment late the next morning, Regal didn't look as rough as Jude expected. He wasn't sure if she'd sweated it all out the night before or if she was still riding the buzz of booze and magic, but he avoided her eyes on the short ride to the Quarter just the same. It only took about ten minutes of wandering the quiet streets to find Celeste Dorcet's place on Rampart, but when they did, it didn't look like much. The sign swinging in the breeze advertised it as MAMA CELESTINE'S VOUDOU SHOPPE, the words painted in a childish scrawl of garish acrylic. Regal peered through the hazy, dirt-crusted window and made an incredulous noise. The inside was like every other voodoo-themed tourist trap, votive candles and copies of *The Serpent and the Rainbow* shelved next to herbal remedies and glass pipes colored with tie-dyed neon swirls.

"You sure about this?" she asked Jude. "You might score a dime bag here, but that's the closest you'll get to any real magic."

Jude—who had gone to watch Tommy's band after leaving the Maple Leaf and was thus still a little hungover—didn't bother to reassure her, just scuffed the toe of his shoe against the sidewalk to direct Regal's attention to the chalk drawing there: two wide V's intersecting in a diamond shape, the inside thatched like a stylized leaf, the outside surrounded by asterisks. To most people, it would look like nothing special, an abandoned game of hopscotch or the incomprehensible marks of a civil engineer signaling the location of a gas main or a sewer line. "This is the veve for Ayizan," he said.

Regal cursed. "Can't believe I missed that," she said. Veve were sacred symbols unique to each loa, signatures and conjuring charms and passwords all rolled into one. Ayizan was the loa of the marketplace and the patroness of mambas.

The bell above the door jingled as Jude walked in, though he doubted the girl at the counter heard it. She seemed focused on the magazine in front of her, white wires trailing down from her ears and disappearing into her pocket. She had a whole goth look going, T-shirt torn at the collar and sleeves, lipstick a dark stain. Her dreads were tied back with a black handkerchief. Piercings dotted her nose, her eyebrow, her lip. Her head bobbed in time with the music, and when she opened her mouth, to Jude's surprise, she didn't let out a death metal screech. *"I'm mad about you, baby,"* she sang, her voice all rhythm and blues.

Jude walked up to the counter where tea pouch labels promised everything from sexual potency to spiritual enlightenment. The girl looked up, her eyes wide with surprise, like she wasn't expecting customers. She pulled the buds from her ears and, sure enough, the music coming from them was soft and easy. "Help you?" she asked.

She was pretty enough and—though still fairly young—old enough that before-the-storm Jude would have made a pass at her, said something about how she probably drove all the boys mad. "What's that you're listening to?" he asked instead.

She bit her lower lip, a flush creeping across her brown skin. "'Wear Your Black Dress,'" she said. "It's by this guy, Willie Egan? I got it 'cause the album's called *The Devil Is a Busy Man* and, y'know." She shrugged and waved her hand around the room, as if that explained her choice. "Wasn't what I expected, but I'm totally in love with it now."

Jude nodded. His mother loved that kind of music, too. It wasn't impossible that he had the same record among his mother's things, back in the house he'd lived in before the storm.

"You guys need something?" the girl asked.

"We're looking for Celeste," Regal said. Something in her tone told Jude she was looking to play bad cop.

Her brow furrowed. "Who? You mean Miss Celestine?" She glanced over her bare shoulder, looking at the beaded curtain that led into the back. "She, uh, she ain't in today."

Jude caught the hesitation, heard the lie in her voice. "Look," he said, before Regal could get started. "We're not here to hassle anybody, okay? We just have some questions. Tell her Leon Carter sent us."

A voice came from the darkness behind the thick glass beads, rolling and imperious like storm clouds on the horizon. "Sweetwater ain't sent you here, no," she said. "He called to warn me you was coming, though."

A hand split the curtain, rings on every well-manicured finger, thick bangles clattering on the wrist. Celeste Dorcet followed. She wore a loose, flowing gown of thin yellow fabric, an embroidered shawl across her arms and shoulders. Everything about her seemed different than Jude remembered, the sound of her voice, the expression on her face, her posture, the tilt of her head. But then, everything about her *was* different. Jude had met *Legba* in Dodge's card room, not this woman.

The girl behind the counter looked from Jude to Celeste, eyes wide and darting. "Miss, I mean, Mama, I'm sorry. I tried to, I —"

Celeste turned to her, a warm smile plumping her already-round cheeks. "They ain't no concern of yours, child, don't you worry. You just mind the store, hear?" She looked back to Jude and Regal, frowning as if she didn't like what she saw. "He said to expect a tall creole drink of trouble. He ain't said nothin' 'bout no white girl look like she got a mind to chew a mouthful of halfpenny nails. Ain't room back here for three."

Jude exchanged a glance with Regal, who made a curt nod that said, *Fuck it, go on then.*

Celeste raised her arm, opening the hole in the strings of beads wider. "Well, young man, you comin' in or you gonna make an old woman beg?"

Beyond the beaded curtain, a short hallway led into a small, dimly lit space, decorated more like a suburban living room than the lair of a voodoo queen. Thick carpet covered the floor; a lumpy, threadbare sofa stretched along one wall. The only other seat in the room—a wicker-framed futon with a thick green cushion— creaked and snapped as Celeste lowered herself into it. A ceiling fan cut lazy circles overhead, most of its lights burnt out, which made the walls feel close, subterranean. A vanilla candle burned on a table in the corner, the kind that always smelled to Jude like fresh-baked yellow cake. An ancient behemoth of a television hud- dled in the other corner, tin-foil-patched rabbit ears on top of it. Celeste had the news on, the sound turned low. She reached over and clicked the knob, the picture squeezing down to a flickering point before vanishing. Faintly, from the front room, Jude could hear the girl making small talk with Regal.

Jude eased himself down onto the sofa, sure that wherever he sat, a spring waited to jab at him. The voodoo priestess picked up a sweating glass of iced tea from the top of the television, drink- ing from it in large, thirsty gulps. "So," she said, gesturing at him with the glass. "Why don't you say your piece so you can be on your way."

Jude considered asking for a drink, but something in her dark, glittering eyes said she wasn't in a hospitable mood, so he skipped the foreplay. "I need to know what you remember from the other night when Legba rode you."

One of her eyebrows, trimmed and plucked within an inch of its life, rose in an imperious arch. "What makes you think I'm gonna tell you a damn thing about that?"

The one thing Jude had found that all practitioners of magic had in common was a reluctance to share anything with those who weren't initiated into their little slice of the magical community. To a mamba like Celeste, a bokor like Jude was about the last person in the world she would willingly discuss the mysteries of her faith with. The trick, he'd learned, wasn't to pretend like you belonged. It was to show that you knew you *didn't* belong, and that you didn't care.

Jude grinned. "What makes you think I'm leaving without getting what I came for?"

She made a derisive noise halfway between a laugh and clearing her throat before taking one last drink from her tea, smacking her lips as she set it down. The gesture seemed false, somehow, part of an elaborate act. "This don't quite sit right," she said. "And I tell you right now, I don't care for you none, neither. But I'll tell you what I know to keep your shadow from off my doorstep." She gathered her dress in one hand, drawing her legs up beneath her. She gripped the fabric so tight that her knuckles whitened. Jude looked up from her fist to her tight jaw, her glaring eyes.

It wasn't anger making her combative, Jude realized, but fear. Was she afraid of what the loa would do to her for telling him things he ought not know? Or was she afraid of him?

"What I can tell you ain't much," she said. "Ain't exactly like you got a clear head when the loa ride you. What you remember is less than the whispers of a dream. All I know from the other night is one minute I'm asking Papa Legba's leave to talk to the spirits, next thing I know it's morning and my mouth tastes like . . ." She made a face. "Legba always rode my husband, Damballah protect us. He liked the pipe Legba smokes, him."

"So if I needed to speak to Legba, you could make—"

Celeste was already shaking her head. "No, no. Don't work like that. Papa come when he come, not when you want. You got a need, you *ask;* you don't *tell* nothin'."

Jude clenched his jaw. "I'm not known for my patience, Ms. Dorcet."

"Hold your water," she said. "I'm getting to it. This about that card game, right?"

Card game? A frisson of suspicion ran up the back of Jude's neck. "Thought you said you didn't remember anything."

"I said it was like a dream, though a nightmare is closer to the truth. I ain't like to forget that room this side of the grave." She gave him a look, a tightening of the lips and a tilt of the head that said that he was one of the things she remembered. "Point is, the next day when I woke up, head full of rum and smoke and bad dreams, I had one thought real clear, in Papa Legba's voice, not mine. It said I had to be ready, because he was gonna need a horse to ride again in a couple, three days."

"Again? For what?"

She shook her head. "Like he would say. Some funeral, I 'spect."

"Why do you say that?"

" 'Cause that's his place. The crossroads between this world and the next. That's why we call on him first of all the loa, so he can open the way. And when you go to your grave? You best hope Papa Legba there to show you the way home."

Out on the sidewalk, Regal had her phone up to her ear, listening and nodding and frowning. She mouthed "Mourning," and then pantomimed a hangman's noose drawing tight, eyes squeezed shut and her tongue lolling out. Jude stifled a laugh and looked up and down Rampart Street, realizing he had no idea where they should go next. It was an alien, unsettling feeling for him. His whole life he'd followed his gift at times like this. The results might have been cryptic—once he'd been drawn to fire hydrants, another time to a certain vintage of wine — but once he understood what his gift was trying to tell him, it had always led him the right way. Living without it made even familiar sights uncertain, a bad dream of his childhood home where the rooms were all out of place, a compass needle forever spinning with no true North.

Regal slid her phone into her back pocket and made a dramatic sigh. "Hope you got some good news," she said, " 'cause His Mourningness is getting impatient."

"She told me where we can find Legba."

"Fuckin' A. Where's that?"

"Dodge's funeral."

Regal pulled in a deep breath and puffed out her cheeks when she blew it out. "Well, that sounds like a whole barrel of fucked up. Good luck with that." She waved off Jude's questioning eyebrow. "I know, I know. Not my idea. Mourning's got me chasing down another lead. Something about the Egyptian god."

"You don't need help with that?"

She waved him off. "Don't worry about me. I can be invisible when I want to be." She yawned, then, abrupt and intense, the kind that looked like it hurt a little. "Jesus, but first I'm going to crash for a while. Unless you've got something in that bag that'll keep me awake for a few days."

"I do, actually, but you wouldn't like the side effects."

"This is me not asking," she said. She pulled tourist Mandy's little pink cell phone out of her back pocket and tossed it to him. "Here. Saved my number in the contacts. Catch up with me tomorrow. You know, if you're still alive." She grinned artificially wide, showing all her teeth. "Sleep tight!"

But he couldn't sleep. He tossed and turned for an hour or so before giving it up as a lost cause and going back to the piles of books and websites he and Regal had spent the morning searching through.

It was like a jigsaw puzzle without a picture. He could sense that an answer, a pattern existed, but the shape of the thing eluded him. He knew one of the gods at the card game had murdered Dodge, and it wasn't too far of a leap to presume that the "big prize" they'd all been playing for was the motive.

What could that prize be, though? What could Dodge possibly offer a bunch of deities that they couldn't attain on their own? And why, he wondered, was it of interest to those particular gods? What did a god of scribes, an angel, a vampire, and a god of the crossroads all have in common? It was a riddle with no answer, a joke with no punch line. He couldn't ignore Regal's insistence on including him in the group, too. He'd been invited to that same table. Whatever united them, it was a connection Jude shared, a link to his long-absent father. Figuring out the nature of the prize wouldn't just help him find Dodge's murderer.

He might also find himself.

CHAPTER EIGHT

THE GOD LIVES; the god dies; the god lives again. Killed by a spear of sharpened mistletoe, or upon a cross of cedar, or in the midst of a sacred ball game. Or he is torn apart by his brother, his limbs scattered from one end of the kingdom to another. Or he collapses with exhaustion during the harvest. Or he is devoured by monstrous giants, leaving only his heart behind. After death, he travels to the Underworld, for three days, or a year, or nine months, or until the world itself dies if the right conditions are not met. The important thing is that the one-who-died always returns, stitched back together by his wife, born of a new mother's womb, rising from the earth with the corn, or the wheat, or the grapevine. Reassembled, resplendent, reborn. Whether in cycles or only once, whether meant to represent the final chapter of the world or the promise of ever-renewing life, these stories, these myths, share one crucial truth: Even the gods can die.

❖

Jude stepped out of the cab and onto Basin Street, where one of the rare pleasant summer days in New Orleans bloomed, a strong breeze sweeping the thick, hot air from the streets, the sky bright and clear and ceramic blue. It was hard to ruin days like this. Yesterday the heat had been nearly unbearable, tomorrow the rain would likely come in torrents, but this day felt like grace, like benediction. In a strange way, it was the perfect day for a funeral.

Unsure where Dodge was going to be buried, Jude started with St. Louis Cemetery No. 1, since it was the oldest one in the city. It felt strange, trusting his only promising lead to what amounted to an educated guess, but without his gift tugging him in the right direction, he had to hope for a little luck. But any vestige of doubt vanished as he walked up to the neutral ground between Our Lady of Guadalupe Church and the cemetery. The crowd, milling around like a casting call for the hallucinations of a drying-out drunk, told him he'd come to the right place.

A centaur—his hair and beard shaggy and wild—exchanged greetings with a nāgiṇī—a white woman in a punk rock leather jacket from the waist up, a huge, coiled serpent the rest of the way down. A fat brown-skinned man with the head of an elephant flicked and curled his wide ears. A hairy giant rested in the shade of an oak tree, his huge bare feet spread out in front of him. A black woman who appeared normal save for the blue flame that burned above her head seemed to be talking to someone high in the oak's branches, though when a mouth formed in the foliage and replied, Jude realized that it was the tree itself she spoke to. Jude saw werewolves and a many-armed goddess of destruction, a Roman god with a face on either side of his head, animals that stood and wore clothes like men, a monkey carved out of stone, and things for which he knew no name. Jude wondered how many of these beings had come to pay their respects to Dodge, and how many were just here for the inevitable debauchery afterward. Jude had no doubt that there would be a drunken wake for the fortune god; Dodge had been a god of New Orleans, through and through.

A tapping noise invaded Jude's thoughts, growing closer until it stopped with a final *clack*. Jude felt a tug at his coat. He turned to find Celeste next to him, leaning on a cane so heavily that her arm trembled from the tension. She wore a suit of pale lavender, her jacket and pants, her trilby hat and tie and gleaming shoes all the exact same shade. Something in the coordination seemed comical, almost cartoonish. She held one hand to her hat, keeping it slanted against her head despite the stiff wind threatening to tear it loose.

"Lend me the strength of them sturdy legs of yours to aid me 'cross the way," she said in a voice not her own, a sonorous patois of French and African accents that Jude recognized from Dodge's card game.

"Legba?"

"That's how they call me, true enough." For a moment, Jude saw the loa himself and not the woman he rode, wrinkles creased at the corners of his eyes, an ancient gap-toothed smile. Legba crushed a knob-knuckled grip around Jude's arm and pointed toward the crowd of deities with the tip of the cane. "They won't wait forever, them."

Jude chuckled and helped Legba across the street, unsure whether Legba held tightly to him for support or to keep him from getting away. As they drew closer, Jude's nostrils were assaulted by the scent of spices and the odor of hot flesh, the burnt ozone of a thunderstorm, the stink of rot. He picked out the other players at the card game from among the restless group. Thoth, still wearing his Jazz Fest T-shirt and jeans, rested in the grass with his legs folded, his bird's head buried in a book. Scarpelli leaned against the cemetery wall, attention focused on a smartphone. He wore a dark suit with a tie the brownish-red tint of a fresh scab. The angel swooped in from above just as the crowd began to quiet, wings snapping, toe tips prancing along the ground.

Jude turned along with everyone else when the doors of the funeral home creaked open, the sound loud enough to be heard from across the street. The pallbearers emerged, six shadowy figures holding a coffin aloft. The gods hushed, and it seemed like the city itself silenced around them, the only sound that of the pall-bearers' footsteps, hooves clopping on asphalt instead of the soft tread of human feet. The smell of sulfur grew overpowering. The wind died down.

When the pallbearers turned in a slow, precise circle to face down Basin, they shifted, changing shape with liquid grace. Within moments, six roughly man-shaped shadows with a black casket hoisted on their shoulders became an ebony carriage and two shaggy-maned horses, pawing at the street and snorting gouts of fiery snot. The wind returned, as if on cue, kicking up the dust beneath the huge wooden-spoked wheels, billowing up into a plume of smoke. Where it blew, images flickered — vague figures, indistinct like something glimpsed in an early morning fog. A single moan hung in the air, a note played on a brass instrument. The note doubled, trebled, and then the dust swept away, and the carriage rolled forward, followed by the shades of a brass band, playing a slow, mournful tune. As one, Jude and the assembled deities fell into step with them. Still leaning on Jude's arm, Legba produced a pint bottle of Old New Orleans Rum, took a long swallow, and held it out with a little shake. Jude hesitated, wanting sobriety when he questioned the loa, but knowing disrespect wouldn't get him anywhere. He tipped the bottle back and swallowed twice before returning the rum.

Jude expected the procession to move across to the cemetery, but it wound its way down to Canal, step by halting step. Traffic stopped without the usual need for a police escort. As they turned onto the busy street and headed away from the river, Jude wondered what the tourists behind their cameras and the locals frozen behind their steering wheels saw. Did they see a normal funeral procession with a hearse and a convoy of cars, or the somber parade of a traditional jazz funeral, the death of a local musician beloved enough to shutdown Canal Street? Did the convoy of deities pass unseen in the darkness between one blink and the next? Then the music and the rum caught his mind and his steps, and, for a time, he thought nothing at all.

If Canal Street was a river, its head was the bustling life of downtown, and its mouth was a broad delta of cemeteries, a city of the dead that sprawled for over a mile, divided, like any city, into neighborhoods. St. Patrick's, for instance, was the poorer part of town, with many of its headstones and iron fences falling into disrepair. Lake Lawn, tucked away on the other side of an interstate overpass, was the resting place of the affluent, huge crypts replete with stained-glass windows and finely crafted statues. In between was Greenwood, a typical New Orleans cemetery with aboveground stone tombs laid out with the regularity of a suburb, like the shotgun doubles where many of those buried had lived and died.

It should have taken Jude at least an hour to walk the three-mile stretch between the Quarter and the cemeteries, but carried along with the funeral procession, it seemed to take no time at all. The carriage took a sharp right at the corner of Canal Street and City Park Avenue, entering a small graveyard that Jude had seen before but always somehow ignored. Ten-foot-high stone walls obscured everything in the small patch of land between the streetcar line and St. Patrick's Cemetery. As Jude followed the deities through the wrought-iron gate, he looked up at the words carved in sunken relief on the arch above: ODD FELLOW'S REST. *Odd fellows,* Jude thought. *That's an understatement.*

The vegetation beyond the graveyard walls had long ago moved past being overgrown. This was the swamp of hundreds of years ago reasserting itself right in the center of the city. The dominant colors in most New Orleans cemeteries were varying shades of gray: marble statues and tombs with crumbling plaster, concrete walls and walkways made of oyster-shell gravel. Here, everything was green. Grass and brambles and vines crept up underfoot while elephant-ear leaves held sway overhead. It seemed larger on the inside than out, which didn't surprise Jude at all; most things were.

Despite the relative coolness of the day, sweat dampened the skin between Jude's shoulder blades and itched at the edge of his beard. Gnats rose in hordes from every disturbance of greenery, every shuffled footstep, and every branch brushed out of the way. They fell on him, irritating pinpricks along his flesh, as if sensing that he alone had mortal flesh to bite. He wandered amid the trees and the graves, awed, falling behind the rest of the procession. By the time he caught up to the gods, they had already reached Dodge's crypt.

The angel perched on one of a row of gravestones facing away from Jude, delicately balanced on the pockmarked granite. Occasionally, the angel's wings shuddered, flinging a fine mist of dew and the scent of spice into the air. Beyond him, Legba leaned on his cane next to Thoth, who still held a book, one of his thick fingers wedged between the pages to mark his place. Scarpelli stood with one hip cocked above the other, his thumbs typing on the device in his hand. His posture, the smartphone, all of it seemed somehow disrespectful, bored.

The ebony carriage waited in a shaft of pollen-filled sunlight, its doors opened wide, its interior empty. Dodge's body must already be in the tomb. Unlike the others Jude had seen, Dodge's burial chamber was not granite or marble, but bronze, centuries of weather coating it with verdigris, a greenish black that spread across its surface like a rash.

A tall, lanky man in a dark, pristine tuxedo unfolded from inside the bronze structure, spinning and closing the doors behind him. Jude's skin went cold at the sight of him. He had no face, no ears, no flesh anywhere on his head, just the smooth bone and rictus grin of a skull. Whorls and blooming flowers of bright paint adorned the glistening surface of his head, like a tattoo, like a calavera sugar skull. That grim visage swept back and forth across the assembled gods, jaws clacking as he spoke, words that Jude either couldn't quite hear or were in a language he couldn't comprehend, and then the skull-faced god stepped up to the carriage and closed the doors. The horses strained in their traces, pulling the carriage forward, and the brass band ripped the solemn air of the cemetery with the first notes of bright, energetic music. Had the funeral really been that brief, or had Jude wandered longer than he thought? The gods began to dance, handkerchiefs waving in the air, second-lining their way out of the graveyard.

Wings snapped and fluttered, the angel taking flight, followed by Thoth in the shape of a small white bird. The vampire was nowhere to be seen. "Shit," Jude muttered. "Shit, shit." He stepped forward, needing to catch up to Legba before he left, too, but a white gloved hand fell on his shoulder and stopped him. A voice spoke into his ear, deep and similar to Legba's, but rasping as though strained by illness. "You looking for someone?" it asked. Jude didn't need to turn around to know that when he did, he'd be looking into the empty eyes of the skull-faced god.

There was a weak flutter of fear in his gut, but he pushed it down. He'd let the fear win in Mourning's office, let fear rule his life for six years—and it had gotten him nowhere.

Maybe it was time to let the old Jude out of the box.

He turned and grinned in the face of death. "Maybe," he said, hoping those empty eye sockets wouldn't see too easily through his bravado, "I'm looking for you. Are you 'angelface666' on Match.com?"

The skull-headed god's jaw clicked as it opened and closed, and a frisson rose the hair on the back of Jude's neck, when he realized what was happening. He'd made a death god *smile*.

"Who I am is either a real long answer," the god said, "or a real short one. Which you want?" He eased back onto the edge of a tomb, his long arms and legs bending at right angles like a thing made of sticks.

"Let's try the short one."

"Then call me Barren."

Jude knew that many of the ghede—the voodoo family who handled death—went by the honorific "Baron." Cimetière, Samedi, La Croix; this god could be any of them or someone else entirely. "You saying I ought to curtsy?" he asked.

The skull-faced god snorted out a laugh. "Naw," he said. "Barren like a field that don't bear no fruit." He slid a gloved hand into his tuxedo jacket and pulled out a silver flask. Barren unscrewed the cap and took a long drink. There was something very unsettling in the way his teeth clinked against the metal, in the way the alcohol seemed to vanish in between the bone of his jaw and the pale gray of the cravat that hid his neck. Jude hoped, desperately, that he wouldn't offer to share. Barren finished and put the flask away, running his gloved hands along his painted skull, like a man smoothing his hair. "No sense in my askin' who you are."

"Because it's obvious?"

"Naw," Barren said, shaking his head. "'Cause you don't know your own self." Barren turned his head away, as if, despite being earless, he heard something Jude could not. "You better figure it out, though. Quick and in a hurry, too. You about run outta time."

"Time? For what?"

"For anything." He turned his empty eye sockets back toward Jude, holes that seemed to fall away to cavernous depths. "You ain't askin' the right questions." He sounded, Jude realized, disappointed.

"What kinds of questions should I be asking?"

Bony shoulders lifted up into a shrug. "I know 'em when I hear 'em."

"Fine. Let's go with the obvious one. Who killed Dodge?"

Barren's gloved hands came together in a soft, patronizing clap. "Better," he said. "But I got no answer to that one." He pulled at his cuffs, an oddly vain, fussy gesture.

Something about Barren's coy, taunting replies burned away the last of Jude's restraint, let his temper off the leash. "You won't tell me who you are—don't know who I'm looking for—why the fuck am I talking to you?"

Again that clicking jaw, mouth gaping open like a serpent's smile. "'Cause I know somethin' you don't," Barren said. "I know who you are."

"Yeah? And who is that?"

"That," he said, "is the right question." Barren reached out, fingers giving a little sleight-of-hand flourish. A large playing card appeared in his hand, which he angled toward Jude. "Compliments of the dearly departed," Barren said. It was a tarot card, THE MA-GICIAN, a robed figure pointing to the sky and to the ground. The man on the card had Jude's face. When he looked up, Barren was gone, leaving him alone with only the dead for company.

The tourist's pretty pink phone buzzed in Jude's pocket with a text. Instead of a number, the phone displayed a series of *X*'s. *Waiting for you out front.* He slid the tarot card into his coat pocket and started typing a reply, but stopped halfway between *right* and *out.* He'd presumed it was Regal, but hadn't she saved her number? It couldn't be her, he realized; she'd have no idea where he was.

Jude rummaged through his satchel, thoughts racing. He had a couple of magical disguises, but none were good enough to fool someone who was actively looking for him, since there was just one exit, and he was the last one still in the cemetery. There were wards and charms he could work to protect himself, if only he knew who—or what—was waiting for him. He considered a handful of ways to escape, and then the old Jude spoke up. *What if that's one of the card players you've been looking for?* he asked himself. *What's it gonna take for you to quit running? How many different kinds of timid little shit are you gonna be?*

Inside the satchel, his fingers brushed against a slim rod, humming with energy. Just a touch filled his veins with fire and swagger like he'd drunk the whole bottle of rum that Legba had offered.

The solution to the worst-case scenario, to *every* worst-case scenario. He grinned. Not even Mourning knew he'd been walking around with an honest-to-Zeus thunderbolt in his bag all this time. Confidence at least somewhat regained, he finished his message, *be right out,* and hit send.

Just outside the gate, a Cadillac—long and dark and low, washed and waxed to a polished gleam—idled next to the curb. The chauffeur stood at the rear door, a tall, thin specter, his posture so rigid it was unnerving. Jude's tongue probed the inside of his mouth to see if he'd bitten his lip. No wound, but he still tasted . . . blood.

The mirror-tinted window rolled down, smooth and whirring, to reveal the vampire Scarpelli. Jude's arm twitched, eager to reach for the thunderbolt.

"Afternoon, Sunshine," Scarpelli said in his high-pitched rasp. His blotchy corpse's skin looked even worse in the daylight. Jude tried to keep his breathing calm, hoping the vampire couldn't smell his fear like people said dogs could. He felt the vampire's eyes traveling up and down his body, judging his fashion sense or looking for the best place to bite.

"Isn't it a little bright out here for you?" Jude asked.

A disappointed click of the tongue. "You watch too many movies. Though I do abhor this heat. Come, get in. I'm here to collect you."

A flash of memory, the doubloon with the drop of blood that Scarpelli demanded of him. "You didn't win that hand," Jude said. The words sounded hollow even as he said them. As though Scarpelli had never broken the rules before.

The dead god smiled wide enough to show his fangs, his gums stained black. "Not to collect you like that, sweetmeats. Not yet." Again the vampire eyed him, his gaze full of some predatory combination of hunger and lust that turned Jude's stomach. "Merely a ride and some conversation. A . . . proposal of sorts."

The chauffeur opened the door, and—though every mammalian instinct he possessed screamed for him to run—Jude eased into the car, the space within frigid and dim, filled with the sterile stink of an industrial freezer. Two rows of benched leather seats faced each other. A young blonde waited inside, wearing a long pencil skirt and a silk blouse buttoned tight against her neck. High as the collar rose, it didn't entirely hide the ragged scar on the side of her throat. Jude saw, then, the pale, unnatural tautness of her skin, the red stain in the whites of her eyes, recognized her as the woman from St. Joe's, the chauffeur as the scruffy-haired bartender. Ghouls. Revenants. The leftovers of Scarpelli's dinner up and walking around, chained to a semblance of life, forced to be his servants.

The woman turned to the small side bar, her movements a detached, near-convincing mimicry of volition, a marionette controlled by a skilled hand. She opened a glass decanter and poured half a glass of some rust-colored liquid, the flow of it smooth and viscous as motor oil.

Scarpelli took it from her as the car rolled into traffic. "Where are my manners," the vampire asked. "Would you care for one? I mix it myself. The trick is, you add the gin when the blood is still hot, so it doesn't fully coagulate." Jude turned his attention to the tinted windows, trying to hide the revulsion he knew must be in his eyes. The vampire giggled anyway. "Yes, well, there's no accounting for taste."

"I thought the same thing just the other day," Jude said, letting some of the vampire's indifferent tone creep into his own inflection, "when Dodge invited an immortal tick to his card game." As soon as the insult left his lips, a feeling of vertigo washed over him, an instinctive repulsion away from the danger he was in, but Jude was desperate. He'd lost his chance to talk to Legba; he needed to goad the vampire into revealing something.

If Scarpelli noticed the barb, he ignored it. "Ah yes, *the game*. Just the thing I wanted to talk to you about." There was something of an eye roll in the way he said "the game," as though the whole experience was beneath him. "I have to admit, I was impressed by your gambit. Quite clever. Just the sort of thing I can make use of when the prize is mine."

"The prize?" This was his big gamble. A bluff wrapped in a mask. He had to seem like he was feigning ignorance about a thing he really didn't know, so the vampire would see through one deception, but not the deeper one.

"Oh, let's not be coy with one another, precious. You know as well as I that whoever leaves the game with the most tokens—which will be this current hand, given your delightful little gambit—will do so as the luck god of New Orleans."

Jude kept his face impassive, even as his mind whirled. He couldn't let Scarpelli know how much he'd just revealed. He thought back to that night, the vampire not bothering to turn his cards over after Dodge showed his own. "Funny," Jude said, "you didn't seem that confident in your hand before."

Scarpelli sipped his drink, rolling it around on his tongue like a fine wine. "That was before your little trick," he said. "I've had time to make some side wagers thanks to you, and with that fool Renaud out of the way—"

"Glad I could help," Jude said, the words spilling out before he could stop them. A glance out the window showed him that the car was moving unwaveringly in the direction of his apartment, and the thought that the vampire might know where he lived made him too jumpy to be able to stomach Scarpelli's gloating. "You have an offer for me?"

All pretense of playfulness slipped from the vampire's face, leaving only cold, calculating hunger in its wake. He drained his glass and held it out to the ghoul without bothering to look in her direction. He reached into his coat pocket with his other hand and pulled out the doubloon from the card game. Jude had to clench his hands into fists to keep from reaching for it.

"So," the vampire said. "Here's my proposition." He turned

the doubloon in an idle circle in his palm. "Your blood is mine, precious. That much is certain. The only question is whether it is more useful to me in your veins, serving me, or on my tongue, feeding me." The vampire snapped forward, far too quickly for a creature of flesh and bone, too fast for Jude to react, so close Jude could smell the blood-soaked gin on the vampire's cold breath. Scarpelli inhaled deeply, eyes squeezed shut. He sighed and sat back, a parody of satiation. "I confess, I can scarce restrain myself. But it's best to let such a complicated, nuanced vintage breathe, isn't it?" He seemed to be talking to himself. For a while Jude sat, heart pounding, staring straight ahead, unable to move, unable to speak.

Petrified. Prey.

It had been foolish to think the thunderbolt would put them on equal footing. If the vampire wished him harm, he'd bite before Jude could even reach into his satchel.

They rounded a corner and drove through the flashing lights of NOPD cruisers and an ambulance. A huddle of uniforms stood around a cloth-covered shape on the ground, some smoking, some talking into the microphones on their shoulders. A leg poked out from underneath the sheet, a shoe with its sole falling away from the toe, like the lolling tongue of a dog.

No. It can't be.

A vision flashed in front of Jude's eyes with awful clarity: the young street performer, his painted jester's mask sweat-streaked and smeared, terror etched on his face.

The Cadillac swept past the crime scene, and Jude forced himself to look back at the vampire. Scarpelli let out a soft chuckle and —perhaps following his gaze, perhaps actually reading his mind— answered his unspoken question. "Not one of mine, sweetmeats," he said. "I don't leave my leftovers out in the street like that."

Jude leaned back into the leather seat, feigning nonchalance, the chilly air of the car seeping into his bones. Even before the storm, if he'd passed that close to a murder, he'd have felt the weight of all the years and the joys and the futures that the victim had lost. The gravity of all that loss would, like a lodestone, point back toward the killer. He wouldn't wonder; he'd *know* if that dead body was Tommy's, would know who was responsible. There was an emptiness in him now, a numbness in his hands where power had once lived. He'd hated his gift after the storm, called it a curse. Now that he was being forced to live without it, he fervently, urgently wanted it back.

Though he'd suspected they were heading in that direction, it was still an unpleasant jolt when the Cadillac eased to a stop in front of Jude's apartment. *So much for all my clever magic keeping my home hidden,* he thought. Jude put his hand on the door handle, eager to be gone. "I hope you're offended when I don't invite you in," he said. Unlike their supposed vulnerability to sunlight, a vampire's need for an invitation to enter a person's home had its basis in reality, not fiction.

Scarpelli pulled a business card out of his coat pocket, used it to wave in the direction of Jude's front door. "That little inconvenience doesn't apply to you, I'm afraid. You know, home is where the heart is, and all that." He held the card—blood-red ink, of course—between two pointed fingers, which he used to tap Jude's chest. "You wagered your heart away, remember?" Jude took the card, an address, nothing more, and opened the door into warmth and sunlight and escape. Before he could leave, Scarpelli spoke again. "Your blood is *mine*, sweetmeats. You can be one of them," he nodded at the revenants, "or you can work for me for as long as you prove useful. Thirty years? Fifty? I'm nothing if not patient."

Jude slid the card into his coat pocket, right next to the tarot card that bore his face. "I'll think about it," he said, hoping it was a halfway convincing lie.

"Think quickly," the dead god said, "I expect your answer by tomorrow night."

"Thought you said you were patient."

The vampire bared his fangs. Only a fool would call it a smile. "I'm also very, very hungry."

Back inside his apartment, Jude opened an Abita and drank half of it in long, thirsty swallows to rinse the taste of blood out of his mouth, then took a scalding hot shower to scrub the feeling of the vampire's gaze off of his skin. Once he felt reasonably clean, he pulled on a pair of worn jeans and an old Saints T-shirt and went back to the pile of books and printed webpages sprawled over his living room floor. He flipped idly through mythology texts and books on tarot, coming to the realization that he'd relied on his magic for this in the past, too, happening across the information he needed instead of tracking it down. He got up for another beer and checked both his landline and the tourist's pink phone, but the only person who had called was his mother, leaving a guilt-trip message on his old-school answering machine.

Where the hell was Regal? She'd changed in the last six years in some way he couldn't articulate. He thought about calling her but decided he needed some time to organize his thoughts, first.

Scarpelli had a doubloon that entitled him to Jude's blood. It was an invasion, somehow, a violation. Shameful and frustrating and infuriating all at once. It felt like being robbed, but worse, as though the vampire had stolen something intensely private, like nude pictures or shitty teenage poetry, something worthy of black-mail. He had to assume that each of the other gods still had one of his coins as well. His blood, his speech, his devotion. Hazy as his memory of that night was, he remembered that much. It wasn't much of a leap to guess that his gift, which he'd lost on the same night as all of those doubloons, was tied to one of the coins.

He took a deep breath and forced himself to think past his own problems. He still didn't know the ultimate purpose of the game, the prize Scarpelli was taking steps to claim. His first thought—the most satisfying one—was that the vampire had killed Dodge.

He'd shown nothing but glee at the mention of Dodge's death, had practically thanked Jude for giving the killer the opportunity.

But it didn't feel right. If Scarpelli killed Dodge, why hadn't he bragged about it, the way he'd bragged about the side wagers he made to undermine the game? For that matter, why restrain himself from killing Jude, if his strategy for winning involved eliminating those with better cards than his? Jude had a hand full of wild cards. The hardest part of Dodge's murder to reconcile with Scarpelli as the villain, though, was the blood spilled across the card table.

There was no way the vampire would let that much go to waste.

Jude closed his eyes and dropped his head back, picturing the scenes he and Regal had seen through the door they'd summoned, everything else that had happened in the past couple of days shifting around in the back of his mind. Dodge's poker hand: four QUEENS and a HIGH PRIESTESS, each one with Regal's face. A fortune god dead on his table, his throat gashed open. Jude's own cards on the table: four blank, one a vague, exploratory sketch. The cryptic explanation of the game's rules. The vampire's reference to Jude's "trick." Jude's conversation with Barren in Odd Fellow's Rest. Several puzzle pieces aligned in Jude's mind with a clarity so perfect, he felt an almost audible click, and his eyes popped open.

He snatched his jacket off the chair where he'd dropped it when he walked in, nearly tearing the inner pocket in his haste to get at its contents. Inside: Scarpelli's business card, and the tarot card Barren had given him. *Compliments of the dearly departed,* he'd said. The card was labeled THE MAGICIAN. The main image on the card was a man pointing to the sky and to the ground, a man with Jude's face. It was the same gesture he'd seen on the sketched card in Dodge's card room, the first card in Jude's hand. It all made sense. The reason the game wasn't over, the reason his cards had turned over blank.

He'd known that calling their game Fortunes meant the gods

were playing with fate, but he'd underestimated them. They weren't just revealing a person's destiny; they were using the cards they were dealt to *change* someone's destiny. These assholes were gambling with people's lives. Everyone except Jude, anyway.

Because if the cards had his face on them, the fate he was gambling with was his own.

CHAPTER NINE

JUDE WALKED up and down the rows in the parking lot of the Riverwalk, looking for a car to steal. Technically, he told himself, he only intended to *borrow* one, since he never kept the ones he took. Not that he'd lose sleep over it if the owners and automobiles were never reunited; he had some very particular criteria he followed in choosing his rides: Cadillac, Lexus, Mercedes-Benz, BMW—anything with the word "luxury" attached to it. Bonus points if there was a self-aggrandizing personalized license plate. He was looking to ruin some rich asshole's day, not screw up some broke person's year.

The little silver Porsche with tinted windows and "UENVME" plates the next row over was perfect.

He used the word Dodge taught him to unlock the door, then a sleep charm drawn with a finger on the dashboard quieted the alarm. He muttered a little prayer of gratitude that losing his gift hadn't cost him the rest of his magic. Once he was in the driver's seat, he dug through his satchel and took out a small tin box filled with long slips of paper. Written on each was a Shem—one of the hidden Names of God—in seventy-two Hebrew letters on one side and a different language on the other side. They were a gift from Mordecai Eichhorn, a rabbi with a nasty dybbuk problem that Jude had solved a few years before the storm. The papers still smelled like the mints the tin once held. He rifled through them, muttering to himself. Since the car was a Porsche, he needed one in German. He found it and slid the strip of paper into the ignition. The engine sparked and revved to life. *If I could mass-produce these,* he thought, *I'd sell 'em to Google, buy an island somewhere, and never worry about any of this shit again.*

Back at his apartment, he'd called Regal after his revelation about the card game and gotten her voicemail. He'd hung up without saying anything, then listened again to the message his mother had left on his answering machine. Paying closer attention this time, he'd heard a tense urgency hidden underneath her typical pleasant, innocuous rambling, the same sense of barely restrained panic that always compelled him to make a trip across Lake Pontchartrain to check up on her. Hence, the need to borrow a car.

Aided by the "Hailing a Cab" section of a Berlin travel guide he pulled out of his satchel, Jude told the Porsche in halting pidgin German what he wanted from it. Its only response was to put itself in drive and pull out of the parking lot, heading for the interstate. At the first red light, it cycled through a few radio stations, stopping on WWOZ, where Allen Toussaint's "Yes We Can Can" was playing.

Haven't heard this song since—shit. Since the day before the storm.

He'd left the city, but he hadn't gone far. Like most lifelong residents of New Orleans, Jude had grown complacent over the years as hurricanes came and went; even the ones that appeared threatening turned aside at the last moment. The names Betsy and Camille were invoked as ghost stories, but storms of that power hadn't been seen since the '60s. Like "the Big One" in California, like nukes launching from their silos, like airborne Ebola, a storm as strong as Katrina was the bogeyman, the monster under the bed, a worst-case scenario too horrible to be contemplated—unbelievable because it was too awful to be real. Six years ago, he'd been aware that a storm was in the Gulf, but he'd planned on riding it out the way he always had, with a bottle of Southern Comfort and a Walter Mosley novel. He'd had no intention of evacuating, had thought then as he did now: that he only needed the car for a quick trip across Lake Pontchartrain to check on his mother. He hoped like hell he wasn't as fucking wrong today as he'd been six years ago.

Once he was satisfied that the Porsche was heading in the right direction, Jude opened the book on tarot he'd brought from home, the MAGICIAN card tucked inside as a bookmark. Holding the card up to the illustration in the book was like a "spot the difference" puzzle on the back of a cereal box. The images were eerily similar, a figure standing next to a table in a garden, one hand raised to the sky, the other aimed at the ground. The magician in the book wore robes of red and white, had the twisted loop of an infinity symbol over his head, and held a candle with a small curl of flame burning at both ends in his upraised hand. The magician on Jude's card stood in the same position, but wore a scuffed leather jacket and a Rage Against the Machine T-shirt, an outfit he'd worn constantly in his misspent youth. Both magicians stood next to a small table, which held a staff, a sword, a coin, and a cup. They were the suits of the tarot, but they were also the tools a practitioner of magic would use. Like Jude's former teacher, Eli Constant.

According to the text underneath the illustration, THE MAGICIAN represented duality, pointing up and down to signify a connection to both Heaven and Earth, the spiritual and the material. Drawing this card during a reading might mean that you were trying to live in two worlds without belonging to either one, or that you were trying to bridge the gap between them. The more he read, the more he had to admit that it was an eerily accurate description of his own life. Before the storm, anyway.

He'd been an outsider even as a kid. His unusual parentage had fucked him up in all kinds of ways that had nothing to do with the magic. The complete absence of a father left him with only half an identity, drifting out of every culture and community he ever wandered into, when it became clear that he'd never really belonged, since no one could tell by looking at him if his dad had been black, or Native American, or Hispanic—though no white person ever presumed he was white.

It went beyond race, though. As far as the world of mortals was concerned, he didn't exist; he had no social security number, no birth certificate, no record of being real. He was "that kid" in his neighborhood: the one who didn't go to school, who stayed out as late as he wanted, who got blamed for whatever trouble was caused. His mother was frequently absent—sometimes merely too distracted to parent, but just as often literally gone—so he'd more or less raised himself. His education had been in the hands of a string of perpetually ditched tutors. There were no family connections to speak of—save for an unmarried, childless aunt who always seemed to forget he existed—and no cultures to claim as his own.

Throughout his life, he'd always felt alone, but that didn't mean he'd been lonely. He was both charming and clever, and he was strange in all the ways that children love and parents hate. He'd had many friends, but none that lasted. Scores of lovers, but never love. He snuck into people's lives just as easily as he slipped out of them. More than his skin tone, more than being a bastard, more than any lack of authority figure or shared experiences, it was what he knew that set him apart. The knowledge that magic was possible, that the gods were real, suffused everything he said and did, and made everything else just that much less important.

When you have a bit of god in you, it can be hard to pretend you give a shit about prom, or taxes, or any of the other things that are important in the mortal world.

So THE MAGICIAN fit him well, as far as having one foot in the material world and another in the world of spirits, but the rest of the description—maintaining the order of the universe, using the four symbols of the tarot (sword and wand, cup and coin) to keep everything in balance—that wasn't him at all. He thought back to the jobs he'd done and the tricks he'd pulled back when he and Regal had been partners, the one time in his life he'd felt like he'd belonged. The only balance he'd protected had been the one Mourning had cultivated. And now? Since the storm, he lived his life trying to make as little impact on as few lives as possible.

So maybe he'd been a magician once, but he sure as shit wasn't one anymore. Which might explain why his cards had turned up blank; even magic cards couldn't reveal your destiny if you'd abandoned it.

The thought of stepping off the path of fate brought an important detail into focus for him. He'd told Regal that being a god meant being trapped in a single identity, and that the only way out was death. It seemed that Dodge had offered a handful of deities a second option, though. Winning the game, according to the vampire Scarpelli, meant becoming something new: the luck god of New Orleans. How many times had he wished for that very thing in the last six years? For the ability to become someone else, *anyone* else, so long as it was a clean start. He understood, then, something about the god who had killed Dodge.

What was a little murder when weighed against the chance to be free?

His mother's room at St. Joseph's Abbey looked—and, more importantly, *smelled*—the same as it always did: a stink of oil paints and chemicals that slapped Jude in the face as soon as he opened the door. The small room was dedicated to artwork. Stacks of canvases three and four deep leaned against the mural-splashed walls; a small bookshelf crowded with art supplies. Even the thin blanket on her small cot was streaked and splotched from being used as a drop cloth.

A huge half-finished painting of the New Orleans skyline at dusk filled the center of the room, stretched across three different panels. The image stunned him, because it simply didn't belong. His mother's work had focused on metamorphosis since he was a child, the natural cycle of a tadpole becoming a frog, the mythic transformation of Daphne into a laurel tree. It was her obsession. Her decision to paint a cityscape all of a sudden was as alarming as if she'd randomly decided to start speaking exclusively in French. More alarming, in truth, because she'd actually done the French thing for a month when he was fifteen.

According to Eli Constant, the cantankerous old sorcerer who'd trained them both before Jude had been born, Lydia Dubuisson had been the most skilled magical practitioner the city of New Orleans had produced in a generation. Something in the act of childbirth had broken her, Eli claimed, which explained why women were so often priestesses and so seldom sorcerers. That sounded like some patriarchal bullshit to Jude, who'd always thought her oddities had more to do with the metamorphic experience of fucking a god than being a mother, but those thoughts always made him feel guilty just for existing, so he seldom wandered down that line of thinking. Regardless of how or why, what really mattered was that at one time, she'd been the heir apparent to the most powerful magician in the city, and these days she'd forget to eat if the monks at the abbey didn't prepare her meals for her. Jude had been way too young, barely ten at the time, to see the spell she'd cast to convince the monks she belonged among them, but as an adult, he was always impressed by its subtlety, at the seamless way she'd been integrated into the daily life of the abbey—almost as though keeping her healthy and safe was an act of devotion.

The sound of a woman humming shook Jude out of his head and back into the moment. Just as he recognized the melody of "Wear Your Black Dress," the song the pretty young woman in the voodoo shop had been singing, his mom danced around the corner of her triptych and saw him. She had bright blue eyes, a generous smile, and the milky-white skin and ample figure that Renaissance artists worshiped. She also—through magic or genes, Jude was never quite sure—looked to be about half as old as she actually was. In his more cynical moments, Jude thought it was her detachment from responsibility that kept her so youthful.

"My baby's come home!" she squealed, and leaped across the room to embrace him. For just a moment, it didn't matter that this was a borrowed room in a monastery, not the house Uptown where he'd grown up, boarded up since the storm. It didn't matter that he was a grown man and had come here because she'd sounded like she was on the brink of one of her episodes, nor that he was waist deep in a rising tide of shit. It didn't matter that, according to the vampire named Scarpelli, he'd traded away his heart on a hand of cards and thus couldn't have one. For just a moment Jude was a child again, caught up in the tenacious grip of his mother's arms, enveloped by the scent of her and the depth of her love for him. He was home.

Then he pulled back and saw the manic, glassy sheen to her blue eyes, and the feeling was gone.

His mother's episodes weren't dangerous, aside from the fact that she might neglect herself. She'd never been irritable or violent as mania sometimes manifested, nor did she suffer from any subsequent crash into depression that could indicate a bipolar disorder. Jude had done some reading after his mother had charmed the third shrink in a row—one of whom had offered to leave her husband for Lydia—into a clean bill of mental health, and had been grateful for the relative simplicity of his mother's mania. If anything, when she went off the rails, it was merely an amplification of her normal behavior: odd obsessions, frenetic activity, euphoria, and a disassociation from the necessities and responsibilities of mundane life. Deciding French was the perfect language, for instance, was the sort of eccentric thing his mother might declare in her normal state. If the same thought occurred to her when she was in the grip of one of her episodes, though, she'd spend a month acting as though it was the only language she could understand, translating every book she owned, and refusing to eat anything but French cuisine. He'd even caught her on the darknet trying to buy a stolen passport just so she could fly into Paris as a French citizen.

A week later, she asked the monks to order pizza for dinner, and the French obsession vanished like it had never happened.

Over the years, he'd learned some of the warning signs that said a storm was on the horizon and came up with a few coping mechanisms to steer her toward calmer waters. The most consistent rudder, he'd found, was to guide her back to the obsession that she'd clung to his entire life: an artistic depiction of the concept of transformation.

He disentangled himself from her embrace and gestured toward the unfinished painting of the skyline. "What's this, Ma? This why you called me?"

She tilted her head to the side; her brow furrowed. "I didn't—" she began, and then, abruptly, smiled and changed the subject. "This is the scary city," she said, curling her fingers into claws and twisting her face into a pantomime snarl. "Rawr. Do you like it?" Jude tried to keep his face from betraying his thoughts, hoping he hadn't inherited his mother's terrible poker face. She was losing time and forgetting things. At least she was still lucid enough to try to cover it up.

He looked at the painting, unsure what was supposed to be so scary about it. After a few moments, he realized that if he focused on the negative space of the image, the gaps between the low clouds and the high-rise hotels and office buildings of downtown became sharp, jagged teeth, a fanged mouth opened wide. *Nope,* he thought. *Don't like this at all.*

He started to ask her why she'd decided the city she'd always loved should be frightening, but she grabbed his hand with one of hers, pressed a finger to his lips with the other. "Shhh," she said. "The one you really have to see is a secret. Can't let the brothers know." Dreading what she had to show him, Jude let his mother lead him to the bathroom door. "In here," she said, "is the very best work I've ever done. It's not finished yet, so try not to see what it *is*, but what it *will be*." With that cryptic request, she put his hand on the bathroom doorknob and stepped back, a coy, unreadable expression on her face.

Inside her closet of a bathroom, a single bare bulb glared on the bright spray of colors on the walls. She'd coated them, floor to ceiling, with a mural of the past few days of Jude's life. She'd perfectly re-created his conversation with Mourning, every detail accurate down to his steaming cup of coffee. She'd left the bright god's face a blank oval of thick reddish brown, broken only by two globs of bright blue to represent his eyes. Above the toilet, Legba clutched Jude's arm while they crossed Rampart Street to join the crowd at Dodge's funeral. Here he was talking to Leon Carter in the alley behind the Maple Leaf; there he and Regal were outlining the summoning circle. In every depiction, Jude's shadow stretched out behind him, emaciated, clawed, somehow sinister. On the ceiling, in dark purple, were the sharp, abrupt lines of a stylized star, or a compass on an old map. At its center, the doubloon with the heart shape that Jude had lost.

Larger than any of the finished scenes, she'd sketched out an outline of the card game in charcoal, recognizable by the round swoop of the table and the twin arches of the angel's wings, by the curved scythe of Thoth's beak and the fat, bald dome of Dodge's head.

Perhaps most distressing of all: she'd painted her bathroom door the exact shade of red as the one he and Regal had summoned.

Jude sat on the toilet seat's lid with a hollow *thump*. On the opposite wall, a cartoonish streetcar curved with the twists and hills of a track that wove, like a roller coaster, through lightning-streaked storm clouds. A figure he didn't recognize stood behind the driver's controls, winged and robed and beast-faced, while in the passenger windows Jude could see Dodge's gleaming head and

Tommy's clown-make-upped face. *What could those two possibly have in common?* he thought.

Everything else, weird as it was, at least kind of made sense. It wasn't the *why* of the rest of the mural that troubled him so much as the *how:* Had someone told his mother what was happening in his life? Or had she seen it herself? But the two figures in the streetcar didn't belong together, unless —

He remembered the body he'd seen from Scarpelli's car, the suspicion that it might be Tommy, and knew with sudden, awful conviction that the young street performer was dead. He still had no idea what might have tied them together, though. Why anyone would kill both a god and a twenty-year-old who spent his days in clown makeup was beyond him.

Whatever the reason, it made him really fucking angry.

After a few more minutes of studying her mural and trying to wrap his head around his mother's sudden ability to spy on his every waking moment — at least, he hoped it was sudden, considering his misspent youth — Jude turned to leave the bathroom, already putting together a list of questions for her in his head. He froze with his hand on the knob, an ornate twist of metal instead of the smooth, round bulb he'd expected. He backed away until his ass hit the ceramic of the sink, hoping to spot some detail that would tell him he was wrong, but knowing he was right. His mother hadn't mimicked the door to Dodge's card game.

The Red Door had followed him.

It took him about twenty minutes to admit it, but after he'd exhausted all his other options, which included banging on the wall and yelling for help, Jude was forced to accept the truth: the fucking door had him cornered.

The bathroom had no windows or any other exits save the door, unless he managed to magically shrink himself and go down the sink's drain. Aside from the fact that every piece of shrinking fiction he'd ever read or watched told him what a terrible idea that was, he couldn't even explore the possibility, because he'd left his satchel sitting on the passenger seat of the borrowed Porsche. All he had on him was a wallet—empty aside from a couple of fake IDs—a handkerchief, and the tourist's little pink cell phone, which had finally died at some point on the drive across the lake, since he didn't have a way to charge its battery. He couldn't wait for his mother to open the bathroom door; during her manic episodes, she sometimes got so focused, she was nearly catatonic. He'd once seen her make a single brushstroke and then stare at it for over an hour, literally watching paint dry.

Plus, there were the metaphysical implications of whether she'd actually be able to open a door that wasn't technically the same door on the other side.

Once he came to the decision to go back through the Red Door, Jude found that his old fuck-you grin was stretched across his face. The old Jude didn't care that it was obviously some kind of trap. He'd always found that the best thing about traps was their tendency to backfire.

Inside, Dodge's card room was just the way he'd left it: stuffy and musty and dark, stopped cat clock on the wall, bloodstain on the table. He found his way back to the stranded seconds he'd come to think of as slivers of time with no difficulty, slipping into each one as though they were steps in a well-practiced dance. He paused within them, testing them against his memory, trying to puzzle out what made these moments significant. The first few were frustrating, oblique, like trying to build a narrative out of random photographs that had no connection. It wasn't until he stood within the sliver where he'd turned over blank cards that he noticed a change. Now only three of his five cards were blank. The first was THE MAGICIAN that Barren had given him. The second showed Jude as a gaunt, bearded old man, leaning heavily on a staff: THE HERMIT.

The card was flipped upside down relative to THE MAGICIAN. Jude didn't know much about the tarot deck, but he knew that a card reversed could be bad news.

Really bad.

"I gotta figure out all this tarot shit," Jude said out loud, more to break the eerie silence of the room than anything else. "Is that what you want? If I promise to talk to a friend about these cards, will you let me go?" He knew he sounded like an idiot talking to the room like it could hear him, but he was honestly a little surprised he didn't get an answer.

Even though he was pretty sure he'd gotten the message he was supposed to receive, Jude moved to the last sliver of time, bracing himself for the stink of blood and the sight of Dodge's corpse. He settled into the moment, found it just as he left it, and turned to go, but—there. Was Dodge's arm flung across the table like that last time? Was there something in his fist?

Jude reached for it before he could stop himself, though he knew that these slivers of time were mere images that he couldn't touch, though every instinct in him screamed that this—this *right here*—was the cheese in the trap. He touched Dodge's meaty, cold hand, and he touched the doubloon clutched in his dead fist, and his gift roared back through him like a long-denied orgasm, every muscle clenching, breath seized in his lungs, pleasure so intense it was just short of painful.

Images devoid of sound or context flashed in front of his eyes, stolen from another life. He stood before a pair of thrones, a king and queen of unspeakable, inhuman beauty. He ran through a forest of eternal summer, sleek and low to the ground and four-legged. He rested his elbows on the rail of a boat, leaned out over the river, and watched the French Quarter being built, docks and ramshackle buildings and streets of dirt. He sat at a card table and made the powerful and the immortal lose and lose and lose. All that loss was his gain.

There was more, so much more, but a sound intruded. The rhythmic clicking of a metronome. No, the ticking of a second hand. *Tick, tick, tick.*

The clock.

Jude wrenched himself free of his gift's trance, surprised that there wasn't a tearing sound when his hand came free of the doubloon. The visions fell away, and he felt his magic draining out of him, that emptiness within him even colder for having just been filled. His breath came in quick, desperate gulps and his heart raced. On the wall, the cat's tail and eyes were flicking back and forth once more. Dodge was solid and present and stinking no matter how Jude shifted around. This wasn't a frozen sliver of time, this was now, and something unpleasant was about to happen. Jude glanced at the door he'd come through, relieved to see that it was still open, still gave him a way out.

The lightbulb above him came on with a harsh pop. As the shadows fell away, he saw that the walls were stained in places, oddly rectangular in shape.

Red stains. Darker and more distinct by the second.

Shit, he thought. *More doors.*

He turned to run for it but hesitated. His gift was right there, clutched in a dead god's hand. Could he really just leave it behind? But if he touched it, he'd be overtaken by the visions again and would likely get caught by whoever or whatever had set this trap for him. Not to mention the fact that the fortune god had a literal death grip on it. Another few ticks of the clock went by while he considered, the stains obviously doors now, each one bright red with an ornate handle, each one somehow unique, a scratch on one, a brass doorknob on another.

Now or never, he thought, and spoke the word that meant *open*. Dodge's hand spasmed unclenched, the doubloon rolling free. The Red Doors all flew open as well. Jude yanked the handkerchief out of his pocket and grabbed the doubloon, bracing himself for the magic to grab him anyway, and letting out a laugh that sounded half-feral when it didn't. Not looking at any of the other doors that had recently appeared, certain that if he did he was lost, Jude hurled himself through the door he'd come through—

—and banged into the sink of his mother's bathroom, bruising, at least, some of his ribs and knocking the wind out of him. His mother stood with her back to him, adding something to the streetcar mural. She was humming again, Nina Simone's "Sinnerman" this time. She didn't seem to notice him. Jude whirled and slammed the Red Door shut, straining for air that wouldn't come, unsure if he could really still hear the ticking of the clock or if it was just in his head. Finally, he gasped out, sucked in a breath, and spoke the word *closed* to the door.

The Red Door to Dodge's card room faded away, became another scene his mother had painted on the door, him and Regal standing outside the voodoo shop looking down at the veve drawn on the sidewalk. Jude lay on the linoleum floor, the doubloon wrapped in a handkerchief clutched to his chest, trying to slow his breathing, his ribs aching with every inhale, watching his mother paint.

A new passenger had been added to the strange streetcar, a young woman with white wires trailing from her ears. The girl from the voodoo shop.

"No," he groaned. "Goddamn it, no."

Suddenly it all made sense. The malevolent shadows his mother had given him in all the murals. The only connection a fortune god, a street musician, and a teenage girl could possibly have in common.

Him.

Dodge first, of course. The next night, Jude had gone to Tommy's show once he'd realized how gloriously normal watching a live band in a crowded bar would be without his gift torturing him with the weight of the audience's lost things. The following morning, he'd seen the girl in Celeste's voodoo shop. He'd gone from one to the next, and his shadow had followed. It was all his fault.

They were dead because someone, some*thing* was stalking *him*.

In south Louisiana, summer afternoons are often overtaken by brief, intense thunderstorms that sweep in, darken the sky, unleash crashing thunder and gale-driven rain for about an hour, and then vanish. On the drive back into New Orleans, the skies opened up over Jude halfway across the Causeway, the long, long bridge that spanned Lake Pontchartrain. Though the Porsche could navigate itself through the falling sheets of water without aid, he turned on the headlights and the windshield wipers, just for appearance's sake. He was already a not-quite-passing-for-white guy in a *technically* stolen Porsche. No sense giving the cops a reason to pull him over.

Having grown up with the howling winds and the booms that pounded the earth every time lightning cracked the sky, Jude usually found these storms soothing, loved falling asleep to the sounds of their fury. The idea that some shadowy horror had been following him and randomly murdering anyone he met really killed the mood for him, though.

Jude's first thought — once the implications of his mother's artwork had fully set in — had been that he hadn't heard from Regal in an alarmingly long time. So once he was safely cruising down the Causeway, he tested a theory that had been tickling at the back of his mind the past few days among all the other, more pressing, unanswered questions. He took the doubloon holding his gift out of his pocket, unwrapped it from the handkerchief, and rested it on his thigh, keeping his bare hand just above it. He reached with his other hand into the satchel, thinking about what he wanted, what he needed. A touch of his thumb against the doubloon and his magic surged back into him, intense, but not as overwhelming as before. The fingers searching through the satchel tingled in their old, familiar way, and he pulled out a car charger for the make and model of the tourist's dead cell phone, the last lingering sensation of loss on it telling him that it had once belonged to the top regional saleswoman of an electronics supply company, who had forgotten it in her rental car when she was in the city for a conference last fall. He grinned and plugged the phone in.

So Dodge hadn't given him a magician's bag after all. He'd given him a *magic* bag, one that held lost things.

No wonder he'd wanted it back.

Jude filed away that little nugget of information with all the other maddening puzzle pieces he hadn't quite figured out the shape of and waited for the phone to get enough charge to wake up. When it did, it started pinging immediately, text after text from Regal, growing more and more insistent as he thumbed through them. When the vulgarities switched away from "WTF" and graduated to more creative swears, Jude quit reading them and called. She answered on the first ring.

"—ing inflamed taint of a ten-dollar whore have you *been,* Dubuisson? You know how much dog shit I gotta swallow with a smile if you turn up—are you *laughing?*"

He was, turned out. A knot in his chest that he hadn't really acknowledged had loosened when he heard Regal's voice, despite the fact that she'd been cursing at him. Maybe because of it. Tommy and the voodoo shop girl were still chains around his neck, but until the feeling had left him, he hadn't realized how awful being responsible for Regal's death had felt. It wasn't a reaction he could explain, so he didn't try, just told her that it was good to hear from her.

"Sure, whatever. So how did the funeral go? Legba show up?"

"He did. They all did, in fact, but it wasn't Legba I ended up talking to. It was Scarpelli."

"The vampire?" She faked like she barely restrained herself from vomiting.

"That's him. He offered—well, insisted really—on giving me

a ride home and gave me some creepy sales pitch about coming to work for him."

Regal made a quiet incredulous noise.

"What?"

"Seems awfully fucking considerate of him, given the fact that you basically took a big steaming dump right in the middle of their magical poker evening. Figured he'd be pissed."

"Surprised me, too. But he was actually glad for the way things went down." He explained how the vampire had suggested that Jude had done something clever, played some kind of trick, and how he'd figured out that what he'd actually done was play a hand that represented his own fate. From there he told her about not being able to reach her and deciding to go see his mother, finding the strange mural depicting the past few days of his life, with its stalking shadows and the streetcar of the dead. He also told her how the door to the card game had trapped him, that his tarot deck poker hand now consisted of two printed cards and three blank ones. Right as he was about to tell her the rest of it, about Dodge and the doubloon and having his gift back, two things occurred to him at the very same time.

First, that Regal was acting strange. Throughout his recounting of his experiences since they'd parted ways in front of the voodoo shop, she hadn't interrupted him or cursed once, just kept using those monosyllabic nothing words that you use when you're encouraging the other person to continue speaking or not giving them your full attention. Like she was writing down everything he said or, worse, like someone else was listening in. He was forced to admit that their whole recent partnership had been off just like this conversation: him telling her what he knew, and her giving him nothing in return. So he kept the return of his gift, such as it was, to himself.

The second realization he spoke out loud when Regal prompted him to keep going, the silence drawing out too long as his mind spun. "The game's not over," he said.

"What?"

"It's just like you said. We're in the *middle* of a poker game. A batshit weird one that uses people's fates, sure, but it still has rules. If I played my own fate, and my cards are slowly revealing themselves—"

"Then your destiny is still being written or whatever you wanna call it—"

"And the hand is still being played. Because until my future is decided, I could be holding the destiny equivalent of a royal flush."

She whistled between her teeth. "That means . . . Christ on a bender, Jude. You might *win*."

Jude chuckled. "Don't celebrate yet. Could be just a busted straight."

She snorted. "This is *your* future we're talking about," she said, playful and cynical. Then her tone shifted to one of quiet alarm. "Oh, dick biscuits. The shadow in your mom's paintings. It's trying to steer you."

"What?"

"We've been working with the theory that the fortune god got his ticket punched because of his cards, right? But what if it was to rain shit down on *you?*" He could practically see her pacing, waving her hands as she talked, as she worked it out in her head. "What if one of these other gods is trying to influence your fate, and thus—"

"My cards."

The rage came out of nowhere, like the storms in summer. He punched the dashboard, hard enough to crack something, and it felt good, so he did it again. He didn't even realize he'd screamed until he heard Regal shouting his name. It wasn't enough that he'd been yanked out of his quiet, miserable retirement and forced into this, not enough that he'd had his magic stolen right out from under his nose, not enough that he was so dangerous to the few people in his life that he might as well be radioactive.

Now some asshole deity was stacking the goddamn deck.

After a few minutes of clenching the steering wheel so tightly that his knuckles cracked, sucking in deep breaths through gritted teeth, he calmed down enough to pick the phone up off the passenger seat, to tell Regal that he was all right.

"Road rage much?"

At her words, all the anger went out of him, replaced by something cold and hard and sly. "I need you to do something for me, Queens," he said. "Can you check on Leon? If that shadow's hunting me like we think, he might be next on its list. I'd go myself, but I don't want to put him in danger if he isn't already, you know?"

She was quiet for just a heartbeat too long. Like he'd made a chess move she hadn't anticipated. "Sure, no problem. You want me to check on your mom, too? If you're being follow—"

"No. I thought of that, too. Sent her somewhere safe." Which was only kind of a lie. He hadn't sent her anywhere, because the abbey was the safest place for her. Even if his shadow had managed to follow or track him there, sacred ground was no joke when it came to the supernatural. On top of that, he'd put up all kinds of wards and protections over the years. If anything managed to get to her there, it was so powerful that Jude had no hope of standing against it anyway. "Besides," he said, as much for himself as for Regal, "she can take care of herself."

"Right. My—uh, folks always said she had a lot of juice."

"Your folks?"

"No, just folks. You know, people like us."

People like Mourning, Jude thought. He made a noise that could have been agreement.

"So what will you be doing while I'm running your errands? Gonna lay low?"

"Thought I'd go back by the voodoo shop and look around," Jude said. "Figure if I can't shake loose whatever's following me, maybe I can at least try to figure out what it is."

She laughed. "And besides, it's not like you can do any more damage there." As soon as she said it, she sucked at her teeth, like she wished she could take it back. "Too bad you don't have that magic touch of yours anymore, huh?"

"Yeah," Jude said. "Too bad. Let's meet up after." He hung up.

There it was, an actual lie. Not withholding the truth, not selecting his words carefully or keeping his theories to himself, but outright deception. On the surface, it didn't make sense. Why couldn't he trust her? Why would she be working against him? He couldn't even be sure that he wasn't just being paranoid, that he might've been out of the game for too long and couldn't read things clearly. All the little clues kept adding up, though. That sudden burst of anger when they'd been drawing the summoning circle. The fact that she'd known where he would be every time someone around him ended up dead. The way she kept treating him like an angle she was working, not a partner. Trying to get him to tell her where his mother lived, when she knew he'd always kept that a secret.

The fact that she'd just called his outburst "road rage" when she knew he couldn't drive.

He pulled out his English-German guidebook and gave the Porsche some new directions, telling it to drop him off at the edge of the Quarter and then park itself illegally somewhere. The Shem that animated it would only last another couple of hours at most. With any luck it would get towed. He reached into the pocket that held his coin. His gift. He'd go where he told Regal and see what he could see. At a touch, his magic swept back into him. He put his hand into the satchel, searching, finding the smooth, thrumming power of the thunderbolt.

And if his shadow turned up where he'd told Regal he was going? Well . . . he had an answer for that, too.

CHAPTER TEN

EVERY WORLD IS a circle with a center, a wheel with a hub on which it turns. Sometimes it is a feature of the natural world—a mountain or a tree. In China they feel the world spin where Mount Kunlun pierces the sky, just as the Lakota revere Inyan Kara in the Black Hills, and as the Anangu of Australia regard Uluru rock. Buddha found Enlightenment beneath the bodhi tree; Odin hung upon an ash named Yggdrasil; and the Serpent wound itself around the Tree of Knowledge in Eden. Where the natural world did not provide a focus, they built one: pillars and obelisks, towers and shrines. The Pyramid of the Sun at Teotihuacan, of Khufu at Giza. The Umbilicus Urbis Romae in Rome, Kaaba in Mecca, the Tower in Babel. Every world has its center, its sacred place where Earth meets Heaven, the point around which everything revolves. Places of Power. Of Truth. Of Sanctuary.

Jude walked the few blocks to Celeste's shop through the last drizzle of the passing storm. He kept his guard up, hurrying his pace and watching the shadows. Watching for more than just the stalker from his mother's paintings.

This part of the Quarter closed down at night once the tourists flocked to the bars and clubs on Bourbon Street. The gas lanterns were few and cast little light, and the thundercloud still overhead added to the darkness, turning the charming, inviting stretch of old homes and wrought-iron fences into a back alley, an abandoned tunnel. A travel brochure photograph in the daylight, an ink sketch from a crime novel at night.

The city wasn't always a safe place, especially since the storm, and no amount of divine parentage made Jude bulletproof. For all her culture and jazz and cuisine, New Orleans also had poverty, addiction, and desperation in equal measure. She was a great place to find yourself, and a terrible place to get lost.

A reality punctuated by the yellow crime scene tape stretched across the voodoo shop's threshold.

After a deep breath, trying to ready himself for what he would find, Jude unlocked the door with a word, ducked under the tape, and stepped inside. The shades were drawn, so the front room of the shop was even darker than the street outside. He reached out without thinking, found the light switch, and flipped it. For a moment, the room didn't make sense. It was simply too surreal how *normal* everything looked, as though nothing particularly unusual had occurred. He'd expected mayhem, but the books remained on their shelves, the herbs and fetishes and candles in their glass cases. The scent of medicinal teas and oils and spices hung in the air, nothing sinister. The bell still tinkled above him when he slid the door shut, a crisp, merry sound.

The magazine the girl behind the counter had been reading still lay sprawled open, as though she had just walked away from it. But the girl herself was missing, replaced by a dark stain on the wood floor, by the numbered plastic placards left behind by the coroner.

Jude *assumed* the blood belonged to the girl in his mother's mural, anyway. There was only one way to be sure.

Jude went down on one knee next to a rack of postcards with cute voodoo doll cartoon characters, took the doubloon out of his pocket, and unwrapped it, then pressed his fingertips to the stain on the floor. His gift surged through him and showed him all that the girl—Renaissance Raines, Renai to her friends—had lost.

Gone was the impulsive decision to enroll next fall in an art school in Savannah, gone was the sense of rightness that came when she dropped out and came home. Gone was the memory of the one class she'd really enjoyed—graphic design—and the lucky break of a part-time job at a local website startup; gone were a series of promotions and job offers, a career in web design. Gone were the first awkward fumblings of romance between her and a journalism intern, gone was the passionate, doomed affair she had with a Puerto Rican barista in the few months she and the intern, who'd become a sportswriter, were split up. Gone was the bittersweet experience of holding her mother's hand through the last weeks of cancer, the pain of her mother's passage, the warmth of her mother's final words, that she was proud of the woman Renai had become. Gone were children and friendships, lovers and rivals. Years of movies and books and makeup sex and looking up into starlight and calling in sick to binge-watch television shows and overhearing a teenager listening to a song she hadn't thought of in years while standing in line at the DMV and Mardi Gras parades and extravagant meals at Commander's Palace and cold Popeyes on a hungover Sunday morning and Jazz Fest after Jazz Fest after Jazz Fest.

She had all of it taken from her, the entirety of the life she was supposed to live, and kneeling there on the bloodstained floor, Jude saw it through her eyes, heard what she heard, knew what she knew.

Saw the moment she lost it all.

She had just come from the back room, where she'd made sure the lights were turned off, the back door locked. She'd already flipped the sign on the front door and pulled the shades closed.

All that was left was to count up what was left in the register, adjust the tally in the spiral-bound notebook under the counter, and she would be done for the night. She had her headphones in, the rippling piano and warbling sax and the smooth, smooth voice of Sunnyland Slim, an old blues singer who was warning her that the devil was a busy man. Something—a noise outside, a flicker of motion in the corner of her eye—made Renai stop counting, pause the song, remove the earbuds. Her pulse ratcheted up, the primate part of her brain leaping into fight-or-flight response over what her rational brain told her was probably nothing. She squinted at the door, saw that she hadn't locked it like she'd thought.

Renai was halfway across the room when a shadow shifted across the wall and knocked her to the ground. As she fell, her MP3 player went flying out of her hand, and in the confusion of the moment, her biggest fear was that it would break, just as something sharp and cold sliced across her throat, as she tried to scream and her mouth filled with blood. Renai hit the floor face-down, struggling but pinned, unable to breathe. Her last thought in this world was that she had forgotten to blow out the votive candles.

Jude fell to the floor as well, the connection to Renai's loss severing when his fingers left her bloodstain, though he gasped in quick panicked breaths that didn't give him any air, like a fish flopping on a riverbank. Eventually—eyes watering, throat raw, heart pounding—he calmed himself enough to force a long, slow breath out, drew in a deep, ragged lungful. For a while, all he could do was lie on his back and suck in oxygen. The only thing that kept him from weeping was the roaring, inarticulate rage that filled his thoughts, the injustice of what had been done to her.

When he could, Jude rose to his feet. Renai's MP3 player still lay where it had landed when it flew from her hand: on a bookshelf across the room. The police had taken her crappy pay-as-you-go flip phone when they'd collected the rest of her things, but this—a device full of pirated music she couldn't transfer to anything newer—they'd missed. Jude picked it up, wrapped the headphones around the slim device, and slid it into his satchel. From his last lingering connection to her lost life, Jude knew where her parents lived. When this was all over, he'd sneak into the Raineses' house when they were away, leave the MP3 player somewhere her folks were sure to find it. Maybe listening to the songs she'd loved would help them feel her there with them, if only for a time.

It wouldn't come close to making up for their daughter's death, of course. Nothing could, not even vengeance.

A sense of conviction rolled over him, that his suspicions about the card game and his mother's paintings had just been proven correct. Whatever had killed Renai had killed Tommy and Dodge, and it had done so because of Jude. He didn't yet know who, or what, or why, but he owed it to them all to find out.

So he could take from the shadow what it had taken from them.

When Jude left the voodoo shop, he stepped out into the street and the sensation of being observed. He couldn't just shrug it off as a lingering effect of experiencing Renai's last moments; this was too potent, too immediate. The gaze touching him felt cold and dark in a way that had nothing to do with the temperature of the air or photons of light. Despite the sweat trickling across his skin, he shivered, expected his breath to plume when he exhaled. Despite the flames dancing in the gas lanterns overhead, he could barely make out the other side of the narrow one-lane street. As he stood there, it grew more focused, more intense. It could only be one thing: the shadow from his mother's painting was here, now — watching him.

And it was coming closer.

Jude fled a few blocks down to Bourbon Street and then slowed, threading his way through the crowd until he'd crossed a couple of streets, and turned onto Orleans toward the river. Every step, every turn, he expected to get snatched off his feet by a sharp-fingered hand made of shadow and malevolence. Every moment he wasn't felt like a small miracle. A quick glance behind him and above showed no signs of pursuit, but the perception continued. He hurried down the wet and broken cobblestones of Pirate's Alley. His pulse refused to slow. Unable to shake the sensation that a predator was right behind him, he went for the nearest sanctuary he could think of: St. Louis Cathedral. Another few dozen steps carried him through the sparse crowd in Jackson Square and to the front door.

He had to whisper *open* to both a padlock and the front door, but once he got into the dim, empty cathedral, he finally began to relax.

Within, the cool silence was a blessing. Christ, he wanted a drink. He grinned a little at the minor sacrilege of his thoughts, moving from the vestibule farther into the cathedral. He paused for a moment while his eyes adjusted to the relatively weak light granted by the multitude of windows throughout the church, large arches of glass along the galleries above him, and smaller, rectangular ones set near the beginning curve of the vault. The floor was a gleaming checkerboard of black and white just like the one in Mourning's office; Jude wondered which of them mimicked the other. Flags hung from the balustrades, one side depicting the countries that had governed New Orleans at various points in its history, while the other bore papal crests, which made the center aisle between rows of pews a representation of the seam between the secular and the sacred authorities of the early years of the city. Twin marble statues flanked the aisle, a cherub holding a seashell so large it took both hands, which served as a basin for holy water. Biblical scenes and moments from the life of whichever King Louis gave the cathedral its name decorated the walls and the highest peak of the vault, Jude knew, but it was too dark for him to see. He thought a remnant of incense hung in the air, but he could have been imagining it. He sat in one of the pews near the altar, maroon carpeted steps leading up to an edifice of white and gold, its sculptures indistinct in the darkness. An errant ray of light illumed the phrase in Latin that graced the top of the altar: *Ecce Panis An-gelorum*.

Behold the Bread of the Angels.

Jude sat in the dark and the quiet for a long while, just trying to come to terms with all that had happened to him in the last few days. The gods, the deaths, the revelations about his own life. Nothing he'd discovered felt like it made a damned bit of difference. Every answer only led to more questions, each more profound than the one before. The last few days felt like a jigsaw puzzle that refused to make sense, not so much because he was missing a piece of the puzzle as it was he had no idea what image he was trying to construct.

Even with his gift returned to him, he couldn't seem to find the right direction, like a drowning man who couldn't tell which way was up and wasted his strength and air swimming deeper. He looked up at the altar, the statues of Peter with his key and Paul with his sword, the tower of angels uplifting a crucifix. "Why?" he asked. "Just tell me, why drag me into this? What the fuck do you want me to do?" He leaned onto the pew in front of him, dropped his head onto his hands. His heartbeat pounded in his ears. The silence of no one answering was deafening.

It was then that the scent of cinnamon filled the air.

PART THREE

WHEEL OF FORTUNE

CHAPTER ELEVEN

THEY ARE INTERMEDIARIES between mankind and the divine, descending from the heavens on outstretched wings. They appear all throughout history, delivering guidance to the lost, rescuing those in mortal peril, bestowing luck to the unfortunate. The ancient Greeks poured out the first few drops of wine in honor of Agathos, a Eudaemon. Timbaru was the chieftain of the Gandharvas, the name by which the followers of Hindu know them. Chitragupta records the actions of all Sikhs, whereas Kiraman and Katibin do the same for Muslims, one recording good works, the other misdeeds. Jophiel, wielding a flaming sword, expelled Adam and Eve from the Garden. Samael is with a person at the moment of death. Uriel guides them to their destiny. Their names are more than identity: they are their purpose, their existence. God Heals: Raphael. The Strength of God: Gabriel. Messenger: Angel.

❧

The angel from Dodge's card game stood on the back of a pew, balanced on the toes of one bare foot with the effortless grace of a dancer. The messenger wore gray linen pants, loose-fitting and tied at the waist like hospital scrubs, and a Kevlar SWAT vest, midnight black and Velcroed tight. A name tag on the vest said "HI, MY NAME IS" along with a symbol written in black marker: ה. It took Jude a second to recognize the shape from his training with Eli Constant, but when he did, he understood the coughing "hey" sound Dodge had used to name the angel: Hē, the fifth letter of the Hebrew alphabet.

Steel greaves and bracers guarded Hē's shins and forearms, ornately made and polished to a gleam; gold bangles decorated the angel's sleek, firm biceps. A look of bliss graced Hē's face, the countenance of one who had achieved enlightenment. That, or one who had partaken of an epic dose of some really good shit. That face, like every other aspect of the angel, was perfectly androgynous: delicate cheekbones, a sensuous mouth, thin hips, broad shoulders. When Hē spoke, it was — like in the card game — with a haunting echo of Jude's own voice.

"Peace be with you," Hē said. Jude couldn't tell if the angel was mocking him, or if that's how his own voice always sounded. Hē came closer, stepping from the ledge of one pew's back to the next with a sure-footed bounce, almost skipping across them.

"Somehow I doubt peace is what your boss has got in mind for me."

The angel stopped at the pew closest to Jude, staring down at him with eyes of empty, perfect white. "You approach a messenger of the Most High with doubt in your heart?" Hē asked. "Apostasy does not suit you."

"Neither does blind faith," Jude said.

"You are in need of guidance," Hē said. It was not a question.

"Guidance is what you give tourists looking for a good place to get gumbo. I'm looking for a little truth."

Hē folded into a crouch, a seemingly effortless swoop that

brought the angel's face uncomfortably close to Jude's own. The reek of cinnamon was almost overpowering. Jude fought the urge to sneeze. "Seek," the messenger said, "and ye shall find." Hē's lips curled back into a wide, childlike smile. The angel burst up from the pew and, with a negligent flicking of wings, floated toward the ceiling, chuckling.

The angel was fucking with him.

Hē swooped a lazy circle overhead before perching, wings folding and furling out of Jude's sight, onto a nearby pew. The angel dug in the various pockets and pouches of the SWAT vest, eventually finding the corkscrew wire and tiny earbud of a radio headset. Once the earbud was seated in place, Hē's attention returned to Jude. "Ask, and it shall be given you."

A dozen questions warred for his tongue, but, ultimately, one was more crucial than all the others. Barren hadn't known the answer, but Hē just might. "Who murdered Dodge?"

The angelic head cocked to the side, listening, and then Hē's mouth twisted into a frown. "You did," Hē said.

Jude's legs went weak. There was that gap in his memory between fleeing the game and waking up in his bed, that strange sense of guilt when he and Regal had summoned the door to Dodge's card room. Could the angel be right? Was he even capable of killing a god? Nothing in his satchel was that powerful. He thought, of course, of the thunderbolt, but—no. He'd seen Dodge's body. The thunderbolt wouldn't have slit his throat, wouldn't have left a body behind.

But then, if the satchel held a thunderbolt, who knew what else might be pulled out of it?

"No," Jude said, more to himself than expecting a response. "That's impossible."

The click of a tongue. "You asked for truth, son of man, and yet you turn away from it." Both hands opened on empty palms, as if to show Jude that the messenger had nothing else to give him. "Your presence and your actions led directly to the death of the fortune god known as Dodge Renaud. As it was not originally his fate to die that night, his killing was unnatural, undestined, and thus . . ." Hē said a word that sounded like "murder" but was slurred somehow, a lisping sound instead of the hard "d."

Relief swept through him, mingled with annoyance and anger. "You said *I* killed him."

"I made no such claim. I said you were responsible for—" Hē broke off and pressed a finger against the earpiece, like an agent of Heaven's Secret Service. "Ah," the angel said, "I see my error. You meant murder, not morðor." A shrug. "It can be difficult to translate a language only a few thousand years old into the Word. My apology."

What I wouldn't give for a burning bush or a couple of stone tablets, Jude thought. He tried to bite down on his frustration. Letting his temper loose would get him nowhere. "The question is still who murdered Dodge," he said, emphasizing his enunciation, "I need to know who killed him."

The angel held up a single, perfect finger. "I think perhaps you have misunderstood to whom you speak. Do you really expect me"—a thumb pressed against the chest of the SWAT vest—"to ask"—a hand waved in the general direction of the ceiling—"to repeat Himself?"

"Not when you put it that way." Jude pressed his palms against his eyelids, trying to squeeze out the headache that was building there. Too much excitement, not enough sleep. He was running on caffeine and desperation, and not even God would tell him why. Except maybe He had, in His own mysterious way. "Can you at least explain what that word you said means? Tell me what I did that led to Dodge's death?"

"Everything has a beginning, an end, and a path to travel from one to another. When everything goes according to plan, we call that fate. But any rule has its exceptions. *Morðor* is the death that should not have happened. It is a wound in the world."

Jude remembered the vision of Renai's lost future that his gift had shown him. He'd thought that since his own destiny was in question, he'd merely seen one of the many potential lives that Renai had lost. If he understood Hē correctly, though, most people had a clearly defined fate, and Renai's killer had committed this morðor, had stolen from her what was *supposed* to happen. Somehow, this felt like an even greater violation.

"You impacted the outcome of the game," Hē continued, "merely by attending. By escalating the stakes, you increased your influence on events. But it was through your choice to play your own fate that the outcome was altered significantly. The fortune god's death, then, is one of the consequences of your actions." A spread of the hands, a "there you have it" gesture.

That much of the puzzle Jude had put together on his own. He'd extended the game until his own fate was revealed, which held the prize just out of reach. Someone was trying to influence his cards by influencing his fate. Apparently, as far as destiny was concerned, that made him partly responsible.

He frowned. *Great. As if I don't have enough sins of my own on my conscience. How do you make something like that right?*

"You cannot," Hē said, which meant either Jude had spoken aloud without meaning to, or the angel could read his thoughts. Either possibility was sobering. "What has been done cannot be undone."

"Says who? My hand is still being dealt. Doesn't that mean—"

"It merely means that you have created a paradox," Hē said.

The messenger's words cut him open and let all his hope come spilling out. He hadn't realized how much he'd believed in the possibility of his own salvation until a hole had been poked in that faith. He found it hard to breathe, and though he tried to hide it, the dismay showed on his face.

The tips of Hē's wings drooped, and the angel moved toward him, stepping from row to row once more, this time without any buoyancy to the movement, still graceful but solemn. Reaching Jude, the angel sat on the back of the pew, legs folded into a lotus pose. "Did you not wonder why your fate was taking so long to be revealed?" Hē asked.

Jude found it very strange to be comforted by his own voice. The angel waited, but he had no answer to give.

With two fingers pressed against the throat, as if checking for a pulse, Hē spoke in Dodge's voice.

"The game tonight," the messenger said, "is Fortunes." Hearing a murdered god's words come from Hē's mouth made the hairs on the back of Jude's neck rise. "You make the best or the worst fate you can."

Above them, the cathedral's bell began to toll the hour. Hē looked up, held rapt and silent while the bell rang. When it finished and the echoes faded away, the angel trembled, head shaking and wings twitching, before turning back to Jude, speaking once more in an echo of his voice.

"Your best possible fate? Winning the game. Taking the prize for yourself." One hand was raised palm up, one half of the scales. "But if you were capable of doing so, your cards would have shown it. You cannot win because you were never supposed to win. Your destiny has always been to lose." The other hand joined the first. "In balance, however, is the fact that you've put all your markers on this one turn of the cards, so the worst possible outcome for you would be to lose. The other players will take pieces of you until there is nothing left."

Despite the despair squeezing Jude's chest and clinging to his stomach, what Hē was trying to tell him clicked. "And having the worst fate would give me the best hand, so I'd win. I'm damned if I do; damned if I don't."

Hands joined together with a soft clap. "Paradox."

"So what, the game just goes on forever?"

A smirk. "Only the Highest is eternal," Hē said. "Which brings me to the guidance I have been sent to deliver. It may not be possible for you to win or to lose, but there is a third option. You can forfeit. You can stop playing before your fate is revealed."

"But Dodge said I can't fold. Are you saying I can break the rules?"

"No. I'm saying one must be alive to play a game."

It took Jude a moment to realize what the angel was implying. "And here I thought suicide was a mortal sin."

"There is a universe of difference between self-harm devoid of purpose and sacrificing oneself for the greater good." The angel's wings stretched with a sharp crack and lifted Hē onto a cinnamon-scented wind. Glowing with an inner light, the messenger spoke louder, to be heard over the sound of feathers pounding against the air. "There is much you might accomplish with your final act, a choice that will allow you to redirect the course of destiny in accordance with the Highest's divine plan. When it presents itself, fear not. You shall not be alone."

That said, the angel Hē burst into a flare so bright that Jude had to look away. When his vision recovered, he saw that the messenger had vanished, leaving him to sit in the empty cathedral for a long while, the scent of spice fading long before the echo of Hē's words left his thoughts.

Jackson Square was bustling when Jude left the cathedral, tourists and street workers alike flooding in now that the rain had passed. He wore a mask that he'd pulled out of the satchel, a nondescript scrap of burlap with rough-cut eyeholes and a potent confusion charm stitched into it. If its magic held, anyone who looked at him would look right past him, would dismiss him as an unimportant part of the crowd, even if they were looking for him. Hopefully, it would be enough to lose the shadow tailing him long enough to speak to someone without putting them in danger.

It was long past time he learned the rules of the game he couldn't win and couldn't afford to lose.

Fortunately, the tarot reader he hoped to find was working, turning the cards for two middle-aged out-of-towners. Opal Brennan was one of the few people in the Square that Jude had more than a passing acquaintance with, the only one who walked that fine line between too cynical to believe magic might be real, and too unbalanced to be trusted. She wore a tank top that showed off the tattoos of roses and briars that twined around her arms from shoulder to wrist, her graying hair pulled up in a tight bun, save a few tendrils that had come loose. The magic of the mask let Jude walk right up behind her without Opal or the tourists noticing. He dropped a note into her purse, written on the back of a donation envelope he'd taken from the cathedral.

Meet me at Lafitte's in half an hour, the note read, *it's important.* It wasn't until he scribbled his name at the bottom that it occurred to him how similar the note was to the text he'd gotten from Regal just a few days before.

Difference is, he thought, *I'll do everything I can to keep Opal out of trouble.*

While he waited for the tourist couple to snap pictures of each other with Opal and pay for their readings, he turned the pink cell phone back on and deleted all the messages he'd exchanged with Regal and, decisively, her number. He couldn't be sure she was actually tracking the phone somehow, nor that doing so represented some kind of betrayal, but it felt that way, and he knew he couldn't entirely trust her either. So once the phone was clear of anything that would lead back to him or to Regal, he dropped it into the empty seat of one of the pedicabs waiting at the edge of Jackson Square for a customer, trusting that the fit young man rocking back and forth on his bike's pedals — whose shirt clung to his back in a way that distracted Jude for a moment with other thoughts — would take the phone on a nice tour of the Quarter once he picked up a fare, and eventually leave it in a lost-and-found somewhere.

Jude watched Opal discover the note he'd left for her, watched her scan the crowd for him and shake her head when she couldn't find him, even though he stood among a crowd watching a street juggler just a few feet away. She looked back down at the note, pursed her lips, and asked the caricature painter who occupied the table next to her to keep an eye on her table for a while. Jude made sure she scooped her tarot deck into the lockbox where she kept the day's cash when she gathered her things.

When she left the Square, annoyance in her gait, and headed toward Lafitte's, Jude went too, keeping pace about a half block behind her, making sure no one followed. That strange sensation of being watched was gone. He felt a quick flutter of voyeuristic thrill at being able to move unseen and unknown through the crowd like this, a pleasure that was quickly tamped down by the thought that his shadow probably felt exactly the same way when it was stalking him.

Opal reached Lafitte's — a bar housed in a former blacksmith's shop once owned by the famous pirate brothers that gave the place its name — without any complications, but Jude waited outside for a few minutes just to be sure, scanning the skies as well as the streets. The building itself was a squat shape of crumbling plaster and exposed brick on the corner of Bourbon and St. Phillip, three storm-shuttered doorways gaping open in the summer air. Inside the darkness did nothing to relieve the heat; low ceilings without overhead light fixtures made it stuffy and cramped as an attic. The jukebox blared over the noise of a crowd that hadn't yet gathered, because despite the heat and the gloom — or maybe because of it — this place would be spilling out into the street in a few hours.

Jude pulled off the mask before he approached the table where Opal sat, staring down at her cell phone and scowling. It came off with a tearing, clenching sensation, like duct tape with teeth, and — if the payment was anything like the last time he'd used the mask — every night this week he'd be visited by a nightmare of pulling his own face off millimeter by agonizing millimeter . . . nightmares he couldn't wake from until he'd completed the ritual.

Magic always had a cost.

He pushed the consequences to the back of his mind and forced a grin, clearing his throat and shuffling his feet so Opal would notice him. He was glad for the darkness and the noise, since it would help keep their conversation private, but it also meant he'd startle her if he wasn't careful. She looked up at him and, still obviously a little pissed at him, struggled not to smile.

"Buy you a beer?" he asked.

"A beer?" Opal said, incredulous at the suggestion, offended even. "Jude, I am surprised at you. I am a lady. I was taught never to allow such a vile substance into the temple of my body." Opal's tendency to drop into the cadences of old money New Orleans, like she was auditioning for the role of Blanche in *A Streetcar Named Desire*, had endeared her to Jude, especially since he knew she'd once lived that life and had walked away from it long ago. The normalcy of it, of her, was reassuring, and he felt his forced grin relax into something more genuine. "I only drink bourbon of the highest quality, and I only drink it neat," she said, "especially when a gentleman is buying."

Jude took one last survey of their fellow patrons as he made his way to the bar. A couple of local drunks murmured to each other at the corner of the bar, sweating as much as the bottles of Abita each of them clutched. The bartender was a white guy, young and clean-cut in a college student sort of way. A pair of couples — three white women and one black guy — took pictures of themselves outside, posing with their go cups as though alcohol on the side-walk was hilariously transgressive. Aside from them, he and Opal had the place to themselves. He nodded at the bartender and or-dered a top-shelf bourbon for her and a rum and Coke for himself.

Jude let his mind wander as the young man made their drinks, realizing that now that he'd gotten here, he had to think of a way to get Opal to show him what he needed to know without scaring the shit out of her. Belief in tarot and mysticism was one thing. Tell-ing her that magic spells really worked was something else entirely.

In the quiet of the cathedral after Hē had left, trying to digest what the angel had told him, Jude had come to a few conclusions. First, that despite what Hē said, it seemed to Jude that some of the other gods at the table thought he had the potential to win. The vampire seemed ready to bribe him into quitting, and something else — either one of the other gods or something working on their behalf — was stalking him, murdering people around him, trying to influence his fate. You didn't go to all that trouble for someone who wasn't a threat. The second conclusion was that Dodge might have had a similar purpose in mind behind inviting Jude to the game in the first place, that the fortune god had hoped to use Jude to stack the deck, only to have his trick turned on him. The third thing Jude had realized — and the reason he'd sought out Opal — was that if he had any chance of surviving the end of this fucking game, he really ought to learn how to play.

By the time Jude made it to her table, he had a drink in each hand and nothing to give Opal but the truth. He searched his satchel for his paperback book on tarot, slipped his cards out from between the pages — THE MAGICIAN and the upside-down HERMIT — and dropped them next to her glass. "Mean anything to you?" he asked. She studied them for a moment, then pulled her glasses down to her eyes and peered more closely at it. She looked up at him, an uncomfortable smirk wrinkling the folds in the corner of her mouth.

"You yanking my chain?" she asked. "You know I take this stuff serious, right?"

"I know," he said, taking a sip of his drink. "What makes you think I'm not?"

Her lips pursed. "They've got your face, Jude. If this ain't a joke — and it's not a funny one, for the record — I'm not sure what you want from me."

With one fingertip, Jude spun the HERMIT card around, so Opal could see the way the image insisted on being upside down relative to THE MAGICIAN. He waited for her reaction, a little bit of fear mixed with a lot of disbelief, before he did it again and again. She started to speak, and then her lips split in a wide, nervous grin. "How did you do that?" she asked.

"See for yourself."

She picked up the card, rubbing it between thumb and forefinger, as if trying to separate it from a twin. She tilted it back and forth, expecting some sort of hologram printing. Brow furrowed, she turned it over. The image shifted, and she cursed and dropped the card as if it had burned her. She checked the room to see if any of the other bar patrons were paying attention to them, cleared her throat, opened her mouth to say something, and then snatched her glass from the table. She finished her bourbon in two swallows, grimacing.

"That trick you do with lost things," she said. "That's not a trick, is it?" Jude frowned and shook his head. "Christ," Opal said. She reached over the table and picked up Jude's rum and Coke, drained it, too.

It was cruel of him, perhaps, to expose her to his world like this, but he didn't have time for a more gradual reveal. He'd always had a feeling she was capable of handling the truth. She was a soothsayer, after all. "You okay?" he asked, less out of concern and more to get her talking again.

"Sure. I'm great. Economy's in a nosedive, we're desperate for a Road Home check that's never gonna come, the mayor's a thief, and the governor's a monster. Not a single damn part of life makes sense anymore, why not throw in a little—" She waved at him and the cards, at a loss for words.

Jude laughed. "Magic. You can say the word; it won't bite."

"No," Opal said. "No, I don't think I will." She toyed with her glass, staring at the few drops of bourbon left as if she'd find an explanation there. "What is it you want from me?"

Jude arranged the cards next to one another, tapping the table with the flats of his hands. "I need to understand what these mean, how they can be used to reveal a person's destiny."

Opal clicked her tongue and shook a finger at him. "Don't show me real-life hoodoo and then talk like a tourist. Tarot doesn't do that. It can't. That's not the point. Reading the cards is about understanding your position in life, your desires, the obstacles between the two. Not about predicting the future."

"What if I told you that in the right hands, they can do just that?"

Opal took a long, deep breath. She glanced down at the cards, and then looked away, like they were shameful somehow. Obscene. Her lips tightened into a thin line. "I guess I'd tell you to find somebody with the right hands," she said. "Shit. You know so much, why don't you do it?"

"Not my gift," he said.

She was close, Jude could feel it. She had the ability, the unusual perspective on the world that would let her see things others would refuse to acknowledge. Some people were born with that vision; some had it thrust upon them by events traumatic or miraculous. She just had to recognize it, to trust that the whisper in the back of her mind was truth, not irreverence or madness.

"Let's try this another way. Can I use your cards?"

She lifted an eyebrow, but took the cloth-wrapped tarot deck out of her purse and set it on the table. Jude flipped through it, searching for the only hand from the card game he could remember, the one Dodge had played, the figures bearing Regal's face. The Queens of Wands, Cups, Swords, and Coins, and the High Priestess—Regal in white robes and an odd hat, two pointed curves and a sphere in the center, sitting between two columns, one white and one black. Jude fanned them out in front of Opal, face-down. "Close your eyes," he said. Opal did so, but not without letting out a short, frustrated noise. Jude reached across the table and pressed the pad of his thumb to the center of her forehead, as though blessing or baptizing her, which, in a way, he was. He spoke the arcane word that Dodge had taught him, the word that meant *open*, and felt something shift within her mind. Opal shuddered and moaned softly, a dreaming sound.

Jude turned the cards face-up and told Opal to open her eyes.

"They're in the wrong order," she said, and then pressed her fingers against her lips, holding them closed. As though she'd said something she shouldn't have.

"Go ahead," Jude said, keeping his voice low, soothing. Hypnotic. "Tell me what you see."

Timid, hesitant, Opal shuffled the cards around, so that they ran, left to right, Coins, Swords, High Priestess, Wands, and Cups. Exactly the order Dodge had played them, when they bore Regal's face. Opal ran her fingertips across the surface of THE QUEEN OF COINS, like a blind woman reading Braille. The card depicted a crowned woman seated on a throne surrounded by fertile growth, looking down at the huge coin decorated with a pentacle that she cradled in her arms. "The first card is the past," Opal said, unsure of herself, a child just learning to read. "A woman of power relying on the strength of another. That's what the coin represents, and why she looks at it with sadness."

Jude had to work to keep his breathing even. That described the Regal he had known before the storm exactly. She'd had her own abilities, her own schooling, but throughout their partnership she'd often deferred to him, to his innate sense of lost things. He'd always believed she was capable of much more.

Opal turned her attention to the next card, THE QUEEN OF SWORDS. Another seated royal woman, this one in profile, billowing clouds in the background. She held a sword in one hand, its point aimed straight up, her other hand held out as if welcoming someone to speak, a gesture that didn't match the stern expression on her face. "The second card is for what is. It shows her place in the world. She has had to arm and defend herself. She has come into her own power. The storm clouds show how difficult this self-reliance has been." Opal seemed to gain confidence as she went, though her voice grew hoarse, as if the experience was taking something out of her as well. "Third is for conflict, for the greatest obstacle in her path."

THE HIGH PRIESTESS had been inverted, like Jude's own version of THE HERMIT. Looking closer at the card, Jude saw that this

Regal wore a cross on her chest, not a crucifix, with the Christ figure on it and taller than it was wide, but a cruciform, two perpendicular lines of equal length joined at the center. She held a scroll and a crescent moon lay at her feet. "She is her own greatest challenge," Opal continued, her cadence slow and distant. "A title stolen or a destiny avoided. A choice she did not make and a choice she will come to regret." Opal's hand trembled over the card, as if she were trying to block it from her view. Not wanting to break the flow of her thoughts, Jude turned it over for her. She closed her eyes briefly and let out a long breath before continuing. When she spoke again, though, her words were clipped, strained.

She couldn't take much more of this.

THE QUEEN OF WANDS held a staff in one hand, a blooming sunflower in the other. At the foot of her throne sat a black cat, its sapphire eyes closed to thin, menacing slits. "The fourth card tells what must be done. She must gain mastery over the order of thought"—here she touched the staff—"and the chaos of nature, of emotion"—here she touched the sunflower. "The black cat is a symbol of Venus in its sinister aspect, but it is unclear. Is this her ally? A harbinger of the conflict to come? I . . . I don't know."

She shoved that card away and pressed her fingertips against the final one, THE QUEEN OF CUPS. Another throne, this one beside a swift flowing river, another queen, who stared intently at an ornate chalice, twin handles curling up to its peak, where its lid rose above the queen's head, its contents sealed away. "What is to come," Opal said, her voice a panicked hiss. "Neither victory nor defeat. Power unused. Abilities locked away. Betrayer? Betrayed? Would she choose differently if she knew? Why—" She tried to say more, but her voice failed her, tears streaking down her cheeks. Jude grabbed her head with his hand, spoke the word for *close*.

Opal slumped back in her chair, drawing deep, rapid breaths, as if she'd just run a race. Her face was flushed, eyes wide and still gushing. Jude took a quick glance around, saw that their conversation had gone unnoticed, despite the tight quarters. The drunks were barely aware of their own words, much less their surroundings. The bartender had his back to them, absorbed in his cell phone. Thankfully, Opal was the whisper-truth-in-a-creepy-voice kind of oracle, not the thrashing-around-and-yelling-in-tongues version. When he turned back to her, Opal's face was split by a wide smile.

"Opal?"

"That was . . . incredible," she said. "I've never seen anything so clearly, never *knew* things so surely. Is that how you— Is that how the world looks to you?"

Jude grinned, but it was a rueful one. "No," he said. "Far from it. That gift is yours alone. I put it away for now, but it's a part of you. It will come back from time to time, if you want it to, if you trust in it."

"If I want it? Oh, yes. I want it very much." She looked at her phone, flipped it open. "I hope I helped. If you ever need . . ." She paused, chuckling a little at the eagerness in her voice. "Well, you know where to find me. Now if you don't mind, I'm going to go home and make Sharon a very happy woman."

"Before you go," Jude said, "let me give you a little something for your trouble." He touched a finger to the doubloon in his pocket and reached into his satchel. The past few years, over $200,000 had gone missing from NOPD evidence lockers. The small envelope he pulled out of his satchel was stuffed with about five grand of those lost thousands. He slid it across the table to her. Her polite "Oh, I couldn't" fell silent when she saw how much was in there. "You and Sharon should take that trip up to Seattle to see her folks you always talk about," Jude said. "You should leave tonight."

Before she could say or ask anything else, Jude was out of his chair and out of the bar, already wondering if Regal would be waiting for him when he got back to his apartment.

And if she'd bring his shadow along with her.

❧

On the long walk home—the shadow thankfully absent—Jude worked his exhausted mind, trying to put things in their places. The first card was for who you were. Jude had been a magician once, trained by Eli Constant in the arcane arts, though the magic had always come too easily to him for Jude to really put much effort into his training. He and Eli hadn't parted on happy terms. Then Jude had started working for Mourning, and then the storm. Jude hadn't been anything resembling a magician for years.

The second card was for the present. When traffic forced him to stop on the sidewalk and wait for the light to change, Jude pulled out the paperback and flipped through it until he found the entry for THE HERMIT. An old man leaned on a staff with one hand and held a lantern in the other, looking down from a mountaintop. Instead of a flame, the lantern held a star. This card represented wisdom, the attainment of knowledge and purpose, a journey undertaken for greater understanding. Reversed, it meant stagnation, refusal to seek answers, an immature turning inward. Jude stuffed the book back into his satchel.

Even his destiny was busting his balls.

He couldn't say it was wrong, though. He'd fallen apart after the storm. Sure, his gift had turned on him, but he'd been a disaster looking for a place to happen for years before that. His second card was as accurate as the first.

Thanks to Opal, he knew what to expect from the next three cards. The obstacle in his path, what he must do, and his ultimate fate. He didn't need divination to know the problem he faced: the game, Dodge's murder, the shadow that stalked him. He was a little curious how all that could be represented on one card. Maybe that was why his cards were taking so long to reveal themselves, not the paradox Hē believed he faced.

All of it whirled around in his mind, Regal and gods and cards and shadows and fate. Jude touched the coin in his jeans pocket and rummaged through his satchel as he walked, searching his various potions and amulets, hoping for some sort of edge. He had magics to make him invisible, or strong, or that would let him leave his body so he could explore the city without endangering himself, but the costs were just too high. Becoming invisible required him to be naked, which would leave him vulnerable in more ways than one. The strength was only a temporary thing and would weaken him twofold once it passed. If he left his body, he had no guarantee of finding his way back.

Other magics were no use at all — a locket made out of the scales of a river dragon that would keep him from drowning, a cardinal's feather that would enable him to speak and understand the language of birds, a powder that changed fire to water or water to fire.

Then Jude's searching fingers found a pearl with some particular magical qualities, and when he got to his street, looking up at the lights on in his apartment, he had an idea, a way to turn at least part of his situation to his advantage.

Not a plan, exactly, he'd never really trusted those. More like a trick. Setting a few things up and seeing how they played out.

It all hinged on the pearl, a comment Regal had made about being invisible, and a card handed to him by a god. Not a tarot card, though.

A business card.

With an address printed in blood-red ink.

CHAPTER TWELVE

OF ALL THE THINGS he'd prepared himself to find when he confronted Regal in his apartment—supernatural thugs and angelic SWAT teams and evil shadow creatures and even a visit from Mourning himself—he hadn't expected her to ambush him with research.

Regal had shoved all his living room furniture into one corner and used the space to pile books and printouts of obscure websites all over his floor. If the research to summon the Red Door had been a high school paper, Regal now had a doctoral dissertation scattered across his living room. A huge standing whiteboard—which must have been a motherfucker to carry up the stairs on her own—loomed over all of it, with the names of the players at the card game written in different colored markers, circled and bisected and connected with questions and arrows, like a schizophrenic's conspiracy wall. Books were stacked on top of each other, Post-it notes poking out from their pages, or held open with the aid of other books. Most of them were his—judging by the gaps on his bookshelves—but some were recent acquisitions from the public library, according to the stickers on their spines.

Regal, dressed in a *Star Wars* tank top and jeans tucked into mid-calf leather boots, stood in the center of this hurricane, half humming and half singing along to "Still Fly" by the Big Tymers —which was playing from a laptop on his kitchen counter—a coffee mug in one hand and an open book in the other.

She turned at his entrance and smiled, a little sheepish at being caught. "Welcome to the Batcave!" she said, her arms spread wide to take in all her work. If it was an act, it was a good one. Even though his skin crawled with suspicion, Jude decided to play along.

"Made yourself at home, didn't you?" He nodded at the mug in her hand. "I'll forgive you if that coffee's fresh."

"Deal." She dropped the book on one of the piles and tiptoed her way out of the mess and into the kitchen. "How'd it go at the voodoo shop?"

You mean the ambush? he thought. "Tell you all about it in a second," he said, instead. "Let me get into some fresh clothes, first."

He slid the satchel off his shoulder and let it flop onto the counter next to her laptop, trying to make the gesture nonchalant, even though it was anything but. His bedroom door was at just the right angle to see the corner of the kitchen from down the short hall, so he was able to watch the bag the whole time he traded his jeans for a pair of loose-fitting gray slacks and tugged on an old Voodoo Fest T-shirt, the skull logo eerily similar to Barren's bone-faced leer.

The closest Regal came to his bait was to set his cup next to the satchel and turn the music down on the laptop. Did that mean she was trustworthy? Or that she'd recognized his act of leaving the satchel unguarded as a test?

Back in the living room, he picked up the coffee and drank, so grateful for the sweet, dark caffeine, that he didn't consider poison or drugs until he'd already taken a swallow.

He'd make a terrible spy.

With Regal sitting cross-legged amid her research, obviously waiting for him to fill her in on what he'd been up to, Jude skipped the foreplay and launched into an account of his past few hours, starting with a lie. He'd decided to keep deceiving Regal about the return of his gift, so he told her that the visit to the voodoo shop had been a waste of time, that he hadn't learned anything they didn't already know. Then he told her about the sensation of being pursued he'd felt outside the shop, how he'd been sure that something dark and deadly had been waiting for him.

Even though he was watching for it, Regal's face didn't betray any hints of subterfuge or hidden agendas at this. Her only reaction was to ask if he thought they were the shadows in his mother's painting, a question he answered with a shrug, admitting that while it seemed likely, he couldn't really be sure.

He told her about fleeing into the cathedral, about Hē's appearance, and how the angel told him that he was caught in a paradox, that he couldn't win the game. He said he'd talked to a fortuneteller in the Quarter to learn a little more about the game he was caught up in, and explained the "past/present/obstacle/turning point/future" structure of the poker hands, but he left Opal out of it entirely, referring to the fortuneteller as a "he."

When he pulled out his cards to show her THE HERMIT, he discovered a third card had been added to his hand: THE WHEEL OF FORTUNE.

A green circle inscribed with arcane symbols dominated the center of the card. On top of the wheel was a sphinx holding a sword, an Egyptian headdress covering up Dodge's bald head. Each of the four corners of the card held winged figures: Hē in the top left; a cross between an eagle and an ibis wearing Thoth's spectacles in the top right; a bloated, dead lion with Scarpelli's face in the lower right; and in the lower left, a bull with Legba's wrinkled old man's face capped by curved cruel horns. The left side of the card held a long, brightly colored serpent, and the right showed a jackal god Jude recognized as Anubis, who guided souls to the Underworld.

Sitting cross-legged and blindfolded in the center of what could be either a circle or a wheel, but was clearly meant to be the card table, was Jude.

It didn't show him anything he didn't already know, but the sight of it still sent a frisson tickling down his spine, a confirmation that the greatest obstacle in his path was the game, the gods in it, and his inability to see what to do next.

Regal's reaction to the card was somewhat more animated. "Fuck the police, Jude! This is it!" She hopped to her feet in a single graceful move that Jude's knees wouldn't have appreciated and lunged at the whiteboard. She wiped off a giant question mark in the middle of the board and wrote "Fortune" in the empty circle left behind. She capped the pen and tapped the word with it. "Right here, this is what all the gods at the game have in common."

Jude opened his mouth to argue, but she waved him off and went to one of the piles. She searched through it for a second and pulled out a few printouts from the Internet. "Here, listen: At least one deity can be found in every culture to whom is ceded the control of fortune or destiny, whether through the art of divination, through the parceling out of luck, and sometimes both."

Despite himself, Jude felt her enthusiasm eroding some of his suspicion, felt himself sliding back into the role of her mentor. Her friend. "Please tell me you didn't just google 'What do angels, vampires, and Legba have in common,'" he said.

She only spared him enough attention to give him the finger without looking at him. "We already know Dodge is a fortune god, and Legba can fit the pattern by being a Trickster figure, but for Thoth—which of these shit-chute piles did I put it—ah!"

Jude tilted his head so he could see the titles of the stacked books she was picking through: *Voodoo Practices of the Caribbean. A Treasury of Saints. The Vampire in Folklore and History. A History of God. Trickster Makes This World.* She snatched up a thick leather-bound tome titled *Myth, Ritual, and Religion,* vol. 2, flipped it open to a pink Post-it, and stabbed the page with a triumphant finger.

"There," she said, "stop with the cunting commentary and read, so you may accept my brilliance and despair." The words she pointed to read "Hermes Trismegistus." She flashed a mischievous smile, like a kid who knew where the Christmas presents were hidden. "Hermes 'Thrice-Great,' get it?" When Jude didn't answer, she rolled her eyes. "Don't tell me I have to explain syncretic myths to a demigod. I swear to your daddy I will punch you right in the dick."

Jude didn't rise to that bait, despite the temptation. "You mean like voodoo, right? The way myths link across cultures through common bonds, like when African slaves were confronted with Roman Catholicism. Instead of converting, they started calling the loa by the names of saints and martyrs that matched up, like St. Peter and Legba."

Regal was nodding as he spoke. "Right, right, exactly. Thoth and Hermes, same thing. That's how a god of scribes belongs at a poker table full of fortune gods."

Jude thought of the visions his gift had shown him of Dodge, memories of being something else long ago. He thought of his suspicions about Mourning, and the questions that Mourning had raised about his involvement in the game. Remembered what Hē had said about the prize they were playing for being the ability to reinvent themselves. Maybe it wasn't just Thoth. Maybe all the gods had gone by different names, had led different lives.

Regal stood at the whiteboard again, redrawing a line between her notes on Legba and on Thoth, scribbling "Hermes," and then drawing an arrow to her notes on "the angel." "Like a lot of Trickster figures, Legba and Hermes are in-between kinds of gods, ferrying communication between the worlds of gods and men. The crossroads, right? Well, that's how the angel fits in."

"Because the word *angel* comes from the Latin for messenger," Jude said, quoting from what Augustus — one of the monks who looked after his mother at the abbey—had once told him. A tingle crept along Jude's scalp and down the back of his neck. Tricksters. It made so much sense, seemed obvious now that it was written in front of him like this. They'd even been playing a game of fate.

Regal gave him a mocking little soft clap. "Look at the big brain on Jude. Plus, what kind of messages do angels bring you? They tell you about your place in God's plan. Your *destiny*."

Jude stepped up to the whiteboard and rapped the vampire's name with a knuckle. "The crossroads, in-between thing applies to vampires, too. They're not alive and not dead. Eat but are never nourished, that sort of thing."

"That's part of Tricksters too," she said. "Anansi, Loki, Hermes? They're always hungry."

"There's one problem with all of this."

"What's that?"

He touched a finger to his own name written on the board. "Me. I'm not a fortune god. I'm no Trickster."

Regal laughed. It wasn't a happy sound. "No. You're just half of one." Jude turned to her, but before he could speak a word of argument, she started counting off on her fingers, like she was reciting a list she'd come up with long ago. "First, you're charming as fuck. Don't give me that look—this isn't a compliment; it's a statement of fact. People like you, even when you're a prick. Strangers trust you. Just about everyone swallows whatever lies you feed them, even when those lies are as ripe as seven layers of dog dookie. Two, your preferred method of conflict resolution is the lie, the trick. The 'Oh shucks, Your Honor, I thought I was banging your sister, not your wife—can't we accept an honest mistake and be friends?' Which would fetch anybody else an ass-beating, but because of point number one, you slide on by, slicker than a greased politician."

She was waving her hands as she spoke, her face getting red, her tone getting more and more intense. Jude couldn't think of another word for the expression on her face other than anger, which didn't seem to make sense.

"Three, you know things, or you did before you pissed it away. That spooky 'lost things' magic touch of yours? That's exactly the sort of thing a Trickster would pass down to his bastard kid. 'Oh, did you lose something of great personal value? I can find it for you if the price is right.'" She poked out her thumb, the one she'd decided to save as her closer. "Last, and the real icing on the cake for me: you're the luckiest son of a god I've ever met. When you're in the car, I never hit a red light. Never. No one else can depend on public transit in this city for reliable transportation, but you've never had to wait for a bus or a streetcar, have you? I mean, Christ, Dubuisson. You're a black man in New Orleans. We've done some shit, you and me. Broken into places we shouldn't've, stolen things. Any black guy I've ever known gets pulled over like once a month, just for existing. Not you, not even when you *deserve* it. Not once have I seen you get harassed by the cops. Things just always seem to work out for you, don't they? You know how I found your number the other day? It wasn't some spell like I told you. I just dialed a random number and you answered. It wasn't me. It was *you*. *Your* magic. Your goddamn luck. You weren't even—"

Her jaw clenched, as she literally bit down on what she was about to say.

"Come on," Jude said. "Get it all out. You've obviously been holding on to this for a while."

She wouldn't meet his eyes.

"Say it."

When she spoke, the Regal Sloan act fell away. No brash vulgarities, no over-the-top attempts to shock him, to keep him at arm's length. Her words were soft. Almost a whisper. "You weren't here for the storm," she said. "Day before the whole world goes to hell, I get a text that you got 'a thing to take care of' and then, poof. Peace the fuck out. Almost a year before I know you're not dead."

She swallowed, shook her head. "Even if it's not intentional. The luck thing. Even if it's just instinct. I was your partner, Jude. I thought I mattered. But you tricked me, didn't you?"

There were all sorts of things that Jude wanted to tell her. That he'd left the city that day because his mother had been on the edge of one of her episodes. That he'd only been half-aware that a hurricane was in the Gulf, something only a native New Orleanian would believe or understand. That it had been over a month before he'd even been able to get back into the city. That once he had, his magic had torn through him so powerfully that he hadn't been able to function for months more.

That he hadn't died, but he hadn't really been alive, either.

None of those things mattered, though. Instead, he went into the kitchen and got a bottle of El Dorado, a twenty-one-year-old rum distilled somewhere in South America that he saved for special occasions, like funerals or an unexpected visit from one of the loa. He poured two shots—one for him, one for Regal—and brought them and the bottle into the living room. He pressed Regal's glass into her hand, and—once she grudgingly took it—he clinked it with his own. He waited for her to look at him, to meet his eyes. "I'm sorry," he said. "It's not enough, but I'm sorry." When he raised his glass to his lips, she did as well, draining her rum and then holding the glass out for another. He poured more for the both of them, and then pointed to the whiteboard with the hand holding the bottle. "So what you're saying is, I got invited to this card game because I am, fundamentally, an asshole."

She choked on her drink, coughing and laughing and cursing all the same time. When she recovered, she squeezed one eye shut and considered him. "No," she said. "Only half."

They endured an uncomfortable silence for a few moments. Jude's thoughts churned, trying to work through the implications of what Regal had said. If he was a Trickster like all the gods at the table, then it was possible that any one of them could be his father. Even the white folks. Tricksters were skin changers. Swapping race was amateur hour if you could go from man to bird to fox as simple as flipping a jacket inside out. Legba or Dodge he could probably handle. The angel was too weird to even consider. The vampire, though? Jude shook that image from his mind and stood, setting the bottle of rum on the counter and gesturing to the mess of books and paper on his floor with his half-empty glass. "So this is what you've been up to since we split up outside the voodoo shop? I thought you had a lead on Thoth. Or Hermes. Or whatever we're calling him." It was an obviously awkward attempt to change the subject, and only worked because Regal was eager to do the same.

"Oh, right. Forgot to mention that before. According to my source, he's got a bookstore downtown somewhere. No sign on the door, only deals in rarities, if you get me."

He did. Most members of the—for want of a better term—supernatural community were born into it, either because they weren't quite human, or because they came from a family of practitioners. Or, like Jude, a little of both. There were a few, though, who were on the fringes. Either they belonged to a family who had fallen away from the traditions, and tried to gather accounts of real magic from the scraps of gossip, family legends, and lies, or they found their way to someone willing to teach them through faith, perseverance, and luck—the way Regal had found Mourning. For those desperate few, a grimoire or amulet of real power would be worth any price, provided they could find the right market.

And if the guy running the market sounded a little odd and told you he was the Egyptian god of scribes, you said, "Sure you are, of course. Love the Nile. What kind of spells have you got for sale?"

"When do I get to meet your source?" he asked.

"Soon as you introduce me to Leon Carter and tell him he can trust me, instead of getting me stoned on horny juice and sending me off to play while you two have a quiet little chat." She shot him a meaningful glance. "He's fine, since you asked."

Jude pretended to finish off his empty glass of rum to hide his grin. "That's not exactly how it went down," he said, "but point taken."

He went back to the counter and poured another couple of fingers of rum in his glass, partly to give himself something to do with his hands, partly to numb that creeping sense of guilt for ever having doubted Regal. Her anger, her distance, her strange behavior. It was all his fault. He thought about what came next and gave himself another generous splash before replacing the cork.

For courage.

"Got anything else planned for tonight?" he asked, trying to keep his tone casual.

"Nothing I'll be sad to skip. Why? What've you got in mind?"

Jude took the business card the vampire had given him out of his coat pocket, the one with his address in red ink. "Scarpelli told me I had to give him an answer for his offer of employment by tonight, and I've got this, well . . . it's not a plan exactly. More of an *idea* . . ."

Regal was already on her feet, shrugging into a leather jacket and wearing a feral grin. "Jude Dubuisson," she said, "you might be a Trickster and you might be an asshole. But never let it be said that you don't know how to show a girl a good time."

CHAPTER THIRTEEN

IN INDIA they were called vetālas. The Greeks knew them as striges. To the ancient Norsemen, they were draugr, the "after-goers." They exist in every culture, always waiting in the night when men are at their weakest. China, Malaysia, Africa, Romania. Jiang Shi, langsuir, adze, strigoi. Vampire. They are the fear of death given shape and will. They are shadows and teeth and hunger. Because they do not know pain, they cannot be harmed. Because they do not hope, they have no weakness. Because they do not live, they cannot die. They are the blood-drinkers, they are the reason you fear the darkness.

Regal's enthusiasm waned considerably during the short drive Uptown to the address Scarpelli had given him, as Jude explained his more-of-a-trick-than-a-plan to her.

"I'd like to revise my previous assessment," she said. "You're not half-a-Trickster. You're batshit, balls-out, Bone Thugs-N-Harmony insane."

"*See you at the crossrooooaaads,*" Jude sang.

Regal snorted. "Not exactly the theme song you want for rolling up against a vampire, especially when your quote-unquote plan involves us immediately splitting up. Haven't you seen, like, any TV show *ever?*"

"His attention will be entirely on me. I'll see to that. Provided you weren't just blowing smoke when you said you could be invisible when you wanted to be."

She waved a hand at him. "*Practically* invisible. But yeah, it'll be enough for what you've got in mind. I'm more concerned about your escape hatch. Please tell me you've got something more solid than 'Please don't eat me' prepared."

He did, in fact, but had neither the time nor the inclination to explain. He opened up the satchel and took out a rosary that an Irish nun named Hyacinth McQuillan had lost nearly a century before — an ornate artifact with marble beads and a silver crucifix — studying it for a moment before slipping it around his neck.

Regal groaned and muttered something pessimistic.

Rosary probably won't help, he thought, *but it can't hurt. Besides, this thunderbolt in my bag is the ultimate exit strategy.* "The first rule of being a Trickster," he said, since he didn't have time to explain the thunderbolt to her, "is to always leave yourself an out. If things turn ugly, I'll give Scarpelli what he wants. I'll tell him I'll work for him. That option sucks — no pun intended — but it's better than the alternative. But it won't come to that."

She worried a thumbnail with her teeth. "I'm just still a little hazy on how you're going to talk him into doing what you want."

Jude touched his doubloon with one hand, trusting Regal's need to watch the road to keep her from noticing, and reached into the satchel. He pulled out the pearl that had sparked his idea for this whole trap. There was something odd about it, some deeper mystery his affinity for lost things was trying to push him toward, but he ignored it and, letting go of the connection to his gift, held the pearl up where Regal could see it.

"With this," he said. "Hold it under your tongue, and everything you say becomes incredibly convincing. Spells you speak become supercharged. It's got a nasty side effect, though. I only used it once, and when I spat it out, I lost the ability to pronounce a couple of words."

"Lost the ability? What does that even mean?"

"Supposively," Jude said.

Regal shot him a look, saw the expression on his face, and sucked her teeth. "Yeesh," she said. "What possessed you to make a thing like that?"

"Didn't make it," he said. "Obviously someone must have lost it, because I found it"—he patted the leather of the satchel—"in here."

"Wait, the *bag* finds lost things? I thought that was your—" She took one hand off the wheel and wiggled her fingers.

"The bag doesn't find them; it's where lost things end up." He slid the pearl into his pocket next to his doubloon, along with a stub of candle and a piece of chalk, and pushed the satchel out of his lap and onto the floor at his feet, suddenly wanting it out of sight for some reason. "And before you ask, I don't know how it works, just that it does. It's funny, you ask most people in this city about their lives, and they'll split it up before and after the storm. Where they used to live, who they used to be. What they lost." He risked a glance at Regal, saw that her jaw was clenching and unclenching. He looked away, watching the houses and oak trees blur by as they drove down St. Charles. "But not me. I'd screwed things up way before the flood. Before I started reaching into that bag, life was simple, you know? My biggest concerns were making sure I saw Kermit Ruffins at Vaughan's on Thursdays. Crawfish boils and Saints games. I had a bunch of non-magical friends, a crappy part-time job at a coffee shop way Uptown on Oak, another one at a bar in Mid-City. The magic? Working for Mourning? That was just an occasional thing, easy cash and a little taste of . . . of being special, I guess. But I got greedy. Saw a chance for power and took

it. Traded a god a blank check, and this is what I got in return."
He took a deep breath and slowly let it out. Decided that if he was
going to trust Regal to guard his back against a vampire, he could
trust her with this. "This was the favor he called in, Queens. This
is why I had to show up at the card game."

Even though he wasn't looking at her, he felt her shift in her
seat, knew her eyes were on him. "Dodge gave you—"

"Regal, stop. Stop the car."

"Why?"

"We're here."

He could tell she had more to say, but Jude was out of the car
as soon as she pulled over, the satchel's strap around his shoulder
and his pulse already starting to ratchet up. The address Scarpelli had given him was a gated mansion on Carrollton Avenue,
a massive, gothic-looking structure that waited down a long,
curved driveway protected by high hedges and floodlights. Two
hundred years ago, Carrollton had been its own town a half day's
walk upriver from New Orleans, built up on the land surrounding the McCarty Plantation. The growing city had swallowed it
up, though, and now it was just a street, its history reduced to a
plaque by the streetcar tracks. Jude suppressed a shudder at the
realization that the vampire wanted to do much the same thing
to him.

Scarpelli's long black Cadillac, its windows tinted and its wax
job fresh, was parked in the curve of the driveway by the front
door. *Guess he's home,* Jude thought, the faint coppery taste of
blood pricking along his tongue. Scarpelli's house and land took up
most of the block between Freret and Zimpel and stretched nearly
all the way from Carrollton to Short Street. Palm trees sprouted up
from the manicured lawn and leaned against the tall fence of black
iron bars. Jude walked along the sidewalk past the front gate while
Regal circled around the back, trying to act nonchalant, certain
that more than a few cameras scanned the outside of the mansion.
The hedges growing against and through the fence hid him from

anyone inside but blocked his view of the house as well. He paced along, feeling like one of the big cats at the zoo.

When they met up on the far side of the house, she hadn't found a way in either. "Any ideas?" she asked.

"I can go right in the front, since I was invited, but—"

"But you need me to go all 'stealth mode.' Think you could boost me up there?"

Jude looked up to where she pointed. Overhead, an oak branch, thick and old, managed to curve out over the fence before its weight pulled it back toward earth. Metal rods held it high above the side-walk, guided it away from the street. The dense canopy of the rest of the tree spread above the branch, shrouding it and the concrete beneath it in darkness. If she could reach it, she was in.

Jude interlaced his fingers and made a stirrup, and Regal stepped into it, lunged up, put her other foot on his shoulder, and just like that, slithered up onto the branch. *Let's hope the rest of this goes so smooth,* he thought. Hissing a whisper up to Regal, he said, "Abra-cadabra time, don't you think?"

In the movies, when you draw a blade from its sheath, it makes this wicked *shhh*ing sound so you know how badass and razor sharp it is. In real life, the sound of edged metal against leather is closer to the noise of playing cards flicking against one another, if it makes any noise at all. When Regal reached to the small of her back—a gesture he'd seen before and had thought she was going for a concealed gun—he heard the quiet *snik* and saw the gleam of a dagger in her hand. It was visible just long enough for him to no-tice that the hilt of it shone pure white, before Regal held it close to her lips, speaking a few words to it too quietly for Jude to hear, and then it, and she, vanished.

But not entirely. The space where she'd been crouched flick-ered, like the air over asphalt on a hot summer day, not something he'd notice if he hadn't already been looking right at her.

Regal's voice came from the branches. "Pretty spec-fucking-tacular, right? I call her Vera."

Jude barely kept from rolling his eyes, remembering at the last second that just because he couldn't see her didn't mean that she couldn't see him. "Be careful in there. I can still kind of see you. Like—"

"Like in *Predator*, right? Vera is so goddamn *metal*. See you on the other side." A rustle of leaves, a flicker just barely seen, and she was gone.

Jude felt a tremor of guilt and suspicion as he turned and made his way back to the front gate. Guilt because he'd worked this into his plot against the vampire, having sensed an artifact of some kind on Regal all the way back in St. Joe's bar a few days ago, and he'd hoped this would force her to show him how to use it. Suspicion because it hadn't been an alien big-game hunter he'd imagined when he'd seen Regal fade out of sight.

To him she'd looked like a shadow.

Jude shook those inklings away. *Neither the time nor the place, Dubuisson*, he thought. *Vampire, remember?* He pressed the pearl to his lips, hesitated for a fraction of a second, and then he dropped it into his mouth and rolled it beneath his tongue. A sudden flush along his skin, coils drawing taut within his flesh, within his mind, told him that the magic had taken hold. Jude wanted something he could not name, not vengeance or retribution or anything so easily articulated as that. He knew only that Scarpelli had taken something from him, something he wanted back.

Whatever the cost.

He considered pressing the intercom button on the gate, but if he could catch the vampire unawares, all the better. He spoke the lock *open* with a word, and with the pearl fueling his magic, the gate surged out of his way so urgently that it almost yanked itself free of its track. As he made his way up the driveway, he tasted blood, a faint presence that grew stronger the closer he came to the house. He found himself tapping his hand against his thigh, realizing after a moment that he was keeping his hand as close to the doubloon in his pocket as he could, in case he needed to dive into

the satchel for the thunderbolt. Like he was a gunslinger just waiting to draw. *Stupid,* he thought, and forced himself to stop. All the
same, he kept his hand near his pocket.

Instead of strolling through the front door, he followed a concrete path around the side of the house where Regal would have
come over the fence, which led to a side door. He forced himself
to keep his eyes forward, to not search the dew-covered lawn for
Regal's heat mirage flicker. Just because he couldn't see a camera
didn't mean one wasn't filming him. He spoke the side door *open* —
softly, so he didn't rip it off its hinges — and entered the cool darkness of the vampire's lair.

Inside, he found an unsettling sterility, the crisp, chilly air devoid of any scent, the furniture ornate and expensive but un-
creased, unblemished. It looked so perfect, so un-lived-in, that
Jude wouldn't have been surprised to find price tags still attached.
Paintings hung on the walls, the generic, impersonal sort of art
chosen by a realtor staging a house for sale. There were no mirrors, no photographs. Silence reigned within, broken only by the
hum of the air conditioning and the refrigerator. Jude tried to picture the vampire's bloated corpse reclining in an armchair reading
or lounging on the plush expensive sofa watching a Saints game,
but it seemed ludicrous. The entire house — like the vampire himself — was a disguise, a shell that held no life within. Jude's very
presence was an intrusion, his sweat and his heat and his pulse an
invasion of the living into the realm of the dead. Jude imagined
wrecking the place, shattering the vase of artificial flowers against
the wall, dancing with muddy shoes on his pristine white couch.

The old Jude's fuck-you grin twisted its way across his face.

He glanced into the kitchen at the gleaming silver tower of the
vampire's fridge and imagined one of two possibilities: either it
was as empty, as sterile as the rest of the house, or it was filled with
a hellish assortment of whatever unfinished meals Scarpelli might
consider worth saving. He decided he could live with that mystery
left unsolved, and made his way deeper into the lie of a house.

Up a set of stairs covered with carpet so thick and clean it might have never been stepped on, Jude found that a large part of the second story had been devoted to a single packed room. Rows of waist-high display cases stretched along the walls and split the room into narrow aisles lit with a dull shine of moonlight through the window high on the far wall. A suit of armor and a wooden globe crowded together in a nook that had once been a closet, the walls adorned with the thin, curved lines of cavalry swords, the straight, squat lines of flintlock rifles, their uniformity broken by the occasional odd shape of an axe head or the jagged edges of an unusual blade.

As he crept down one of the rows, he discovered that the cases mostly held coins, some the shiny full moons of recent mintings, pockmarked by the faces of rulers both familiar and foreign, others with chipped edges and smoothed, indistinct faces, gnawed by time. Jude's breath rasped in his own ears, amplified by his nervousness, by the silence. He felt the urge to run his hands along all of these artifacts, since they were just so much steel and silver without his magic to overwhelm him with the stories of their loss or flashes of memory from their previous owners. If this were a movie, he'd yank one of those swords free, probably an out-of-place katana, but when Jude pictured it, all he could imagine was a clatter of falling swords and spears and shattering glass, and him standing in the ruin of the vampire's collection when Scarpelli found him.

He turned to leave and something flickered in the corner of his eye—maybe Regal, maybe just moonlight across a polished coin—startling him. He whirled, his hands plunging into pocket and satchel for his magic and the thunderbolt, but the instant his fingertips brushed against the doubloon, a sensation of loss roiled through him with such intensity that it knocked him to his knees and drove any other thoughts from his mind. Pain and grief and guilt, more than anyone should have to bear. Gun smoke and blood and shit and the burn of barely choked-back vomit. Screams and screams and screams.

Jude grit his teeth and forced himself to his feet, following the thread of loss across the room to its source, a wooden box about a foot long and half as wide, smooth and varnished to a slick gloss. The cover was engraved with the initials A. E. C. and a symbol Jude recognized as denoting a curse. Alphonse Elijah Constant— Eli as he preferred to be called—the magician Jude had apprenticed under in his youth. Bracing himself for what the box might contain, Jude snapped open its clasps and removed the lid. Inside, a revolver, a worn and heavy-looking chunk of steel, lay nestled in the velvet-lined depression that matched its shape, along with a round metal disk and some kind of clamp. There were spaces for six bullets: two were empty, and one had been fired already, some unusual nostalgia driving someone to keep the brass shell casing.

He didn't know what Eli had done to this weapon, but there was only one way to find out.

Just touching the gun grip hurt with that mingled sensation of hot and cold that came with either scorched or frozen flesh. He forced himself past the pain, waiting for his affinity for lost things to reveal the revolver to him. There was nothing but pain for several long breaths, and then, like a dam breaking, the entire history of the gun roared into him in a torrent.

It was a Smith & Wesson Model 3 American, assembled in 1880 in Springfield, Massachusetts, as part of a bulk order for the U.S. Cavalry. It found its way into the hands of Joseph Wright, a thirty-year-old veteran of the Fifth United States Colored Cavalry, the son of a free woman of color and a Creole—the old kind, the descended-from-a-rich-French-dude kind of Creole—plantation owner. After the Civil War, he was assigned to another regiment and headed north, where he and the revolver met. Increasingly disgusted with the treatment of the Sioux at the orders of his superiors, he deserted his unit soon after and returned home, to New Orleans, haunted by the things he had seen and done as a soldier.

When he was nearly mad with guilt and alcohol abuse, Joseph's mother begged Eli Constant for aid. In a ritual that lasted three days and turned Joseph's hair entirely white, Jude's former teacher drew the sins of Joseph's life as a soldier from him like lancing the infection from a boil and sealed them in the steel and wood of the instrument of his worst crimes. Doing so cursed the revolver so that it would unleash Joseph's sin on anyone who tried to use it for violence, with dire consequences. Joseph, free of the crippling burdens of his guilt—though never from the memories of what he had done—lived to be an old man, but more importantly a peaceful man, preaching against violence and enriching many lives. In 1930 his eldest son, packing some of his father's things in preparation for a move, lost the revolver, and it had hidden itself among other antique instruments of war for nearly a hundred years, until Jude's magic sniffed it out.

Jude gasped in a breath and tore his hand away from the gun, away from the coin in his pocket. He jammed the revolver back into its case and snapped the clasps shut. He wanted, desperately, to leave it there where he had found it, but it bore his teacher's name, and it was a curse he could not, now that he knew it existed, leave free in the world. Besides, hideous and warped though it was, it was a lost thing.

So he picked it back up, then put it into his satchel with all the others of its kind.

Jude quickly explored the rest of the upstairs, a series of closed doors that opened onto empty, unused rooms, wondering how much, if any, of his experience with the revolver Regal had seen, how much she'd have understood if she had seen it. He supposed it didn't much matter. After tonight, he'd either trust her enough to tell her about the doubloon and the thunderbolt and everything else, or he'd be leftovers in Scarpelli's fridge. He crept down the stairs to the first floor, footfalls silent on the thick carpet, where—

now that his eyes had adjusted fully to the darkness — he found a small door set beneath the stairs.

He eased the door open, wincing at every creak and groan, and found the last thing he expected: stairs leading down.

The jokes and comments about New Orleans being below sea level were not hyperbole. That fact, combined with the absorbent clay that made up much of the subsurface geology of the area, meant that the architecture of the city simply did not include basements. Sewers and foundations might delve beneath the surface, but nowhere in the city would building beneath the earth be anything other than an exercise in both futility and stupidity. If it didn't flood outright, the walls would buckle from the constant pressure of rainwater during the first summer.

And yet, here were stairs carved out of stone leading down into an eerie blue light, and the taste of blood was more powerful here, twisting Jude's stomach. The stone walls bore regularly spaced, crypt-like alcoves, though they were filled with ornate carvings — re-creations of Renaissance pietàs or depictions of martyrs' deaths — instead of the piles of bones and skulls he'd expected, which made it feel like he was descending into some perverse chapel as much as a catacomb. The strange light came from blue flames dancing in wall sconces that seemed to produce no heat; Jude's breath misted in the frigid air. The taste of blood grew stronger until his saliva felt thick and warm and viscous in his mouth. He fought the urge to spit.

Abruptly, the tunnel leveled off and widened into a large, circular space — what he'd call a cavern if he didn't know he was beneath Uptown New Orleans. In the center of the room, a squat table of rough-hewn marble rose from the floor.

The vampire named Umberto Scarpelli loomed over a naked tattooed woman, who lay on the table like a sacrifice upon an altar. She was thick, her flesh rounded at her hips and stomach, that particularly sexy shape of a New Orleans woman nurtured by rich foods and a sensual palate. The tattoos covering her body seemed to be abstractions at first. Evenly spaced rectangles of gray marked her belly and thighs, large swathes of green and brown curved and undulated from her large breasts down the length of her body, a web of lines spread up her neck and across her shaved head. When Jude saw the unmistakable white eggshell swoop of the Superdome on her stomach, the rest of the images fell into place. She was tattooed with the city, partly the skyline, partly a map, partly something else.

A slurping, gurgling sound hung in the air. Scarpelli's back bunched and flexed as he fed. Jude flashed on a memory of a night years ago in City Park, grunting noises and a van rocking back and forth on its shocks. Burning flesh and inhuman strength and two small bundles of meat that had once held innocent life. Eli had always said you'd never forget your first vampire. Ice ran through his veins. Scarpelli looked up from the naked woman's neck, his eyes pools of crimson, the lower half of his face a black stain. And then he did the most terrible thing of all.

He smiled.

The horror of it freed Jude from the shock that bound him. He dropped to one knee and dug in his pocket for his chalk. He used it to trace a circle around himself on the floor, forcing his hand to be patient. If he broke the line by lifting his hand, or by scuffing it with his shoe, or letting his concentration waver, or any of a hundred ways, the magic would be useless. He sucked in one long, continuous breath as he drew, stopping only when it was complete and his lungs felt like they would burst. He held this breath as he wrote four symbols at the compass points, released it as he placed the stump of candle at the seam where the circle had begun and joined itself. With a snap of his fingers, the candle burst into flame. He tossed the chalk behind him, outside his drawn circle, said the word that meant *close*, and the spell was complete; he felt its protection tighten around him, a pressure against his skin.

When Jude looked up from the marks on the stone floor, the

magic that Eli Constant had taught him so long ago, Scarpelli stood a few feet away, tucking his shirttails into a pair of trousers that strained to contain his bulk. In the short moments it had taken Jude to draw his ward, the vampire had dressed and had even cleaned the blood from his face. "Finished?" he asked.

Jude had counted on the amused contempt he heard in Scarpelli's voice. The dead god could have interrupted Jude at any point, snatching him out of his half-worked spell before Jude could flinch, much less escape. The trick, Jude had hoped, was in how pathetic he must have looked crawling around on the floor, how weak and hastily erected his magic must seem. Jude nodded, not yet wanting to reveal his voice.

Scarpelli crossed the distance between them with a shiver's quickness, a flurry of teeth and shadow. He struck what appeared to be thin air with a wet smack, recoiling with an expression of shock that would have been comic if not for its immediate shift to one of malice. Scarpelli hissed past yellowed fangs and pounded his fist against the barrier of Jude's magic. In order to hide the terror that wormed through his belly and to spite the pain that flared in his temples each time the vampire lashed out against his spell, Jude flashed the vampire a bright grin and winked right in the dead god's face.

Rage drained away from the vampire's expression, replaced by something unreadable and cold. "Well, well," he said. His voice grated in Jude's ears, high-pitched and harsh. "How interesting." Scarpelli stretched his head back and inhaled deeply, his jowls flattening and expanding like the throat of a toad. A bloated tongue slithered across moist lips. "Oh, sweetmeats. Something has changed about you. Something . . . delicious. Something familiar." Red-tainted eyes rolled to the ceiling for a moment as he sniffed the air again. He clicked his tongue and grinned. "Oh, of course. You haven't changed, have you? You've just brought along a friend. Appetizer or digestif?" He raised his voice and spoke over his shoulder. "Oh, Friend Appetizer? You smell delightful. A bit familiar, even. Have I eaten anyone you know? A brother or father perhaps?"

Even though he was desperate to know that she hadn't run away, Jude didn't dare look away from the vampire to see if Regal really was in here with them, or if Scarpelli could merely smell her on his clothes. Nor could he entirely blame her if she'd fled. She didn't have the protection of his circle, only the thin armor of her pseudo-invisibility. If he made any move to reassure himself and she was here, though, it would be the end of her.

"Don't blame yourself," the vampire said, his tone mockingly conciliatory. "It was a good trick, however you did it, sneaking your naughty conspirator in here. Almost fooled me. But the nose knows, no?" He pressed one nostril closed and giggled, that high-pitched tittering sound that put Jude's teeth on edge. "Yes, a good trick," Scarpelli said, continuing as if Jude weren't there. "Not nearly as good as this, though." He pressed a long-nailed fingertip against the invisible barrier of Jude's spell. "No mere half-breed could keep me at bay with such a simple working. What are you truly, I wonder?" He held up a hand when Jude opened his mouth to speak. "No, don't tell me. I want to savor it. I want your taste to be a surprise." He ran the tip of his bloated tongue along the tip of one of his yellowed incisors. "I want you to know that I'm really going to enjoy this," he said. "Not just feeding off whatever power lurks in your veins, although that'll be nice, too. I'm going to enjoy watching the light go out of your eyes. Soon, precious. Soon. That candle can't have more than twenty minutes of life left in it. Just like you."

Jude darted a glance down. The flame sputtered above a lump of wax that had seemed much larger not long before. The piece of chalk had vanished. The vampire giggled once again and pulled a white cloth from his sleeve, shaking it in the air like a celebrant at a second line. "Now that we've taken care of that," he said. "Come. Come and let me introduce you to the city of New Orleans."

Jude's gaze traveled to the stone pedestal where the painted woman lay. Had he killed her? No, her breath plumed in the cold air. He also saw scabs at the woman's neck, on her thighs, in the crook of her elbow, in a line down her belly, and in her groin just above her sex. They were not the dainty puncture marks of a Hollywood vampire but wicked tears in her flesh, the ravening bites of a savage, hungry beast.

"Beautiful, isn't she?" Scarpelli said, running one monstrously elongated finger across the woman's cheek, a horrific parody of tenderness. "She will be my greatest achievement."

"Funny," Jude said, his pronunciation a little hesitant with the pearl clutched beneath his tongue. "All I see is more death."

Scarpelli's titter dragged a cold blade down Jude's spine. "Not death," he said. "I am giving her life. The life she has always wanted." The vampire was, Jude realized, drunk on the woman's blood, his eyes heavy, his speech sluggish. Like a tick, he had fed and now needed to curl up and sleep. Then things clicked for Jude — the ritualistic, half-healed bites on the woman's flesh; Scarpelli's swaggering claims that the game no longer mattered; his mother's painting of a fanged, monstrous New Orleans skyline — and he understood what Scarpelli was doing, spoke the words as soon as he thought them.

"You're turning her, aren't you?" he asked. "You're trying to make the city a vampire."

"Not trying, sweetmeats. Doing. It's going to be glorious." Scarpelli dipped a finger into the woman's still gaping wound, licked the blood from his elongated nail. "And the best part is, no one will notice. She already lures people in with sex and drink and the promise of freedom, and grants them those things even as she drains the life from them." He turned a burning red gaze in Jude's direction. "Brilliant, isn't it?"

Jude could see the bleak poetry of it. He knew, as everyone in the city did, of at least one person who had fallen into the very trap Scarpelli described. Especially since the storm, people here let the drinking or the drugs or the sex, once a *celebration* of life, become the *purpose* of life. The night took over, and they grew thin and wasted, as though something ate them from the inside out. Most didn't last long. The simple, predatory beauty of Scarpelli's plan was that he wasn't changing anything. He was just making it literal.

"You about a dumb motherfucker," Jude said. His balls tightened as soon as the words left his lips, but he tried to keep his diction ignorant, to push forward with his bluff. "Couple of tattoos don't mean shit. She ain't a city just 'cause you say she is. How you figure she any kind of special?"

The vampire tilted his head to the side, as though he hadn't fully understood the question. After a moment, he shook his head. "You think like such a mortal," he said. "Observe." Scarpelli lifted the woman's legs, bending each first at the knee and then at the hip, curling her limbs into the lotus position. He crossed her arms as well. Each movement seemed to realign the lines and colors on her flesh into some new combination, as though she had been painted with not one map but many.

What he did next gave Jude a headache just to watch. The vampire pressed one hand into the crease of her groin and lifted her leg with the other hand, bending the joint at an impossible angle. Instead of breaking, though, the woman *folded*. The vampire continued with her other leg and the rest of her body, collapsing the woman in on herself in a kind of grim origami. Jude looked away when he realized that at some point in the process she had become weightless and paper-thin. When he forced himself to look again, the woman had vanished, replaced by a book, its spine shimmering with a soft intermittent glow.

The vampire turned a look of absolute victory toward Jude. Behind him, Jude saw a chalk *X* on the stone wall that hadn't been there a moment before. His pulse raced. Now or never.

"No," Jude said.

Scarpelli set the book down on the altar and caught his tongue between his teeth in a leering smile. "No to what?"

"To all of this. To your offer of employment, to this perversion of my city, to anything and everything you stand for. The answer is no. I won't allow it. I'll kill you here and now if I have to."

Scarpelli laughed, high and tittering and filled with glee. "Kill me? *Me?* Please, precious, tell me how."

"I've dealt with your kind before."

"You may have killed some fledgling with the dirt of the grave still moist beneath his fingernails, but don't think we're all such easy prey. I am so very old, and you are so very human. Stronger beings than you have tried to make an end of me, and I can still remember how each one of them tasted."

Jude forced a smile onto his face. He reached behind his back, the way he'd seen Regal do time and again when reaching for her dagger. "Vampires rise at noon and sleep at midnight," he said, "or you used to, back when people woke at dawn and slept at dusk. You cannot cross running water, or abide the scent of garlic. In the hands of a true believer, a symbol of faith will weaken you. Stakes carved from the heartwood of an ash tree will bind you, silver will cut you, and fire will destroy you." The words poured out of him, slick as a sheen of oil. He felt the old Jude's confidence filling him, the swagger that came with always having an ace up his sleeve.

Or a pearl under his tongue.

Scarpelli rolled his eyes, made a masturbatory gesture. "Thank you for the lesson in folklore, but what does that have to do with anything? You have none of those things, and even if you did, I am faster and stronger and more powerful than you will ever be." Despite his words, the vampire's gaze was focused on Jude's arm, on the hand out of sight.

"It's not about the objects themselves that matters. It's what they represent. It's what they reveal about your nature. Silver, garlic, running water, fire. All symbols of purity. That's what hurts you. That's what will unmake you. Something pure. Because you are nothing but a corruption of life."

Scarpelli's grin slid from his face. He licked his lips with his thick hanged-man's tongue. "Maybe you're right," Scarpelli said. "Maybe. But you've evaded my question. What weapon of purity did you bring?"

With his free hand, Jude tapped his chest, right above his heart. "Right here," he said.

Scarpelli laughed again, his condescension returning. "*You?* Oh, Jude. Your blood is diluted with mortality. You have no faith; you believe in nothing. I can smell the taint of sin on your soul. Purity? Oh no, precious. Oh no." He chuckled. "You nearly had me going."

At Jude's feet, the candle's flame succumbed to the inevitable and snuffed out. The vampire, bluffed by the empty hand behind Jude's back, didn't move.

"As you say," Jude said, "I'm not pure. But my hatred of you? My desire to watch you burn?" He let some of his magic slip from him, felt his words burning in the frigid air. He smiled the old Jude's fuck-you smile. "*That's* pure. And if you don't be-lieve me . . ." He spread his arms wide, showing his empty hands, betting it all on one turn of the cards, on one throw of the dice. "Come and have a taste." He stepped backward across the chalk line he'd drawn, pointed to the floor, and shouted the word that meant *close*, putting all the force of will behind it he could sum-mon. Then he looked up, met the vampire's red glare, and waited to see if he would live or die.

Scarpelli looked down at the book on the stone altar, caressing its cover before turning away. Just as before, the vampire launched himself through the air faster than the eye could follow and, as before, slammed into the barrier of a protective circle. This one wasn't a three-foot loop around Jude, though. While the vampire had been focused on gloating and threats, Regal had used the chalk to make a larger circle around the entire room connected to the original one Jude had drawn.

Not to keep the vampire out, but to cage him in.

"You are a clever little meal," Scarpelli said, once he'd lashed out at the barrier a few times. "I don't know if it's your arrogance, or your naiveté, or the pleasure I get waiting for you to stumble. Whichever it is, I find your fumbling little efforts so endearing. What *can* you be plotting?"

"You're talking a whole lot of shit for someone in a cage."

Scarpelli clapped his fleshy hands in a gross imitation of childish glee. "Oh, I *love* this game." All pretense of amusement slid from the vampire's expression, leaving nothing behind but cold, naked rage. "How long do you really think this pitiful ward will hold me?"

"Just long enough," Jude said, "to fuck with your plans."

"Ah, ah, ah," Scarpelli said, shaking an admonishing finger. "I think you overestimate your own talents." He stalked the confines of the chalk circle like a jungle cat at the zoo, drawing his nails along the empty-air barrier with an unnerving screech. "I won't bother to ask if you've considered that by locking me in here with this"—he gestured toward the altar and the book he'd unfolded into a woman—"you've done nothing more than assure that I'll continue to turn the city uninterrupted. Surely you've thought of that already, clever boy that you are. I won't ask if you've any idea of the powers aligned against you, or if you know who you can trust. I won't even ask you, out of the goodness of my heart, to consider my offer one last time." He *tsk*ed and shook his head. "That one you've already answered. No, what I want to know most is"—he cupped a hand around his ear in exaggerated pantomime—"do you hear what I hear?"

In spite of himself, Jude held his breath and listened. From the top of the stairs came a rhythmic pounding: *thump-thump-thump, thump-thump-thump,* THUMP, THUMP, THUMP, *thump-thump-thump.*

Shit, Jude thought, *SOS.* He took the stairs two at a time, propelled forward by the sound of Scarpelli's grating, tittering laughter. When he burst out of the stairwell and into the pristine living room, his first thought was: *Scarpelli's gonna need all new carpet after this.* Ghouls—about a dozen of them—crowded the expansive, sterile living space, dropping chunks of putrefying flesh onto virginal carpeting, smearing what few bodily fluids the vampire hadn't drained onto walls and furniture. They were so rotted that it was hard to say which had been male or female, white or black, which had died young or old. They shambled and swayed in exactly the aimless, apathetic way that horror movies had trained him to anticipate semi-sentient corpses might move once their bodies started to degrade.

The stench lodged in his sinuses, in his throat, so powerfully that Jude feared it might never leave.

Since they hadn't seemed to notice him yet, Jude had time to consider and dismiss the idea of using the thunderbolt in such tight quarters, to wonder madly what one should call a group of the undead—a rot? a hunger?—and to scan the room for Regal, before he decided the first and best thing to do would be to lock the door that led down to the vampire's cage, so one of his puppets couldn't come and let him out as soon as Scarpelli called.

He touched the knob behind him and spoke the word that meant *close,* forgetting the pearl's amplification in his haste, the word sealing the doorway shut with a grumble of shifting rock. The room suddenly went silent, and every corpse's cataracted gaze angled toward Jude in a synchronized glide.

The movies had prepared him for what that meant, too.

They came at him in a shuffling mass, desiccated hands clutching, mouths gaping wide in soundless cries. Jude had time enough to change his footing, to scan the room one last time for Regal's flickering presence, and then the ghouls were on him, grasping hands and filthy, bloated flesh.

At first, it was all he could do to avoid being mauled, backing away from their clutches and shoving them away. When they pressed him up against the wall, any further retreat cut off, Jude hit one of them, desperation giving him such strength that he felt skin split and bone crumble beneath his knuckles. Another one lunged at him, grabbing his extended arm and bearing its full weight against it, pinning him against the wall. As if sensing his moment of weakness, a ghoul darted forward, blackened teeth snapping together inches from Jude's cheek. Jude's veins ran with ice water.

Demigod, Trickster—none of that would matter if these things ripped his throat out.

A knife blade sprouted from the ghoul's left eye socket, the decaying corpse yanked back from Jude and hurled away. Regal, panting from the effort, filled the suddenly empty space next to him. "Thanks," Jude said.

"Don't mention it."

Together, they tried what spells they had, shouting words of transformation, words of control. Even supercharged by the pearl, magics slid away from the ghouls and died, finding no form to change, no mind to coerce. Magics designed to cut and to maim had no effect on their nerveless flesh. The first ghoul recovered enough to grab Jude by the neck, its implacable strength drawing him closer to its grinding jaws.

Rage overtook him, that anger he'd always gone to such lengths to subdue, billowing up from his stomach like a physical thing, like heat and acid and thunder in the blood. He'd endured too much these past few days for it to end this way, in the clutches of these things, these castoff bundles of meat and rags that had been full human lives not long ago, the petty insults and grand hopes and the *life* that had been reduced to a shambling, ravenous machine.

Which was what Scarpelli had in mind for the entire city.

There were no words for the hate he felt for what Scarpelli represented. No way to speak the pure, smoldering desire to see the vampire destroyed that Jude felt. Except, in the midst of these clutching fingers and grinding jaws and his own blinding rage, suddenly there *was* a word, thrust forward from somewhere deep in the recesses of Jude's mind, a word that had the same twisting shape and roiling cadence as the words of opening and closure that Dodge had taught him.

Burn.

It spilled off of his tongue like lit gasoline, took shape as flames spewing from his open mouth. When the fire touched the first ghoul, it went up like so much kindling, as though its rotting flesh had been soaked in alcohol. Jude drew in a deep breath, his throat scorched ragged, the taste of cayenne and smoke and burnt sugar, and he spoke again. Through a red haze, he saw the living dead consumed, collapsing under their own weight as his magic ate through torn skin and the putrid, bloodless meat of their flesh.

Burn, he said. *Burn. Burn. Burn.*

An open-handed slap connected with his jaw, knocking his head back. The pearl rattled against his teeth, went solidly down his throat like a dry-swallowed pill. Something slipped away from his mind, a phrase he and his mother had shared in his youth, a way of saying *I love you* known to just the two of them. He knew it existed, but not the words, and then it was gone even from memory. The pearl's price had been paid.

Regal stood over him — when had he fallen to his knees? — visible once again, her face sweat- and soot-streaked. She was yelling that they had to get out of there, so he let her guide him to his feet and out the side door, smoke heavy in the air and fire crackling all around them. They made it halfway across the lawn before they fell to the grass, the dew blissful against Jude's skin. Beside him, Regal retched and rasped for breath. Eventually she pushed herself up until she knelt over him. "Not that I'm not grateful for the sudden show of force in there, because I am. But Christ, Jude. When in sweet hell-fuck did you learn to breathe fire?"

He didn't have an answer for her, or at least not one that she'd want to hear. Because he had the feeling that he'd always been able to, that it was a part of who — and what — he really was. He was content to lie there and contemplate his place in the world, but Regal forced him to his feet and into her car before the fire department got there, not that it would matter. Whether they saved the building or let it burn to ash, Jude knew the stone walls and frigid air of Scarpelli's subterranean tomb would keep the vampire safe.

Still, he thought, watching the glow in the side-view mirror recede as they sped away, *it would have been nice to watch that fucker burn.*

CHAPTER FOURTEEN

THE NEXT MORNING Jude woke to heaven, the scent of fresh chicory coffee and the sizzle of breakfast cooking. He'd slept with the rosary still around his neck and decided to leave it there, a good luck charm if nothing else. He changed into a Tipitina's T-shirt and a pair of faded jeans, both of which were reasonably clean, and left his bedroom just in time to see Regal click off the stove and pour the contents of two skillets, an omelet from one and hash browns from another, onto a plate. She looked up at him and gave him a sheepish sort of grin, the closest she'd come, he presumed, to an apology for the way she'd invaded his apartment of late. If she hadn't obviously showered and changed clothes, Jude might have thought she slept on his sofa. "Coffee's in the pot," she said, as she squeezed past him on her way out of the kitchen, already scooping a forkful of food off of her plate. Jude surveyed the wreckage of her breakfast preparation, noting that she'd only cooked for one.

"Where's mine?" he asked, knowing she'd hear the smile in his voice, even though her back was to him.

She mumbled something with a full mouth, something that sounded a lot like "In the fridge, fucknuts."

"But I saved your life, Queens."

She swallowed and raised her eyebrows with exaggerated innocence. "Really? Let's zoom right past the part where you saved me from a life-threatening situation you got me into in the first place, and ask: Did you save my life in nineteen-fucking-fifty? No. It's twenty-eleven. Women can vote, black man's in the White House, and you make your own breakfast, hero. And be quick, it's already the crack o' noon, and I want to check out this bookstore before the thunderstorm they forecast rolls in."

A glance at the clock told him she was right, it was just shy of noon. He wasn't surprised he'd woken up so late, because he hadn't slept well at all. He made himself a cup of coffee and started on his breakfast—half a carton of takeout shrimp-fried rice dumped into a hot skillet with a couple of eggs fried on top, the breakfast of champions—and while his hands were busy going through the motions, his thoughts turned to the night before.

After Regal had dropped him off at his apartment, he'd crashed into bed and fallen right to sleep, plagued by dreams of fire and shadows, culminating in a strange one where he'd lain on a prison cot eating dozens of hard-boiled eggs, one after another, surrounded by everyone he knew chanting that Trickster was always hungry, while the vampire Scarpelli loomed over all of them wearing mirrored sunglasses and shouting in a Texas drawl not his own that what they had here was a failure to coagulate, and Dodge told him that sometimes nothing was a pretty cool hand.

After waking from that bit of madness, Jude had given up on sleep and gone to the pile of research Regal had left on his floor, scooping up anything that talked about Tricksters. Reading about those myths in the context of his own life was, simply put, weird, like studying a mental disorder and seeing a list of your own personality traits and idiosyncrasies. Tricksters were liminal creatures, always living in the edges of one world and the next, never quite one thing or another. They were also agents of change, able to take on the role of creator or destroyer with ease, whichever was more useful for upsetting the status quo. Tricksters shared a complete disregard for any societal rules about sex or gender. Tricksters were often pansexual, cross-dressed out of necessity or whim or inclination, and were sometimes capable of physically shifting from one sex to another. When they were victims, it was usually through the fault of their own appetite or lust—which they had in spades. When they were angered, it was usually with disastrous consequences.

So much of Jude's life made sense when viewed in this light: the way he'd bounced enthusiastically from one passion project to the next, his compulsion to stick it to the rich and powerful, especially if he was able to show how foolish and petty and human they were, his long list of love affairs, men and women both, which he always ended disastrously when things got too routine, and his capacity for "Hulk smash!" levels of rage.

As it turned out, he'd belonged at that card game all along.

Regal finished eating and carried her coffee mug over to the whiteboard, staring at it and bobbing her head as she debated with herself. Jude devoured his rice and eggs, watching her, wondering what was going through her mind, grateful that they'd gotten her problems with him out in the open, wishing he could shake those last lingering scraps of suspicion that kept him from being entirely honest with her. After practically licking the plate clean and pouring another cup of coffee, Jude asked where this bookshop was.

"Not far, actually. On Perdido Street, over by the Superdome."

"And what, exactly, are you hoping to find there?"

She gave him a wry frown. "I'm hoping we're greeted by a dude wearing a name tag that says, 'Hi, I'm an ancient Egyptian god of scribes and also a Greek Trickster, ask me anything,' and he sells us a copy of *How to Solve Creepy-Ass God Problems for Dummies.*" She took a sip of her coffee. "On sale."

"Seems a little on-the-nose, don't you think?"

Regal snorted. "After last night? I'll be thrilled if you don't burn the damned place down with me inside it."

Regal drove Jude downtown to an abandoned building on the corner of Perdido and South Rampart. It rose three stories from the pavement, isolated all around by wide streets and parking lots. One of the exterior walls was left bare where another building had been torn down, the brick and mortar showing like a scab, a scar. Around one corner, a fire escape clung with all the tenacity of the moss and kudzu Jude found in the back, where a chunk of the third-floor wall had fallen away, covered by wood as though the gap were just another window. It had the look of "historic preservation" or, in common language: a building that the Historic District Landmarks Commission wouldn't let anybody tear down, but one that nobody would pay to revitalize, either. It had stood empty for so long that even the plywood used to seal the windows looked aged, the padlocks on the doors more rust than metal. Jude's first impression was of the single tower of a sand castle that managed, through luck or providence, to survive the tide.

Amid the thick, reaching weeds and the knee-high mounds of rubble at his feet were the remnants of a red-and-black checkerboard floor, its individual tiles splintered and swept or stolen away. A tentative drizzle of rain plucked at his hair, more a suggestion than any actual threat of a downpour, as though the heat of midday sapped the will of even the clouds overhead.

After a few moments of fumbling around with locks too aged for even his magic to open, a whispered spell of Regal's revealed a third door where before there had only been a blank wall, and a glowing neon sign above it that read: LIBROS PERDIDOS.

"Sounds like the place," Regal said from behind him. "You gonna wait for an invitation?"

He knocked twice before he reached for the knob. It shook in his grip, like many in New Orleans, unseated by years of the wood shrinking and swelling around it. A quick shove showed that the door was unlocked. Jude led Regal inside into a dark and stifling room where the lack of air conditioning trapped the heat, entombed it. The long, mournful creak of the door announced their presence to anyone within. Jude felt the irrational urge to call out, to shout into the dust and emptiness that they were here.

Jude crept past abandoned counters, his sneakers silent on the bare concrete floors. Interior walls had been gutted, Sheetrock ripped away, leaving only the skeletal wood framing. He couldn't tell if this had once been a restaurant or a storefront, or if it had some other purpose. He now smelled the decay he had expected outside, rot and the dank scent of black mold, all too familiar since the flood.

"You sure Thoth is still here?" he asked. "Maybe he moved after the storm."

"Lost books sounds right to me." When she saw Jude's puzzled expression, she rolled her eyes. "The sign on the door, genius. Means 'lost books.' I guess you never studied with a bruja, then." She kicked at a chunk of wood and sent it skittering. "Does seem pretty hopeless in here."

Jude pointed to the staircase on the other side of the room, a perilous contraption of sagging wood and questionable construction. "There's always that," he said.

She bit her thumbnail. "Empty building; creepy, dangerous stairs? This is feeling too damned familiar."

"Who you telling? Do I get to be the one to go stealth mode this time?"

Regal looked at him strangely, then shook her head. "Nope. Lost that dagger escaping the burning building you tried to drop on my head, fuck you very much." Something in the tone, in the look, didn't sit right with Jude. He tried to push it away, reminding himself that she'd risked her life the night before guarding his back, that she could have left him to the tender mercies of a vampire and his horde of rotting minions if she'd so chosen, but that squirming of suspicion remained nonetheless. Especially when she gestured, with both emphasis and derision, for him to go first.

As Jude started up the stairs, they bowed and trembled beneath his weight, groaning as if they were about to collapse. He tried to swallow past a lump in his throat, a clench of fear that grew with each lurching step, with each vision of himself stepping into empty air, arms pinwheeling, before a short abrupt plummet. He might be half man and half something else, but he was pretty sure the man half could still die all the way. With slow movements and his breath held the entire time, Jude made it to the top of the stairs.

This door opened with a blast of cooler air and a soft, inviting light that illuminated a long hallway cramped along its length and height with books. A dozen feet in, this hallway branched off in another direction, and a few feet down that one, two more split off, all of them filled to the brim with old, faded spines in a variety of languages. Jude signaled to Regal that they should split up and check the different paths. She nodded, pressing an upright finger across her lips.

Despite this caution, his footsteps creaked on the polished cypress floorboards as he threaded his way through the maze of bookshelves. Looking closer, Jude saw that the shelves themselves were made of books, that the archways overhead were formed by volumes stacked so tightly together that they held each other in place, that the entire structure of walls and stairs were formed solely from books artfully arranged and piled.

A library fort, Jude thought, *I'll be damned. Leave it to the god of scribes to be the biggest nerd on the planet.* He couldn't decide if he was more impressed at the construction, condescending toward the inefficiency, or just plain jealous.

The light came from a phosphorescent shine that glowed from some of the books' spines in a synchronized dance, like candle flames all swaying in the same gentle breeze.

Checking over his shoulder to make sure Regal couldn't see him, Jude slipped his hand into his pocket to touch his coin. As the magic poured into him, he brushed a knuckle against one of the books, and just as when he touched the revolver from the vampire's room of antiques, he was seized by the knowledge of the book's loss.

The book's title was *Isle of the Cross*. In the summer of 1852, in a tavern in Nantucket, a lawyer met an author with a failing career. The lawyer told the author the story of a woman he knew, Agatha Robertson, whose sailor husband had abandoned her and their daughter, returning years later to reveal that he had married another. This tale so inspired the author that he wrote a novel with Agatha as the protagonist, only to have his publishers Harper and Brothers reject the work, effectively ending his career. That author's name was Herman Melville, and when he burned the manuscript of *Isle of the Cross*, Thoth preserved it on these shelves.

Jude pulled away from the vision, his heel scraping against the wall of books as he stepped back. A tremor ran through them at the disturbance, a shudder that threatened to topple the precarious balancing act around him. He heard a rustling, like the sigh of trees in a high wind. He let go of his doubloon and lowered his hand, slowly, not wanting to disturb the books further, not wanting to suffocate beneath a pile of literature any more than he wanted to break his neck at the bottom of a busted staircase.

"Careful," Regal hissed from the next aisle over. "The hell was that?"

"Sorry. This hall is a tight squeeze."

"Then suck your gut in or go back. We'll never make it out if these bastards start falling."

The last shreds of his fading connection to *Isle of the Cross* told Jude more about the collection itself: that it was ancient and had gone by many names, that it had started with the burning of the library of Alexandria, that it had grown when the Maya codices were destroyed by Diego de Landa, and when Hanlin Academy burned, that it collected worthy works that had gone unpublished or whose authors had died when they were still unfinished.

And that it was, somehow, incomplete.

A brush of fingers against his doubloon sent Jude back down a different aisle than the one he'd taken, tugging him along until he found a rectangle of darkness at waist height, an empty space on the bookshelf, the absence of a single slim volume. When his hand entered the gap between the books, he felt—faintly, more like memory than actual sensation—the one that was missing: frigid air and blue flames, slashing fangs and the taste of blood.

A couple of pieces came together in Jude's mind. The glowing spine of the book Scarpelli was using to turn the city. The name of the bookstore. The peculiar properties of his satchel. The Red Door to Dodge's card room ignoring the restrictions of space and time.

Without allowing himself to consider that the absurd idea that popped into his mind was very likely impossible, Jude pulled off the satchel and set it on the ground, knelt beside it, touched his doubloon with one hand, and reached in with the other, letting that fragile, tenuous connection to the lost book guide him. He stretched, his arm going in past the elbow, then to the shoulder. The air touching his arm went suddenly cold, and a creeping shiver that came from childhood swept over him, that knowledge of eyes watching from the closet, of claws stretching forth from beneath the bed. He touched a slim leather-bound book, grabbed it, and snatched his hand free, slamming the satchel's flap closed like he was cutting off pursuit.

His gift sent the history of the book flowing into him: it was a journal of sorts, a series of maps of south Louisiana compiled by Jean-Baptiste Le Moyne, Sieur de Bienville, in the early 1700s. Beginning with hesitant, preliminary sketches of the Gulf Coast and ending with the first official design of New Orleans drafted by Adrien de Pauger in 1721, each individual piece held great historical value. As a whole, though, it contained within it the entire conceptualization of a city. If a city had blood and bone, this slim journal would be its DNA. After Bienville's death, the collection passed down from one family member to another before being swept away in the 1927 flood, when it found its way to Thoth's library. Jude couldn't quite tell if the vampire had bought, borrowed, or stolen it.

He eased his way out of his magic's grip, starting to get the hang of accessing it through his doubloon instead of through his own will. The journal he slid into his satchel, not wanting to leave it where Scarpelli could find it again, hoping that in reaching past the wards Regal had drawn, he hadn't liberated the vampire. Or worse, given Scarpelli access to his bag. He stood and pulled the strap back across his shoulders, turning around just as Regal came around the corner of the aisle.

She didn't, Jude noticed, look surprised to see him. Had she been watching him and backed out of sight when he'd stood up? Was he just being paranoid? Before he could say something to try and tease the truth from her, she waved an urgent "come here" gesture at him and whispered, "Come on, I found something."

She went back the way she had come so quickly that Jude had no choice but to follow. After a few twists and turns, she brought him to a dead end, the hallway coming to a stop with another wall of books stretched straight across. She pointed a thumb at it. "So here's the thing. When I first saw this, I immediately turned around. Building can't go on forever, right? But then I thought about it. Unless my sense of direction is totally fucked, we've been going toward the middle of the building, not the outside."

Jude nodded. "You're right. You find any more like this?"

"Nope. All the others seem to curve toward this, like—"

"A labyrinth."

"Exactly." She held her arms out, gesturing at the walls of books. "So if this is the center of the mouse maze, where's the cheese? Any of these books look special to you?"

Jude peered closer at the titles, really just trying to shift his posture so he could reach into his pocket without Regal seeing, but something in one of the titles gave him an idea. He stepped back and looked at the wall as a whole, and it seemed even more likely that he was right. "Hey, Queens?"

"Yeah?"

"If you're nerdy enough to build a labyrinth out of books, what would you need for it to be complete?"

"I don't know. Minotaur?"

"What? No. Christ, that would be awful. You know how bad those things stink?"

She backed up until she could see from his perspective, thinking. He knew she got it when, after a moment, she barked out a laugh. "Secret door?"

"Yep."

"So what? You think we find the right book and—" She pantomimed tilting the top edge of a book back from the shelf and made a clicking noise.

"Or . . ." Jude stepped forward and spoke the word for *open*. One of the books slid in about half an inch—*The Infinite Page of Reality*, a novel by Jorge Luis Borges—and the door made of books creaked open. They walked through into a huge space, dimly lit and stretching up far higher than the building's confines allowed. If the space they'd just left had been a labyrinth, this was the inside of a lighthouse, a tower with a staircase of books spiraling along the wall to the top.

It reeked of cinnamon.

The next few moments happened very quickly. Jude saw Hē standing over Thoth—who lay supine with blood gushing from his ibis neck—a blade that curved in a shimmering arc on either side of the angel's fist, a stream of brackish water fountaining up from the wound and into Hē's gaping mouth. Regal shouted a curse—not a vulgarity, but an actual curse—a vicious word that would strike the angel blind or cover Hē in painful boils if it took hold. Jude followed the same impulse, though the word that rose to his tongue was the word from the night before, the one that meant *burn* and, remembering where they stood, he choked it back before it fully left his lips, reabsorbing its power in a swallow that left a scorching line down his throat.

The stream rising from Thoth slowed to a trickle and then stopped. Hē's mouth snapped closed then, the draining of some vital essence from Thoth now complete, and the messenger whirled, the strange weapon flashing as it left Hē's hand. Jude lunged for Regal, who was concentrating on some complicated hand gestures whose meaning Jude could only guess at, knocking her to the floor as the angel's blade whispered over them, the wind of its passage tickling the hairs on Jude's neck.

A cracking of the air signaled Hē's wings unfurling, and, gasping for breath because of the flames he'd swallowed, Jude came to his feet at a run, the angel already rising out of reach. Jude dug in his satchel, unsure what he sought but hoping that he had some magic that could trap or wound the angel. A glance toward Regal showed that she was back up and searching along the wall that they'd had at their backs when they'd come in here just moments before. *Looking for another way out?* Jude thought, but then saw the line of shredded paper that the angel's weapon had left as it scraped across the wall of books, and realized that Regal was looking for Hē's blade.

The angel had risen almost to the top of the tower, moving toward a skylight at the summit, and Jude had just enough time to consider the consequences of casting the thunderbolt at the angel and missing, when both of Hē's arms swept forward, a curve of blade flickering out from each hand in a swooping arc. Jude saw in the same instant that they weren't actual blades at all but some kind of magic—some weaponization of light or will—and that Hē hadn't aimed at him or Regal but at the walls themselves.

The angel slipped through the skylight and away as those shining blades ripped through priceless volumes, tearing and ruining and violating, but more importantly, *undermining* the walls of the tower. Books started raining down; the entire structure shook beneath their feet. They'd never make it out the way they'd come in.

Only one way out, Jude thought.

He ran to Regal's side, pulled her off the stairs she was already scrambling up. "Too high up!" he shouted, and hurried to the door they'd come through.

"You *crazy?*" she yelled, her voice coming out a panicked shriek.

"Might be," he muttered, yanking the door shut. He closed his eyes and concentrated, his hand on the door made of books. He pictured what he wanted, strained for the change he needed, *felt* the ornate twist of a knob in his palm. Without opening his eyes, trusting that the magic had worked as he wanted it to, he said the word that meant *open* and wrenched open the Red Door to Dodge's card room. Regal rushed through behind him, and he slammed the door shut just as the tower collapsed behind them.

Crazy like a fox, he thought.

For the next few moments the sudden silence was broken only by the two of them gasping for breath.

Regal recovered first. "Yay, we're saved?" she said, in a quiet, sarcastic voice.

"Everyone's a critic." He rose from his hands-on-thighs crouch and tried the door, but it wouldn't budge, still buried beneath a mountain of lost books. He closed his eyes, trying to focus, but as the adrenaline leaked out of him, the enormity of what he'd just witnessed crashed down on top of him.

Hē had murdered Thoth. Any inclination Jude might have to second-guess that thought — to consider the possibility that the angel had somehow been framed, or that the strange fountain had been some kind of rescue attempt — came crumbling apart when he ran through his vision of Renai's last moments, her strange thought about blowing out the candles making far more sense when viewed as her rationalizing the sudden scent of cinnamon in the voodoo shop.

It all came into focus, like a stubborn knot unsnarling and unspooling when just the right thread got pulled. If Hē killed Thoth and Renai, then the angel — a fallen angel, it would seem — was the shadow in his mother's painting and had also been the one who killed Dodge, and so that whole message-from-on-High that Hē had fed him in the cathedral was suspect, including the proclamation that Jude couldn't win the game.

But right then, just when Jude started to feel a little hope, the clock on the wall started ticking.

CHAPTER FIFTEEN

A **ONE-EYED GOD PIERCED** by his own spear and hanged from a tree in order to gain the knowledge of writing. A humble god crippled by disease who cast himself into a bonfire, that he might be transformed into a new sun after the old one perished. A healer god, stabbed and beaten and executed, so that he could redeem the sinful. A titan chained to a boulder, his liver eaten by an eagle each day, regenerating each night, after he gave man the power of fire. Again and again, the lesson is the same: Only through pain do we gain knowledge. Only suffering grants us wisdom. Only in sacrifice can we become powerful.

"Shit," Jude said. "Shit, shit, shit."

His words unconsciously coordinated with the ticking of the cat clock on the wall. They only had less than a minute before the other doors started to appear. After that, Jude could only guess what would come next, but he assumed that the other gods would return to their seats—the ones still alive anyway—and the card game would resume. And his last cards would reveal themselves before he'd had a chance to make his fate a winning one.

"I'm guessing that's not good," Regal said.

Jude didn't bother to answer, just tried the door again and found the way still blocked. He took a calming breath, trying to still the anger and fear that twisted in his gut. His pulse slowed, and the knob started to vanish from his grip, like a hand clasped in a dream, slipping away upon waking. The red of the door faded away into dingy floral wallpaper.

Tick, tick, tick.

Jude kicked the wall. It felt good, so he did it again, but obviously it did nothing to solve his problem. *Think, stupid,* he hissed at himself, *you just made this work.* Up until Thoth's library, the door had shown up as if it had a mind of its own, as if it were following its own whim. Hadn't it? No, not exactly. He'd summoned it with a circle—and the thought of trying to do that from *inside* the card room was a violation of physics he couldn't wrap his brain around—but he'd also made it appear that first night, during the game. It had vanished when he'd entered, had only come back when he'd turned over those blank cards and tried to—

"Escape," he said, not realizing he'd spoken aloud until Regal agreed that yes, escape would be nice, thanks. When he glanced at her, she was scanning the room, her fingers curled in a rigid, unnatural gesture that looked like some combination of a martial arts pose and a letter in sign language. A half-dozen or so balls of light orbited her hands, each about the size of a quarter and whirring and crackling with energy. She shifted her weight from one foot to the other, like a cat preparing to pounce.

Tick, tick, tick.

Jude stopped trying to control his fear, let it come flooding back in. He let himself imagine what would happen if the gods returned with them still in the card room, let himself remember the way they had laughed at him when he'd been forced to wager away the pieces of himself he couldn't afford to give up. The panic that had risen in him as he backed away from the table, silently begging to be somewhere, *anywhere* other than here. Clinging to those feelings, Jude did purposefully what he'd done before only by instinct: he reached for the Red Door and yanked it open, shoving Regal through into hot, humid night. He risked a glance behind him and saw the vampire Scarpelli framed in a doorway of his own. Smiling.

Jude dove through the door and slammed it shut, colliding with Regal in his haste and sending them both sprawling onto a wooden porch. With the soft *poomf* of a roman candle, the orbs spinning around Regal's hands went flying off in uncontrolled arcs, streaking away to collide against trees and cars and streetlights with silent detonations that crumpled hoods and shattered glass. A car alarm started blaring.

Guess that's what she was planning on doing to Hē, Jude thought. *Wonder if it would have worked.* Out loud he said, "We've got to get out of here," as he struggled to his feet.

"Duh," she said, waving away his offered hand and standing on her own. "Soon as we figure out where in bumfuck Egypt you brought us."

The overly rich stink of rotted fruit came to him on the hot breeze, peaches left on the branch until they had fallen to the dirt and spoiled. The sagging and busted porch they stood on jutted into the overgrown yard and wrapped around to the back of the house, which had cracked and fading pink paint on the outer walls and kudzu dangling off the rain gutter. To the left of the door, the spray-painted circled *X*—the symbol that let rescue crews know that the house had been searched, and whether any bodies had been found—remained, just as it had the last time he'd been here. The house he'd grown up in, where he'd lived just before the storm. The house that had once been home.

"I know where we are," Jude said. "Streetcar's that way."

Regal walked with him the few blocks to St. Charles, talking the whole way about how strange it was that jumping back and forth to Dodge's card room had taken hours, but felt to them like just a few minutes, how she needed to go straight to see Mourning and tell him what they'd learned, how much she wished she'd been able to find the angel's weapon before the tower of books had come down on them. Jude nodded and murmured, but he felt drained, exhausted in a way that ached all the way down to the bone.

His luck held, because the streetcar came rumbling down the track right when they got there, Regal already on her phone calling for a ride to take her back to her car as Jude climbed inside. He collapsed into his seat and hoped the streetcar's rocking sway didn't lull him to sleep.

Jude still had questions; he knew *who* killed Dodge, but still couldn't quite figure out *why*. His own fate was still in question, and the schemes of the other gods were still in motion. He couldn't concentrate long enough to make sense of any of it, though, and nearly missed his stop in the midst of his distraction.

When he stepped off the streetcar, the barometer had dropped, a chill in the air warning that the storm that had been threatening all day was about to break. By the time he made it back to his apartment, the rain started to come down, the wind howling.

Must be a bad one, Jude thought, when he discovered that his power was out. Not that he needed lights to crash into his bed and sleep for ten hours, which is what he felt like doing. So, once his eyes adjusted to the darkness, he picked his way across the research still stacked in piles across his living room floor, making his way toward his bedroom. He dropped the satchel on the kitchen counter as he passed, already kicking his shoes off. The first one thumped against the floor, but the second one made an odd sound.

As though it had struck and come to rest against something— or some*one*—that Jude couldn't see.

Jude whirled for his satchel, touching the leather just as a strong hand grabbed him and yanked him back, knocking his bag to the floor. He heard some of its contents spill out, heard a grunt of breath behind him. He needed a weapon, needed to know what he was facing. He didn't taste blood, didn't smell cinnamon, but then he realized that it didn't matter. Whether his assailant was vampire or angel or anything else, everything burned.

He started to speak, to call on the flames that had destroyed a room full of ghouls, hoping it would be enough to save him without the boost of the pearl's magic aiding his own, but a sudden twist of urgent pain in his gut stole his breath. *Now?* he thought. *This is happening to me* now?

Because until the cold, sharp agony retreated and came again and again, Jude mistook what was happening to him for a sudden, painful bowel affliction. Had thought he was about to crap his pants in the middle of a fight.

It wasn't until he smelled the blood that Jude understood that he was being stabbed.

The strength trembled out of his legs, and he fell to the floor, barely noticing the impact, realizing what was happening to him now, his hands pressed tight against the sticky, hot fluid gushing from his abdomen. He gasped for air that wouldn't come, strained with all his might toward some magic spell, some last-second rescue that he knew had to be coming. He tried to speak past a mouthful of blood—his own, not the mere taste that signaled the presence of a vampire—a gurgling froth that came with every failed breath.

It occurred to him that he'd done so many things wrong, that in the view of more than a few people, he deserved this.

And then, to his great surprise and against every effort to the contrary, Jude Dubuisson died.

PART FOUR

CH∆PTER SIXTEEN

THE SOUL MUST BALANCE the weight of its heart against the feather of truth in order to pass into the realm beyond. Or it must cross a bridge as narrow as a knife's edge, or brave a mountain pass where the mountains clash against one another, or it must pay the boatman to ferry it across the river, which is a river of blood, or of tears, or of waters of forgetting. Or it rides a horse that gallops across the ocean's surface, or sails in a boat made of glass. Or it must descend into a frozen pit, or climb a vast mountain to the celestial spheres. It undertakes a journey that may last three days, or a year, or four, or that is outside of time entirely. The soul's destination is a meadow, or a field, or a green lawn, or hunting grounds, or an island, or the first home of mankind, where the food is plentiful and disease does not exist and it is always summer. The valorous dead are carried from the field of battle to a great feast, the benevolent find themselves in a garden of eternal joy, and the wise become one with all. The sinful dead face their punishments in a maze, a lake of fire, or a dark and frozen cave, or they are returned to the world, given another birth, another life, another death, in which to redeem their mistakes. Or the dead are simply dead. Their bodies rot and join the soil and nurture the ecosystem that sustained them. Their energy returns to the universe, their elements the same as the living and dying stars. Death is the beginning of a journey, a doorway to another world, one part of an eternal cycle. It is never truly the end.

Jude stood out in the rain wearing his only suit and didn't know where he was or why he was there. The rain shrouded the world around him as completely as if he were engulfed in fog, the noise of the city drowned out by the static roar of the wind, by the hiss of rainwater against hot concrete, the brick and neon of the buildings across the street almost invisible through the thick downpour, curtains of rain undulating like tall grass in the wind, like waves against the shore. He felt like he'd just been doing something incredibly important, but couldn't remember what it was.

Jude reached for his cell phone, not even sure who he intended to call, but found his pockets empty. No keys, no wallet, no phone — nothing. Lightning flared, freezing the falling rain in its camera flash, and in that same instant thunder roared, the strike so close it shook Jude down to his bones. He checked his pockets again, patting himself down like a cliché of confusion.

An inarticulate dread began to creep through his thoughts. It occurred to him that, despite being soaked to the skin, he didn't feel cold at all, didn't feel the slightest discomfort from the driving wind. Maybe he was dreaming. What other explanation could there be for wandering around during a storm in a suit and tie with nothing in his pockets? He closed his eyes, willed himself awake, and opened them to the wind and the rain and the familiar shelter of a streetcar stop.

The ground trembled beneath him, a constant thunderous rumble, growing stronger instead of fading away. Light burned his eyes, not the flicker of lightning, but a steady shine. A rush of motion, a squeal of brakes, and an odd streetcar came to a halt in front of him, battered and worn like the archaic cars on the St. Charles line, but not green like the cars he'd ridden all his life. This one was painted a glossy black.

The streetcar's doors folded open and Barren leaned out, raindrops splashing against his floral painted skull.

"Didn't I tell you that you were about outta time?" he asked, his tone both rhetorical and scolding. "Now look at you." He shook his head, a slow gesture that would have been grave if not for his mocking death's-rictus grin. "Well, come on in before you catch your death. Again."

Wavering flames danced in the glass and iron cages of antique gas lamps, lighting the interior of the streetcar with a gloomy, entombed sort of illumination. Thick cushions of molded leather covered the seats, the dark reds and browns of a coffin lining. The air smelled of candle wax and a pungent oil that almost hid the faint, lingering bite of bleach. One other passenger sat in the last row, face hidden by the shadow of a hat brim. Jude started toward the back, curious, but stopped when Barren, behind him, cleared his throat with exaggerated impatience.

"Where you think you going?" Barren asked. When Jude turned to face him, the voodoo loa had changed: his flower-decorated skull now naked, bleached white bone, his tuxedo replaced by wool robes. Ashen gray wings arched from his shoulders, almost brushing the streetcar's ceiling. Torchlight seemed to reflect from somewhere deep within his eye sockets, his lipless mouth no longer a grin but a snarl.

Jude had no answer for him, could not find his voice. The music punctuated the silence and the space between them. Barren rubbed his thumb against the first two fingers of his hand. "Nobody rides for free," he said, at last.

Jude searched his pockets again, knowing he would find them empty. Pants and coat both nothing but damp cloth. He opened his mouth, wanting to explain, but nothing came out. He struggled, like trying to find a word that had escaped the grasp of his mind, but it was as if speech itself had vanished, a vast gulf yawning between his thoughts and his tongue. Straining so hard that that he trembled, he managed only a wheeze, a gasp that might have only been the moan of the wind outside.

A strong hand grasped his shoulder, and the tension eased. A voice, heavy with a Haitian accent, spoke from behind him. "Leave the boy be," it said. "He got enough to deal with, him. Don't need to put up with your meanness, too, no."

Jude turned and saw that the other passenger on the streetcar was Papa Legba, his mouth wrinkled into a smile, his body as gnarled and weathered as an oak root. This wasn't the body of one of his houngan; this was his true face.

It was then that Jude began to realize—perhaps a little belatedly—that he was well and truly fucked. He opened his mouth to thank the voodoo god, but Legba frowned and shook his head.

"Won't do you no good," he said. "Not now." He pointed to Barren. "You got to pay the fare. Everybody do."

"How come it's cruel when *I* say it?" Barren asked. "I said the same fucking thing."

Legba frowned, all the lines on his face bending toward the floor. He kept his eyes on Jude but spoke to Barren. "It is how you talk, you know this. You are meant to guide them, but you delight in taunting them."

"You just don't know how to have fun anymore."

In the periphery of Jude's vision, Barren made a rude gesture, which Legba seemed to both notice and ignore. Their words seemed well-practiced, as though they had had this argument many times before, and they needed only to recite their lines. It was strange, seeing two gods bicker like an old married couple.

Outside, the storm pounded against the streetcar, the wind and the rain making it totter back and forth like a drunk, like a ship on the high seas.

"Open your mouth," Legba said. It took a moment for Jude to

realize that the loa was speaking to him, but he saw no other option but to obey. Legba motioned for Jude to lean down, to lower his head to the wizened god's level. When he did, Legba reached inside Jude's mouth and touched his tongue. Legba's fingers, warm and tasting of tobacco and rum, scooped the sensitive underside of Jude's mouth and pulled something out. Jude hadn't felt it there until Legba touched it, something hard and flat and round. The entire moment had an eerie echo in Jude's memory like a parody —an inversion—of Communion.

"There it go," Legba said, holding up the wet coin to Jude's eyes: one of the doubloons from Dodge's card game. Jude thought at first it would be the one that held his gift, but this one had a stylized tongue stamped into the metal. It took him a moment to recognize it as the wager that Legba had demanded. The loa pressed it into Jude's palm. "Go on now. Pay the fare so we can be on our way."

Barren—once again wearing the floral-painted skull and tuxedo—waited with his hand out. Jude couldn't understand why Legba had given him the doubloon back when the game was still being played, but then he didn't understand much of anything that was happening to him, just that he was alone on a streetcar with a couple of loa. He dropped the coin into Barren's upturned glove. The skull-headed god looked down at it and chuckled, flicking the doubloon up to the back of his hand, where he walked it across his knuckles. "Slipping me the tongue on the first date," he said, feigning the breathless drawl of a shocked southern belle, "and here I thought you were a gentleman." He pivoted on his toes, giggling as he fell into the driver's seat of the streetcar. He pulled a lever and the engine chugged to life, pounding beneath the floor like a clutching, struggling heart.

Legba pulled at Jude's sleeve, turning him away from Barren and toward the back of the streetcar. "Leave this rooster to crow at his own foolishness," he said. "There is much you must understand." He led Jude down the rows of seats with slow and cautious footsteps as the car lurched down the tracks, buffeted by the storm. Legba sat and pulled one leg on top of the other, his ankle balanced on top of his knee. It was a surprisingly nimble gesture for one as old and frail as he appeared. He held out a hand to the seat next to him.

Barren, without turning his attention from the window in front of him, yelled over his shoulder, "Don't listen to that old fart's bullshit, Jude! This rooster up here got the biggest cock of all the loa. You ask anybody!"

Jude smiled, and beside him, Legba laughed. "He clever, I got to admit," Legba said. He took a hand-carved wooden pipe from his coat pocket, chuckling and shaking his head as he knocked it against the heel of his polished dress shoe. "Least, he think he is." From his vest pocket came a clump of dried leaf that he pressed into his pipe with a thumb. Jude stared, half hypnotized, half hoping Legba would produce the bottle of rum they'd shared at Dodge's funeral. He couldn't remember ever in his life wanting a drink as much as he did in that moment. The loa reached into the lantern swinging overhead and plucked a flame free as easily as stripping a leaf from a branch. He used it to light his pipe, taking short puffs on the stem until smoke rose from the bowl, smelling richly of a combination of tobacco leaf and ginger root.

The memory of sharing a drink with Legba at Dodge's funeral sparked another memory in Jude, but as soon as it came to him, it vanished. He struggled to hold on to it, sure that the memory was somehow important, but his thoughts felt as elusive as his voice. Why couldn't he remember how he'd gotten here? Why couldn't he say anything?

Legba took the pipe from between his teeth with a quiet click, used it to point at Jude. "The thing you must understand," he said, his words quiet and grave, "is that you have died." Jude felt no surprise at these words. No sudden increase in his pulse, no rush of heat along his skin, no amusement at the silliness of the idea. Nothing. That probably wasn't a good sign. "This is why you cannot speak," Legba said. "Why you cannot remember where you were before you came to me. These things are difficult for the newly dead."

Legba stared out the window as he spoke. Following Legba's gaze, Jude saw that they were on the Riverfront line, hurtling between the levee wall and the river. The voodoo god waved a hand at the window, seeming to indicate the levee and the buildings peeking over it and everything else.

"Here, in this place, the dead have many choices. Many gods willing to guide them to the place at the end of their path. I have returned your token so that you have no obligation to me. So that you may believe the things I tell you, and trust that I seek no gain from your misfortunes." Legba turned away from the window, his ancient eyes now boring into Jude. "From here on out, you may follow whichever course you choose. You may even stay, if it suits you. But if you choose any guidance save mine, you will be lost. I promise you this."

The car squealed as the brakes caught, the gas lamps swinging so hard they nearly slammed into the roof. "First stop," Barren yelled from the front. "Elysian Fields!"

The party spilled out of the large house and into the well-manicured lawn, a black-tie affair. The revelers outside, whispering pairs or bullshitting groups, seemed unconcerned with the storm raging just beyond the borders of the house and its grounds, as though certain the wind and the rain knew better than to bother them. Every light in the wide two-story house burned, a warm glow emanating from the windows and the open front door. From that door wafted sounds of joy and laughter and jazz and conversation, all mixed together in one energetic murmur. As Jude walked out of the rain, through the high stone gates, and onto the gravel path that wound a lazy meander to the porch, a warm summer breeze blew into his face, sweet with the scent of magnolia blossoms and fresh clipped grass.

He'd been here before. Not the sprawling plantation house, but the end of Elysian Fields Avenue, the edges of the Quarter and the neighborhood called the Marigny. Any other time he'd walked down this street, from the streetcar to one of the bars on Esplanade or to catch the Krewe du Vieux parade that ran through the Quarter, this had looked like nothing more than an intersection and a tiny neutral ground, a thin strip of grass and a couple of spindly trees. He stood for a moment, amazed that something like this had been hidden from him. He wondered what other wonders he might have walked past, unknowing.

Papa Legba leaned on a cane beside him, the colors of his suit muted, as though he had stepped out of a poorly developed photograph. "Come then," he said, "you may as well have a look around." They followed the walkway toward the house, the god limping, Jude strolling with his hands in his pockets. Their steps fell on gravel with brittle crunches, an ashen dust rising in their wake. None of the party guests stopped them, or questioned them, or seemed to even notice them. Jude helped Legba up the steps to the porch and followed him inside.

The interior of the house matched the outside: wealth and extravagance, charm and mirth. The doorway led into a huge, crowded ballroom, floors of dark wood polished to a mirror's shine, twin staircases sweeping along each end of the room to the landing above. Satin curtains hung in heavy drapes from each of the windows, smooth and dark as an expensive red wine. Gray plaster covered the walls, artfully crumbling in places to reveal the red brick beneath.

The chandelier hanging from the ceiling was not the glittering thing of crystal and light that Jude expected, but a massive bronze sculpture: seven winged figures holding trumpets to their lips, flames crackling within the bells of the instruments. Jude couldn't be sure, but one of them could have been Hē. Other statues decorated the room; plaster men and women leaning out of the walls, arms lifted over their heads in exaltation or prayer and marble cherubs at the base of each stairwell. Above them all, on the landing, a band played a slow, mournful song that Jude thought he knew but couldn't place. The singer had a bluesy twang to his voice, somehow very familiar. Jude didn't recognize him until he smiled, a lopsided, boyish grin.

Tommy.

"*Yes, the devil is a busy man,*" Tommy sang, "*boy look like he always stay on my trail. But it don't matter what I try, the devil he gets right in my way.*"

The swarm of guests swayed to the music, moved by the sound but not quite dancing. They laughed and talked and drank, the men wearing suits or tuxedos, the women in elegant gowns from a variety of time periods, here a simple piece of slinky fabric, there a construction of lace and volumes of fabric. Save for a few exceptional riots of color that proved the rule, everyone wore black or white or some combination of the two. The scene had a patina of antiquity about it like an antebellum ball, but unlike that era, the divide between guest and servant was not a line between black and white. Jude searched the crowd—the drinking, laughing, arguing, smoking, kissing, seething crowd—and saw skin colors of every shade, everyone enjoying the party. There seemed to be only drinkers, only feasters, no one to mix the drinks, no one to serve the food. Curious, Jude made his way to the back of the ballroom, creeping along the wall as he went.

It was only when he reached the far side of the room that he noticed that Legba had stayed behind, leaning on his cane.

The hallway beyond the ballroom was dark, like a tunnel underground, the noise of the celebration behind him muted to a dull pounding. As Jude's eyes adjusted, he saw slivers of light along the floor at regular intervals, closed doors, private parties. The lights winked out, one by one, as Jude approached. He came to the end of the hallway where he faced a final door, the glow beneath this one shining brightly enough that he could make out the red paint that covered it. He felt like he should know it, but the thought flickered away when he tried to grasp it.

When Jude opened the door, its rusted hinges squealing, the light spilled out, blinding him, though he still felt nothing, no anxiety, no surge of anticipation at what might be revealed. When he could see again, he saw floral wallpaper, the pattern like that on Barren's skull, faded and curling at the seams. A cat-shaped clock clung to the wall, sharp horns sprouting from its head, the lower half a sinuous, scaly curve. The felt of a poker table glared bright green, the color of money, like the eyes of someone he knew. Memory assaulted Jude, sudden, heavy, and sharp. He remembered this room full of gods, the air thick with smoke and noise. He also remembered it cold and empty, the silence of the grave, a dark stain on the table and the stink of blood. He remembered turning over the blank cards dealt to him by a fortune god.

He *remembered*.

Dodge Renaud sat at the far end of the table, fat and bald and ever smiling, a deck of cards in his hands. He wore his tie loose and his shirt unbuttoned as though proud of the gash across his throat, the slick and gaping second mouth. He shuffled with deft, sharp motions: cut, riffle, cascade. The angel Hē perched on the edge of the seat to Dodge's left; a handsome young white man sprawled to his right, chair leaned back on two legs, running shoes flopped insolently on the card table. As Jude watched, stricken by the return of memory—memories of Dodge, memories of his own—Dodge paused to take a drink. The liquor oozed out of his wound as he swallowed, but the fortune god seemed not to mind. He looked up at Jude with eyes as cold, as hard, and as green as cash—quick as the snap of his shuffling cards.

" 'Bout time you got here," he said.

CHAPTER SEVENTEEN

FEAR, JUDE KNEW, lived in the body. Adrenaline in the blood, the painful clench of a frenzied heart, a tight fist in the abdomen, stomach dropping and balls shrinking, the prickle of flesh as hair stood on end, tongue dry as old leather, vision sharp and pinpoint-clear. Standing in a room with gods and feeling none of those things finally, truly convinced Jude that Legba hadn't lied when he told Jude that he was dead. The only way he couldn't feel fear in this moment is if he had no body left to feel it with.

"Pull up a chair," Dodge said. "We'll play a few." Jude slid into the seat across from the fortune god, remembering the blank hand of his own fate. Dodge shuffled, spreading the cards into fans in each hand, a chaotic sprawl, bridging them back into order. "What's your pleasure?" he asked. "Five-card draw? Atlantis? Crazy eights?"

Jude opened his mouth, strained to speak, but despite the return of his memories, his voice still eluded him.

Dodge's smile faltered for a moment, then burst again into its fluorescent glare. "Oh, right," he said, "the speech thing. Don't worry, it'll come. Not your real voice, 'course. Nothing with any power. Ain't nobody would stay dead, otherwise." He laughed at his own joke and dealt two cards, face-down, to everyone at the table but himself. "Hold 'em, then. No need for talking."

Jude looked at his cards, not at all surprised to see that he'd been dealt two blank cards. Neither Hē nor the other god had bothered to look at their cards—the young man was too busy thumb-typing on his cell phone, and the angel was staring intently at Jude with those unnerving eyes. Jude wondered if Dodge knew he sat at the same table as his murderer. Without a voice, he had no way to ask. Dodge flipped a chip from his stack to the center of the table, waited, cleared his throat, then shook his head and took one from Hē's pile as well. "That's small and big blinds," he said, "bet's to you, Jude."

The chips in front of Jude were nothing but cheap plastic. He scooped up enough of them to cover the blind and tossed them forward. Dodge raised his eyebrows but continued. He added more of his own chips to the pile, then dealt three cards in the center of the table, face-up: THE MAGICIAN, THE HERMIT, and THE WHEEL OF FORTUNE.

This was ridiculous, and Jude tried to say so, trying to force lungs that weren't there to squeeze a voice out of a throat that didn't exist. He remembered the power his voice had held, a word to open any lock, another to summon flame—words of healing or destruction. He remembered the magics he had once called forth with such ease. And now this, humbled and muted, playing a childish, castrated version of the game that had cost him and Dodge and who knew how many others their lives. He was more than this. He was a demigod, a Trickster. A trickle, a faint shadow of that rage he had once felt smoldered in the center of him.

Jude tucked his two blank cards together and tore them in half.

Dodge set his cards on the table, his smile vanishing. "You try to throw somebody a rope, and they hang themselves with it. You wanna play the hard-ass, you go right ahead." He snatched his scotch up off the table and gestured in Jude's direction with it, the ice clinking against glass. "He's all yours."

The young man finally looked up from his cell phone and gave Jude a devil-may-care grin. "So here's the *real* game. Most folks get whatever afterlife they've got coming to them, but you, you lucky son-of-a-gun, you get to pick your own." His words had a rich, sonorous quality to them, as if he were always just about to break into song.

Hē made a scoffing noise, before speaking with an echoing memory of the voice Jude had left behind. "Always games with you. This choice is no game. Besides, he's already made it."

The young god dropped his feet to the floor and sat forward. "How you figure?"

"He wears his choice around his neck."

Jude reached up to his throat, found the rosary he'd pulled out of the satchel hanging there. He'd been wearing it when he died.

The young god laughed. "Wearing a symbol don't mean shit. If it did, these"—he kicked one of his feet back up to the table, showing the tiny wings growing from the ankles of his sneakers—"would make me an angel."

Hermes. Hermes was Thoth, and Thoth was dead. Which meant that Hermes got to live. Had Hermes and Hē *planned* this? Or was the Greek god just making the best of a bad situation? Either way, Jude didn't trust him, not one bit.

Hē turned back to Jude. "As a being granted free will by the Highest, you are able to choose the eternity that most appeals to you." The angel lifted both hands palms up, a soft light emanating from them. Jude noticed a second Red Door—or maybe the same door in two places at the same time, the thing was impossible to predict—behind the angel that he was fairly certain hadn't been there a moment before. Mist curled across the threshold from beneath the door; given what Hē was, however, maybe those were wisps of cloud. Jude couldn't be sure, but he thought he heard a choir singing, soft and reverent. "Seems to me, when Paradise is on the table, it is an easy decision. It is not always so readily offered."

Hermes threw his head back, groaned, and shook his fist in front of his groin, pantomiming jerking off. "Oh, blow me," he said. He now also had a door behind him, from which emanated the rich, loamy scent of fields in the summer, the salt of ocean breezes. "You ever notice how much Paradise's people like to talk about Hell? You wanna know why? Because Paradise is fucking *boring*. You want to spend eternity contemplating how sparkly white your holy robes are, you go with Feathers over there. But don't think about slipping those robes off and getting frisky with one of the hotties from the choir, or you'll get a fast elevator drop down to the hot place. That's where their real creativity goes. Now Elysium? That's where you want to be. No sorrow, no toil. Instead, you get great food, strong wine, and the dress code is a little, uh . . . less restrictive, you get me?"

Dodge chuckled. "You left out a thing or two, Herms. You make the Summer Isles sound better than a slow fuck on Christmas morning. I'm sure you just forgot to mention that you ain't had a new guest in, like, millennia. And then there's this." He clapped his hands twice. Hermes' handsome young face twisted and stretched into the long-beaked bird's head of Thoth. "If you still looked like this, would you be trying to convince him that Aaru is where he needs to be?" He shook his head, clapped again, and Thoth became Hermes once more. "I think you could sell redemption to the devil, son, quick as you hustle, but Jude here ain't buyin', are you?" This last was directed at Jude, who had no answer, even if he could speak.

The fortune god stroked his chins, a mockery of contemplation. "No, Jude knows where he belongs. Where he's always belonged; just like me." He aimed a thumb toward the door at his back. "What they ain't said, what they don't want you to know, is that you ain't *gotta* go nowhere. That party out there? It's always happening. Sometimes it's Mardi Gras. Sometimes it's New

Year's. Saints game tailgates, hurricane parties . . . hell, sometimes just because." Dodge winked. "You lived in Heaven all your life, little one. Why's a small thing like death gonna make you leave?"

Jude stared at the table in front of him as though trying to bore a hole through it, just so he wouldn't have to meet the gaze of any of the gods who sat there, watching him. How did you even begin to make a choice like this? He'd done so many things wrong in his life, failed so many people. Surely neither Heaven nor Elysium would have him, no matter what Hē or Hermes said.

He realized he still held the torn cards in his grip, had held on to them through each of the three gods' sales pitches. They were still blank. Suddenly, the realization of what these gods were attempting hit him: He might be dead, but his fate wasn't decided yet—the blank cards proved it, and these three were trying to influence his hand by taking him out of the game, by presenting him with a choice he didn't have to make.

But he already had the only guide he trusted: Papa Legba.

Jude flipped the cards around so Hē, Hermes, and Dodge could see them—breaking the spell of the con they were trying to work on him; it felt like giving them the finger. Hermes rolled his eyes, Dodge barked out a laugh, and Hē just stared. "Guess that's that," Dodge said. "Y'all know the way out." The angel went first, unfurling cinnamon-scented wings and vanishing in a flare of painfully bright light.

"Showoff," Hermes muttered as he faded from view. Jude was left sitting at the table with the murdered fortune god, only the ticking of the monstrous cat clock breaking the silence.

Dodge seemed uncomfortable with the quiet. "That was a good play," he said at last. He swept the cards together again, started to shuffle them. "You already learned the most important lesson: Don't play any game you can't win." A sly, knowing grin slanted across his face. "Be honest, though. I almost had you."

It took effort to not let Dodge's charisma win him over, to not let him charm away Jude's control.

The fortune god sighed. "It's too bad you lost that bag I gave you." He seemed to be talking more to himself than to Jude. "It's old, maybe older than the world itself. Some things are . . ." He paused, seemed to struggle for the right words. ". . . are too important to vanish entirely, even if they get lost. They gotta go somewhere, and that fucking bag is where they end up." Jude thought of the thunderbolt, the strange artifacts whose purpose he'd never been able to decipher, of the way he sometimes felt like he was reaching into a vast space when he searched for something in the bag. "If I had what's hidden away in that bag, then I could make myself whole again." He grinned. "Meet the new boss, same as the old boss, y'know?"

The door behind Jude creaked open. A heavy hand grasped his shoulder, carrying with it the scent of rum and tobacco. "We must go," Legba said. Jude was halfway out the door before he realized he'd risen to his feet and followed Legba without conscious thought. Was his will slipping away already?

"Later, gator!" Dodge yelled at Jude's back, laughing once again. "See you soon!"

Jude followed the loa down the hallway and toward the crowded ballroom, leaving Dodge behind, alone with his booze and his cards. He felt nothing. And why should he? He could do nothing for the fortune god, could do nothing for himself. They were both dead. Even the semblance of anger he'd gathered had now fled. Only the numb detachment of death remained.

Coming out of the dark into the light and the noise of the main room, Jude saw the surroundings differently than he had on the way in. Though they retained their beauty, they had also now taken on a funereal quality. The satin curtains and hardwood floors became the lining and the confines of a coffin. The brass containers decorating the chandelier, once vases, were now urns. The marble statues of frolicking cherubs and graceful acrobats had become the mournful angels of gravestones, while the plaster walls and the exposed brick of a retro artists' studio Uptown now looked like they had been taken from the aboveground tombs of New Orleans cemeteries.

As Jude and Legba slipped through a mob of dancers, Jude recognized many faces among the dead. Tommy, the street juggler, laughing as a woman in a ball gown guided him through the steps. The bartender and the blonde that Scarpelli had murdered and turned into ghouls. His aunt Sara, years wiped from the face he remembered.

Jude reached out to each of them, but they swept past him, seemingly unable to see him. Then there were people he had never met — faces he had only seen in visions, the lost his talent had sought out. He knew that their joy was merely a memory, a shade of the life they had once known. He knew, too, that if he stayed, he would join them and, in doing so, would regain a pale shadow of laughter just as he had remembered anger.

Something drew him forward, though, out into the night and onto the gravel path, which he now saw was made of crumbling bone and ash, the remains of anyone buried in a New Orleans tomb, different in function — but not form — from brick ovens. The type of tomb where his own body likely lay. He tried to step more lightly, but it was hopeless: his every footfall was a grinding, crushing sacrilege.

He walked down this path of ruin until he reached the gate between this illusion of life and the streetcar that would take him to the world beyond. He hadn't seen Regal among the spirits, nor his mother. He hoped that meant they were still alive. He knew that if his mother had died, she would have chosen to stay here. She loved the city, had loved Mardi Gras more than Christmas. Jude couldn't lie to himself the way these dead did, staying behind here in this halfway place.

He had to know what lay beyond. Jude followed Legba through the gates into the hot, wet night and toward the waiting streetcar.

Behind him, the dead drank and laughed and danced.

The black paint of the streetcar glistened as Jude approached, a flickering, greenish iridescence like the sheen on an oil slick or a beetle's carapace. He heard arguing, raised voices: Barren's and that of a woman. When Jude came around the front of the car, Barren filled the entrance, arms folded across his chest like a bouncer barring the door. The person he argued with, a young black woman in a white frilly thing of a dress, bounced on her toes, straining to reach her pointing finger into the skull-face of the loa, her bright red canvas sneakers untied and slipping from her heels each time she pounced forward.

"I'm ready to go!" she shouted. "I changed my mind, and I want to move on!"

Something about her felt familiar, but Jude couldn't place her until he saw the white wires trailing down from her ears, recalling the brief echo of an overheard song. *I'm mad about you, baby,* she'd sung, back in Celeste Dorcet's voodoo shop.

Renaissance Raines. Renai, to her friends. Part of the reason he hadn't recognized her was the absence of her piercings. The memory of her came coupled with a burden, the sense that when he was alive, he'd been responsible for her death.

Legba made hushing noises as he and Jude walked up. "What is all this commotion?" Legba asked, his Haitian accent calm and quiet.

The girl dropped to her heels and turned, her eyes wide and shocked. When she saw that it was Legba who had spoken, her entire posture slumped, bent neck, drooped shoulders, a toe dug into the dirt. When she spoke, her voice matched her dress, abashed and kittenish, like that of a child. "He won't let me on," she said. "I want to go with you. I'm ready to go, but Baron Samedi won't let me."

"Nobody rides for free," Barren said, his exposed jaw clenched shut.

"But I paid already," she said. "You know I paid. How else could I have gotten here?"

Legba made a clucking noise with his tongue, cupped her smooth face in the palm of his gnarled and knotted hand. "You chose this place, child. You. Not me, not him, not any of the ghede. You. There is always a cost when we make a choice. You gave us a coin and we led you here. Always a cost, you understand?"

She nodded, her eyes welling up with the memory of tears. With a heaving sigh, she backed away from the streetcar, making room for them to pass. Legba nodded at Barren, who stepped into the car and sat in the driver's seat.

"Come, Jude," Legba said. He gestured toward the stairs. Jude wondered what Renai's fate would be, if she would be able to re-enter that place of joyous self-deception, carrying as she did the memory of sorrow. Or would she become one of the legends of the city, a haunting presence whose reason for weeping was lost to history?

No, he thought. *No more lost.* Jude tried to speak once more and failed again. He rapped a knuckle against the side of the streetcar, to get the attention of the loa. He pointed at Renai, then to the entrance, then to himself.

Legba frowned. "You only paid for one," he said. "Only one." He tapped the tip of his cane against Jude's pants pocket. "You have no more coin, remember? You can't pay. Unless —" He touched his tie, making certain it lay flat within his vest. Something sly and hungry passed across his ancient face. "You have another form of payment? Something else we might trade?"

Jude shook his head. He remembered someone, the vampire maybe, saying something about side wagers. He made a circle with his fingers and pointed at Legba. Pantomimed holding a fan of cards, laying them on the table. Repeated the gesture of the circle and pointed once again at Legba.

Laughter came from within the torch-lit confines of the streetcar, Barren's throaty chuckle. "You know what he's saying, Pops," Barren said. "You know you always like to double down."

Legba's wrinkles spread into a grin, understanding the gamble that Jude was taking. The voodoo god had returned the doubloon he'd demanded, so if Jude lost, Legba would gain nothing. But the game hadn't ended yet. Even in death, Jude's destiny had yet to be fully revealed.

He might yet win.

"My gamble is this," Legba said, reaching into his vest pocket and taking out a silver dollar, "I wager that you will win. When your fate is revealed, it will defeat the current high hand." He pressed the silver coin to his lips, and then handed it to Jude. "If this occurs, then you will owe me a favor."

Jude nodded and kissed the coin as well. A tremor ran through him as the contract bound him to the loa. Renai hit him with a hug so intense that he staggered. He handed her the coin, and she flicked it, spinning, toward Barren's laughter. As all of them—Jude, Legba, and Renai—entered the streetcar, Legba repeated his earlier words, as if speaking to himself. "There is always a cost."

Renai spent the first few minutes of their journey thanking him, unconcerned that Jude found it impossible to speak. She seemed more than capable of carrying the conversation herself.

"I never really believed in an afterlife, you know?" she said, phrasing it as a question but not even pausing for the answer Jude couldn't give. "I mean, I hoped, but I always kind of figured when you were done you were done. Mama Celestine told me all about the loa, but she never said anything about all of this." She waved a hand, vaguely indicating the streetcar and Legba, perhaps the entirety of the afterlife. "So when I got to that party on Elysian Fields, I thought, *This is it. This is as good as you can hope for.* But it wasn't. It didn't change. I could barely spend a day there; can you imagine spending eternity doing the same frivolous thing over and over? But you rescued me from that. And now we're moving on to

— Well, to I don't know what. I wish Mama Celestine had told me more about what that was going to be like, because she was sure right about Papa Legba and Baron Samedi. Do you know what comes next?"

She looked at him, her eyes so open and earnest that Jude was glad he had no voice to answer with, that he could only shrug. He had offered Paradise, and Hermes, Elysium, but if those existed, then so did Hell, so did Tartarus. Jude had no idea where the loa were bringing them, but he knew there was no guarantee that it would be anywhere pleasant.

"Can't talk yet, huh? Don't worry, it'll come. It's funny, I don't really sound like myself anymore. Like, you know how people always say they hate hearing their own voice recorded, because it sounds different than in your ears? It's kind of like that." She searched his face for something and seemed unable to find it. "Anyway," she said, "thanks again. I owe you one."

Jude opened his mouth to tell her that that was a dangerous thing to say, but she'd already turned to stare out the window and, besides, Jude didn't have the words yet. He followed her gaze outside, saw that they were heading back to Canal Street, but beyond that he couldn't even guess where they were being taken. He knew far less about these things, it seemed, than he had believed.

Renai twisted her headphones cord around her finger, winding it into a tight coil. Jude wondered if the music player still worked, or if, like everything else, it was simply a shadow, a memory of what once was. Seeing the expression on her face, recognizing in the tight line of her lips a nervousness he couldn't feel, Jude couldn't decide whether or not he should be grateful for the lack of feeling the newly dead were granted.

Of course, even if he *should*, gratitude was another thing he couldn't feel anymore.

The car swerved, pulling a tight turn onto Canal, facing the Mississippi. Beside him, Renai relaxed. "Oh," she said. "The ferry, get it? We have to go across the river. Styx, I guess."

That wasn't the right river, of course. Nor would a voodoo loa have any reason to lead them to another pantheon's Underworld. What struck him as significant, though, was where they had come to a stop. The squat glass tower of the Aquarium rose out of the night to one side of them, the Riverwalk on the other. There were no tracks beneath them, not in the world of the living.

So where were they headed?

In the driver's seat, Barren spun a wheel just at the edge of his reach, the flames overhead growing brighter, crackling in their iron lanterns. A thrumming energy filled the vehicle, growing more and more intense. Renai grasped at Jude, her nails digging into his arm, her breath coming in quick gasps.

Jude looked to Legba and saw that one of the loa's hands gripped the seat in front of him while the other mashed his hat down onto his head. Without any warning, Barren threw a lever forward, and the car surged at the river, sparks flying as high as the windows as its metal wheels ground against cement. Jude and Renai were slammed back into their seats, her arms squeezing tight around him.

The streetcar slipped through a break in the concrete wall and ripped through a parking lot, bouncing up over grass, not slow-ing—indeed, seeming to *gain* momentum—and then they shot up the rise of the natural levee and flew into empty space, falling to-ward the churning waters of the Mississippi River, pitch-black in the dead of night.

Renai shrieked just before they hit the surface, when the street-car—ignoring any potential buoyancy it might have had—sank through the muddy water like a stone. Jude patted her hand, pre-tending concern he didn't—couldn't—feel, thinking that his deathly calm might extend to her. It seemed to help; though she still clung to him, she only let out a slight whimper when the sen-sation of falling was arrested by the sudden thump the car made when it came to rest on the riverbed. And yet, she shrieked once more when Barren pulled a handle and swung open the squealing doors, a roar of river water pouring in.

As the torrent rose around them, past their ankles, the benches, the cushioned backs, all the way to the hanging lanterns, the flames hissing out one by one, Jude decided that the absence of fear was, after all, a gift.

CHAPTER EIGHTEEN

IN **SIBERIA,** you must face Erlik, a dark and evil old god, who will swallow your soul into his porcine maw if you are judged unworthy. In Varanasi, you stand before Chitragupta, who has recorded your every deed on Earth in meticulous detail. In Naples, your fate is decided by Aeacus, Rhadamanthus, and Minos, who will send you to the Fields of Elysium, the Meadows of Asphodel, or the tortures of Tartarus. Mictecacihuatl and Osiris, Freya and Odin, Ereshkigal and Supay. With mirrors, with feathers and scales, with records in books or on clay tablets or written on the back of your eye, you will be remembered. Your name, your sins, your virtues. None will be forgotten.

Without lungs, of course, neither Jude nor Renai had any true need for oxygen, and so when the car filled with water, they did not drown. The dead girl, though, caught for too long in the seam between the world of the living and the world beyond, believed differently. She held her face and nose to the ceiling, trying to get one last sputtering gasp of air, then thrashed and flailed when she had to release that imagined breath. Jude waited, patient and un-sympathetic as the grave, for her to recognize the illogic of her fear, caged by her panicked grip on his arm. At last she relaxed, her mouth gaping open, her earbuds popping out and floating along-side her head.

"Oh," she said, quiet and flat. "Okay."

When she released his arm, Jude followed Legba and Barren out of the streetcar, into the watery valley of the Mississippi bed. The silt-thick waters blocked out any light from above, but with-out eyes, Jude didn't actually need light to see. Catfish slithered among thin grass, their whiskers trailing from wide mouths like Chinese dragons. The current howled around him, a hurricane wind beneath the waves. Debris littered the soft mud, car tires and planks of wood, battered musical instruments and shoes, pirogues and rowboats with shattered hulls, a child's rocking horse, its springs so encased with rust, it looked like a species of spiral coral. Though he kept his mouth closed and knew his senses were mere illusions, he could not avoid the cold, stale coffee taste of the brack-ish water, the stink of rotting things.

Renai floated beside Jude, her faith in her body strong enough to make her spirit too buoyant to walk along the murky riverbed as he and the two loa did. Jude took her hand and towed her along with him, following their guides to a sunken steamboat half sub-merged in the river's bottom. Barren had again changed his ap-pearance, his painted skull now replaced by a canine's head, some-thing feral in the slant of its ear and its shaggy fur.

"Down you go," Barren said, once they had reached the wreck, his thick tongue lolling between his open jaws. "Down, down, down." He held out a gloved hand when Jude stepped forward. "Whoa there, brah. You lost your manners along with your voice? 'Ladies first' mean nothing to you?" He beckoned Renai forward with a teasing curl of his fingers. "Come along, child. Let's get you settled."

Barren led the way, descending a staircase into the depths of the sunken wreck. Renai turned to look back at Jude—a fragile smile, a pitiful attempt at bravery—and then she swam after him, her red sneakers flashing as she kicked her way down.

"It was a noble thing you did for that girl," Legba said. "I wonder if you know how much." He poked the tip of his cane into a knothole. "I think no. I think you do not understand what you risk." Legba's eyes rose up to meet Jude's, a deep, hungry stare. "You think you are dead, what more can you lose, yes?"

Beneath them, muffled but still clear, Renai cried out, first a shrieking burst of fear, then a long, throaty moan of pain. Legba held Jude back as she cried out again. "But there are some things, Jude," he said, before releasing him, "worse even than death."

Jude took the stairs two at a time in a headlong plunge, chasing Renai's screams. At some point, he splashed out of the river water and into a pocket of air. He followed Renai's wet sneaker prints down a hallway and into the vast room of what had once been the steamboat's cargo hold. Water flowed across the ceiling before falling in a thick column—a hypnotic roaring, frothing, gushing whirl—that vanished into a ragged hole in the center of the floor.

Even without flesh, Jude could tell that the room was frigid, a cold that wasn't physical but primal. On the far side of the pillar, their images distorted by the water's refraction, Barren crouched over Renai, who knelt, slumped back onto her heels. Beyond them were two ornate thrones, far too large for any human, carved of a single massive piece of wood.

Jude ran toward them, skirting around the column of water just as Barren faced the empty thrones, raising something red and wet above his canine head. Gleaming balance scales stood between him and the massive seats, metal plates hanging from thin delicate chains. Renai, still on her knees, had her back to Barren and whatever absent deity he made sacrifice to; she held up a mirror as though trying to find something in its reflection. A dark stain spread across her chest, down among the folds of her white dress. Jude took a step forward, uncertain. Though tears still lined her cheeks, she smiled. Jude looked back at Barren, at his hands.

He held a human heart.

Words came from his muzzle, a harsh, guttural language that Jude didn't recognize. The heart steamed in his hands, still warm from the heat of Renai's imagined body. Barren placed the girl's heart on one side of the scale with a reverent, almost fearful tenderness. Then, licking the blood from the fingers of one hand, he pulled the pin that held the balancing mechanism in place. A single feather lay on the other plate. It shimmered with vibrant, shifting colors, shining as though lit by an inner fire.

The scales dipped and rose, back and forth, finally coming to rest with the feather weighing the same as Renai's heart. The dead girl began to laugh, her face shining—literally, a beacon of radiant joy. "Thank you," she said, looking into the mirror. "Thank you, thank you, thank you." She stood, almost too bright to look at, handed Barren the mirror, and moved to the side, her trial complete.

Something about the scene tugged at Jude's memory, the heart and the scale and the feather, but he couldn't quite place it. And then Barren returned his attention to the thrones, his dog's head turned in profile to Jude, and the image clicked into place.

Anubis. The Feather of Truth. The funerary rites of ancient Egypt. So Barren was both Anubis and—if Renai was right about him—Baron Samedi, the way Thoth was also Hermes. Was anybody who they said they were?

Legba spoke from beside Jude, his appearance sudden and startling. "This is why it is better that you came with us," Legba said. "The others, they will try to convince you that Paradise and the Fields of Summer and Ginen are different places, and maybe they are if you believe they are. But you trust Papa Legba. Everything come together, in the end."

228 • BRYAN CAMP

Barren, whoever he was, turned his dog's—no, his *jackal's*
—head, unleashing a feral grin in Jude's direction. He crooked
a gore-stained finger, beckoning. "You're up," he said. "Don't
worry. I'll be very gentle."

Jude moved to where the god directed, floating as though in a
dream. He turned his back to the thrones, facing the rushing wa-
terfall. A sense of vertigo swept over him, the whisper that came
at the edge of a cliff, teasing you to jump. He didn't realize he'd
stepped closer to the rushing plunge of water until Barren stopped
him with a hand on his chest.

Jude had time to glance down, curious, and then watched as a
claw, bent and dagger-sharp, tore through to the center of him. He
heard the rending of cloth, the wet suck of ripping flesh, saw the
spurt of dark blood, even smelled the coppery scent of it, before
he felt the pain. When it came, it was greater than anything he had
ever known, second only to the cacophony of lost things that had
overwhelmed him after the storm.

Jude sank to his knees—would have collapsed if Barren's hook
of a claw hadn't held him upright. The jackal-faced god handed
him a thick slab of stone—obsidian polished to a mirror's shine
—then swiped with his claw again and again, making a shredded
mess of Jude's chest.

"Hey, boss," Barren shouted over Jude's head, "this one's got
no heart!" Jude heard a rumble, like far-off thunder, a reply just at
the edge of his hearing. He held up the mirror, as he had seen Renai doing, and aimed it at the empty thrones.

Smoke rolled off the obsidian, black and stinking of a pyre. The
reflection showed two seated figures, male and female—or one
that shifted back and forth; Jude couldn't be sure which. The man
wore thick robes and sandals, and held a spear in one hand and
a short scepter in the other. A frown glowered beneath a bushy,
curled beard, and a withered, puckered hole marked where one of
his eyes should be, a sickly green pallor clinging to his skin. The
woman wore a long, sleeveless red dress that hugged her body.

Jude couldn't be sure whether she had two arms or four, or whether it was shadows or frostbite that stained her legs black. Despite the cold paleness of her cheeks and the animal skull she wore like a helmet, she smiled, genuine and bright.

At his feet, or hers, or theirs, three dogs lounged, or one dog with three heads. Two ravens perched above them, one on each throne, or just one atop a helm of black metal shaped in the likeness of a raven's head. In the instant it took Jude to take all this in, he also saw that they were speaking, could hear the words once he could see the movement of their lips. They spoke as one, their voices mingled together, the cold scrape of a closing tomb door, a lily petal against a cheek, harmonious opposites.

"Then we have no choice," they said. "Send him to the Devourer."

Without ceremony or protest or a word of regret, Barren plucked Jude from the floor and shoved him into the crush of falling water. Jude gasped, forgetting in that instant that he could neither drown nor fall to his death. Far, far below him, through such black depths that nothing should be visible, Jude saw something that inspired fear even in the dead. A fear not born of the body, but a piercing dread of the soul.

In that abyss, Jude saw something formless, something of many forms. Something that hungered, that personified hunger. Something at the bottom of all things. Something with *teeth*.

Hands pulled Jude back from the brink of destruction, yanked him gasping into that cold room at the bottom of the Mississippi, with the empty thrones and the scales for weighing a heart he didn't have. When he looked up, he expected to see Barren grinning down at him, either with Anubis's jackal muzzle or Samedi's skull. Instead, he saw Renai, her mouth pulled into a tight line of grim determination. Again he heard that rumble of speech that hovered just at the edge of his comprehension. Renai, though, seemed to understand it, because she turned to the thrones, her feet set, her hip cocked, shoulders wide, every inch of her defiant.

"No," she said. "It's not right." More grumbles of distant thunder. "Because it's impossible. I wouldn't even be here if it wasn't for him. There has to be a mistake."

What was she doing? Jude searched the floor, found the mirror where he'd dropped it. He shuffled toward it on his hands and knees, unable to summon the strength to stand. He had to know what—*Death,* he forced himself to admit; who else could it be? —what Death was saying to her. She couldn't throw away eternity for someone like him. Just as he came within reach of the mirror, a glossy patent-leather shoe and a long, long stretch of tuxedo pants blocked his path. Jude looked up into Barren's skull-face, saw that the loa held a finger up to his lipless mouth, bidding Jude to be silent.

Behind him, Renai was speaking again. ". . . a chance," she said, "to find what he lost." A brief growl of hunger. "Yes," she said. "I agree."

Barren moved, and Jude lunged for the mirror, snatching it up and turning it toward the thrones where Death was seated. *No,* he wanted to say. *Don't let her do this.* But his voice would not come, no matter how hard he strained. He glanced at the column of water, the descent into the Devourer's maw. If he threw himself down there, then she couldn't sacrifice herself for him.

Too late. Renai stood in front of him, her eyes radiant, the front of her white dress a red and bloody mess, her heart in her hands. Barren leaned down beside her, whispered in her ear. She nodded. The loa turned and reached down to Jude, slid something into his pocket. Somehow, the skull winked.

Renai knelt and studied Jude's face. "I think after this you'll owe me one," she said, and pushed her heart into the gaping wound in Jude's chest. The pain was exquisite, dragging Jude to the floor.

The obsidian mirror filled Jude's vision, its darkness the re-

THE CITY OF LOST FORTUNES • 231

flection of Death's single immense eye. He dropped into it, and it swallowed him whole.

Jude fell through darkness for a tiny piece of forever.

Of course, words like "fall" and "dark" were constructions of a consciousness still rooted in the flesh, still concerned with bodily motion and the perception of light. Jude began—once he could understand his surroundings past his sublime terror—to experience heat and pressure, as though his soul was being squeezed in a giant hot fist. Tighter and tighter, hotter and hotter, far past what flesh could endure, body crushed and burnt to a fine, dry powder, the dust to which we must all return. Jude fell through darkness and pain, hoping only for oblivion.

Pieces crumbled, began to burn and flake away. Memories went first, then thoughts. Jude lost bits of personality, the passage of time. Lost desires, first complex ones, like wishing things had turned out differently, that questions had gotten answered before the end, then simpler ones, like wishing for release, then desire itself. Jude no longer questioned fate, no longer had the capacity to hope that the agony would end. Finally, Jude's sense of self vanished. Nothing separated the observer from the darkness, the pain from the sensation of it. Only the concept of Jude remained, among darkness and pressure, heat and pain.

Darkness. Pressure. Heat. Pain. And then, for one eternal instant:

Nothing.

PART FIVE

THE FOOL

T IS DIVIDED into: shen, the mind; yi, the intellect; zhi, the will; hun, the essence that leaves the body after death; and po, the essence that remains. Or it's split into the nephesh, ruach, neshama, chaya, and yechidah: the breath, wind, life, and singularity of a living being. Some see it as anatta, a continuum of changing states, never a single thing, eternal in its constant evolution. Others see it as left and right, one side who speaks, the other who obeys. Yet others believe in the ib and the sheut, the ren and the bâ, the ka and the akh; the heart, shadow, name, essence, and power of a person. We are never a single existence, but a collective. A school, a flock, a pride. An ensemble of voices, sometimes in harmony, sometimes discordant. In life, the many are one; in death, the one becomes many.

Jude returned to life—to identity, to pain and darkness and heat, to flesh—in an explosive moment of conception.

A heart seized in a chest, two lungs stretched and burned, joints popped and muscles strained. Jude drew in one ragged breath, hot and thin, and let loose a howl, agony and fear and rage and life pouring out. Wood splintered, and Jude fell, turning sideways, scraping a cheek against rough stone. Jude gasped, and struggled, and realized that the return to life meant a return to a body that was trapped. Entombed. So Jude spit out the word learned from Dodge, the magic that meant *open*, and was rewarded with light, with cool, fresh air.

Wriggling headfirst through the door that had opened — arms either pinned or numb but useless either way — soaked and crying, out of heat and darkness and into light, reborn into the world in the middle of a cemetery, pushed out of a womb of marble and granite. Jude lay on the ground, face in the sunlight, arms spread wide, weeping. Gave thanks, not knowing or caring who was thanked, only able to repeat the words over and over again. Eventually, breathing and heartbeat slowed, and the stiffness, the all-body ache settled to a slow throb. Jude laughed and wept a little more, and then a deep and abiding calm set in.

A shape occluded the sun, too quick and deliberate to be a cloud. Jude squinted against the glare, eyes burning and slow to adjust to the light, and laughed again. Imagined what it must have looked like to whatever tourist or cemetery worker who saw a tomb door swing open and a person come slithering out.

"I know this looks strange," Jude said. "I know what you're thinking. But I'm not a zombie." Realized even as the words were spoken that they might be lies. Jude's vision cleared enough to show the stranger, revealed the crisp lines of a well-tailored tuxedo, pristine white gloves, and a floral-painted skull.

"Don't be ashamed of it, sweetheart," Barren said. "Some of my best friends are zombies."

Jude groaned and rose, staggering, to stand, and in doing so noticed something. Bright red canvas sneakers. A white frilly thing of a dress. A body not Jude's own. A woman's body. Reaching out with proprioception — one's awareness of one's own body, a word this mind knew but Jude had never heard before—Jude considered herself. She felt healthy and strong, quickly shaking off the shock of waking up in a hot tomb and falling three feet to the concrete with a vitality Jude hadn't felt in years. In truth, the sudden return of youth was a more profound change for Jude than waking up a woman. Jude still had memories of being a man, but felt no discomfort or strangeness in her current body. When Jude recognized the shoes, a terrible thought occurred to her.

"What did you do with Renai?" she asked Barren.

"Nothing," Barren said. "She's in there with you. Or more accurately, you're in there with her. Her body, her mind, her soul. Little bit of Jude tagging along for the ride."

"How little a bit?"

Barren chuckled. "The essential bits. Thoughts and personality and memories. Think of it like a computer. Renai's the hardware and the operating system and the hard drive. You're just a flash drive with some Jude software." He looked back over his shoulder and shouted, "Hey, Sal! Found 'em!"

I'm in her mind, Jude thought. *That's how I knew about proprioception.*

We did a project in school, Renai thought, her mental voice like someone half awake.

"Is she in any pain?" Jude asked.

"If I know my trade—and I do—then she is currently experiencing a state of constant but mild euphoria, observing a series of unusual, disconnected events that nevertheless seem to have attained a powerful resonance and are imposing upon her a message of cosmic significance and awe. Which is how she'll stay, if you don't shake her around too much."

"So, the good news is, I'm not dead. Bad news is, I'm possessing an epically stoned teenager watching *The Wizard of Oz* synced to *Dark Side of the Moon.*"

Barren leaned against a nearby tomb. "Only technically," he said. "I'm pretty sure she's nineteen."

As Jude opened her mouth to reply, a shadow swooped overhead, accompanied by the rustling of wings. The image on Jude's mother's paintings flashed in front of her eyes, the darkness that had stolen the lives of Tommy and Thoth, Dodge and Renai. Her stomach tightened and her fists clenched, the word for *burn* rising in place of her answer to Barren. But before she could articulate the magic, she saw that it was not an angel but a black bird the size of a cat that fluttered down and perched on the skull-headed god's shoulder.

Jude gagged on the power rising from her belly. She turned and spat the taste of cayenne pepper and crème brûlée onto the gravel, a thin curl of smoke rising from her mouth.

"Kinda twitchy, aren't they?" the bird said.

Barren sighed and tilted his hand back and forth. "Little bit," he said. "All we got, though." He tilted his jawbone in Jude's direction. "You got any clue what's going on?"

The bird spoke first. "Fuck no they don't. I heard they were in front of the Thrones. I forget my thrice-be-damned name down there, and I *belong* there. Smart money says they're all tangled up hell to breakfast in that brain of theirs. I bet it'll be at least a day before she can walk and talk at the same time without shitting herself."

"I'll take that bet, little raven," Barren said. "Jude's only about half as clever as I'd like, but they're both of 'em hard as coffin nails."

Despite the crystalline blue sky above and the solid ground under her feet; despite the pleasure of breathing in the familiar, humid air of New Orleans, thick with the scents of growth and bloom; despite her deep and complex joy at simply being alive, so unlike the numb sterility of death; despite all of that, the skeleton and the raven talking about her like she wasn't there began to piss Jude off. A flush rose across her skin, a heat that had nothing to do with the summer's humidity. "Standing right here," she said. This protest went ignored, even after she repeated it. They hashed out the details of their wager, gambling on whether Jude's resurrection would grant her anything other than a second, messier, death.

Jude didn't know if Renai had been capable of magic in her previous life, or if returning from the dead or having Jude riding along inside her had granted her the ability, but she felt the magic raging within, the arrested spell still burning at the back of her throat, an explosion building in her stomach. Before, she would have pushed the magic and the rage down, would have forced herself to be calm and patient. But she stood next to the tomb she'd been buried in. What did she really have to lose?

She barked the word that meant *close,* the sound of it concussing the air like a thunderclap. Barren's teeth and the raven's beak both clicked as they snapped shut. Her pulse still throbbing in her head, Jude closed her eyes and took a deep breath, enjoying the momentary silence. Even as it occurred to her that she had used magic on a god, it also occurred to her that it had *worked.*

From the back of her mind, Renai thought, *That was sick.*

Jude smiled and opened her eyes.

Somehow, Barren's fleshless skull managed to convey amazement. Jude ignored him, and the raven as well, deciding to see how far she could play out this trick. She brushed the dirt away from her clothes as best she could, cursing the dress for its lack of pockets, though it's not like Renai's folks would have buried her with a cell phone. She knelt and tied her sneakers, and then decided she'd stalled long enough to make her point.

She turned her attention back to the silent god and the raven. "So," she said, "here's the deal. Now we all know that I don't like being ignored, and we all know that I can do what I just did. That's new information for the both of you. In the interest of sharing, I'd appreciate it if you two told me some things that I don't know. Just so we're even. That sound good to you?"

The bird bobbed his head, a quick, nervous gesture. Jude was surprised at how easy it was to read the animal's body language. Barren tilted his forehead down, the barest impression of a nod. It would have to do. Jude spoke their mouths *open*.

Barren stretched his mouth in a wide yawn, the joints cracking. "Not bad," he said. "Not bad at all." He reached up and poked the raven. "You lose."

The bird hopped from his shoulder, gliding to the outstretched hand of a stone angel. "Yeah, yeah, bite me," he said as he settled his weight on the carved finger. He dug his beak between his feathers, the motion somehow as rude as a middle finger. He aimed his sharp face in Jude's direction. "My name's Salvatore. Go ahead and call me Sal, everybody does."

"Okay, Sal, tell me about yourself." Jude wiped sweat from her forehead with the back of her hand. Somewhere in the cemetery, a jazz band played, slow and solemn. Jude wondered what they had played at Renai's funeral.

"I'm a raven, for now."

"No, shit. I mean what are you doing here?"

"I'm supposed to keep an eye on you."

Not, Jude noticed, to protect or guide. To *watch*. Jude leaned against the hot granite of a tomb and toyed with the end of one of her dreads. Hunger rumbled, a loud and shifting thing, in her stomach. Barren lit a cigar, smoke making a thin haze around his floral-painted skull.

Things always had to be difficult with the gods, evasions and word games and pissing contests. Since Jude had received the invitation to Dodge's card game, she'd felt like the whole world was fucking with her, playing games with her life. If that was the way it was going to be, then let the games begin. Jude launched herself at the bird, her hands closing on feathers and fragile bones; with him in her grasp, she could feel the beating of his fluttering, delicate heart.

Sal's needle-sharp beak darted at her, stabbed Jude's hands and wrists three times, four, in the instant it took to snatch the raven from his perch and throw him into the tomb Jude had crawled from when she awoke. Jude slammed the door shut and held her weight against it, fueled by frustration and a kind of terrible joy.

A small riot came from within the stone box, scratching and curses and flapping wings. Jude looked at the cuts on her hands, stinging but minor. Barren had dropped his cigar, was bent over, shaking with laughter. Through the granite door, Jude heard shifting, claws scratching, and then something much heavier than a bird threw its weight against the door, nearly pushing it open. Jude shoved back, then spoke the word that meant *close,* shutting the lock with a sharp click. Whatever Sal had become howled, hurled itself against the door over and over again, and then, panting, fell silent.

"Hey, Barren," Jude said, nearly shouting so she could be certain Sal would hear. "You wanna hear a joke?" The skull-headed god was nodding, still laughing, holding up a hand for Jude to stop. Jude banged her hand on the door of the tomb twice, hard enough to bruise, yelled, "Knock, knock!" When there was no answer, she did it again.

Sal grunted. "Fine, fine, who's there?"

"Cream."

"Cream who?"

"Crematorium, you dick. That's what you're locked inside. You don't want to talk now, but I bet you'll be amiable as hell if I let you slow-cook a couple of days."

Another round of pounding against the door. "Or I could let you out now, so long as you give me some straight goddamn answers."

Moments ticked by as Sal tried to call Jude's bluff. Then, after giving one last halfhearted thump against the door, he whined, low and whistling, like a dog. "Fine," Sal said. "I'll play it straight, okay? Just let me out."

Jude spoke the word *open* and a long, lean shape slipped to the ground, a sandy-coated mutt of a dog with his tail tucked between his legs, ears flat against his head, tongue lolling from his muzzle.

In this form he looked familiar in some inarticulable way, but to Jude, one dog looked pretty much the same as another.

"Told you," Barren said, "tough as a coffin nail."

"Go blow a corpse," Sal said, settling back on his haunches. "Seriously."

Jude gave him a minute to recover, remembering exactly how hot the inside of that tomb was, and then she cleared her throat to get Sal's attention. "Sent by *whom*, to keep an eye on me *how?*"

"I'm supposed to make sure you don't just take the resurrection and run," he said. "That you keep your side of the bargain." Jude pressed a hand against her own chest, felt the heart beating there. The bargain. Renai had given up her heart. But what did that mean for her?

"What's my side of it?" she asked.

"You gotta go back," Sal said. "Once you find your heart, you gotta put it on the scales."

Jude swallowed. There was no way to ask this that didn't sound bad, but she had to know. "What happens to her if I fail?"

Sal's muscles twitched, his back shaking from his neck to his haunches, a gesture Jude saw as a shrug. "Depends on what mood the boss is in. Maybe she gets tossed to the Devourer. Maybe she gets pumped full of angry mojo and gets sent after you as an avenging spirit. Maybe she sticks around and becomes a psychopomp, like me."

Psychopomps guide the dead to the Underworld, Renai thought.

Thanks, Jude thought, *that one I knew*. "How long do I have?" she asked.

Sal looked up at her with liquid black eyes, then dropped his head to stare at his paws. "You have as long as you were on the other side," he said. "That's how these things work, you know? It has to balance. However long you were dead, that's how long you have to live."

"How long, Sal?"

"Two days," he said. "You got until midnight tomorrow night."

Jude slid right past the revelation that she'd been dead for two days and into accusatory rage. "You," she said, turning on Barren. "You did this."

Barren spread his hands wide, spoke around the cigar clamped between his teeth. "You could say that. No need to thank me."

"Thank you? *Thank* you? I ought to shove that cigar up your bony ass!"

"Easy there, tiger." He took his cigar from his mouth, tapped some ash from the tip. "You see how you're standing here tossing around meanness instead of being nothin' at all? That's 'cause me and mine done you a favor." He shook his head. "That was a neat trick, shuttin' me up. Impressive, even. But don't confuse yourself. Don't think for a second it means we're equals. You got no idea." He leaned in close to Jude, smoke filling the slits of his nose, his cavernous mouth. Something immense lurked in the absences of his eyes. "You think we helped you out 'cause of *you?* It's all part of the game, Jude. Fuck or be fucked. I lay with the boys and I lay with the ladies, but gettin' laid is a world away from gettin' fucked, you feel me?" Barren stepped back, took a couple of puffs from his cigar. "You wanna stay friends with the ones you got, times like these. We clear?"

Jude swallowed against the constriction of her throat. She nodded. "Yeah. We're clear."

"Good," he said. "Now. I ain't usually on the side of law and order, but I'm guessing the next step is to check out the murder scene."

The hair on the back of Jude's neck stood up. She'd already seen where Renai was killed. Had someone else died? "What? Whose?"

There was a brief, uncomfortable silence. Sal lifted one of his back legs and scratched at his ear. "Yours," he said, then muttered, "dumbass."

❧

Jude hesitated outside the door to her apartment, unsure now that she stood here if she really wanted to go inside. No police tape blocked the door like it had at the voodoo shop, but then Jude had been the only person to come into this building for years. No surprise that the body hadn't been discovered in just two days. She remembered, now, those few dark moments, the raging thunderstorm, the unseen assailant, the knife again and again. She didn't know if she could really look at a corpse that had once been the face in the mirror without going mad. Renai was a soothing presence in the back of her mind, a playful reminder that hearing voices in one's head sort of solved the whole insanity question anyway.

Sal sat beside her, canine ears perked forward. "What's the holdup?" he asked. "You think they might still be in there?"

"Well, shit, Sal. I do *now*." The plan, such as it was, that they'd ironed out on the way back to her apartment—the work of a few hours of creative resource gathering, given that she'd been resurrected without any cash or streetcar tokens—was for Jude to search the satchel for some way to fight something you couldn't see, while the psychopomp sought the killer's scent, both for identification and tracking. Her biggest hope was that, with her enemies thinking Jude dead, she'd have the element of surprise this time.

She listened at the door for a minute or so, but heard nothing inside except the sound of the air conditioning clicking on. Sal let out an impatient sigh.

"Are you sure you can do this?" Jude asked him.

"This shape ain't just for the pretty face," he said.

"Fair enough." Jude spoke the lock *open* and stepped inside, the psychopomp at her heels. She held her breath, bracing herself for a wave of stench that didn't come. Not that the apartment smelled nice, exactly. Dishes had been left in the sink for a few days and the cloying odor of dried blood hung in the air, but nowhere near the heavy, rotting corpse stink she'd been expecting. It was easy to see why.

The corpse of Jude Dubuisson was gone.

Sal went straight to the bloodstain, his nose pressed to the hardwood floor, sniffing audibly. Jude did her best not to hover over Sal, trying to keep calm. She picked at a seam, a nervous gesture that was Renai's, not Jude's. After a minute Sal huffed and sat back on his haunches, his ears low against his head. "Well, this is damned peculiar," he said.

"Any idea what happened?"

"All I can really tell is what you already know. Somebody got killed right here and then carried away."

"Carried away? By whom?"

"My guess would be Cafard."

Jude shrugged to show that she didn't know who that was.

"Scavenger god," Sal said. "Every place that's got enough of us godly types to be worth a damn has got some bottom feeder that handles the mess when one of us so-called immortals turns out to be, you know, *not*. But you do *not* wanna go find her, believe." Sal turned his head to the side and let his tongue loll out in an expression that could only be disgust. "Scavenger gods ain't much for hygiene. Kinda like this place." That last was muttered sotto voce.

A suspicion that had been worming its way through Jude's thoughts returned. "How sure are you that I am who Barren says I am? What if this is a trick? A spell to make me think I died, another to change—"

Sal rose to his feet and shook, a whole body gesture, like he was flinging water off his fur. He stilled and looked up at Jude. "Look, believe me, I wish that was the case. If you were just transmogre— transpara— if they just did some hoodoo and gave you ladybusiness, I could leave you here and go back to the day job. But that ain't the way it is. I know Barren is as slippery as they come, but you ain't no trick. This nose don't lie." He pressed his muzzle into Jude's palm, snuffling. "This is Renaissance Raines, body and soul. Jude Dubuisson's scent is all over this place and his soul"—

Sal lifted his noise into the air, paused for a second, and then, letting out a surprised little grunt, tilted it toward the books still piled on the living room floor — "is right over there."

Wait, what? she thought.

Following the psychopomp's nose like a pointing finger, Jude moved aside books and papers until she found the doubloon stamped with a stylized heart that contained her gift. She glanced back at the spot where she'd died and tried to picture it. The stabbing, the fall, and then? Someone going through her pockets, tossing this over their shoulder when it wasn't what they sought. She held the doubloon in her bare hand but didn't feel anything, no surge of lost things, nothing. Replaying the moment of death in her mind was disturbing, but even more so were the implications. An invisible attacker wielding a knife.

Maybe she'd been right to be suspicious of Regal all along.

"Sal," she said, "you're going to have to help me out here. This isn't exactly my realm of expertise." She held up the doubloon. "This is my — is Jude Dubuisson's soul?"

The dog cocked his head to the side. "Yep."

"Then how am I in here?" She tapped her temple. "Barren said we were sharing this body. I figured that meant my soul was hitching a ride."

Sal chuckled. "Oh, hell naw. You'd have a whole mess of conflict going on if we'd'a put Jude's soul in Renai's body. Jude's soul is male, for one. Demigod, for another. You think your thoughts and your meat is all you are? Shit ain't that simple. That whole body and soul di-whatcha-call-it? The fifty-fifty split? Life is more complicated than that. It's like this: What makes you *you?* Most people figure it's your brain. Memories and experiences and whatnot. And when you die, you got a little ghost brain that leaves your body and goes up to heaven, right? Wrong. Brain stays put. Brain ain't you. Brain ain't even the whole of you when you're still alive and in the body. You also got an energy, an engine that drives you from before you're born until after you're dead. That's part of what I do. I collect bits and pieces of that energy so it can be stitched together into something new and stuck in a baby about to get born. That's soul.

"But even that ain't you. The part that was around before this life and goes on into the next one, the essential part, the eternal part, that's what's riding around in Renai's mind and body right now. Got all kinds of names. These days we just call it 'essence.' Barren gave you that computer talk?"

Jude nodded, and Sal made a scoffing noise in his throat.

"That's bullshit. He's just trying to be modern. Used to do one that was all about steam locomotives. You ain't a program. You're a song. Play it from a record, sing it out loud, repeat it in your head; it don't matter. It's always the same song." He flopped onto the floor, his head resting on his paws. "But hell, I ain't good at the metra— uh, mystical—"

"Metaphysical?"

"Yeah, that. The important thing is, we ain't gotta track down your killer; what you got in your hand is all we need. We bring that back down to the Thrones—" Sal stopped talking, his head snapping up, his ears erect and tense. "Aw, crap."

"What?" Jude spun around in a slow circle, scanning the apartment. "What did you see?"

"The brain stays put," Sal said, repeating a part of his crash course in metaphysics. "If Cafard ain't took you, then someone else did. And if they got enough soul and enough know-how, they can, like, jump-start you. Only it ain't you, remember? It knows what you know, acts how you might act, but the essence of you is gone." He stood up and started to pace. "The Thrones don't send just anybody back. Even if you got a pretty little savior like Renaissance here."

Aww, Renai thought, *good doggie.*

"If they gave you a second chance to bring them your soul, they probably didn't want you rattlin' around up here without your training wheels. I don't suppose that thing in your hand is one of a kind, huh?"

Jude heard echoes of the gods demanding their own pieces of her: devotion, passion, blood, heart. All of it sounded a lot like soul to her.

Sal could see the answer on her face. "Shee-it. Guess we gotta follow this nose of mine after all." He paused, then turned his face down to his paws, only looking up at Jude with his eyes. "After you, uh, freshen up, that is."

"What?"

"I know we're on a deadline and all—'scuse the pun—but that body spent the past few days in a tomb, Jude." Sal lifted his nose to the air and gave a couple of delicate, poignant sniffs. "You're a little ripe."

After a quick phone call to the abbey to make sure Lydia was okay and one to Regal that went straight to voicemail, Jude showered with her eyes closed, coaxing Renai to come forward and handle things. Partly because she wasn't entirely sure where the line between guest and intruder was drawn in their relationship, but had a feeling that getting naked and handsy in a body that wasn't her own would cross it. But also because, when raiding the closet for some clothes that would fit a nineteen-year-old girl, a giggling thought of Renai's about getting into Jude's pants had flittered up from the back of her mind. That combined with Renai's memories of the first time they'd met left Jude feeling both flattered and skittish. So she was both scrubbed clean and happy that the experience was over when she left her bedroom, dressed in a "Save Our Cemeteries" T-shirt that had been too tight for Jude Dubuisson's body but hung loose on Renai's, and a pair of women's jean shorts belonging to a few-night stand—a history professor by day and a

French Quarter tour guide by night, if Jude remembered correctly —that Jude hadn't known were still in her closet.

Happy, anyway, right up until the moment she realized that the satchel had been stolen along with Jude's corpse.

It took about fifteen minutes of cursing and scouring the apartment before she stopped searching, but, in truth, she'd known it was gone the instant she saw the handful of magics that had spilled across the counter when the thief had snatched it up. It made sense, in a way. Jude had figured she'd been invited to the game because of something in the satchel, some lost thing that would enable the winning god to remake him- or herself into the luck god of New Orleans, so whoever had broken in here had probably had theft as much as murder on their mind.

Which explained why they'd searched Jude's pockets and why they'd taken the body: they were going to reanimate it and ask it where whatever it was they were looking for was hidden.

Jude shuddered. It was a horrible concept to consider, so she didn't. Instead, she made an inventory of the handful of magics left to her, aside from the physical charms and verbal spells she still seemed able to perform:

- the doubloon holding her gift, which only seemed to work when in contact with Jude's body;
- a dragon-scale amulet that would let her breathe underwater;
- a pair of magically loaded dice that would show whatever number you wanted, if you knew how to roll them properly;
- a jar of kraken ink that would leave an indelible stain on anything it touched;
- an ancient Chinese coin, round with a square snipped out of the center, that did some very useful things to ATMs;
- a puzzle box Jude had never managed to open;
- and the journal of old maps that had come from Thoth's library.

Jude was very happy to see that the journal hadn't fallen back into Scarpelli's clutches, but as lucky breaks went, it didn't inspire much confidence. It's not like the thunderbolt or a magic wand had fallen out.

Least it's not a total loss, Jude thought, reaching down for something that had spilled off the counter onto the floor. *The killer left us this, too.* Not only was the MP3 player miraculously not broken; it had half a charge left of its battery.

Ooh, Renai thought, *is that mine?*

Sure is. I was going to leave it for your folks so they'd have something to remember you by.

Fine as hell and thoughtful, too, Renai thought, her teasing tone somehow conveyed without a voice. *Why are all the good ones married, gay, or disembodied voices inside my head?*

You were a lot shyer the last time we met.

Death is a real confidence booster.

Sal coughed.

When Jude looked at him, the psychopomp licked his chops and then tossed his head toward the door. "If you two are done flirting," he said, "we kinda got some things to take care of?"

"Can you hear what we're thinking?"

"Nah. But pheromones don't lie."

Jude scooped the assorted magics and the MP3 player into an old gym bag, stuffed a handful of cash and streetcar tokens into her pocket, and followed Sal down to the street, where a black gleaming car idled at the curb. Jude cycled through a number of emotions in the space of a few seconds: a spike of fear at first, which calmed when she didn't taste the blood that would signal a vampire, then fear returning and skyrocketing right into panic when she remembered that the taste thing had belonged to another body. She readied herself to shout the word that meant *burn* and then run like hell, but then the car door opened, and the vehicle's shocks groaned, the chassis rocking back and forth as someone huge and heavy levered themselves out of the front seat: a gray hand, followed

by a suit coat, a bald gray head, and a massive body, with אֱמֶת —
the Hebrew word for truth — etched onto that cracked and craggy
forehead.

It was a golem dressed like a Secret Service agent, mirrored
sunglasses and all.

The golem's voice wasn't the resounding boom that Jude expected, but a rasping, hissing whisper. "Mourning sent me to collect you," the golem said.

Jude's thoughts raced. "Collect — oh, you must be looking for
Jude. He's upstairs. I'm just taking his dog for a walk. You can go
right on up. C'mon, boy." This last was said to Sal, who hesitated
only a fraction of a second before yipping and trotting along at
Jude's heels. They didn't make it far. A single gray palm blocked
their path.

"Very specific instructions. Collect the first person to leave."
The golem opened the rear door and waited. Jude considered her
original plan of yelling the word for *burn* and running, but quickly
dismissed it. Fire wouldn't do much to clay, and the golem moved
much more swiftly and smoothly than anyone that massive had
any right to.

Be interesting to see if Mourning recognizes me, Jude thought, re-
signed, and slid into the back seat.

"Dog stays," the golem said. "Not cleaning dog piss off my
seats."

It was very disconcerting to see a dog roll its eyes in disdain,
but Sal did it. To Jude, he said, "Might take a while to track this
scent anyway. I'll let you know when I find something."

Before Jude could argue, the door slammed shut, the car leaning alarmingly back and forth as the giant got in, and then eased
away from the curb. Just like that, she was on her way to see the
last person in the city she wanted to see. Aside from her murderer,
anyway.

It occurred to her then, too late, that they might be one and
the same.

CHAPTER TWENTY

THE GOLEM DIDN'T SPEAK much on the short drive downtown. Jude, hoping the magically animated statue might reveal something about Mourning's plans, asked why Regal hadn't been sent to pick her up. "Sloan woman don't work for Mourning no more," the golem said, which gave Jude enough to think about that she didn't say another word until they parked illegally on Canal Street.

"Why are we stopping?" she asked, sticking with the "I don't know what's going on—I'm just a teenage girl who walks the dog" plan until she knew it wouldn't work. The golem said nothing, just opened her door and waited, patient as the grave, for Jude to get out. When she did, the golem closed the door, locked it with a *chirp-chirp* from a key fob, and motioned with one massive hand for Jude to follow.

The golem led her around the corner of the building to a maintenance entrance. A homeless man in dirty, ragged clothing huddled against the door. As Jude dug in her pocket for some change, the man turned his face, revealing gray-streaked dreadlocks and the thin-wired spectacles of a scholar, dark mournful eyes that looked straight through Jude, a gaze turned inward: the zombie musician, Leon Carter.

Inside, Renai cursed.

Jude knelt beside Leon and reached out to grasp his shoulder. The contact sent a shock between them, an electric current of pain that knocked Jude to the ground. Though he looked whole, inside the musician was nothing but a raw, seeping wound. Leon jerked his head back and forth to a beat only he could hear, like an addict's convulsions. Jude didn't need a magic talent to tell her that Leon had lost something profound.

But what? Hadn't Regal said Leon was fine?

"What are you doing?" the golem asked.

Jude looked up at the broad, impassive face. "We have to help him," she said. "Don't you know who this is?"

"A nuisance. Like you." The golem pulled open the maintenance door, shoving Leon out of the way. "Let's go."

Jude stood and wiped the dirt from the seat of her shorts. She realized that Leon wasn't staring inward like she'd thought at first. He was watching the Canal Place building, his eyes traveling up and up, as though his vision could penetrate the floors that separated Mourning's office from the street.

Mourning, she thought, *of course.* "I don't know what he's done to you," she said to Leon, not caring if the golem heard, "but I promise I'll make it right." The golem ushered her none too gently into the cool and quiet of Canal Place, all but taking her hand and walking her to the elevators. Inside, Jude looked at herself in the mirrored walls, pleased to see that the wound from when Hē had killed Renai had healed without leaving a scar. She thought the young woman would be pretty pissed when she realized that the holes for all her piercings had closed up too, though.

Renai was too worked up about Leon to notice. *This is bad,* Renai thought. *This is so bad. The loa are gonna be beyond pissed. What's wrong with him?*

I don't know, Jude thought, *but I'm going to find out. What's Leon got to do with the loa? I know he made a deal with Legba but—*

Not Leon Carter. He's just the vessel. I'm talking about High John.

The golem pressed the sunburst medallion that granted access to Mourning's office into place, and Jude braced herself for the crazed dance of the elevator's travel. To Renai, Jude sent the mental equivalent of a confused shrug.

High John de Conquer? Renai thought, somehow making her mental voice sound incredulous. *He's King fucking Arthur as far as the loa are concerned, get it? We have to help him. You think death was bad? I don't even want to think about what Legba would do if he knew we saw this and didn't try to make it right.*

I said I'd help and I will, Jude thought. *Just try not to freak out in here, okay?*

Renai somehow managed to make an incredulous sound in her mind. *Whatever, dude. Can't be worse than death.*

As the elevator stopped its sickening sway and came to a stop, its door dinging open, Jude tried to keep her next thought to herself, that Renai was wrong, that what awaited them in this office might just be worse than death.

Jude couldn't decide if it was a good sign or not that the golem didn't follow her into Mourning's waiting room. The horned little man behind the desk didn't even look up when the elevator doors closed and vanished, simply said, "Mr. Mourning is not in at the moment. I'm afraid you'll have to come back later."

Jude's face flushed, rage coming on fast and hard, gripping her and shaking her down to the bone, like a fever. Tricked, maneuvered, murdered, robbed, and now whatever was going on with Leon, and Mourning was at the center of all of it. She didn't know why an angel was killing people or what it had to do with fortune gods and her own fate, but the being on the other side of that door did. She didn't really want to be here, but she'd be damned before she let this little prick send her away without a fight.

She'd only taken a few steps into the room when Scowl appeared from behind his desk. He bobbed from side to side as he walked, blocking the way between Jude and Mourning's door. From the waist down, Scowl had the hairy, naked hindquarters of a goat, his genitals swinging free, large and obscene. Jude closed the distance between them.

"You should not be here, Dubuisson," Scowl said, all pretense of absent-mindedness gone from his voice.

So much for the innocent little girl approach, Jude thought. "Tell me about it. But Mourning sent his goon after me, so here I am. Whether you like it or not, I'm going in."

"I sincerely doubt that," Scowl said, looking up at her, showing no discomfort despite the way he had to crane his neck back. "I am under my employer's protection, now. None of your cheap tricks will have any effect. Now go."

Jude lifted her hands and started to turn away, as if she'd been bluffing, then spun and kicked Scowl square in his naked balls, hard enough to lift him off his cloven hooves. The satyr, the imp —whatever he was—went down in a heap, and Jude stepped over him on her way past. A better person would feel no satisfaction acting in such a way, but Jude's essence, the core identity that apparently transcended time and even death, had always been a bit of a bastard. The corners of her lips twitched, the ghost of a smile illuminated by the glare of Mourning's office as Jude threw the door open.

As always, the first step inside was blinding, the inhabitant's presence like the white-hot center of a cutting torch flame. When her vision cleared, she saw Mourning lounged back in his seat, bare brown feet propped up on the desk. He wore a pair of crisp eggshell linen pants and an oxford shirt as black and glossy as oil, those sapphire eyes betraying nothing, not surprise at Jude's entrance, nor anger or disappointment at the way the door had slammed open. He merely held up one immaculate finger, the casual dismissal freezing Jude mid-step. Mourning kept his attention on the elegant ivory curve of a telephone receiver in his other hand. "Do we have an understanding?" he asked. "Good. See to it."

Mourning hung up, and the phone vanished as he turned — chair swiveling without a sound, feet making a smooth and effortless glide to the floor — his piercing and weighing gaze toward Jude. A Cheshire cat grin curled across his face, his skin the same reddish brown as the clay that Jude had walked on beneath the Mississippi, and he spoke, not to Jude, but to whoever occupied one of the other chairs in the room, hidden by the high back. "Look who has joined us," he said, his voice purring, lisping, hypnotic, "just as I promised."

A list of the worst possible people to be sitting in that chair ran through Jude's mind, but the person waiting for her when she crossed that checkerboard floor certainly wasn't on it: Celeste Dorcet.

Careful Jude, Renai thought. *I've got a bad feeling about this.*

Renai might have been quoting a movie, but she was right; Celeste wasn't herself. Clearly, a loa was riding her. Whoever it was wore a three-piece suit in dark reds: scarlet vest, wine pocket square, even a tie pin capped off with a garnet. Something in the insolent smirk, the overtly casual drape of one leg over the other knee, told Jude that it wasn't Legba. No matter their name, their presence here meant that Jude had been played. Probably from the very beginning.

Of course, she'd had that impression for a while now.

"Such a grim visage, M. Dubuisson," Mourning said, using the gender-neutral honorific of a single letter, polite to a fault. "Perhaps a cocktail will remedy that. Mr. Cross, I trust you will have the usual?" Mourning held out his hand as he stood, gesturing for Jude to take a seat in the leather armchair next to the loa in red. Mourning moved to a fully stocked bar that hadn't been there a moment before, glass ringing against glass as he pulled down bottles of rum and cognac and bitters.

Jude sat, the leather groaning around her, her fists clenched between her knees. "Coffee for me," she said, not surprised to find a steaming cup of chicory already waiting at her elbow, but a little unnerved when her first taste revealed it to have been served black, the way Renai's soul and this body liked it, not the cream-and-sugar way Jude preferred.

This guy is good, Renai thought.

You have no idea.

Mourning brought Cross his drink: half a glass of neat rum, into which he poured black sand from a small burlap sack with a faded label that read HAZARD POWDER COMPANY in a semicircle around two crossed cannons.

Jude and Renai shared a moment of revelation with the clarity of a fired pistol. Only one loa took his rum with a chaser of gunpowder: Kalfou, the dark and angry side of Papa Legba — the Petwo half — sinister in all the ways Legba was benevolent. Calling himself Mr. Cross was a joke that came from his title: Mait' Carrefour, Master of the Crossroads and Closer of the Ways. When Haitian slaves studied Roman Catholicism, they recognized Legba in St. Peter, the keeper of the keys to Heaven. When they looked for Kalfou, they found Satan.

Jude took a sip of her coffee and wished she'd asked for something stronger. And yet, the rich scent and the burst of flavor and the lingering bitterness combined in a sense of protection and family, a connection to a whole host of good feelings that were not Jude's, but were a conspiracy of this body's tongue and sinuses and synapses unveiling Renai's memories of early mornings with her father as a child. Memories that Jude allowed herself to take comfort in, even though she knew they were stolen.

Mourning leaned against his desk, taking a long swallow from a glass of amber-colored liquor with a sigh of delight. He glanced at the watch on the inside of his wrist, and his full lips quirked in a quickly smothered frown. "Now," he said, "I trust you are prepared to discuss the exceedingly grave and urgent matter for which you were so—crave pardon—indecorously requisitioned?"

"Love to," Jude said, managing to fill her voice with far more confidence than she felt, "but aren't we missing someone?"

"I confess, I am at a loss as to who that might be."

"Regal Sloan. Where is she?"

Mourning exchanged a glance with Cross. "Much as it pains me to admit it, M. Dubuisson, I do not have that particular piece of information at my disposal, nor anything as might regard Ms. Sloan at present. She is no longer employed under the auspices of this organization, nor has she been for quite some time."

"But she's the one who brought me the invitation to the card game."

"Correct. I engaged her as a courier, as I believed—correctly as it happens—that a previous acquaintance might more readily secure your diligence and confidence, but I did so in an entirely unaffiliated capacity. 'Freelance' was the term she preferred. If you will recall, I attempted to obtain your services in a similar fashion, an entreaty you resoundingly decried."

Jude took a long swallow of her coffee to keep from screaming. The steaming liquid went down hot, and the fact that the pain felt good was probably not a good thing. The whole thing had been a lie. Or worse: a trick. And Jude had walked right into it. Swallowed the bait, took the hook, and then, when she was of no more use, she'd been gutted like a fish. Fire bloomed in her belly that had nothing to do with the hot coffee.

Two can play that game, Queens.

"Fine," Jude said, "you win. Regardless of how I got here, you got what you wanted: me in a room full of deities gambling to be the next luck god of New Orleans, and at least one of them is murdering the others while they wait for my hand to be revealed. I've got a day left to live and no more outs left to play, so it's time to stop fucking around. What's the scheme? What is it you want me to do?"

Mourning blinked, a slow flutter of his eyelids. "I must beg your indulgence once more," he said, the hissing of his sibilants becoming more pronounced. "Your reference has caught me unawares. To which 'scheme' are you referring?"

Cross snorted and emptied his drink in one swallow. "He means *your* scheme, podna. He don't get it yet. He's trying to get you to reveal your master plan."

"Ah, so I see," Mourning said. "You have mistaken me for a creature engaged in a finite enterprise. I am no Atropos, to shear off the thread when it has reached its appointed culmination." He pantomimed with two fingers a pair of scissors snipping closed. "Nor am I the watchmaker so oft alluded to, building my little wind-up toys and watching them run." Mourning spun his glass around and around in a tight circle. "No, beginnings and endings bore me in every conceivable way, M. Dubuisson. I am precisely what is indicated just here."

At this, he leaned over and gave the nameplate on his desk one sharp rap with his knuckle.

"Management. I exert my influence over the machinations of others, disrupting or enhancing as the situation warrants. So while your presumption that I have built this entire house of cards of my own volition is flattering, it presupposes that I have the capability or the desire to do so. Simply put, the game did not originate by my design, M. Dubuisson, nor do I have anything more than conjecture as to how it will conclude." Mourning circled back around behind his desk, moving with the casual grace, the rolling-hip gait of an alley cat. "My concern is not which of the deities is ultimately victorious. It is in ensuring that whoever holds the winning hand is in some way indebted to me. Which leads us to the nature of our current palaver. Mr. Cross?"

Cross launched to his feet as if sitting still so long had been painful. Two long strides brought him to the bar, where he took the bottle of rum and left the glass. Gunpowder or no, he bit the cork out, spat it on the floor, and drank in gulps from the bottle. "Bright Eyes here likes the sound of his own fuckin' voice, don't he? I think he done talked enough for the three of us. Word is, you pissed in the vampire's cornbread, got him riled up but good. That true?"

"I stopped him, if that's what you're asking."

Cross huffed, an indignant, offended sound. "You full of cacca-shit. Words ain't nothin' but stanky breath without something to show. So how 'bout it? You got something to show me aside from them pretty titties of yours?"

Jude tried to think of something, anything else she could give them that would count as proof, but even if the satchel hadn't been stolen, she only had the one compelling piece of evidence. She dug through her duffel bag and took out the journal of maps she'd stolen from Scarpelli. "How's this for proof?"

"For a dead vampire," Cross said, "that looks a hell of a lot like a book."

Jude couldn't ignore the bait, even though she knew that's exactly what it was. "Never said I killed him," she said, "just that I stopped him." Jude tossed Bienville's maps onto Mourning's desk, her anger starting to get the better of her. "He was using this to turn the city. I'm not sure how." Mourning snatched it up with the fluid, predatory speed of a striking hawk. He studied its cover and spine as he eased into his chair, opening the journal and turning its pages with languid, casual flicks of his hand. At one point, he pressed his nose to the crease between pages and made an audible sniff.

"Ah," he said after a few tense moments, holding the book out for Cross. "You see how clever our mutual adversary has proven himself? Scarpelli is attempting to access the city's four qualities of being." Cross examined it in much the same way, but whereas

Mourning had been efficient and delicate, almost effete, Cross treated the journal with a savage disdain.

While he was occupied, Renai whispered to Jude, *Any idea what they're talking about?*

I think so, Jude replied. She started to answer more completely, but realized that even sharing thoughts back and forth like this, it would take too long to consider and articulate into words. So, she tried something else. She opened up a part of herself to Renai, letting part of the demigod essence riding along in the young woman's mind flow into her. The experience was something like recalling a dream days later: a series of thoughts and impressions that were suddenly there, as if they'd been waiting there all along.

Most people—even those who think they understand the supernatural—really have no idea how complex and how strange things can be. Humans easily recognize the gods that are most like themselves. But in the same way that gods come in a variety of shapes and sizes, no one type of consciousness has an exclusive right to godhood. Animals have their own gods, and so do trees, and computers, and storms. There are deities of mountain and ocean for whom a single prayer has lasted longer than the whole span of human existence, and there are virus gods, microscopic and fierce, whose entire immortalities pass unnoticed before our eyes.

Cities, too, can be gods. Some of the ancient city-gods have been asleep for centuries, places like Byblos and Nin, Samarqand and Ilè-Ife. There are other older cities that are still awake, mad old London and reserved Beijing. Jerusalem, who argues with herself in four different voices, and Mexico City, who only answers to the name Tenōchtitlān. The younger cities—Sydney and New York, Tokyo and Brussels and Chicago—are bursting with energy and myth, trying to figure out who exactly they are. New Orleans might be young and small among city-gods, since most cities take centuries to develop enough history and charm and myth to attain an identity, if ever, but the Crescent City has been a god almost from her very beginning.

Sal had said that humans were composed of more than body and soul, that the ephemeral aspects of existence could be split into at least two parts — essence and energy — one that was eternal and one that got recycled. Jude had been taught a similar thing, long ago, about cities. That their souls, for want of a better term, were three-part in nature: Strength, Luck, and Will, represented by physical aspects of the city. In New Orleans, strength was a musician whose name Jude had never learned; Luck was a fortune god named Dodge; and Will was a magician, the man who had taught Jude all of this: Eli Constant. Mourning seemed to be implying that there was a fourth aspect that Eli hadn't told Jude about.

In the handful of seconds it took for all of this to flow into Renai, related pieces of knowledge washed back into Jude. The three-in-one concept of a soul seemed immediately familiar to Renai, like the human experience writ large. She'd learned, having been dead longer than Jude, that our own consciousness was more like a braid than a thread: the essence and energy that Sal had mentioned, but also a third piece, a thing that stayed with the body when you died — a thing the dead called your "voice." If essence was your identity, the part of you that made you *you*, and energy or soul was the spark that gave you life, voice was your ability to impact the world, the part of you that didn't just observe or exist but the part that *changed*.

The part that could make magic.

That part of you stayed behind when you died, which was why the newly dead could not speak. In fact, none of the dead could speak in the truest sense of the word; they merely shared ideas and concepts via something closer to telepathy. What Dodge had told her, in that card room in the afterlife, made more sense now, that if the dead could speak, none of them would be dead. That loss of voice, of the ability to impact the world, was the most crucial line between life and death.

Jude was shaken from her shared daydream with Renai by Cross slapping the journal onto Mourning's desk and growling, a low, pissed-off rumbling deep in his chest.

"I trust this satisfies the condition of our arrangement?" Mourning asked.

"Yeah, yeah," Cross said, "deal's a deal." They shook, and then Cross turned to Jude. For a fraction of a second, the loa riding Celeste was revealed, as young as Legba was old, hat pushed back on his head by a pair of horns, black tears leaking from his eyes. Jude blinked, and the red-suited figure wore Celeste's body once more. "Be seeing you," Cross said, with a flick of his hat brim that seemed, somehow, vulgar. He went to the door and then was gone.

Jude and Renai and the bright god shared an uncomfortable silence, the last embers of daylight fading away from the view at Mourning's back. "Now," Mourning said, gliding to his feet and returning to the bar without making a sound, "shall we discuss your recompense immediately, or do you require a measure of fawning gratitude to accompany it?"

What, Renai thought, more a statement than a question.

He's talking about payment. I did him a favor. He can't have a debt like that hanging over his head.

Maybe he can help us with High John! Jude felt Renai's body perk up, posture straightening, toes curling, with an excitement that wasn't Jude's, a reminder that she was only a guest in this body.

A handful of things clamored for Jude's attention: that she needed to track down the corpse of Jude Dubuisson and the killer, who she'd all but decided had to be Regal; that she needed to help Leon somehow, that—thankful as she was that she'd managed to keep her thoughts about Mourning away from Renai—she thought the bright god was more likely responsible for Leon's condition than he was the solution; that she no longer saw a path through the next couple of days that didn't end with her soul devoured by gods or back in front of the Thrones.

All of this, yet what came out of her mouth was "How about

you start by explaining what Scarpelli was doing with that damned book?" Renai groaned in the back of her head.

Mourning finished making his drink and returned to his chair. He ran his tongue along the edges of his teeth before he spoke. "Four qualities comprise everything that exists: you, the chair you're sitting in, this office, the Sazerac in this glass" — he smiled without humor — "even me. Anything that is a real and true object shares these fundamental elements: its relationship with other objects in space, the changes in those relationships over time, the ability to influence other objects, and the object's understanding of itself. Simply put, to exist, a thing must have shape, duration, impact, and essence. This object we collectively refer to as 'New Orleans' is in jeopardy because these qualities are in jeopardy."

He paused, a teacher waiting for his more obtuse pupils to catch up.

"Take my drink, for example." He shifted his grip on the glass, holding it with this thumb and two fingers, turning it so the amber liquid caught the light. "It has a shape, dictated by the container which holds it. It has a particular duration, a series of moments from the one where I concocted it to the one where I consume the last of it. I taste it, and it gives me pleasure; its alcohol numbs my senses just slightly, and so it influences the world around it through its existence. It also has an essence, the degree to which it aligns itself to the ideal cocktail. Four qualities in harmonious equilibrium, allowing my drink to exist. If one of those qualities is forced to change" — he let the glass slip from his fingers, where it shattered against the chessboard marble floor, the scent of liquor and anise bursting into the air — "they *all* change. New shape. New duration, new perception, new essence, you see?"

He reached across the desk to Bienville's journal, turning to Pauger's map, the design that laid out and named the streets of the French Quarter, the original city. "This is the shape of the city," he said. "This is the glass she's poured into. Symbolic, most assuredly, but symbols matter. Symbols can be corrupted. Or destroyed. Or even, rarely, restored." Mourning made a twisting gesture with his hand and held his glass once more, not a drop spilled. He sipped, delicate as a hummingbird drinking nectar, and leaned back in his chair, the leather creaking.

Everything slid into focus. She didn't have the entire picture yet, but viewed in this light, so much of the past few days made more sense. Scarpelli hadn't cared who the card game declared the next Luck, because he'd planned on changing the shape of the city into one where only he could assume that role. The other gods were willing to gamble on it—and kill for it—because being the Luck of New Orleans wasn't just a title; it meant you were a fundamental influence on the destiny of an entire conscious, magical city. And the big question, the one that had plagued Jude for as long as she'd known the nature of the prize: Why would Dodge give away such power? Why have the game at all?

Answer: He hadn't had a choice.

She pictured the glass shattering against the floor, and news footage of the levees breaking and the lake flowing in. The shape of New Orleans had changed six years ago, her body pierced and wounded, and so her soul and her essence and all the rest had to change as well. Dodge had the winning hand; if Jude threw the game—not that she had any concept of how to do that yet—if her fate wasn't triumphant or tragic enough to overcome the hand Dodge had played, then he would be the city's Luck once again.

Mourning said symbols could be restored. But what would that even look like?

"What about Leon Carter?" Jude asked, except she hadn't really meant to say the words out loud. That had been Renai, pushing from the back of her mind.

Mourning laughed, a sound so rich and pleasant it nearly disguised its own cruelty. "Ah yes," he said, "the lamentable Mr. Carter. He has indeed found himself in a situation of most grievous vexation." Mourning reached into the empty space beneath his desk and pulled out a small black case. Renai lurched forward so frantically that Jude had to clench her hands on the armrests to remain in her seat. Renai was either a Sweetwater Carter fan or had siphoned knowledge of the case's contents from Jude's thoughts, but she certainly recognized it. Mourning spun the case around and, with precise, emphatic, gloating gestures, flicked open one clasp, and then another, and then eased open the lid to reveal Leon Carter's brass horn.

The one he'd told the crowd at the Maple Leaf he'd traded his soul for.

"A lesson may be gleaned, here," Mourning said, "concerning the ineluctable perils of storing one's more ephemeral qualities within a physical receptacle. I confess, my sole intent in acquiring this particular item lay entirely in securing the allegiance of Atibon Legba, but as a result of this" — he tapped a finger against the journal — "bringing so swift an accordance with Mr. Cross, I find myself without any true purpose as regards it."

Knowing that there must be some trick hidden here, some tripwire she hadn't yet seen, Jude responded cautiously. "So, let's just call it a fair trade, then. The book for the trumpet."

Mourning feigned a pained expression. "Perhaps you have misconstrued the nature of our discussion, M. Dubuisson. I have already dispersed the agreed-upon remuneration for this trifle, and, with a far more valuable asset than a mere musical instrument, I have revealed to you the nature of this city's predicament — indeed, the nature of all things. No, if you hope to gain possession of Mr. Carter's horn, I fear I will accept only one specie in exchange . . . *You*, M. Dubuisson. As has been true for quite some time, it is my most fervent desire for you to be engaged in my service once again."

Do it, Renai thought. *Let's be real here — you're already dead. You can save High John right now if you just say yes.*

Doing her best to tune Renai out, Jude considered what she knew of the bright god who referred to himself as "Management," including who — and what — she suspected Mourning might be:

another Trickster in a city rotten with them—one who, like the Scorpion on the back of the Frog, could only do what was in his nature. Jude reached down into the duffel bag at her feet and pulled out the pair of magically loaded dice. A petty hustle to try against a god, but Jude's bag of tricks was getting pretty light. "Why don't we make it interesting?"

Mourning tapped his lips with a finger. "What did you have in mind?"

"One throw. Five or a seven and I walk out of here with the trumpet, free and clear. Anything else and I'll come work for you in exchange."

Mourning released a sharp bark of amusement. "A marvelous suggestion," he said, "but ultimately without merit, as I fear your definition of 'interesting' seems exclusively one wherein there is no increased reward for me. May I counter?" He didn't wait for a response. "One cast of the dice, as you said, but if the sum is anything other than five or seven, then your term of service is dictated by the dice. Shall we say, one year for each pip?"

Something was wrong here. Mourning had agreed too easily, had to have some counter-trick of his own planned. Before Jude could think of some way of climbing out of the shit pile she'd talked herself into, Renai seized control of her own mouth. "Done," she said.

Mourning smiled sharp enough to leave a scar.

Renai faded into the back of her mind, a sensation of chagrin, maybe, but not guilt; as far as she was concerned, this simply needed to happen. No matter the cost.

Mourning gestured for Jude to make the throw. Heart sinking, Jude stood and rolled the dice in her hand. She tried to tell herself that this was a good omen. Surely Mourning knew that no matter what the dice read, if Jude failed she was lost. Mourning wouldn't be able to collect his years of service, not unless he descended into Hell and dragged Jude's soul back from the Abyss. In a way, Jude *couldn't* lose. So why, then, was the blue-eyed god's smile so wide?

Jude blew on the dice in her fist to activate the spell and released them, holding the number seven in her mind. The dice danced and clattered and bounced across the glass, first two, then four, then a handful. Jude lowered her head, unable to watch. When the rattling stopped, she forced herself to look. Dice covered the table—well over a hundred—each marked with a single black dot.

"Most unusual," Mourning said. "But a deal is, as they say, a deal." He closed the trumpet case with an abrupt *snap-snap* of the clasps and spun it so that the handle was next to Jude's hand. When Jude picked it up, it was far lighter than her destiny ought to be. "While I would much prefer it if you began immediately," Mourning continued, "I understand that you are as yet under obligation to others. Shall we reconvene when you have resolved your dealings, then?"

He searched Jude's face, clicked his tongue at what he saw there.

"If it brings you a measure of solace, M. Dubuisson, know that your former teacher made a similar arrangement with me some time ago. The outcome was identical." At those words, Jude stopped trying to count the dice, knew exactly what Mourning meant, understood how Eli had become the Magician of New Orleans. Knew how much of a debt she herself now owed to Mourning.

Two hundred years.

Mourning plucked two of the dice from the table and cupped them in his fist, his gestures as deft and as theatrical as any stage magician's. He held this hand out to Jude, unfurling his fingers. The two cubes resting on Mourning's palm had reversed their colors: solid black with white pips marking their values. "As a show of good faith—a signing bonus, one might call it, were one so inclined—I will reward you with an equal measure of knowledge as I paid for the journal. One question"—he glanced at the watch on the inside of his wrist—"and then I really must consider our business concluded."

At this point, only one question really mattered. "My last card," Jude said, "what should I turn over? What fate do I need to win?"

If she hadn't just endured Mourning's gloating, preening joy, she might have believed the expression of sorrow that twisted across the bright-eyed god's immaculate face; it was that good. For once, Mourning spoke without ornament or elaboration.

"You *can't* win," he said. "Losing this game has always been your fate."

Jude clenched her jaw to stop the laughter that threatened to bubble up from deep within her, the desperate, panicked kind that wouldn't end if she let it even start.

The deck was stacked. The game was rigged. As it always was. Jude felt a part of herself shift, stretching muscles long unused, relaxing a clenched fist to reveal the old Jude, the bastard who always came out on top and didn't give a fuck who got burned in the process. The old Jude grinned.

"I was hoping you'd say that," she said.

Not waiting or caring for a response, Jude snatched up the trumpet on her way out the office door. It dumped her out into a restroom—bleach struggling to overcome urine and harsh fluorescent light—in the Aquarium of the Americas, just a few minutes' walk from where she'd left Leon. She passed through the entryway where a two-story fountain murmured—a trickle of water spilling over huge, overlapping bronze scales belonging to some metal leviathan—out into the heat and the view of the Mississippi, her steps quick and her thoughts whirling.

She found Salvatore waiting with Leon, the dog-shaped spirit lying at the zombie's feet. "This is so bad," Sal said. "Legba's gonna shit *fire*. Do you know who this is?" The psychopomp didn't look up until Jude snapped open the case and showed him Leon's trumpet. When he saw it, the dog leaped to his feet. Leon just stared, head still bobbing back and forth. "Where was it?" Sal asked. "How did you get it back?"

In a swift, self-deprecating rant, Jude caught Sal up on all that had happened in Mourning's office and what it all meant. Sal turned one dark eye up toward Jude and sighed. "You just can't win for losing, can you?"

It was worth it, Renai thought. *If it saves High John, you didn't lose. Not really.*

Don't play any game you can't win, Jude thought, quoting Dodge. But Mourning and everyone else said it was her fate to lose. So how could she avoid playing? Just like that, the answer — or at least the beginnings of one — rolled through Jude's mind.

It wasn't a *plan* so much as a *trick* — and Jude couldn't do it alone.

Sal made a high-pitched, anxious whine and tugged at the trumpet case, reminding Jude of what she'd come here to do. She'd hoped Leon's personality would return as soon as the zombie's fingers touched the brass of his trumpet, but aside from a long, gasping shudder, Leon showed no reaction when she pressed the horn into the musician's hands. Even bending stiff fingers to the buttons and raising the mouthpiece to his lips had no effect. Jude turned to Sal, hoping the psychopomp might have some advice, since souls were his area of expertise, but one look at the pacing, whining dog told Jude he wouldn't be any help.

He needs the music, Renai thought.

I know, Jude thought, *I'm trying, but —*

No. Renai seized control of her body once again, casting Jude to the side as though she were no more than a passing thought. Which, in a way, she was. Renai dug through the duffel bag and came up with the MP3 player, said a little prayer to Legba when she saw it still had some battery left, and twisted the buds deftly and gently into Leon's ears. She scrolled through the menu until she found Leon's first album, *Sweetwater,* in a playlist of New Orleans artists labeled, simply, HOME. She cranked the volume all the way up and hit play.

Long, low notes drifted from the headphones' speakers, muted by Leon's ears. A flicker of recognition passed across the zombie's eyes, a shift that could almost be felt in the air around them. Sal must have felt it, too, because he stopped pacing and dropped to his haunches.

Leon's fingers twitched on the buttons, his tongue trembling across cracked and swollen lips. The first notes he played were hoarse, discordant, the death rattle of some wading bird. Leon bent low and tried again, this time managing a weak, hesitant riff. The musician rose to his feet, cracking his knuckles and rolling his shoulders and shaking the headphones out of his ears. He closed his eyes, and where Jude expected to see pleasure or relief, the look on Leon's face was one of pure determination. The zombie drew in a long, deep breath, pursed his lips against the mouthpiece, and blew a note the angels on Judgment Day would envy. Fingers stabbing the buttons, cheeks puffed out as taut and round as baseballs, Leon leaned into his horn and played. As his song grew louder and stronger and more intricate, Jude felt a weight from her heart vanish, unsure if it belonged to her, or Renai, or both of them. Leon Carter played himself back from the brink of ruin, and the sound of it was pure joy.

When Leon finished, Jude looked down at Sal, who was, for once, speechless. After a few long moments of silence broken only by the sounds of the city around them, the corners of Sal's mouth tugged back into a doggie grin. "So," he said, "you guys wanna go and see a dead body?"

CHAPTER TWENTY-ONE

HE IS TRAVELING on a road that will become famous for his experience: blinding light, scales falling from his eyes, and a conversion to aid those he once persecuted. He is preparing for battle, weighing the necessity of fighting against the honor of making peace, when he realizes that his chariot driver is, in fact, the embodiment of the universe. He is meditating beneath a tree, withstanding the onslaught of the demonic army sent to distract him and the lust spirits sent to seduce him in order to achieve true Enlightenment. He returns from the mountaintop with the Law burned into stone tablets by Celestial fire, his hair turned snowy white by the shock of what he has seen. She bites into the fruit that the Serpent convinced her to taste, and immediately knows what is good, knows what is evil, knows that she is naked. He is hunting and stumbles upon the goddess unclothed; he is a stag pursued and then devoured by his own hounds. Knowledge can come suddenly, or gently. A light from on high or a voice from within. It can transform or destroy or condemn or embolden. The only thing an epiphany cannot be is denied.

From the street, Audubon Park seemed filled with ink. The lights had been shut off, and the oak canopy overhead blocked out any of the weak moonlight that managed to penetrate the clouds above. The summer air was sticky and cloying, even at night. By day, the park spread itself open, a bright and verdant garden. Once twilight fell, though, it became a pool of shadow in the bend of the river, a dark place for doing dark things.

Jude thought of her mother's depiction of Scarpelli's New Orleans, the shadow with teeth, and shivered. The vampire's mansion, or what was left of it, was just at the end of St. Charles; the park was practically his backyard. Behind her, as though designed for contrast, Loyola University's front lawn shone like the dawn, floodlights burning away the night, illuminating a statue of Christ, his arms thrown wide, comforting.

On the streetcar ride Uptown, Sal had told Jude and Renai that he'd found the corpse of Jude Dubuisson, alive and refusing to talk, hanging from a tree deep in the park. Before Jude could ask if Sal had seen who had taken the body, Sal told them that he'd fled as soon as he saw the corpse, not wanting to take the risk of getting caught. His exact words were "Screw discretion and valor — running away was the better part of staying the fuck alive."

So it wasn't exactly a surprise when, after Jude told Renai and Sal her idea for how to proceed, the psychopomp plopped his dog's haunches on the sidewalk and licked his muzzle. "This is as far as I go," he said.

"You're kidding."

"'Fraid not. I look like a warrior to you? Psychopomps are guides, genius. I got enough juju to drag you back downstairs if you make a run for it, but that's about it. I'm a lot of things, but

274 • BRYAN CAMP

impervious to harm I ain't. So don't take this personal or nothing, but consider yourself guided."

"Would you do it for a Scooby snack?"

"Get bent," Sal said, but his lips tugged back in a doggie grin all the same.

"What, then? If I'm hanging from a tree in there, I can't do this without you."

Sal whined and started wagging his tail, not the happy one, but the agitated "don't know where that scary noise is coming from" wag. "You're good with lost things, yeah?"

"If I'm in my own body, I am. You help me with that, I'll owe you. What did you lose?"

"Me." Sal scrambled to his feet and started pacing, an unnerving thing to see a dog doing. If he were a human, he'd be chain-smoking. "You ever see *It's a Wonderful Life?* Jimmy Stewart, Donna Reed? Course you have, everyone's seen that fuckin' thing. Well, I'm Mr. Potter. Not, you know, literally. I'm what happens if Jimmy was him. Shit, I'm not saying this right."

"You were human once," Jude said, trying to keep Sal talking, "and an angel showed you what the world would be if you'd never been born."

"Close enough. And it was better. Way better. Wonder if that shit-heel got his wings for that. Anyway, that's how I ended up doing this part-time psychopomp gig. Not much work for a fella who ain't supposed to exist. I'm fine with it, really. Mostly. Once you make the choice, it all goes away like it never was, 'cause it never was, you know? But lately I've had this . . . itch, I guess. This feeling that there was one good thing in that crap life of mine that I miss, even though I don't remember it."

Jude squatted down, so her eyes were level with Sal's. "I promise you that if I survive all of this with my abilities intact, I'll do whatever I can to help you."

Sal's wag was a happy one now, fervent and bouncing. "Jude, I could just lick you."

"I'd rather you didn't. How about we shake on it?"

His dog's paw was halfway raised when he realized Jude was smirking at him. "Aww, dammit. Why you gotta ruin the moment?" He shook himself. "Okay, stand back. For what you got planned, I gotta change."

Sal opened his mouth, first a yawn, then a gaping stretch, jaws straining with the effort. Sides heaving, he coughed and hacked, a dark shape wriggling in the back of his throat. Sal spat it free, and then sank to the concrete, deflating, suddenly nothing but fur and teeth. The dark thing shook itself and stood on two spindly legs, revealed the raven shape Sal had worn when Jude first met him. The raven folded one wing and did a little bow. "Not bad, huh?"

Jude gave him a golf clap, poked the empty skin with the toe of her sneaker. "Does that hurt?"

Sal flapped his wings, drying the dog's saliva from his feathers. "Nah. Getting the dog out of the bird, though? That hurts like hellfire. I should know." Jude laughed. She turned away from Sal's furry remains and looked back at the park. Her former body was somewhere in those acres of trees and darkness according to Sal's nose, and hopefully the satchel as well. She had almost nothing in terms of planning or backup, and no weapons to speak of.

But she was half Trickster. She'd always been more lucky than good.

Jude tied her dreads back with a handkerchief, made a "follow me" gesture to the psychopomp, and stepped into the first of the park's shadows. Sal spread his tail feathers in a wide fan and then hopped, with a couple of bouncing flaps of his wings, onto her shoulder. "Let's go see a man about a corpse."

Damn, Renai thought, *good line. I had a whole thing about "going to raise hell," but his is better.*

It was then, with her backup treating this like an action movie, that Jude accepted that she might very well die again before the night was over.

Though her vision eventually adjusted to the darkness, only

Sal's whispered instructions kept her from wandering in a blind circle. She followed the psychopomp's directions — trying not to think about the fact that he normally led the dead to their just rewards — past the indistinct shapes of public restrooms and picnic shelters — some brick, some fitted stone — quaint in the daylight but little more than ruins in the night. She stumbled around squat clumps of shrubs and over the limbs of oak trees that had sagged to the ground under their own weight, blundering through the obstacles that seemed to her like a charcoal sketch on tar paper, lines and clots of black on black. She had ways of conjuring up some light, but they were more likely to reveal her to her enemies than illuminate her path. Water gurgled somewhere out of sight, an artificial fountain in one of the ponds that pockmarked the greenery.

Her heart leaped against her chest, her every footstep careful, her limbs straining to move, to run, her whole body trembling in anticipation. Not with fear. She *should* be afraid, she knew, picking her way through the darkness toward whichever god waited for her in the night, whichever deity had killed her once already. The first attack had been a coward's strike, though, an assassination. Killed unawares, like a sick dog. Things would go differently this time. Instead of the acid bite of fear, Jude tasted the cayenne and burnt sugar flavor of flames on her tongue.

Jude rounded a curve in the path and saw light up ahead, felt the sauna's heat-like pressure against her skin that told her magic was being performed. It didn't feel like Scarpelli's cold, sterile magic, nor did the light have that echoing choir quality that Hē produced. Not one of the enemies she knew about, then. Someone else. Some*thing* else. She stepped off the path and into thick, damp grass, walking toward the light. The chirping insects around her fell silent, replaced by the sounds of flames crackling, of drums pounding, of voices chanting.

Jude peered through a gap between branches and saw who she

faced, and suddenly wished she had something—*anything*—more martial than a bottle of ink in her duffel bag.

Three figures capered around a bonfire in the small clearing: a hulking, vaguely man-shaped thing made of vine and branch and bark, like an oak tree that had gained sentience; an emaciated, filthy man with the head of a canine, rabid saliva frothing from his jaws; and Celeste Dorcet, wearing the red suit she'd had on in Mourning's office, but with bare feet and Jude's magician bag slung over her shoulder. The drumming was the sound of the tree-man thumping oaken arms against his own trunk. The canine-headed man slapped the ground and tore up fistfuls of grass and earth, howling. Between one blink and the next, Jude saw the loa who rode Celeste, a handsome young man with horns curving up from his forehead: Cross.

Within her mind, Renai let out a little gasp of dismay.

I take it you know them? Jude thought.

Cross you've already met, Renai thought. *The one riding the tree is Grand Bois, the loa who presides over nature. The third one is Baron Criminel, who is the Petwo side of Barren, like Cross is for Legba. They are the three sorcerers, and that means there is some serious dark magic happening here.*

"Sheee-it," Sal muttered in Jude's ear. "You gone and pissed off just about every death god in the city, ain't ya? Got you trussed up good, too, just like I said."

Almost hidden within the canopy of the oaks overhead, hanging by a rope or a vine by one ankle—his unbound leg tucked up behind the other and his arms restrained behind his back—was Jude's corpse. An odd gag or mask of some kind obscured the lower part of his face. Jude felt a small whisper of pride, when it became obvious that the body, even devoid of the essence that rode in Renai, was refusing to cooperate. Apparently being a little bit of a bastard went straight down to the bone.

Jude dug in her pocket for the doubloon and held it up to the raven, who snatched it with his beak. Sal's weight vanished from her shoulder in a flutter of wings that sounded thunderous to Jude's strained nerves. If the raven was discovered before accomplishing his task, the whole fragile plan fell apart.

What we need, Renai thought, *is a distraction.*

No. Stick to the plan. Shove me out and then run like hell.

Your "plan" is more a loose collection of ideas that boil down to "try not to die." And what it needs, like any good plan, is a diversion. Besides, I feel crappy about that dice thing in your boss's office. Good luck!

And then, without a chance to offer any word in protest, Renai cast Jude out of her mind and body with the ease of shoving aside an unpleasant thought . . . which, in a way, was what Jude was.

It was very strange to be a being of pure essence. Some quality of the Underworld had let Jude practice self-deception about having a body, but now there could be no illusion, no hiding the lack of form, of substance. For one thing, there was a great sensation of detachment. Things were happening that should interest Jude but didn't, somehow:

Renai stepping into the bright clearing, deepening her voice and swaggering her hips in an impression of Jude that was simultaneously hilarious, eerily accurate, and unflattering.

Cross pointing, shouting, and the two other loa moving forward, Bois extending a snare-like tangle of vines from one of its sharp-barked hands, Criminel dropping to all fours.

Renai yelling the word that meant *burn* and throwing a wave of searing flame at the two loa, and then running into the trees — not the way they'd come, but deeper into the park.

And yet, Jude's gaze turned inward, into the essence of what it meant to be Jude Dubuisson. It was a mess. A conflicted, wounded thing. The parts that ought to be strong were made weak by pain; the parts that ought to be clever were hobbled by doubt. And straight down the center, a jagged, ugly scar. For an entire life, one side of Jude had pulled away from the other, a being of two worlds trying to decide which one to belong to. A duet fighting to sing a song written for one, discordant and competing and off-key. Tearing a soul apart wrestling with a decision that—Jude realized for the first time—didn't have to be made. Because Jude had never been merely one soul or the other but *both*, and so both worlds were Jude's for the choosing.

The structure of Jude shifted, and the rift between the old Jude and the post-storm Jude began to close. Between the mortal and the divine. Became the swaggering, hungry, sly, provocative, and subversive creature Jude was always meant to be. The thorn in the side of the tyrant. The trap awaiting the prideful and the wicked. Neither creator nor destroyer but both.

Hanging there in the space between male and female, alive and dead, between human and god, the Trickster's song that was the essence of Jude Dubuisson restored itself to harmony.

With the rush of an indrawn breath, Jude slammed back into himself: hanging upside down among enemies, bound and gagged and with a stabbing ache in his side, but himself and whole once more. The pain revealed itself to be not a phantom of his attack, but the raven jabbing him over and over again with his beak, trying to drive the doubloon deeper into the wound between his ribs. Jude jerked against his restraints, trying to tell Sal that it had worked, that he could quit poking him already. The attempt to speak scraped his rough, dry tongue against a foul-tasting burlap pouch filled with herbs that had been stuffed into his mouth: a gris-gris bag, the magic that had restored a semblance of life to his corpse. Among the catalog of bruises and wounds across his body and the danger to his friends, the nasty bag of dried leaves and ground seeds filling his mouth was a minor inconvenience, but in terms of escape, it rendered him helpless.

If he couldn't speak, he might as well still be a disembodied essence without a voice.

A rasping howl cut through the night, brash and heavy with a drunken glee. "Ain't I told you," Criminel said, his words coming from somewhere Jude couldn't see, "ain't I told you he'd come looking for his body, even if he ain't got nothin' but his dick in his hand?" It took Jude a second to realize that Criminel wasn't talking to him, but to the tree-shaped loa. Jude strained his neck back until he could see them. Bois had one of its tree-branch arms stretched out behind it, clutching a struggling Renai and dragging her through the underbrush.

Criminel dug a toe into Renai's ribs, a casually cruel gesture. "Except you ain't got no dick in that body, do you?"

They thought, Jude realized, that she was him or, rather, that Jude's essence still rode inside her.

"Not unless she ask nice, she don't," Cross said. He and Criminel shared a laugh that made Jude's skin crawl. He strained against his bonds, trying to loosen their grip, only rubbing his wrists raw against the vines in the process. Below Jude's head came a creaking groan, a massive pine swaying in a strong wind. Criminel glanced up into what Jude assumed was Bois's face.

"The fuck you know?" Criminel snapped. He looked back down at Renai. "He says I should just cut you and be done with you," he said. "But we danced that dance already, you and me." He pulled a knife from a sheath on his belt, studying it with menacing idleness. "Maybe this time we'll see about making it stick." He held it up for Renai to see, giving Jude a better look, letting him recognize the blade by its white hilt.

The dagger Regal had used in Scarpelli's mansion.

So it was Baron Criminel that had been the one waiting for him in his apartment, the knife in the dark. Had they stolen it from her? Or was she working with them? A mixture of frustration and guilt and betrayal washed through him. Somehow, he knew, he'd fucked everything up. And now they were going to kill Renai, because of him. Again. Though he knew that his struggles were fruitless, he continued to strain against the vines that gripped him, sweat— maybe blood—running down his back, pooling in his palms. He grunted into his closed mouth, telling them all to go do something unpleasant with their mothers.

Cross stood, abruptly, and spun in a circle. For a moment, Jude didn't see the horned young man's face, nor the face of Celeste, the voodoo mamba. Instead, he saw Papa Legba's wrinkled, ancient frown. Then it was gone and Cross was in control once more. He snatched Jude's satchel off his shoulders and threw it to the ground next to Renai. "Don't forget what we come for," he said, the menace in his voice aimed at Criminel, not Renai.

The satchel. That's what this was all about. The gods at the card game had been gambling for something inside, something that would let them become the Luck of New Orleans. Cross must not have been able to find it. If Jude found it for him, maybe he could trade it for their freedom. Or at least Renai's.

Of course, if he had the satchel, he'd have the thunderbolt again.

"Now," Criminel said, "I ain't gonna ask you nothin' but the one time. And when I ask, you gonna sing." He reached down and grabbed a fistful of Renai's dreads, yanked her head back in a torturer's stretch. Even twisting in the trees, Jude could see the fear in her eyes. "You hearin' me, fool?"

No, Jude thought, *not again.* Renai had suffered enough for him. This he simply could not endure.

Rage surged through him and swept away everything else, a wave that rose from his stomach, crested in his pounding heart, and broke against his clenched teeth, the magic surging through his veins and churning in his gut, straining to be called forth into wrath and ruin, expanding against his skin until Jude feared he would burst. He longed to scream defiance, to vent his anger and let curses of terrible potency spill from his mouth. If he was to die, let it be on his feet, with a smile on his lips and mischief in his eyes, like the bastard of a magician he'd once been. Like the Trickster he was born to be. The burning thunder inside him became painful, a cramp in his belly and shards of glass in his throat, a fever across his skin.

Before, he would have fought to quiet this rage, to overcome it. But now that he knew himself as he never had before, he knew that his wasn't the anger of a man losing his temper, but of a Trickster overcome with indignation. A righteous fury. He closed his eyes and took a long breath. Held it. Let the fury and the power overtake him. Let himself tremble at the moment of crisis, a coiled spring, the instant before an explosion.

He relaxed in his bonds, tension easing out of his body like spilled water. Magic radiated from his skin like sunlight, hot and pure. This was the opposite of the chill of the Underworld, the dark emptiness of the Devourer's maw. It wasn't despair, nor was it acceptance: it was looking destiny in the eye and giving it the finger. This was the essence of him, the thing no one could take away. So what if they tortured him, killed him? He'd been dead before. If being swallowed by the Devourer was his fate, he'd carry the flame that had kindled within him back to the depths and burn the fucker's throat on the way down.

Bound, threatened, outmatched, and bleeding, and still Jude grinned that old fuck-you grin.

He reached out with a part of himself he'd always denied. Felt something respond, and with a sense he had no name for, he grasped it, caressed it, and *twisted*.

And felt his luck change.

He swung by one foot in gentle, erratic arcs like the pendulum of a clock that no longer kept time, the vine creaking with every change in motion. He'd loosened the knots in the vines tied around his wrists in his struggles, slickened them with sweat and blood, but still they held. At least, until his magic put the weight of his swing and the sliver of free movement and a particularly harsh yank of his arm all into perfect alignment, just enough for one hand to—suddenly, blissfully—pop loose.

Moving without much thought, relying on luck and instinct and a passionate desire to cause the bullies threatening Renaissance Raines a great amount of harm, Jude pulled off the rag that kept the gris-gris bag sealed in his mouth; dug out the moist, small burlap sack; and spoke the word Dodge had taught him that meant *open*.

The remaining bonds around his wrist and the loop around his ankle loosened. Jude twisted as soon as his limbs were free, as he dropped to the earth, and managed to turn just enough in his brief plummet to avoid breaking his neck. He struck the loose dirt and thick grass with a bone-jarring thud, an impact that knocked the breath from him, a gasp of red-hot vapor forced from his lips. A spasm shook his chest as he fought to draw in more air. He sprawled in the dirt, arms splayed wide, desperate but unable to stand. Criminel appeared above him and lifted him by the front of his shirt with an effortless strength.

Criminel's snout twisted in a sneer. The whites of his eyes seemed filled with blood. He opened his mouth—to say something vulgar and threatening, to speak the words of a spell—but Jude didn't give him the opportunity. He drew back a fist, the one that still held the gris-gris bag, and shoved it as far as he could down Criminel's throat, yanking his arm back just as Criminel's jaws snapped shut, scraping a layer of skin off of his knuckles on the canine fangs.

Jude shouted the word for *close*, sealing Criminel's mouth shut tight, just as he'd done to Barren in the cemetery. The loa dropped Jude, who landed on his feet and backed away, skin flushed and heart thumping. Criminel fell to his knees, clawing at his lips, making choked, gagging noises, his breath coming in shudders.

Jude turned toward the tree loa and started to laugh, amazed that he was still on his feet. Bois made a hesitant move toward Jude, his long, multiple limbs held up in what, moments before, would have been menacing but now looked cartoonish. Jude raised a fist slick with blood from his split knuckles and—muttering the word for *burn*—spat fire into the open palm of his other hand. He gave the wooden creature his best "don't fuck with me" stare. *Gotta give me points for showmanship, at least,* he thought, forgetting for a moment that Renai could no longer hear his internal dialogue.

Bois, big as he was, looked from Jude's fist to Criminel sprawled on the grass and back to Jude, and turned to flee.

His path was blocked by Cross, who hadn't been standing there a moment before. Fresh tears of tar leaked from Cross's hate-filled eyes. He made a savage chopping gesture at Bois and spoke the word that meant *close*. The wooden loa reached out to Cross, his words like wind through the leaves, but Cross's magic was already taking effect. Groaning and creaking in a way that seemed somehow painful, Bois became still, became just another tree. Cross smirked and turned his attention to Jude.

"Look," Jude said, "if you're in the middle of something, Renai and I can just come back later."

Cross appeared in front of him and, with negligent flicks of his fingers, extinguished the crackling flames from Jude's palm and jabbed him in the stomach with one slim hand. Though the body he rode stood no higher than Jude's chest, Cross's blow knocked him back a couple of steps, made him struggle for balance, yet Cross seemed surprised that Jude stayed on his feet. The spike of adrenaline in Jude's bloodstream started to recede, replaced by waves of increasing pain. His mind raced. He had no tricks left, and the satchel was far out of reach. There was something, though, something he'd pulled out of the satchel back before he'd been killed. He reached into his shirt and pulled the rosary of marble beads and silver crucifix from around his neck. He held it up so Cross could see it. "Don't make me use this," he said. "Just give me back the bag and let us go."

Cross chuckled, implacable and callous as distant thunder.

"Don't let the horns fool you, podna," he said. "I ain't no demon to get exorcised by the likes of you."

Exorcism, Jude thought, *that's it.* He knelt down and scooped a small, thick chunk of oak branch off the ground. He threaded the loop of the rosary around the stick, wrapping it around and around, and then held the ends tight with his throbbing, bleeding hand.

"Fuck you playin' at?"

Jude gave the stick an experimental shake, the rosary beads clattering against the oak. It wasn't the best asson — the ceremonial rattle of voodoo rituals — but it might just serve. Especially if the loa in question was already looking for a way in. Jude shook the improvised rattle as hard as he could and sang out at the top of his lungs:

> *Papa Legba, open the gate for me, ago eh*
> *Atibon Legba, open the gate for me*
> *Open the gate for me, Papa, so I may pass*
> *when I return I will thank the loa!*

Legba started fighting Cross within Celeste as soon as Jude started chanting, as soon as he called upon the loa to open the way. Celeste's face shifted from a horned young man's, to her own, to an old smiling man's and back again — so swiftly that they all started to look like the same face. She doubled over and trembled, though Jude couldn't say whether it was from pain or from ecstasy. Nor could he be sure which of the loa would end up with control of her body. He picked up his satchel, his whole body protesting the motion.

Jude opened his mouth to say something, but Renai called out from the edge of the clearing. "No, it's cool," she yelled. "I'll just untie myself from these creepy fucking magical vines!"

Jude left Cross and Legba to their struggle and hurried over to Renai, pausing as he stepped over Criminel to reach down and grab Regal's dagger, strangely grateful that they'd cleaned his blood from the blade. "Language, young lady," he said as he reached Renai's side, grinning, until he saw the expression on her face. He dropped to his knees and hugged her, whispering soothing noises.

"Please, Jude," she said, hushed as though she was afraid of being overheard, "I don't want to die here."

He tucked the dagger away into his satchel, spoke the knots in the vines *open*, and helped her to her feet. There were questions he wanted answers to, how Criminel had gotten Regal's dagger, what Cross knew about what the gods wanted from the satchel, why he'd felt it necessary to have him killed, but none of them were as important as getting Renai out from under these dark trees and back into the light.

They ran from the clearing and didn't give the immortals behind them a single glance back.

By the time they were out of the park, Renai had recovered her composure enough to pull away from Jude, to retie the bandanna around her dreads and give him a "the hell were you thinking" glare. Jude pretended not to see it. Sal came swooping out of the shadows to perch on Jude's shoulder. "That," he said, "was the dumbest, most reckless, and ill-advised, stone-cold badass thing I have ever *seen*." He looked at Renai. "Right?"

She shrugged. "S'alright. I was tied up for most of it."

"What next?" he asked. "The night is young, right, Jude?"

Jude's stomach made some alarming noises. He looked down and saw that his shirt was still all torn and bloody from the knife wounds that had killed him. He reached into his satchel, his gift running out from within him to his fingers once again, as it should be. He pulled out a Beatles T-shirt that a seventeen-year-old Tulane hopeful had lost on a college visit to the city last year. He traded it out for his bloody murder shirt, and this time it was Renai who pretended not to notice that he'd taken off his shirt.

"Way I see it," Jude said, "you two had my back against some kind of voodoo god royalty back there. Least I can do is buy you a meal."

CHAPTER TWENTY-TWO

AFTER SAL HACKED up his dog-shape from somewhere inside his tiny raven's gullet, a short walk down St. Charles and around the bend of Carrollton brought them to Camellia Grill, a late-night diner that had been a staple of night owls and half-drunk college kids since the mid-'40s. Jude had been both, at one time or another.

A line often stretched out the front door due to the limited countertop seating, but Jude's luck held, and he and Renai and Sal walked right in and claimed a few stools. The only other customers were a handful of tourists — who advertised themselves by wearing Mardi Gras beads in the middle of summer — and a younger white couple sharing an order of fries and laughing over whatever they were showing each other on their phones.

In a way, the place seemed to be a bubble from the past, the small kitchen of flattop grills and mini-fridges behind the counter staffed entirely by gregarious black men in white chef's jackets and bow ties — many of whom had worked there for years — who gave you daps to let you know they were your waiter before taking your order.

When their waiter, Dante, turned and flashed his gold-toothed grill at Jude, the hunger in his stomach shifted like a living thing, and Jude found himself ordering without any semblance of control: enough food for two meals, with coffee and a chocolate freeze (which was like a milkshake only better in some inscrutable way) to drink, and a slice of apple pie warmed right on the grill to finish it off. The waiter called their requests out to the cooks, who shouted the order back. If Dante had any problems taking an order from a dog, he gave no sign; indeed, he seemed far more concerned with flirting with Renai once he'd determined that she and Jude weren't "a thing." She gave him the sweet eye right back.

"Mind telling me where your scrawny ass is gonna keep all that food?" Sal asked. "We can't exactly bring to-go boxes where we're going."

"Sure," Jude said, "right after you tell me why Dante didn't blink when a stray dog plopped his furry ass on his bar stool and asked him how it was hanging."

Sal's ears twitched. "Anybody here's a stray, it's you." He leaned forward and lapped at the cup of ice water in front of him.

Another couple of white folks walked in, a middle-aged woman and a young man, who acted like fist-bumping his waiter was a ridiculous inconvenience and started telling Dante what he "needed" to eat before the waiter had a chance to introduce himself. Jude could see Dante repressing the urge to tell the prick to go fuck himself as he turned away to get their drinks.

"And?" Jude asked Sal.

"And I'm a *death* spirit. People get a glimpse of me, they pretend they didn't, and then they immediately try real hard to forget that they did." He gestured with his muzzle in Dante's direction. "You ask him what I look like? He'd describe the most bland person you've ever met. Ten minutes after we leave, I won't even be a memory. Why you think I'm letting you two drag me around topside like this? Just talking to you like people is worth the ass-chewing I'm gonna get when we get back."

Jude had to resist the urge to scratch Sal between the ears, settled instead for patting him on the back, halfway between a human gesture of camaraderie and a doggie "who's a good boy" thumping on the side. When he touched the psychopomp, Jude's gift reacted as it had before the storm, alerting him to the presence of Sal's loss without overwhelming him, handing him a thread he could follow if he chose to tug on it. It felt familiar somehow, a loss he'd touched before, and then it occurred to Jude why Sal had seemed familiar when he'd seen him back in the cemetery where Renai had been entombed.

"You were the guard dog at Dodge's card game," he said.

Sal's head drooped, like Jude had just accused him of pissing on the carpet. "Was wondering if you were gonna remember that," he muttered. "Starting to think we all looked alike to you. Like I said, this psychopomp gig is only part-time. Sometimes I carry messages for the dead back to the living. Sometimes I work security." He made the dog-shape's equivalent of a shrug. "It's a living."

Jude didn't answer, really only half listening, distracted by the hunger worming through his insides, by the fierce itching of the scabbed-over stab wounds that stretched across his chest and stomach, by the desire to throw something heavy at the asshole down the counter. Sal had warned him that part of the magic Cross had used to restore life to his corpse would supercharge his healing, but that it wouldn't be pleasant . . . and not without its own price. He was tearing his napkin into little strips to keep from scratching.

He hadn't caught the change in Sal's demeanor, so it was a surprise when the psychopomp apologized, his voice heavy with guilt. "I shoulda just done my job," he said, like he was trying to convince himself as much as Jude, "but I didn't know you, and I had no idea it was gonna turn out like this and—"

"Shhh," Renai said, smoothing back the fur on his head in a way that managed to seem comforting and not demeaning. Jude hadn't even known she was listening. "Look, nobody's upset with you, okay? Why don't you just start from the beginning?"

Their food arrived, and — after assuring the psychopomp that he was listening — Jude tore into it with an intensity that made even a seasoned waiter like Dante raise an eyebrow. "Ain't nobody gonna take it from ya," he said, chuckling. The first few mouthfuls, instead of satisfying, felt like they fell into an abyss as complete as the Devourer's maw. Sal, whose guilt hadn't kept him from snapping up his own meal, started explaining even though his mouth was full.

He hadn't been hired by Dodge to guard the game, nor — as Jude had assumed — to jump out and startle the players as they arrived. He hadn't been working for the fortune god at all: it was Legba who'd asked him to be there . . . to keep Jude away from the game entirely. Dodge had taken Sal aside when he arrived and made him a side offer. If he'd make a show of keeping Jude away and then let him in anyway, the fortune god had promised the same thing Jude had promised outside Audubon Park: to help him find what he'd lost when he abandoned his former life.

"And now I feel like such shit," Sal said, a whine coming into his voice, "because now you're dead and she's dead, and Papa was trying to keep it all from happening. I let him down and I let you down, and here you are buyin' me a cheeseburger like I ain't stabbed you in the back."

"I didn't get stabbed in the back," Jude said, after swallowing the last of his pie. "I got it in the stomach, wanna see?" He made as if to lift his T-shirt.

"Jude, don't be such an asshole," Renai said. "Can't you—"

"No, I'm making a point. Did you stick a knife in me? No. That was Baron Criminel. Did you tell him to do it? No, again. Cross did that." He jerked his head toward Renai. "You didn't have anything to do with what happened to her, either."

Across the counter from them, the young prick with the older companion was telling her a story about getting caught being drunk at work, after he'd had a few too many at lunch with his boys. "I said to myself, 'This is it, I'm gonna get fired.' How crazy is that, right?" He spoke with the casual, confident disregard of wealth, of someone who had never actually been fired before, not even—by the sound of it—in this account of showing up intoxicated. Like someone who had never had his will subject to the whim of someone else's. The kind of person who had been related to every boss he'd ever had, who was simply waiting his turn to be the boss himself.

Jude's hunger had subsided to a dull ache, but the itch on one of his wounds had grown to a full-on burn, like someone had poked a soldering iron into his flesh. He reached under his shirt and the skin there was hot, feverish. "I can't forgive you," he said to Sal, "but only because there's nothing to forgive. You couldn't have stopped me from getting in that game even if you'd tried."

Sal chuckled and started to say something, but Jude lurched to his feet and hurried for the bathroom, his hand clutching his belly, the pain becoming suddenly unbearable. *This can't be right,* he thought. Just before he left the loud, hissing grill area of the kitchen and made his way back into the prep area, all gleaming stainless steel tables and cooking utensils, he heard Dante tell someone, "Told that boy he was eatin' too fast."

This pain had nothing to do with what he'd eaten, though. It was in his skin, not his stomach. Once he closed and locked the men's room door, he pulled his shirt up and off, wincing as the motion stretched the muscles near the part of him that burned. In the streaked and dirty mirror that hung over the bathroom's one sink, Jude examined the wounds that had killed him. They were each about the size and shape of a lipstick kiss left behind on a barroom napkin, puckered with pink-tinged scar tissue and crusted over with reddish-brown scabs. Tentatively, he touched the one that was the source of his concern and found a small, hard bulge beneath the skin of his solar plexus. His heart rate, already elevated from the pain, cranked up into panic. He started imagining what the loa might have shoved in there — just like Sal had done with the doubloon — when it was still an open wound, magical tracking devices or explosives or eggs.

That last one made his vision go a little gray at the edges.

Grinding his molars together against the pain, Jude probed the area around the lump and felt it shift. Before he could talk himself out of it, he sucked in a breath and dug at the scab with one fingernail while the other hand squeezed. For a moment, all he managed was searing agony, and then, a squelch of pus and blood and something hard and pea-shaped and about the size of a dime popped out of him and went *plink-plink* inside the porcelain of the sink. Relief made his knees a little weak.

A handful of toilet paper pressed against the reopened wound stopped the surprisingly thin trickle of blood oozing out of him, the itch of reknitting flesh resuming immediately now that he'd removed its obstacle. He peered into the sink and saw, in the drain trap, the pearl that he'd used against Scarpelli — the one he'd accidentally swallowed and then forgotten, assuming it would dissolve in his stomach, like the fabled earring Cleopatra had drunk with her wine. As he washed his hands and let the water rinse off the pearl, he pieced together what must have happened. One of the knife wounds must have pierced whatever digestive organ held the pearl, and his body had been forcing the object out like a splinter, as part of Cross's resurrection magic.

Jude fished it out of the drain and dried it off along with his hands, its sense of loss tickling along his fingers, its promise of a greater mystery that he'd felt outside of Scarpelli's mansion and ignored. Curious, Jude let the knowledge of it flow into him. It tore into his mind and his soul, an electric charge that shook the room, like a lightning strike so close it lifted the hairs on your arms.

Jude now saw what the pearl really was, understood how it could amplify spells and charm minds the way that it did, why it imposed the penalty that it took. He pulled his magic away from it, awed for a moment by the power that he held in his hand.

And then he tucked it away in his pocket and eased his shirt back on, already moving forward, already trying to think of how he could use what he'd just learned.

When he left the bathroom, the door to the ladies' room across from him was the Red Door to Dodge's card game.

Waiting.

By the time he made it back to his stool, Sal and Renai had finished eating, and the psychopomp was polishing off a slice of pie of his own. When Jude saw it, he felt a lurch, impossibly, of his hunger returning. He took Dante's teasing in stride, making a joke about the bathroom being off-limits for a while, and asked for a refill on his coffee. Renai was trying to ask him why he'd run off like that, but Jude's attention was drawn to the young asshole at the other end of the counter. As Dante served him his sandwich, he held up his index finger and reminded the waiter that he'd ordered cheese fries, too. "How hard is it to serve a whole meal at once," he said to the woman next to him, not really a question, not at all concerned with the fact that Dante was still within earshot.

A spike of the anger Jude had felt when the loa were threatening a defenseless Renai coursed through him, less intense, but no less righteous. Something in that raised finger, that privileged, unspoken demand, seemed to Jude to be everything that was wrong with this city, with people in general. He reached out again with that part of himself he'd always tried to hold back, and suddenly everyone in the room seemed filled with light.

The asshole white kid glowed brightest; even the air around him seemed incandescent. Compared to him, most everyone else in the diner seemed a bulb on a dimmer switch, but a couple of the patrons—one of the cooks and one of the tourists lined up at the register to pay—looked like candles at the bottom of a well. Just by focusing on them, Jude's gift whispered to him, like it had evolved somehow into something more. The tourist, though he looked reasonably healthy, had profound blockages in his arteries, would be dead before New Year's. The cook's younger brother had dropped out of school and fallen in with their cousin, slingin' and bangin', and would lead to their house getting shot up and the family tearing apart, which would cause him to lose his other job at a repair shop, which meant he and Cherise, his girlfriend, would default on her student loans, which meant the speech therapist degree she was in school for would sink them further in debt long before it had a chance to pull them out of it. It was then that Jude realized that he was looking at their fortunes: the better and worse for most of them, the institutionalized benefits and harms for some.

Seeing with the eyes of a Trickster.

His hunger yearned toward the welding torch glare of the wealthy kid, and as he had with his physical hunger, Jude let it off the leash. He drew in the excess luck burning off of the man until he felt swollen with it, something like breathing in and something like drinking down but as different from them as they were from each other. He took and took until he could take no more, until his strange new hunger was, at last, sated.

And then he reached out in a different way and *twisted*.

He diverted some of the glowing stream of good fortune into the dark wells of the tourist and the cook, pouring and pouring until he felt like he had enough juice, until they each shined a little brighter, just enough that he could see down the twists and turns of destiny that lay ahead of them, both the choices they could make and the unavoidable impacts that could swoop in from outside. He couldn't touch their choices, but the things beyond their control, everything from the flat tires to the genetic predispositions, those felt flexible to him, somehow. Mutable.

The tourist, Charles, was relatively easy. Jude gave him a little push as he made his way out the door, and a few weeks from now at a company basketball game, instead of a sprained knee he'd tear his ACL. The injury would require surgery, which would reveal his blocked arteries, which would save his life.

The cook—also named Charles, but named after his father, so

everyone called him C.J.—took far more effort. It seemed like every twist or change Jude made only briefly impacted C.J.'s life. It took a split condom to make a drastic shift: if his girlfriend Cherise got pregnant, C.J.'s sister would be working an extra shift to try to help them pay for a crib instead of in her room when the family home was attacked in a drive-by, wouldn't be paralyzed, wouldn't turn C.J. against his younger brother. Even that drastic shift wasn't a huge change: C.J.'s brother still ended up in and out of prison, C.J. and Cherise still struggled, but it made things better.

Then Jude turned his attention to the rest of the room, tossing out twists of good fortune like Mardi Gras throws, a twenty-dollar bill found in a pocket here, a job offer there, a string of good tips, a chance meeting in a bar, a left turn instead of a right, a last-minute bump up to first class. He pulled good fortune away from one person and lit the room up like a Christmas tree.

Then he went to work on the asshole, sending him a string of bad luck over the next couple of weeks that would make him think the universe had suddenly turned against him, which, in a way, it had. Jude took a certain amount of sadistic pleasure chipping away at his pride: a flat tire that led to him getting mud splashed all over his favorite designer shirt, a misunderstood order that cost his boss a lucrative contract, a drunken stumble that chipped a tooth, a mild case of food poisoning that lead to diarrhea on a first date, and—when Jude remembered that he had to pay for the meal the three of them had just eaten—a lost wallet.

In the same way that Jude couldn't make a significant, positive change in C.J.'s life without following him around and pouring lucky breaks into him for the next few years, Jude couldn't ruin the asshole's life, either—not without following him around like a curse. The machinery of the world was too well greased in his favor, a reservoir of good fortune that he thought of as the life he deserved. But Jude wouldn't have destroyed him, even if he could have; the guy wasn't evil, just a dick.

Still, when Jude slipped a hand into his satchel and took a hundred out of the prick's lost wallet, most of which he'd leave for Dante, Jude didn't bother to hide his smile.

He'd always been a little bit of a bastard.

Alone in his apartment a few hours later, after he'd given up on trying to sleep, Jude considered his next move. After they ate, Jude had animated a car with a Shem from his collection and sent Renai and Sal across the lake to his mother at the abbey. He'd lied to the psychopomp and told him that he had one more piece of his soul to track down before they could go back to the Underworld, but needed his help in keeping Renai safe; lied to Renai and told her that he wasn't really sure they could trust the psychopomp, and wanted her to keep Sal out of his hair while he did some digging.

In truth, he wanted some time to think without Sal hounding him, literally, about returning to the grave, and he didn't trust himself to spend the night in his apartment with a determined pretty girl who he knew had the hots for him. Especially one who wouldn't hesitate to use the "but it's my last night alive" argument against him. The Trickster in him was pretty pissed he'd sent her away on *his* last night alive, but then the Trickster in him had a few thoughts about the whole "last night" thing as well.

So he'd gotten down the El Dorado from the high shelf, drank the twenty-one-year-old rum straight from the bottle, tried not to scratch his healing stab wounds, and considered his options.

Option One: the Thrones. He'd given his word to return to the Underworld and put his heart on the scales. If he did it now, he ensured that Renai would get the final reward that she'd earned, would go on to a blissful afterlife. Even Sal hadn't known what would happen to her if Jude screwed up that deal. It also meant that Jude's fortune would be, ultimately, average.

He'd found his cards in the satchel, unsurprised to find that the fourth one, the one that showed his turning point, his moment of truth, was THE TRAITOR, which depicted a man hanging by one foot, a nimbus of light around his head. Only one card remained.

If Jude's fate was merely to die before the game ended, before the gods at the table ripped him apart for their promised pound of flesh, well, then, that was that. He'd just be dead. He'd forfeit a soul he no longer owned, would be beyond anyone's harm. If that happened, maybe Dodge would win, restoring him to life and his role as the Luck of New Orleans and returning the city to what she'd been before the storm. But somehow Jude didn't think so. He thought maybe one of the other gods would claim that title. Regardless, option one boiled down to give up and die.

Option one sucked.

Option two: the Red Door. It waited for him right there in the living room in what had always been a closet. He was glad it had stopped trying to ambush him and decided to be patient. He was less happy about using words like "decided" to describe the actions of a door.

Going through the door now would trigger a paradox, according to Hē — although Jude didn't really trust anything the angel had told him at this point — and would trigger his downfall according to pretty much everyone else. Of course, that's what they *said;* the gods had all told him he couldn't win, and then did everything they could to force him to quit, which were the actions of worried players.

Except, that wasn't entirely true. Legba hadn't told him to quit; he'd tried to keep him out of the game entirely. In fact, now that he thought about it, the loa almost seemed to be on Jude's side. He certainly didn't seem to be playing to win like the others. Jude checked to see how much rum was left — curiously little — and thought it would have been nice to share a drink with the old loa before the end. You could never tell which version of him would show up, though: Legba or his dark twin, Cross.

Which, he realized, explained why Legba didn't seem to want the title at all. He didn't. He just wanted to keep Cross from getting his hands on it.

Option two was better than option one, but it still had way too many variables.

Option three: the Dagger. Jude got no sense of loss from the thing, which meant that Regal had *given* it to Criminel, which meant she'd had some part to play in his murder. With a bit of magic, he could use the traces of herself Regal had left on the dagger to track her down. To ask her some of the questions he'd kept to himself these past few days. To get a little vengeance before he died.

It would take the better part of a day to gather the ingredients and work the spells, though. Which meant getting revenge would be literally the last thing he did, and force him into choosing from options one or two. That was assuming she'd stayed within the city, of course. If she'd fled to Peru already, he'd never find her in time.

Option four: the Magician. Eli Constant's name kept coming up—the revolver Scarpelli had in his display case, the deal for two hundred years of service with Mourning, his role as part of the city's soul along with Dodge and the journal of maps—but the man himself was suspiciously absent. Jude kept expecting him to turn up spouting all the answers in that infuriating, didactic tone he'd always used back when he'd been Jude's mentor. But if anyone would have valuable insight into this whole mess, it would be Eli. Then again, there was also a reason Jude hadn't gone to see him yet, why he'd avoided him since the storm and for years before that—a reason he was Eli's *former* student. If he chose option four, there was a chance that Eli would take one look at him and send him straight back to option one, involuntarily.

Jude realized, as he put the cork back into the neck with one swallow of rum left in the bottom of the bottle, that he'd made his choice. *It's been almost twenty years*, he thought. *The old man has to have forgiven me by now.* But easy as it had been to deceive Sal and Renai, he couldn't lie to himself. He'd stolen a summons intended for Eli, back when he'd been his student. That's how he'd met Dodge, gotten the satchel, and become the person he'd become. By betraying his mentor and sneaking his way into the ranks of the powerful. Why should Eli forgive him? He'd never really forgiven himself.

He stumbled toward the bathroom, hoping a hot shower might be enough, along with the booze, to put him to sleep at last. After all, he had a busy day tomorrow, a day of reconciliation, or maybe one of reckoning.

Or maybe just his last day on Earth.

PART SIX

THEY ARE the ones who live in the hut on the edge of the village, or in a cave deep in the forest, or at the summit of an isolated tower, or in the deepest basement of a nondescript building on a street that has no name. They have always been with us, as the tenders of fire, or the keeper of tales, or the healers of the sick. During the daylight hours, they make medicines and aid in childbirth, they tell us when to reap and when to sow, and they teach us how to give honor and how to mourn. In the night, they interpret our dreams and keep the darkness at bay if we respect them, invite it in if we do not. They keep our secrets, whisper misfortune on our enemies. They see that which would blind us, do what we can't bear to do, learn what we dare not know. We call them shaman or bruja, magus or bokor, kalku, onmyōji, magician. We revere or revile them; we beg them for help or burn them alive. We fear them, not because of their power, but because of their humanity. They are what we could be if only we had the courage, or the madness, to pay the price—and there is always a price.

❧

Jude stepped out of a borrowed Cadillac on the corner of Dauphine and France into the squeezing heat, squinting against the sun's glare. After telling the Caddy to park across the street and wait for him, he turned in a slow circle, trying to get his bearings. It had been a long time since he had been in the Bywater, and something about having his gift yanked out of him, stuffed into a doubloon, and then shoved back into him had played hell with his sense of direction.

He frowned, realizing just how long it had been since he had been out here, thinking of the obligations he had let slip. Surely he could have made some effort to reconnect with Eli, especially in the storm's wake. Death—or resurrection, or some combination of the two—gave him a new perspective on how he had acted since the flood, made a mockery of his self-imposed exile. Regal had been right, back in the Clover Leaf. He'd been hiding, from everything.

Speaking of which, Jude thought, and pulled on the burlap mask whose magic let him hide in plain sight that he'd used to sneak to the meeting with Opal. *No sense leading Hē straight to Eli if I'm still being followed.*

He recognized the house with the lime-green siding on the far corner and, like a wandering compass finding true north, he knew where he was. As he walked, he saw yards with waist-high grass, the homes beyond dark and abandoned. Here and there a spray-painted *X* remained on the wall next to the front door despite the efforts to cover them: a date in early September 2005, the number of bodies found. He checked every time, unable to stop himself. Mostly they were zeroes. Far too often they were not.

The scent of hot pavement seemed to wash out all others, as did the sound of rushing traffic on St. Claude just a few blocks away. Halfway to Royal Street, Jude stopped next to a white shotgun house, glanced down at the short concrete steps that led up to the front door. He found the pentagram etched into the stone riser, just as he'd remembered it, its dual points aimed down. Aimed up, he'd been taught, signified evil, the horns of the devil. Like this, it meant protective magic.

A small gate of wire-link fence separated him from a long walkway into the backyard, bordered by the house on one side and a high wooden fence on the other, overgrown and dark. He could walk through the shade and the grass and into the back, where an ancient swing set rusted, empty chains dangling, its rubber seats long since rotted away.

Families had lived in this house for generations and never met their neighbor, never even seen his house. Jude closed his eyes and spun in a circle three times, whispering the invocation with a measured cadence. He reached out, just so, and grasped a wooden latch. He opened his eyes, his hand clutching something that he couldn't see. He lifted and pulled, and the gate swung open, taking with it the image of the yard and the grass and the trees overhead. Even at his most jaded, the wonder of this never ceased to amaze him. A front gate that was a hole in the world.

Beyond lay cypress trees and a clapboard house, a path formed from single planks of wood raised over the swamp, and a wisp of smoke rising from the chimney. This had been the edge of New Orleans once, and within this seam of magic it stayed that way. Jude had never quite understood how this ground avoided being drained when the land around it was all developed. The impossibility of it, he'd been told, was what made it work.

He pulled the mask off and stuffed it back in the satchel as he stepped through the opening. If Hē had followed him in here, there was no hiding from the angel, and if the mask fooled Eli, the magician wouldn't react kindly to a stranger finding the way to his home.

Of course, Eli might not respond well to the sight of Jude, either.

Jude found Eli's shack just as he remembered it, the precarious walkway over the duckweed and the cypress knees, the Spanish moss twisting and wispy as a cartoon witch's hair, the towering pines stretching back to a time when this was where civilization ended, the seam between a newborn city and virgin wilderness. It stank with the rich, living rot of a bog in summer. The song of cicadas threatened to drown out his thoughts, a continual, droning *rant-rant-rant* like a living car alarm bellowing from every tree.

Hanging from the cypress nearest the front porch were bottles, dozens of them—maybe as many as a hundred—glass tinkling softly against glass, a rainbow of colors shimmering amid the leaves. Jude stared for a moment, puzzled. He couldn't remember them being there before, but it had to be a problem with his memory, he thought. In all the years Jude had spent under his tutelage, Eli had never changed anything about his home, had insisted that consistency was necessary for his magic to work right. He had refused even the modern touch of a doorknob.

Jude knocked. Over the cacophony of the insects, through the wood of the door, Jude heard a solid, mechanical *click*. The sound of a revolver's hammer being thumbed back.

Before it occurred to Jude to reach into the satchel for a weapon of his own, the door thumped and swung open with a long, agonizing creak. The room beyond looked exactly as Jude remembered it, though he only gave the surroundings a cursory glance. Nor was he very concerned with the dark mouth of the revolver's barrel aimed straight at his chest. No, the woman wearing frayed jean shorts and a thin, sleeveless T-shirt from a local all-girls' school who held the gun dominated his vision: short, with deep-set eyes of molten brown, like honey. Spikes of auburn hair plastered with sweat to the sides of her head. Full lips twisted into a grimace.

Regal.

For a long moment, the drone of the cicadas seemed to fade into the distance, and all was silent save the rasp of Jude's breath and the *tink-tink* of glass bottles brushing against one another in the breeze. He knew he should say something, but he genuinely couldn't think of a single thing to say. She clicked her tongue at him, like she was getting a dog's attention. "Don't know what the game is, boo," she said, "but I ain't playing."

Jude nearly laughed. "That's rich coming from you," he said. "Looks like you've been playing games since the beginning, Queens."

Her eyes narrowed. "That is eerie as shit." She chewed at her lip. "Piece of advice? Don't pretend to be someone who's already dead."

Jude started to answer, to try and convince her that he really was the friend she'd betrayed, when the anger bubbled up from deep within him and he realized he didn't give much of a damn whether she believed him or not. He hissed the word that meant *open* at her revolver. The cylinder dropped down to the side, spilling bullets to the floor. Her eyes stretched wide, and Jude stepped forward and snatched it out of her hand. He emptied the remaining rounds into his satchel, snapped the cylinder shut and put the safety on, then slipped the revolver into his satchel as well. He fought the urge to wipe his hands on his pants.

"Fuck me with a blowtorch," she said, "it really is you."

"It really is me," he said, reaching into his satchel for the dagger with the white hilt. "Piece of advice? Don't try to kill someone who's already dead." Regal looked at the dagger in his hand and then into his eyes, and did the last thing he'd expected her to do.

She passed out.

It only took her a few minutes to come to, but that was all the time Jude needed to secure her wrists and ankles with a couple of lost silk scarves he pulled out of his satchel so that he could search the small cabin for his old teacher. He discovered neither the man, nor his corpse. If Regal had killed him, she'd dumped him in the swamp for the gators—something Eli had threatened to do to Jude many times, over the years.

When Regal shook awake, she glanced down at her bonds, closed her eyes, and groaned. "No," she said, "don't tell me I fainted like a wuss."

Jude had to grind his back teeth together to keep from smirking. "Regal—"

"Got the vapors like some floofy dress-wearing Jane Eyre *bitch*."

Jude squatted down so he was eye level with her and spoke the word for *close*. Her jaw snapped shut. "There are things that will happen now," he said, "and things which will not. What will *not* happen is you will not start running your mouth fast enough to slip in the string of the words that activates one of Eli's defenses. Nor will you distract me enough to get the upper hand. What *will* happen is that I will ask you some questions and wait patiently for the full and truthful answer." He picked up the dagger from the floor, examined it, and stood. He backed away from Regal, not turning away from her for a second, and set the dagger on Eli's workbench. "I also will not hurt you or even threaten you. If you choose not to answer me, I'll leave you as I found you, hidden away in this sad little shack." The words were pouring out of him now, unplanned, inspired. His Trickster nature taking over and spreading it on thick.

"Nod if you understand what will and what won't happen here."

She nodded.

"And will you answer my questions?"

She thought for a moment, lips pursed, before shrugging and nodding.

"Good enough," he said, and spoke her mouth *open* once more. He dragged the cabin's one chair over to face her and eased into it. "So. Where's Eli Constant?"

"Dead."

Jude swallowed down a burst of cayenne and burnt sugar. "Did you kill him?"

She seemed offended by the question. "Of course not. I'm—no. No, I didn't kill him."

"So you just set him up to be killed?"

"No! I didn't have anything to do with his death."

Jude lifted up his shirt to show her the pale scars pockmarking his flesh. "Why do I have trouble believing that, Queens?" He followed an impulse, an instinct about what she was doing here. "You wouldn't be the first student of magic to kill her teacher to take his place."

"He wasn't my teacher, you dick-juggler! He was my father."

When Jude looked for it, he could see the remnants of Eli in her. The shape of their eyes, if not the color. That wry quirk of the lips when they were laughing on the inside—at you, not with you. He leaned forward, the chair creaking beneath him. "Tell me what I need to know," he said.

"It's a long story."

"I've literally got all day."

Regal's real name, she told him, was Alafair Constant. She'd been a teenager when Jude and Eli parted ways, had asked her father if she could take Jude's place as his apprentice. After Jude's mother, though, Eli had sworn to never train another woman. Regal seemed to think it had more to do with the fact that she was his child—not his daughter—that mattered, but whatever his motivations, Eli refused to teach her. This only made her more determined to learn, of course, so she'd taught herself, studying Eli's books when he was out, seeking out those back alleys and back rooms where she could discover something, *anything* about magic.

Which was why, when she'd started working with Jude and with Mourning, she'd had to come up with another name. To become someone other than Eli Constant's little girl. And so Regal Sloan had been born. She had a feeling that Mourning had known who she was all along, though, because after the storm, Mourning started grooming her to fill the hole Jude had left behind. Teaching her things, giving her gifts like the dagger. It had been nice, for a while, but then she'd started getting suspicious.

So, with the help of the dagger, she'd started spying on Mourning.

She'd learned enough about his intentions to know that he didn't care who won the card game, even if it was a monster like the vampire or Cross, only that the winner was in his pocket. So she'd told him she was quitting. Mourning didn't seem bothered by her leaving, just asked her to perform one last task for him. In return, she'd get to keep the dagger.

Her eyes wandered around the room as though searching for something out of place or unable to meet Jude's gaze, and after a few moments, she looked back at him. "And that was the first time I betrayed you," she said. Despite himself, despite his anger and hurt and suspicion, Jude believed the guilt he heard in her voice.

"Because your last task was to deliver my invitation to the game?"

"No. Well, yeah, but not exactly." She rubbed her thumbnail against the pad of her index finger, worrying it back and forth. "You were the task, yes, but no, the invitation Mourning told me to give you wasn't yours. It was meant for him. You were never supposed to be at the game, Jude."

Now that he had seen through the eyes of a Trickster, Jude could see the twisting brilliance of it. In one deft move, Mourning had pushed him and Regal back together, had shifted the nature of the game in such a way that whatever Dodge was planning would be disrupted, and pulled Jude — and with him the satchel — out of hiding. By keeping himself out of the game, Mourning had put himself in exactly the position he wanted to be in: in control. You didn't need to be as strong as a horse to pull a wagon; you just had to be able to hold the reins. And unlike everyone sitting at the table, Mourning had nothing to lose.

"So if that was your last job for Mourning —"

"Why did I pretend I was still working for him? Because you actually showed up, with that magic touch of yours. It's like you said back at St. Joe's when I gave you the invitation: There's a change coming. And I'll be damned if I get left behind. My father was the Magician of New Orleans. It's my birthright, and I'll do whatever it takes to claim it. That includes lying to you so I could use your magic to find what I need. That includes giving a voodoo god my dagger so he could steal the satchel from you, because Mourning promised to name me the Magician when this is all over, and slippery as he is, he's a man of his word. Even knowing you might die. Even after you'd just saved my life."

She twisted her wrists in her bonds, showing her empty hands. Partly a shrug, partly a gesture of defeat. She fell silent.

Part of Jude wanted to untie Regal—he couldn't call her Alafair, that was a woman he'd never met—and ask for her help. To forgive and trust her. Part of him wanted to reach out with his magic and drain every last ounce of luck from her, to litter her next few days with calamity and misfortune. Part of him wanted to drag her to the porch and toss her in the swamp. He wouldn't be killing her, just leaving her in a position where death was the most likely outcome.

Just as she'd done to him.

Instead, he moved past it, focused on the reason he'd come to this shack in the first place: Eli Constant.

"What I don't understand," he said, "is why this is happening now. First Dodge gets murdered, and now Eli is dead. You weren't really clear on that, either. How did he die? He'd always said that he'd live—"

"As long as the city lived. Yeah, he told me that, too. Turns out it works both ways."

When the implication of what she'd said hit him, Jude was glad he was sitting down. It wasn't happening now. It had been going on for six years. "The storm," he said.

Regal's lips compressed to a grim line, and she nodded. "My father went years ago, just a couple of months after the storm. Said he couldn't stand the silence, after she died."

"She?" Jude could guess what she would say next, but needed her to say it out loud. Needed to know for sure.

"New Orleans," she said. "The storm, the flood. It killed her. She's been flatlined for six years, and this shit-heap game is supposed to be like those paddles on TV—you know, 'Clear!' and *bzzt*, the heart's beating again? Give her a new Magician, Voice, and Luck god and she'll snap right back."

The last piece of the puzzle slid into place. The reason Mourning needed Jude, needed his gift; why the city was vulnerable to Scarpelli's attempt to turn her; why Cross had wanted the satchel so badly. New Orleans died six years ago.

And when you died, you lost your voice.

Tears glistened in Regal's eyes, her fists clenched at her sides. "I begged him to leave. Told him he wasn't the city's Magician anymore, that he didn't have to lie down in his grave and die. But he refused. Said he would never turn his back on this place, even though everyone here with enough power to leave had turned their backs on him, even though—" Her voice cracked as she restrained emotions Jude could only guess at.

Regal clenched her jaw and turned away, unable to look at Jude, or not wanting him to see the tears coursing down her cheeks. He stayed quiet, knowing that she needed to say her piece, and while he didn't owe anything to her, he owed Eli Constant that much, at least.

"My father was the most powerful, wise, and selfless person I have ever, or will ever, know," Regal said, speaking in the clipped cadence of barely restrained contempt. "But when he died, he was nothing but a foolish old man. Because of you. He told me, 'Jude will save us.' Over and over. 'Jude. Find Jude Dubuisson. He will save us. Jude will save us.' But you didn't. You didn't even try."

Jude rose to his feet and went back to Eli's workbench, picked up the dagger that Regal had traded back and forth in exchange for his life, one way or another. He dropped it to the floor next to her. "This belongs to you," he said. "When I'm gone, you can use it to cut yourself free, and we'll be square."

"Just like that? How do I know this isn't some kind of trick?"

"Because I'm not done. I've got too many knives at my back already, Queens. I can't afford for you to be one of them." He reached down, pressed a finger against the hollow of her throat, and said the word for *close*. "I'm sorry," he said, "but I just don't see any other way."

As he walked away, out the door and down the long pathway across the swamp, back into the stink and noise of modern New Orleans, Regal cursed at him, an impressively vulgar and creative stream of obscenities, and then, when she realized what he'd done, the potent kind of curses, magics that should have blinded him and covered him with boils and broken his limbs.

But none of them had any effect. He'd left her with the power of speech, but he'd locked away her Voice. She might be the daughter of the Magician of New Orleans, but now she would be incapable of magic.

And just like that, all his options went away. Revenge against Regal, finding Eli, done and done. And if Eli was dead, Dodge couldn't win the game, couldn't be the city's Luck again, so New Orleans couldn't return to the city she'd been before, no matter what Mourning had said about symbols being restored. Which meant deliberately losing the game in the hope that his sacrifice would let Dodge win was no longer an option.

Leaving him with just one path: the Red Door.

CHAPTER TWENTY-FOUR

JUDE DECIDED that even if walking through the Red Door was inevitable, he didn't have to do it right away. He had a whole day to prepare, to call in favors, to experience the city that he loved one last time.

He went back to his apartment and dressed for the occasion, solid black slacks and a pinstriped black dress shirt, a dark gray vest decorated with purple, green, and gold fleur-de-lis that he wore every year on Mardi Gras day, a solid dark purple tie, and a pair of black and white oxfords. Last, but not least, the burlap mask to hide him from Hē's gaze.

Sharp as a knife, he thought to himself as he rolled up his sleeves, slung the satchel around his neck, and made his way downstairs to the Caddy he'd animated with a Shem to bring him to Eli's cabin. For a moment, the options for how to spend his last day alive overwhelmed him, but then a rumble in his belly decided for him.

Beignets at Café du Monde—crispy, deep-fried squares of dough, covered with sticky-sweet powdered sugar and washed down with hot chicory café au lait, rich and bitter and thick; pecan-crusted gulf fish at Commander's — a pan-seared trout filet, flaky and steaming, with crushed sweet corn and sweet wine–poached blue crab, a delicate mélange of sugary and brine and herbs; a Surf and Turf po'boy at Parkway Tavern — a feast of fried, spicy shrimp stuffed inside a roast beef sandwich, with thick, savory juices soaking into crusty French bread; a snoball — a Chinese takeout container filled with crushed ice drenched in chocolate syrup on Plum Street; and a cup of cappuccino and a slice of spumoni at Brocato's.

And everywhere he went, Jude got lucky.

With the same senses he'd used in the Camellia Grill, Jude found those graced with an overabundance of fortune and those down on their luck, and used his powers to tip the scales, trading lucky breaks for misfortune and vice versa.

There were exceptions, of course. A fantastically fortunate older white guy who recognized that he'd been blessed — that "the universe smiled on him," as he called it — and did his best to share the benefits with those around him, giving to charities and literacy programs and treating his employees with compassion. A couple of unfortunates who were real assholes and deserved every pound of crap the universe dumped on them. Those few Jude left as they were.

Everyone else, though, felt the push of Jude's influence on their fate, in one way or another. Each time he gave the life of someone in need a little *twist*, he felt a little more at peace with himself, and every time an overconfident, privileged ass-clown got knocked down a peg or three, Jude kept a taste of that good fortune for himself.

For what he had in mind, he'd need every scrap of luck he could hang on to.

As he followed his stomach back and forth across the city; as he crossed the river in a sprinkling of rain to ask Leon Carter to do him a favor that night; as he called Regal to make a deal; as he got the Caddy to drive slowly past the house where he'd grown up, the mask seemed to fool Hē, but somehow the Red Door continued to track him. Always in the corner of his eye, always just a few steps away. Bathroom doors and kitchen doors and fire exits and once, just for variety, an empty frame in a building under construction. Between one blink and the next, they were exchanged with a splash of red and an ornate twist of a doorknob.

Soon, Jude promised it, *soon.*

Evening was coming on when Jude finally turned the Caddy toward the Causeway—toward Renai, and Sal, and his destiny. Jude stared out at the setting sun as the clouds caught fire and the surface of Lake Pontchartrain burned into his retinas. He watched brown pelicans as they fished, gliding straight up, turning a slow, graceful arc in midair, then a tuck of the wings and a darting plummet that ended in a tight, comic splash.

He thought about Regal then—and about Cross and the vampire Scarpelli—and wondered if his traps had managed to hold any of them for very long. He thought about Renai and Sal, and what he was about to ask of them. He thought about his mother and all that she'd endured on his behalf. He considered the contents of his satchel, the revolver and the thunderbolt and his cards, pondered the wisdom of trusting his life, his soul, to a handful of lost things. He let it all tumble through his mind, the threats and the shadows, the players at the card table and the humans caught up in their dance, magic spells and hurricanes and city gods and trumpet players and absent fathers and fate and luck and life and death and the everlasting game that kept changing its rules.

He thought about the place, and the life, and the myth called New Orleans.

A pelican kept pace with the Caddy, its long pinion feathers twitching in the wind as it angled up and out of sight. Jude wondered if the fish saw the bird's shadow just as it was too late to do anything about it. He pictured the moment, the realization that the sudden gloom was something more than a cloud passing in front of the sun, the frantic struggle to change direction, and then the snatch into a hungry gullet and into darkness.

He knew the feeling.

Jude guided the Caddy into the parking lot at St. Joseph's Abbey, where it pulled in right next to the Lexus he'd animated to send Renai and Sal across the lake. *Brother Gus is gonna have a hell of a time explaining this,* he thought. As if summoned, the monk walked out of the church on the other side of the gravel parking lot, heading Jude's way. Remembering just in time, Jude yanked off the burlap mask, not sure what it would show Gus—not sure the monk could handle seeing actual magic performed right in front of him. He slipped it back into the satchel as he got out of the car. After tonight, he'd never have to hide from Hē again.

Brother Augustus started speaking before Jude had a chance to. "Good to see you, my boy. Your mother's guests arrived last night. We put them each up in a spare room in the retreat center." He frowned, seemed to gather his words. "Will they be leaving with you this evening?" He tried to hide the hope in his voice, but it came through.

We're all leaving one way or another, Jude thought. To Augustus, he said, "Why, have they been a hassle?"

Augustus held his hand out, indicating they could talk and walk at the same time. "Not at all; Ms. Raines is a delightful young woman." He opened his mouth to speak, then—Jude guessed by the expression on the monk's face—actually bit his tongue.

Jude sighed. "What did Sal do?"

"I'm not sure Mr. Vittori is all there. I saw him— I believe I saw, at any rate— I believe I saw him . . ." He lowered his voice to a near whisper, even though they were the only two people in sight, much less earshot, *"defecating outside."*

Jude choked back a laugh when he realized that to the monk's eyes, Sal probably looked like a man. "He's kind of a free spirit,

I'm afraid. Real big on the natural order, you know? Probably thought he was saving water or helping your garden or something. Don't worry, we'll head out soon."

Augustus nodded, probably a little more enthusiastically than he intended. "I believe they're having dinner with the other brothers; would you like me to have them meet you in your mother's room?"

"I'd appreciate that, yes."

The privacy would give them a chance to talk, for Jude to say something that he should have said a long time ago.

His mother's room, still reeking of turpentine and oil paints, had undergone a transformation since he was there last. The frightening, vampiric cityscape was gone, as were many of the paintings that had previously crowded the space. Now a single canvas sat on an easel in the center of the room: a self-portrait of his mother painting another, smaller image that he needed her to paint, a request he hadn't made yet. Her bathroom door was the Red Door to the card room again—though now, Jude noticed, it was facing inward. Jude felt a little stab of filial guilt, knowing that she had to have added the scene of his murder to her mural, that she'd had to witness that.

Her strong arms wrapped around him before he knew she was there. "My baby came to see me before his big night," she said. "You make your poor mother so happy." She slipped something small and flat into the watch pocket of his vest. "Before I forget, here's what you asked for." She put his hand over the pocket and patted it, keeping Jude from checking to see if it was what he needed. Besides, she'd be offended if he didn't trust her.

"I didn't ask for this, Ma. How did you know I needed it?"

She waved a hand at him, like the question was irrelevant. "You were going to ask. Same difference." She scooped a brush out of a cup, swiped some gold paint off a nearby palette, and dropped to the floor with her legs folded, stretching in an awkward yoga pose so she could use the brush to paint her toenails.

Jude squatted in front of her, so he could look into her face. "But, Ma, it's not the same. Not at all. How do you know these things?"

She peered up at him, blew a few strands of hair out of her eyes with a puff of breath. "Well, because of you, silly. You think I could carry around a tiny little Trickster in my belly for nine months and not end up a mad old fortuneteller?" She made a scoffing noise in the back of her throat.

It took a couple of deep breaths before Jude could trust himself to use his voice, to ask the question he'd never permitted himself to speak. "Mom, are you telling me that you know who my father is?"

She crinkled her brow. "Didn't I just say? Trickster."

"No, I meant— I thought you knew which one." Jude sighed. "Never mind."

"Oh, the names don't matter. They're all Trickster deep down." She smirked at him. "Just big ol' sacks of righteous indignation, sneaky smiles, and bellies that are always growling. And, you know, lust." She nudged him with her shoulder, playful. "Barely took any seduction at all for me to turn your daddy's head." She whistled between her teeth. "And he was a *looker*, you bet. Just like my— honey, what's wrong?"

Jude realized then that his eyes were brimming with tears, that he was trying to speak but couldn't get past the lump in his throat. "Seduced?" he managed at last. "Not—" He gestured inarticulately with his hands, unable to even say the word.

"What, rape? I'm a woman, Jude. I know the word." She dropped her paintbrush to the floor and wrapped him in an embrace. "No, sweetpea, no. It wasn't love between us, not exactly, but nothing like that. It was . . . nice. And when it was over, I got what I wanted in the first place. I got my sweet boy. Stole him right away from the gods and brought him home with me."

Something broke in Jude, and he started sobbing in his mother's arms—great, painful heaves of breath bursting out of him, as the topography of his existence shifted in his mind, in his heart. A guilt that he'd always borne sloughed away from him, leaving an ache behind, like the muscles bearing a heavy load cramping when the weight was finally set down. He wept, while his mother made soothing noises in his ear, until he was done.

And then, wiping his face on the handkerchief that his mother had taught him a gentleman always carried, Jude stood, feeling like he rose to his full height for the first time in his life.

From the doorway, Sal cleared his throat. "Hope we're not interrupting nothin'," he said.

"Puppy!" Jude's mother shouted, bouncing to her feet. "Here, puppy, puppy! C'mere, boy!" She slapped her paint-stained hands against her thighs. Renai pressed the back of her fist against her mouth and giggled. Sal glanced up at Jude, sighed, and moved obediently forward, letting Lydia scratch him between the ears, seemingly unaware or uncaring that the dog she was petting was capable of speech.

"Hate to be the buzzkill here," Sal said, "but we really oughta be getting you two back downstairs, don'tcha think? We only got till midnight." He licked Lydia's fingertips and made a noise of disgust. "Does this chick know she's covered in paint?"

"About that . . ." Jude said. "What would you say if I asked you both for a favor?"

CHAPTER TWENTY-FIVE

HE WEARS a jester's cap and many colored clothes, talks in riddles and in rhyme. Or she speaks the truths no one else dares speak; she is the child who cries out that the Emperor is wearing no clothes. Or he is Falstaff, a font of drunken wisdom. They are Loki or they are Raven; Coyote or Prometheus or Quetzalcoatl. He is the bringer of fire and she is the bringer of pain, the gambler who dances with chaos, with madness, with change. The ghost in the machine is his. The uncertainty principle. The exception that proves the rule. Hers are the unintended consequences, the lucky breaks, the reversals of fortune. They are man and woman, both and neither. They bring wisdom through mockery, truth through lies, life through death. Liar. Thief. Trickster. Fool.

It took surprisingly little effort to convince Sal and Renai to help him. Renai seemed to be up for anything, had only needed to be reassured that, yes, the satchel really did work the way he promised it would—even though Jude himself hadn't known for sure that it would work until it did. Though, to be fair, nothing was too hard a sell when your other option was death.

With Sal, Jude had to remind him that one of the many benefits of his trick working was that Jude would be around to search for that piece of a lost life that he'd promised the psychopomp he'd find. And that if it *didn't* work, he needed Sal there as an insurance policy, to drag him out of the card room and down to face the Thrones' judgment as he'd sworn—which Jude couldn't do if the other players devoured him. He failed to mention the part where he was far too much of a Trickster now to take any comfort in the promise of Death's embrace.

And so, with only an hour left to live, death trotting on four paws at his side, dressed to the nines and brimming with the luck he'd skimmed off the overly fortunate, Jude kissed his mom good-bye, shouldered the satchel full of lost things—his bag of tricks —slipped the pearl into his mouth, felt his lips stretch into his best fuck-you grin, and reached for the twisted, ornate knob that would open the Red Door.

A provocative, swaggering confidence whirled within him, filling him, leaving no room for fear or doubt. For the first time in a long time, maybe ever, he felt the hand of destiny, knew that he stood exactly where he was supposed to be.

The knob turned; the door opened on a haze of smoke, the tinkle of ice against glass, the faint hint of cinnamon, the hungry grins and appraising stares of the assembled fortune gods and the empty seat, waiting, once again, for Jude.

As he stepped inside with Sal right behind him, Jude was unable to stop himself from meeting, and matching, the gods' smiles. If he went by their expressions, every single god at the table believed they had a winning hand. Scarpelli had a distracted air about him, staring into space, his too-long fingers splayed across his cheek, his victory a foregone conclusion. Though Hē appeared focused on balancing a feather on a fingertip, Jude saw that those stark white, pupil-less eyes were constantly moving, evaluating. Legba smiled around the pipe stem clenched between his teeth, but there was a tension in him—the shadow in his eyes named Cross. Hermes wore a smirk, his feet propped up on the card table, busily typing away on a cell phone, Thoth's spectacles pushed back into his hair, the glass replaced with red and green lenses.

Aside from the gash across his neck, Dodge remained just as he had been that first night, fat and bald and ever smiling, his fluorescent grin cranked up as bright as it would go. "Shut the door, little one," Dodge said. "You're letting out all the luck."

Hē spoke as Jude took his seat, in that haunting voice that was an echo of his own, though the angel's words were directed at Dodge. "You're going to let this walking blasphemy bring his beast in here?"

Sal started to say something, but Jude cut him off. "He's my seeing-eye dog," Jude said.

Hē's head whipped around, those impossible eyes boring into him. "You are not blind," the messenger said.

"Sure I am," Jude said. "How the hell else would I have ended up here?" His skin felt swollen with stolen luck as he eased into the chair. The heat of his magic surged through his veins. He gathered his cards into a tidy stack, covered them with his hands.

Legba chuckled and nodded. "I do believe the boy is starting to get it," he said.

Hē's face puckered with distaste, but Dodge laughed that booming, joyous laugh. "Let the dog stay," he said. The angel looked ready to argue, but Dodge kept talking. "This is still my game. I might be dead—my word might mean dick out among the living—but until the last card is turned, this is still my game. My rules."

"Speaking of things being over," Scarpelli said, staring with his corpse eyes at Jude. "Why don't you go ahead and flip those cards, sweetmeats? You are merely an appetizer, and I'd just as soon be about my meal."

"Yes," Hē said in Jude's own voice. "I should like to end this game as well." Hermes and Legba murmured their agreement. Jude was supposed to be afraid, he realized. And because he wasn't, he was making them nervous. His smile stretched wider. Jude gathered his cards, flicking and twisting his wrist just so. He arranged the speech, the narrative, he had crafted during a long phone call with Opal Brennan, his tarot-reading friend from the Quarter. Made his move.

Jude turned over the first card, THE MAGICIAN, and tucked the pearl under his tongue so that its magic would influence his words. "This is for who I once was," he said. "A man caught between two worlds, between power and vulnerability, between divinity and mortality."

He turned over the second card: THE HERMIT, reversed. "Who I have been. A self-centered and lost soul who turns away from enlightenment."

The third card: THE WHEEL OF FORTUNE. "This stands for those assembled here, the fortune gods, the Tricksters, the obstacles in the path. The challenge I must overcome if I am to succeed."

The vampire tittered, the noise setting Jude's teeth on edge. He swallowed and took a deep breath. He had to stay calm despite the throb of his pulse staggering through his veins, despite the fortune god magic whirling like a compass needle in his mind, searching for the one moment he needed to find.

The fourth card: THE TRAITOR. "This is my moment of enlightenment and triumph. This is when I learn who I am, what I'm capable of. Everything hangs in the balance."

Something about the card or Jude's explanation agitated Hē, sent a flutter across those spice-scented wings.

Scarpelli giggled again. "We'll see about triumph when you turn that last card," he said. The gods — the ever-hungry Trickster gods — leaned in, their attention focused on Jude's hands, waiting for the image to be revealed. Only Dodge watched Jude, those money-colored eyes staring coolly into Jude's own.

Jude's magic found the moment at last — this moment — the instant his fate hinged upon. He seized it and, with every ounce of luck he possessed, *twisted.*

With a touch, he changed the card on the table, exchanging it for the one in his vest pocket.

Jude flipped over the final card, THE FOOL. Moans and curses rang out around the table. It depicted Jude in patchwork clothes —a staff over his shoulder, magician's bag slung on his back, Sal leaping at his heels—smiling as he stepped over the edge of a cliff. "This is my future," Jude said. "This is my fate. This is who I am: the Luck of New Orleans."

As one, the gods turned to Dodge. Jude could see it in their faces, could feel the disbelief radiating from each of them. Jude looked from vampire to fallen angel to loa to thief and knew that if his gamble failed, his only hope was a swift death, and swifter oblivion. His gaze caught Dodge's, and Jude saw that the murdered god knew what Jude had done—that he might have known what would happen all along. Jude's heart seized, fear piercing him at last. He had thrown the dice, he had played his hand, and he had lost both times. He pulled in a breath to speak the word for *burn*, his signal to Sal that the whole thing had turned to shit.

But then Dodge began to laugh.

"Well, I'll be damned!" he shouted. He thrust his hand in Jude's direction. "Let me be the first to congratulate you."

Numb, waiting for Dodge's trick to become clear, Jude reached across the table and touched hands—flesh to spirit flesh—with the dead fortune god. His gift surged within him, identifying all that Dodge had lost. Jude saw a childhood that lasted for hundreds of years. Dodge running with the others of his kind—the fae—through virgin forests of endless summer in a world before, or beyond, the world of man. He saw a time in France, where Dodge Renaud was Reynard the Fox, the Trickster of fable. He saw when Dodge came to a newly born New Orleans, his father's stolen pouch in hand and head full of plans, so many plans. They stretched out into the next century, rebuilding the city, revitalizing it, healing her wounds, ensuring that she would survive storms and turmoil and a growing darkness on the horizon. He saw the night when those plans came to an end, when the card game meant to draw out the lost voice of the city went so very wrong.

The night Dodge was murdered by a fallen angel named Hē.

Dodge's grip tightened on Jude's hand and yanked him to the floor. Jude felt the wind of passage on the back of his neck, heard the whistle of something sharp slicing the air as he fell, as one of Hē's blades went whispering past his head. His vision narrowed to a fine point, adrenaline and magic flowing in a torrent through his veins. Knocking over his chair as he tumbled to the ground, Jude's satchel fell with him, flopping open. Jude lunged for it and dug inside, his fingers tingling as they led him to the lost thing he sought, as he reached down deep, past the elbow, up to the shoulder, brushing past a young woman's dreads and clasping her wrist and pulling her out in one convulsive heave, dragging Renai into the card room.

"The angel," he shouted, "shoot the angel!"

Hē leaped onto the table, scattering drinks and playing cards, wings spread wide, the smell of cinnamon overpowering, lips overflowing with incoherent babble. Jude pushed himself to his feet as Renai aimed the revolver he'd taken from Regal and squeezed the trigger. The hammer dropped onto an empty cylinder with a pitiful *click*. She tried again, and again—*click, click*. Jude let out a long, slow breath that burned like fire and readied himself to speak his flames at Hē. But then the gun bucked in Renai's hands and a roar ripped through the room. Hē swiped a hand through the air, knocking the bullet away with the same motion, the same nonchalance, of someone shooing away a fly. Renai fired twice more with the same result, as the fallen angel stalked closer, ignoring the young woman with the pistol. Hē snatched Jude into the air by the front of his shirt, like a puppy held by the scruff of its neck.

Jude grabbed the messenger's wrist with his bare hand, and again his gift tore through him, revealing what Hē had lost. Jude

saw Hē in Paradise, receiving a name, a purpose. Hē. Five. Fifth.
He saw Hē protecting Issachar, the fifth tribe of Israel. Saw the angel sicken the livestock of Egypt in the form of the fifth plague.
Saw Hē handed the Fifth Trumpet, the one that would unleash the
First Woe at the End of Days. Hē took the trumpet, felt its dread
power, and felt an impulse never felt before. Wanted to know why
such a thing had to be, knew that angels were created without a
voice with which to question, much less the autonomy to do so.
Felt the desire to question that choice, too, the wisdom of creating
beings to be entirely servile. And as that question formed in Hē's
mind, for the first time in the messenger's eternal, obedient existence, Hē's angelic feet touched the ground.

Jude saw all that and more, knew now why Hē had always spoken in an echo of his own voice, understood why the messenger
had become a murderer, saw who had led the angel to the game in
the first place.

The fallen angel howled into Jude's face using the voices stolen from the victims Jude had seen on his mother's wall. Sal leaped,
growling, at Hē's back, but those massive, beautiful wings flexed
and struck the dog-shape to the ground. Over the angel's shoulder,
Jude could see the other gods, relaxed around the table, content
to watch, merely enjoying the show. Hē raised a hand—fingers
curled around one of those blades of light—to Jude's throat, to
add his voice to Tommy's and Renai's and Dodge's and Thoth's.

Jude breathed deep, gathered his rage and his magic, and with
a single word spat fire into the angel's face. Hē hurled him to the
ground. Jude rolled on the floor and came up running, the satchel
swinging loose in his grip. He darted through the door that led to
the mansion on Elysian Fields and ran down the hallway, sprinting
for the ballroom and—he hoped—space to maneuver.

So far so good, he thought.

Jude burst into bright light and music and laughter, the never-
ending party of the dead. He cursed and shoved his way through
the crowd, brushing up against person after person, their cold

spirit-forms searing his hot flesh, and then he shouted, the force of his living voice demanding their attention, clearing a space before him. He nearly reached the door that would have let him escape into the Underworld proper, but it slammed shut in front of him. He turned around, looking across the ballroom, where Hē towered in the hallway that led back to the card room, wings stretched overhead, murder in those haunting eyes. Renai dangled from the angel's grip, alive and awake, but too terrified to move. Sal came limping down the hall behind her. Smoke rose from Hē's face where Jude's fire had burned without leaving a mark.

"C'mon, Jude, don't run," Hē said, using Tommy's voice. "Don't fight it." A hand petted Renai's dreadlocks. When the angel spoke again, the voice had switched to Renai's. "It's nice in here with us."

"You have to be stopped," Jude said, reaching into his satchel as Hē came closer, already dreading what came next. His tingling fingers found what they sought, and pain lanced up his arm as he grabbed it. "What you're doing is wrong."

"It's not wrong," Hē said in a gravel-filled drawl that took Jude a moment to guess must belong to Thoth. "It's the nature of things. We all become one in the end." The angel was just a few steps away. Sal still pulled himself toward them, all the way across the ballroom, moving way too slow to make it in time.

"Renai, now!" Jude yelled, pulling Eli Constant's cursed revolver free of his satchel and hurling it toward her. Renai lunged against Hē's restraining grip as the revolver flipped, end over end, toward her hands. Jude didn't have much luck left, but he reached out once more, *twisting* and hoping this last gamble would pay off. As the last trickle of his stolen fortune dwindled away—

—the revolver's grip landed with a smack in the palm of the angel's hand.

"Jackpot!" Hē said, Dodge's voice now. "You kiddin' with this shit? How many guns you gonna try before you think of something else?"

"This one's different," Renai said, nearly a whisper.

"Renai, no!"

"Quiet!" Hē snapped in Dodge's voice, aiming the revolver at him. Jude assumed the proper position, hands in the air. "Don't you see, Jude? I've already won. I'm going to take your voice, and then I'm going to take the voice of this city. When I'm through, the whole world will know what it means to be kept silent." The fallen angel turned a beatific, pitying expression down to Renai. "How is it different, child? Tell me, and I'll give you back your voice."

Tears running down her cheeks, the young woman told the angel what Jude had told her, that the cursed revolver held all the guilt and pain of a wasted life, that in the right hands, it was powerful enough to kill a god.

"Really?" the fallen angel said, switching to Jude's own voice, no mere echo this time, but the very voice Jude heard when he spoke. "It does feel special. Let's find out." Sal shouted and Renai shrieked and Jude spoke the word for *burn.*

And Hē squeezed the trigger.

The revolver imploded, a pulling in instead of expelling out, an eerie rush of silence instead of a roar of sound. There was a brief vacuum of wind, a churning of light and shadow, and the revolver thumped to the floor where Hē had stood. The angel was gone.

Should have known better than to trust a Trickster, motherfucker.

Eli's curse had been twofold: for the revolver to visit the pain of its original owner on any innocent soul who touched it—if it hurt for him, Jude realized, it would have been agony for Renai—and to make it a magnet, a trap, for sin. If a wicked person ever tried to use it, it would drain the sinfulness out of them. For someone like Hē, whose very essence had become twisted and corrupt, it was a black hole.

In the end, they'd told the angel the truth: in the right hands, it could kill a god.

"You did good, kid," he said to Renai as he helped her to her feet. "Tears were a nice touch."

"Yeah? I was worried I was gonna oversell it."

"I'm cool," Sal said, a doggie whine in his voice. "Nobody worry about the wounded animal. Everybody loves a tripod dog."

Before Jude could say anything, Renai rolled her eyes and turned on him. "Are all psychopomps such babies? If only you were able to, I dunno, *fly*."

Sal blinked. "Oh."

While the psychopomp hacked up his raven's shape, Jude took out his handkerchief and used it to pick up the cursed revolver. *I fucking* hate *guns,* he thought. To Renai, he said, "Violent means always lead to violent ends."

She rolled her eyes. "It's 'violent delights,' Romeo."

Jude grinned. "That's what I said."

She ignored him. "What now?" Renai asked, flinching and giggling when Sal hopped onto her shoulder.

"Now, we see if I really am fortune's fool."

When Jude walked back into Dodge's card room, he found everyone still seated as he'd left them, as if nothing special had happened. The vampire stared at something on his cell phone, Hermes —based on his hand gestures—was in the middle of telling Dodge a dirty joke, and Legba had pulled his straw hat down over his eyes and appeared to be napping. Each of the gods had a red door behind them, the same arrangement that had appeared whenever he'd spent too long in this room. Their own personal entrance to the card game.

Jude collapsed into his chair, his body weak and trembling, the revolver like a lead weight in his hand. He let it fall with a thump next to the spread of his cards and folded his hands, one on top the other. For just a moment, as he considered the muscles and joints that were already starting to ache, he regretted leaving Renai's youthful body for his own. He wanted to ask the gods why none of them had left, but the room seemed pregnant with some possibility, so he waited and watched, looking from deity to deity, and then to the pile of coins and other markers in the center of the table.

Then he realized why they had stayed: He had beaten the gods at their own game. He'd won.

And now they had to pay up.

Jude scooped together the markers that Hē had scattered, hiding his revulsion at the teeth Scarpelli used, and stacked his doubloons in front of him. He remembered what Dodge had said, way back when he'd first started this hand: *Too small a wager means you forfeit the choice.* Which meant, if he understood things correctly, that he could demand whatever he wanted of them, as they had done to him. He felt like a kid at Christmas, unsure which present to start with. Then he saw Sal perched on Renai's shoulder, remembered that he didn't have much time. He also recalled whose fault that was.

He turned to the vampire first. Scarpelli picked at his nails as though he'd never been more bored. "Demand of me whatever you wish, sweetmeats; without a Magician or a Voice, this city is still dying. Today? Tomorrow? How long before she slips away for good? Before she rises as my thrall? You'll have nowhere to hide from me then, and I'll drink your good fortune from you drop by drop."

Jude smiled. "You've missed the point, vampire."

"Oh? And what point would that be?"

"That I've found my heart." Dodge and Legba both chuckled, getting it before the vampire did.

Scarpelli made a snort of derision and twirled his finger in a slow circle. "Well, la-di-da," he said. "How wonderful for you."

"I found my heart," Jude repeated. "And it's here, in this city." Scarpelli's eyes narrowed. Clearly beginning to understand, he rose from the table . . . and then above it, the mass of his bruised corpse body lifting into the air, his fangs bared. Even Legba pulled away.

"New Orleans is my home, vampire," Jude said, his voice calm and certain. "And I don't remember inviting you in." Before Scar-

332 • BRYAN CAMP

pelli could say anything—threat or plea or parting barb—before he could lunge toward Jude, before he could even change the expression on his face, he vanished, leaving behind nothing but a lingering taste of blood.

"We'll discuss your debt later," Jude said, deadpan, almost starting to enjoy himself. He glanced down at Sal. "Is it wrong that I hope that hurt?"

Legba spoke before Jude could address him. "Before you make your demand of me," he said, "perhaps we should discuss this." The loa dug in his pocket and pulled out the silver coin Jude had given him in exchange for Renai's passage through the Underworld. "If you will recall, I put my money on you." He shrugged. "It is as I warned you: There is always a price."

Jude laughed. "I was thinking the same thing," he said.

Legba hadn't expected Jude to be amused. "Have I said something humorous?" he asked. Something flickered behind his eyes, a presence Jude recognized: Cross. From behind him, Sal muttered something that sounded like "Careful."

"Not at all. I was just thinking how nice it is when you've paid in advance." Jude told Legba then, how he'd found Leon Carter —making sure to emphasize that he knew Leon was High John de Conquer—bereft and abandoned and with his trumpet stolen, and how he'd traded away two hundred years of his life in order to get it back. He hoped that Renai wouldn't mind that he'd left her involvement out of it. But if she did, he had an idea how to make it up to her.

Papa Legba and Mait' Carrefour struggled, briefly, for dominance, but the old, benevolent side of the loa won and remained in control. His eyes crinkled up into a smile. "Then I owe you my thanks and consider the matter settled." He used a cane to lever himself to his feet and, frail though he appeared, moved quickly toward his Red Door.

"Forgetting something?"

Legba turned around, feigning surprise. Jude gestured at the markers left on the table.

Legba grinned again and popped himself on the forehead with the heel of his hand. "Curse this senile ol' head of mine," he said. "Forget it if it wasn't sewn on so tight." All pretense slid away from him. "What is your demand?"

"These two," Jude said, pointing to Sal and Renai. "Escort them back to the Thrones and plead their case on their behalf. Salvatore shouldn't be punished just because the heart he was sent to find happened to belong to an immortal, and Renai can't be held responsible for vouching for a Trickster. Surely the Thrones will listen to you."

Legba licked his lips, considering. "The psychopomp will be little trouble. But the girl, I fear, has been away from life too long to return to it. Nor would she fare as well against the scales, given her time in company such as yours."

Sal poked Renai in the shoulder with his beak. "Ow," she muttered, "what?"

"Tell him," he said, through gritted teeth that ravens didn't possess.

"Um . . ."

"Yes, child?"

"I've been thinking. I'm not sure I'm ready to try to move on after all. I might be good at what Sal does. Guiding dead souls, I mean." She grinned, far too full of mischief and beauty and goodness to be gone from this world. "I mean, if he can do it, how hard can it be?"

"I'm only part-time," Sal muttered from her shoulder.

"Next time you see Barren," Jude said, "let him know we're going to have a talk about what happens when Baron Criminel plays with pointy things."

Legba said nothing, merely smiled a grandfatherly smile, tipped his straw hat to Jude, and led the two psychopomps through his Red Door. On the way out, Sal turned back. "Be seeing you, Jude," he said. "It's been real." Then they were gone.

Hermes started talking as soon as Jude looked in his direction. "I'm merely here as an observer," he said, "as any arrangements you may have made with Thoth were rendered null and void at the moment of his untimely demise." His words were as precise as a lawyer giving closing remarks, his tone as slick as a used-car salesman working the lot. Jude imagined none of this "null and void" bullshit would have come into play if Hermes-slash-Thoth had won.

"Of course," Jude said, cutting off whatever the Greek Trickster was about to say next. "That makes perfect sense." Hermes touched his tongue to the corner of his mouth, the hint of a smile wavering around his lips. Jude couldn't tell if Hermes knew Jude had seen through his shtick, or if he thought he really was that good. Either way, he played along. "In fact, I ought to give you something for your trouble."

Jude picked up the revolver, though its touch, the sight of it, filled him with revulsion. The thing had ended a god, was nothing but an instrument of destruction. Hermes went very still but didn't flinch, didn't speak. Jude thumbed open the cylinder, dumped the remaining bullets onto the green felt of the poker table. He snapped the gun closed and slid it across the table to Hermes. "You're the god of travelers, right? And thieves? Take that on a trip with you. Take it far away, and then lock it away somewhere no thief can get it." Jude scooped up the bullets and dropped them into his satchel. "I'll hold on to these. Whatever you do, don't lose that gun. I never want to see that fucking thing again." Jude had a feeling that the next time he put his heart on the scales before the Thrones, having anything to do with that revolver would weigh pretty heavily against him.

Hermes picked up the gun with two fingers as if worried that its touch would soil him, too. He tipped a curt nod and faded from view, not bothering with the door, his smile the last thing to vanish.

Which left Jude alone with Dodge.

"Not bad, little one," Dodge said, "not bad at all. I ain't seen a cheat that ballsy in ages." Jude rolled the pearl against his cheek, grateful for the aid its magic had given his voice, the word for *burn* still on the tip of his tongue. Part of him was still waiting for everything to turn ugly, for Hē to return and rip open his throat — was still waiting for the moment he'd have to light the match and run like hell.

"How did you know?" Jude asked

"That you cheated?" Dodge shrugged and picked up the stump of his cigar. "It's what I'd have done. What everyone in the room was trying to do. What I can't figure is how you did it. Where in the name of Oberon's nutsack did you get enough power to change your own fate?"

"I didn't." Jude reached into his vest pocket and pulled out the card hidden there, the one that held his true fate. "I used up all my fortune twisting chance so none of you would notice when I traded this" — he held up the card Dodge had dealt him — "for the Joker I had hidden in my pocket." The one his mother had painted over with the image of Jude as the Fool.

"Ha!" Dodge laughed and laughed his smoker's wheezing rumble, tears coming to his eyes.

"I figured you'd all be looking for something big," Jude said, when the dead god had quieted enough to hear him. "So I went with something small."

Dodge, still chuckling, shook his head. "Ain't no such thing as a small magic," he said. He reached across the table and took the card he'd dealt him out of Jude's hand, turning it to show him: THE FOOL, exactly as his mother had painted it. The fate he'd created for himself.

"I don't understand," Jude said.

"The fuck you think magic is? It ain't always about calling down storms and bringing the dead back to life, Jude. It's about *tricks*. Changes in perception. You fooled a room full of fortune gods. What you call that, if not big magic?" He licked a thumb and rubbed the corner of Jude's card, swiping away some of the fresh paint. "What if it smeared?"

"Then I'd have been fucked," Jude said, and joined Dodge's laughter. It worked. It actually *worked*. He'd changed his fate. He tried not to think about what that fifth card might have been, otherwise. The relief was almost tangible, a warmth in his body as powerful as any magic.

Dodge tipped his glass back, draining it, and then his smile turned cold and hard. "You know we ain't done yet, right?"

"Yeah. I had a feeling." Dodge was, after all, as much a Trickster as anybody else in the room. Being dead didn't change that. The only thing separating Dodge from the others, apparently, was that Dodge hadn't underestimated Jude. "So what's your play?"

All illusions of coarseness or obtuseness smoothed away. "I can't move on if I'm still me." He tapped the FOOL card. "Ask me for this. Make your demand of me to make you what I am. Once you're the city's Luck, I can shed my skin like Thoth did and become something entirely new. It's a win-win for the both of us."

"What makes you think I'm not her Luck already?"

"In name only, chief. You got the stones for this gig, I'll give you that, but you ain't got the juice yet. Let me give it to you." He reached across the table, a harsh light emanating from his skin. "Just one touch," he said, "and my divinity is yours." To Jude's eyes, Dodge shone as brightly as Mourning—brighter. If the overly fortunate pricks he'd stolen luck from had been noon on a cloudless day, looking at Dodge now was like staring straight at the sun.

Jude's hand started to move before he caught himself. He stifled a grin.

Bastard almost got me, he thought. "And what else?" he asked.

Dodge quirked an eyebrow, but he kept his arm outstretched, his expression sincere.

"What else comes with your divinity is what I'm asking. How much of *you* comes along for the ride? Just your luck? Or will I have your thoughts and goals and impulses rattling around in the back of my head? Or is it like the loa and their priests, with you holding the reins and me as the horse?" Jude crossed his arms, watched as the mask of compassion Dodge wore splintered, replaced by an ugly, hungry smile. "You going to possess me, body and soul, like a vampire with a fresh corpse? If I take your hand, who walks out of that door, Dodge? Me or you?"

The room filled with the scents of a forest: pine and earth and a hint of rain. When Dodge spoke, his mouth was filled with the needle-sharp teeth of a fox. "Which door would that be?" he asked, his voice now tinged with a French accent.

Jude stood, pulling the satchel onto his shoulders as the doors began spinning around and around the room like a top and the walls turned into a candy-apple smear, as if the two fortune gods stood in the eye of a hurricane.

Dodge's room, Dodge's rules.

The dead fortune god shrank in front of him, his bulk melting away, leaving his face sunken, starvation thin. Tawny fur sprouted from his bald head, his cheeks, the backs of his hands. The room stopped spinning, and suddenly everywhere Jude looked—the walls, the floor, the ceiling—was made of identical red doors.

"I wish there was another way," Dodge said, "but you know as well as I do, death sucks. And I can't abide it any longer. I won't. If it helps, I promise you won't feel a thing."

If ever Jude needed his luck to hold, it was now.

"Tell you what. I've got something else I need to take care of. Let's just say you owe me one," Jude said, reaching out with his magic, *twisting* his luck, feeling for the one particular thread of one particular lost thing.

And found it.

"Don't get up. I'll show myself out." With that, Jude closed his eyes and reached behind him, for the doorknob his gift tugged him toward, the one where he heard, faintly, the sound of a trumpet being played.

From across the room came the scratching of claws against table felt, as Dodge rushed at him, realizing too late that Jude already knew the cardinal rule of being a Trickster. Jude flung open the door, filling Dodge's card room with the sultry, sticky, potent air of a New Orleans summer night, with the music of Leon Carter's trumpet. It was the sweetest sound he'd ever heard. Second only to the sound of the Red Door slamming shut for the last time, behind him.

He grinned at Leon—and Regal, who was standing beside him—and, knowing they wouldn't entirely understand and not caring, said, "Rule number one: Always leave yourself an out."

CHAPTER TWENTY-SIX

JUDE WAITED until the red faded away entirely from the maintenance entrance of Canal Place before turning his attention to Leon and Regal, the source of the music and the lost thing that had guided him home: his trumpet and her lost voice.

Sweat dripped from the musician's dreadlocks, and his shoulders sagged when he lowered the horn from his lips. He must have been playing for an hour straight, at least. They stood there in silence for a moment, musician and con man and sorceress, zombie and Trickster god and mortal, all of them standing at the crossroads, each living in the seam between one world and the next.

Don't you just love it when a plan comes together? Jude thought.

"Is it done?" Leon asked.

"Yeah," Jude said. "Just about."

"What's left?"

"What's left is this douche-canoe and I have an arrangement to settle," Regal said. "How 'bout it, Dubuisson? I'm here, as requested."

Suspicion crept across Leon's face, perhaps knowing who Regal had once worked for, certainly recognizing what building they were standing outside of. "What's she mean, Jude?"

"She means," Regal cut in, "that dick-nuts here called me up and promised that if I showed up to this spot and waited with you — you're awesome, by the way, big fan — that he'd give me what I most desired. So, you know" — she tapped her throat — "any time you're ready."

"Are you sure that's what you really want?" Jude asked.

She rolled her eyes. "This is unadulterated fuckery," she said. "I don't even know why I came."

"Because I'm charming as shit," Jude said, rolling the pearl around beneath his tongue. "But that's not the million-dollar question. We're trying to figure out what it is that you want most in this world. The goal you were willing to do anything to achieve. Remember?" He tapped his finger against his lips, realizing a moment too late whose gesture he was copying. "Oh yes, I know. Your birthright."

He looked into Regal's eyes, into Alafair Constant's eyes, and spoke through the pearl beneath his tongue: "You are the Magician of New Orleans."

A hot wind swirled around them, energetic, alive. It centered on Regal, tousling her clothes and her hair, spinning faster and faster, a hurricane's gale now, that roared and danced and lifted her feet, briefly, from the ground. It pulled tighter against her, a corkscrew of motion that no longer touched Jude or Leon, that vanished inside of her, only evident by the expression on her face that it twisted inside her still, an ever-winding coil of energy. Standing this close to her, Jude felt the presence of the power coursing through her like a physical thing, like the humming of a high-intensity wire.

She was silent for a moment, and Jude basked in it, relishing the anticipation of her reaction. When she spoke, it wasn't quite what he was expecting.

"That was such a dick move," she said.

Jude's face fell. "What?"

"The fuck good is the title without access to my *magic,* you . . . you . . . you *bastard?*"

"Hold that thought."

While Regal spluttered in surprise, Jude turned to Leon, suddenly realizing there was a complication in what he had to do next. The musician seemed content to just wait out whatever was going on, but when you were a zombie who hung out with voodoo gods, you must learn to take weird shit in stride. "Leon, you mind putting your trumpet away for this?"

He quirked an eyebrow but did as Jude asked. As soon as Leon bent over, looking away from him, Jude fished the pearl out from beneath his tongue and cleaned his spit off of it with a fold of his shirt. He braced himself for the loss of language to come, but nothing happened.

Must not have said anything she disagreed with, he thought.

When Leon finished closing the clasps of his case and stood, Jude took the zombie's hand and rolled the pearl into his palm. It glowed softly in the night. "Swallow it," he said.

"Dude, what the fuck," Regal said.

Leon hesitated.

"I'm serious," Jude said. "Trust me, Sweets."

The zombie slipped the pearl into his mouth and tossed his head back as though he were dry-swallowing a pill. Jude pressed his hand flat against Leon's chest and spoke the ancient word that meant *open.* He felt the pearl spread itself wide, like a flower blooming.

The changes were so gradual and subtle, Jude might have missed them if he weren't looking for them. Light flickered in the depths of Leon's eyes where before the cold impassivity of the dead lurked. A solidity hung in the air, as though Leon grew steadily heavier, more imbued with gravity. Vibrations shuddered through the ground at Jude's feet, through the wall behind him, through the air in his lungs and in the marrow of his bones, waves of energy with Leon at their center. The weight on his heart of New Orleans's loss lightened, eased. When it was gone entirely, Jude felt like he could breathe for the first time in years.

"What was that?" Leon asked, his voice infused with a depth, a resonance, beyond anything a human throat should be capable of. "What did you do to me?"

"What it was," Jude said, slipping his hands into his pockets and leaning against the concrete wall of Canal Place, "is what you are now. The Voice of New Orleans. Lost for far too long, but found at last."

"What does that mean?" Leon asked, nearly whispering, as though afraid of his own words.

Jude shrugged, scuffed one shoe with the toe of the other. "It means that New Orleans is alive again. She's got her Luck, and she has her Voice, and she's got her Will back, too. Well, mostly, but I'm getting to that. What it really means is up to you, Sweets. To all of us. You're the Voice of New Orleans now. You speak for her, and she speaks through you." He nodded at Regal. "Just like she's the Magician of New Orleans, who makes the city work for her and lets the city work through her."

Regal started to say something, but Jude answered the question he thought she was about to ask. "Me? I'm the city's Luck." Two pairs of eyes widened in shock, and Jude grinned and kept going. "Which is a wicked story that we don't really have time for right now." He bounced to his feet, pretended to look at a watch he wasn't wearing. "Hey, Queens, you know the medallion that gets you into Mourning's elevator? You got one on you?" Regal slipped it out of her pocket and held it up for him to see. "Mind if I borrow it?" he asked.

"Sure, no problem. Soon as you give me my magic back, fuckwit."

"Deal." One long stride closed the distance between them. Jude snapped the sunburst medallion out of her fingers with one hand, touched her at the hollow of her throat with the other, and whispered the word that meant *open,* restoring the part of her soul that was her voice, and with it, her magic, her ability to enact change in the world. He shot her a wink and turned toward the doors to Canal Place.

"This has been fun," he said. "We three should get together again soon. Really get to know each other." He watched their reflections in the window as they exchanged a combination of startled glances and shrugs that said that he'd managed to shock them, confuse them, and change their place in the world in a handful of moments. The Trickster in him—he was pretty much Trickster down to the bone now—was thrilled. "Gotta go clock in now, though," he said over his shoulder. "The new boss is a real ball-buster, I hear."

He whispered the door to Canal Place *open,* paused when Regal and Leon both said his name at the same time. He spun on his heel. "Yes?"

"You don't want some backup in there?" Regal said, with a nervous glance up in the general direction of Mourning's office.

"Yeah," Leon said, "he ain't no one to be triflin' with."

Jude knew how foolish he must appear to the both of them. How cocksure and very, very likely to die. But if he'd learned anything from watching the other fortune gods at the card game, it was that playing the role of Trickster didn't really work if you only went halfway. If you gave them even half a chance to call your bluff.

"Don't you worry about him," Jude said, patting the satchel hanging at his waist. "He and I are about to come to an understanding."

When Jude stepped into the waiting room, Scowl, the ram-horned secretary, glanced up from the papers on his desk and greeted Jude, for the very first time, with a smile.

"Come on in, Mr. Dubuisson, come on in. If you'll just take a seat, I'll see if he's ready for you."

Jude forced himself to lounge on the uncomfortable wooden bench Scowl gestured toward, hands clasped behind his head, legs stretched out in front of him, and tried to ignore a sinking feeling in his gut. He'd been expecting some form of retribution for the last time they'd met, but this? Was Scowl fucking with him? Everything but the secretary's demeanor was the same, the tidiness of the desk, the archaic rotary phone that he spoke into, even the fussy part of his hair. But the change in attitude was baffling.

Scowl replaced the receiver with a soft click and turned that unusual smile back to Jude, who noticed for the first time that the secretary's teeth were filed down to sharp points. "He will see you now," he said, waving a small hand toward Mourning's office.

Jude stood, unable to resist the parting shot that escaped his lips. "Glad to see that swift kick in the stones helped dislodge the stick in your ass," he said. He was nearly to the door when Scowl spoke again, saying only Jude's last name, all civility gone from his voice. Jude turned. Scowl stood on top of his desk, his hairy legs bent underneath him, a fist gripping his disproportionately huge cock.

"When he's done with you," Scowl said, thrusting his goat's hips, "I'm going to shit on or fuck whatever he leaves behind. Whichever is more unpleasant for you." Braying laughter followed Jude through the door.

Mourning waited behind his desk, shimmering like starlight in the darkened office, framed by the skyline of New Orleans. For the first time, Mourning's radiance wasn't overwhelming. Those sapphire eyes, though, were still far too bright. Far too knowing. Jude wondered if his eyes looked the same, now. He thrust his hands into his pockets and stood, calm enough to wait, to force Mourning to speak first. The bright god stared at Jude for a long moment, studying him.

"It seems you have me at a disadvantage, sir. I do not recall instigating this particular assignation and, thus, your presence is unanticipated. As my assistant has been so inappropriately remiss, might you be so inclined to redress this imbalance and grant me the pleasure of your name and a succinct summary of your situation?"

"This a joke?"

"Most assuredly not." The smile Mourning gave was meant to be disarming, but Jude had dealt with enough Tricksters that night to see right through it.

"Jude Dubuisson, Mourning. Talent for lost things? Tracking down a fortune god's murderer? None of this ringing any bells?"

"Ah, yes. Dubuisson. New Orleans. That business with the card game." Mourning flipped through a thick file that hadn't been there a moment before and clicked his tongue as he read. "As for my inability to recognize you at a glance, you must consider the scope of my influence." Without looking up, Mourning snapped his fingers. The skyline behind him changed in a camera flash, New Orleans becoming the brightly illuminated skyscrapers of Chicago. Another snap, another flash, and the city outside Mourning's window was San Francisco. Snap, Tokyo. Snap, Prague. Snap, Mumbai. Snap, Johannesburg. Snap, Algiers. Snap, Mexico City. A final time, and the skyline was New Orleans once more. "As illustrated, Mr. Dubuisson, my managerial interests are perhaps more global than you were aware. Do forgive me if I require a moment to distinguish your particular entanglements from my other enterprises." Mourning closed the file and steepled his fingers in front of his mouth. "Now, am I to presume that this unscheduled visit indicates that your conflicting engagements have been satisfactorily resolved?"

Jude dipped his head, a silent, grudging nod. This was the true game, the true contest, and he couldn't lay all his cards on the table. Not just yet.

A wry frown bent the corner of Mourning's lips, a gesture so unusual that Jude thought it might be genuine. "How laconic of you," he said. "How terse. Might I request some measure of elab-

346 • BRYAN CAMP

oration, if only to secure my own intense curiosity? I assure you, you currently have the full thrust of my not inconsiderable attention."

"The fallen angel Hē murdered Dodge Renaud, and others, in an attempt to find and consume the lost Voice of New Orleans. I stopped those plans. Made an end of the angel."

"How fascinating. And how menacing. You say you managed to slay this creature?" Mourning glanced down at his desk, tracing his finger in a circle along the glass. "You needn't have exerted yourself further by presenting yourself immediately. A night's respite is the smallest balm you should grant yourself after such an ordeal. Let us preclude more intricate elaboration of your imminent duties until the morrow, yes?"

"No."

A flash of anger ran across Mourning's face, so quick, so intense, that Jude almost believed he'd imagined it. "Beg pardon?"

"I said no. Let's get this over with."

Mourning said nothing, but if the expression on his face wasn't yet another mask, Jude had actually managed to surprise him. Another first. "Very well, then," Mourning said, smoothing out an imaginary wrinkle on his bleach-white tie. "By all means. You are, of your own accord, obligated to me for a period of service of no less than two hundred years, beginning" — he turned his wrist to look at the face of his watch, waiting for a specific moment — "now. Do you concur?"

"That was the agreement."

When Mourning looked up from his watch, Jude thought he might be truly seeing the blue-eyed god for the first time. There was a hunger in the curl of his lips, something cunning in the slant of his eyebrows, in the way he leaned back into his chair. "Now, then. As I am once again the director of your actions, I should very much like to divest you of some of the more — ah, shall we say — demanding responsibilities that have come into your possession of late." His gently mocking tone vanished, the mask sliding completely away to reveal something old and hard and dark. "Give me the Voice of New Orleans."

"I can't do that," Jude said.

Mourning went very silent and very still. He stood, his hands balled into fists, knuckles pressed to the surface of his desk. When Mourning spoke, his voice was as cold and sharp as a blade. "Can't? *Can't?* You find yourself in the fortuitous position of not needing to concern your conscience with questions of can and cannot, should or should not. There is simply that which you *do*, which, at further benefit to you, is simply what I *tell* you to do. Give me the Voice. Now."

"I gave it away," Jude said.

A jagged crack snaked its way across the glass of the desk. Mourning's tongue flicked out and ran along the pristine whiteness of his teeth. Jude could see a burning aura burst around the bright god, knew his rage before he smelled the burnt cloves stink of it. Mourning stood and clasped his arms behind his back. "You. Gave. It. Away."

"Yeah," Jude said.

"And the subsequent right to proclaim the next avatar of luck for this city? Did you so generously donate that to the common welfare as well?" Though Mourning stood on the other side of the room, Jude could feel the waves of heat coming off of him, the pulsing, tangible presence of a bonfire.

"Not exactly."

"What, exactly, did you do?"

"I named myself."

Mourning released a sharp bark of a laugh, though it contained no humor. "Of course you did. How else could you have managed to survive that particular tangle of fortune? I must admit, I did not anticipate such an expedient resolution of so convoluted a situation. I'm impressed, truly." Mourning spread his hands wide, as though welcoming Jude in for an embrace. "However, you needn't tax yourself further. You have neither the discernment nor the capability to sustain that role. Likewise, there is no need to strain your powers of deliberation in determining a suitable successor. The decision has been resolved on your behalf. Transfer the mantle to me."

"Sorry, but no."

The air around Mourning began to waver, the space between his fingertips crackling and sparking. "You will explain yourself. You will choose your words very carefully." He leaned his fists against his desk again, a jungle cat preparing to pounce.

Jude managed to keep his hands in his pockets and his voice relaxed by summoning every ounce of courage and every scrap of luck he possessed—his own luck now, the last of his stolen good fortune used up in Dodge's card room—even though his heart pounded and his balls shrank. His last shred of humanity—his fear—screamed at him to flee, but he ignored it, and it quickly died. He wasn't a human, not even a demigod. Not anymore. He was Trickster.

And Trickster lived for this shit.

"I swore to work for you," Jude said. "I agreed to be 'engaged in your service.' But I never said I'd be obedient. I never promised to be prompt or disciplined. You gave me a task that I have chosen to respectfully decline. If you ask again, I'll tell you to go fuck yourself. I swore to work for you, but being a good employee was never part of the agreement. If you don't like my performance so far—" Jude shrugged, unable to stop the grin from spreading across his face. "Fire me."

Mourning's desk shattered into a cloud of glittering sand, which was caught on a wind that swept through the office and whirled around the two of them. Like thousands of tiny blades, the sandstorm of glass cut and gouged, devouring the armchair Jude usually sat in, scouring a round groove in the marble floor. The stone beneath Mourning's feet cracked and buckled, his perfect, chiseled features cracking as well, betraying his emotions at last, revealing his rage. "Mr. Dubuisson," Mourning said, his sibilants coming out as a hiss, "you do not know who you are fucking with."

Jude took as deep a breath as he could with the wind screaming hot and furious around him. He struck out, over and over with his gift, *twisting* the moment with the last dregs of his own luck to keep Mourning's maelstrom of wind and glass at bay. If he failed, even once, it would tear him to shreds. Despite all of this, Jude stood his ground and spoke the simple, deadly truth. "Wrong on both counts, Mourning. Jude Dubuisson died. I'm someone else now. Someone new. And I know exactly who you are. You're Quetzal-coatl, the Feathered Serpent. You're Loki, god of fire and deceit. Typhon, Serpent of the Abyss. You're Raven, the bright-plumed bird who stole fire from Heaven. S. Mourning: the Star of the Morning, First of the Fallen. Lucifer."

Black wings arched from Mourning's back, proud, strong wings shimmering with the rainbow iridescence of an oil slick, shivering and then striking against one another like a thunderclap.

For a brief instant, Jude regretted that he hadn't asked Leon and Regal to come with him. They couldn't have helped, but it would have been nice to have an audience for this. Even the powers of an entire city were no match for this. Jude had just one chance, one power that might conceivably stop a god as old and as mighty as Mourning.

"I stand corrected," Mourning said, his voice cutting easily through the keening wind. "You know me well. And yet, with all this knowledge, you choose to enter my domain and challenge my authority? What weapon, I wonder, could you have stumbled across to make you so brazen? What blade, what fang, do you believe could threaten me?"

Jude reached into his satchel and pulled free the thunderbolt, felt it come alive in his hand. "Recognize this?" The whirlwind tearing around the office died, a glitter of glass falling, tinkling, to the marble floor. "The thunderbolt that cast you out of Heaven?

That drove you from the slopes of Mount Olympus? Wanna see if third time's the charm?"

Holding the thunderbolt felt, Jude decided, exactly how he'd imagined gripping a lightning strike by the balls would feel. It crackled and burned and roared, filling him with a terrible strength but constantly twisting and writhing in his fist as though it wanted to strike him instead. If Jude tried to wield it, it might very well kill him. If he unleashed it here, unrestrained, it could take out half of the French Quarter along with Mourning. He needed to walk the middle path between too timid and too reckless. It was the only way.

Mourning's laughter hissed like a serpent's scales winding through dry grass, like a whetstone sliding against a knife. "You lash out at me, at *me*, with a weapon that has already failed twice?"

But his laugh and his words were hollow. A bluff.

"Never said it was a weapon," Jude said. He gave the bright god his best fuck-you grin, and Mourning blinked, *flinched* even, because Mourning knew the same truth about the thunderbolt that Jude did.

It wasn't a weapon; it was a key.

Jude thrust the thunderbolt forward, spoke the word that meant *open,* and let the power he'd kept hidden away in his satchel serve its purpose at last: to punch a hole through the fabric of the world. Jude had expected wind and noise and fire, but a terrible silence came through from the other side of the door he'd opened, a profound and dreadful gravity. Everything in Mourning's office leaned toward the opening now, a subtle shift in the angles and seams, turning the space around them into a funnel.

The world on the other side of that door was filled with beige modular cubicles, always a Wednesday afternoon three hours before the end of the day, with a stack of reports on the viability of forming an action committee to research the findings of a previous committee's decision to produce more detailed, hourly reports on the decisions of action committees that had to be scanned for errors that were never there, typed into a computer that could only access the company filing system, surrounded by the murmur of a thousand other employees in gray suits with gray ties, whose low voices spoke only to repeat the findings they had read in their reports.

Or it was a waiting room—DMV, doctor's office, you were never really sure—your ticket always ten numbers away, a woman on the phone next to you loudly recounting the minutiae of her day, a litany of mundane household tasks and petty disagreements that never had a point or a conclusion but were regaled with the excited tone of meeting a celebrity; "Hey Mickey" playing on the PA speakers over and over, the name of the band always on the tip of your tongue.

Or it was sitting in a car waiting for a train to pass, traffic on either side of you blocking you in, nothing but mindless matching games on your phone, nothing but overly aggressive car commercials on the radio, the graffiti on each train car always the same pointless squiggle, a train that stretched to the horizon in one direction and all the way to Pittsburgh in the other.

Or it was a weekday stuck on a living room sofa, the television only ever showing debt reduction commercials and law firm commercials and an episode of a soap opera you'd somehow already seen before.

It was never a prison cell, or a cage, or a trap. Nothing that would compel you to escape, no puzzle to engage your mind. It was simply unchanging. Relentlessly, perpetually boring.

Hell for Tricksters.

And it dragged at Jude and at Mourning and everything else in the office. Jude stood near the event horizon of its pull, was backing away step by agonizing step, but the bright god had dug his hands and feet into the marble floor right next to the door itself, was twisting and distorting as the world on the other side tugged at his very essence. Jude's mind whirled, unsure how he could loosen the bright god's grip without putting himself in danger. The thunderbolt still twitched and blazed in his hand, waiting for its final command. If the rift was open too much longer, it would begin to grow, could change the entirety of New Orleans into that beige sameness.

The door to the waiting room banged open and Scowl came rushing in, and Jude saw his chance. He reached out and seized Scowl's immediate future and, with the last of his strength, gave it one mean little *twist*.

Scowl's hooves skidded for purchase on the marble floor as he saw what he'd rushed into and tried to reverse direction too little, too late. The horned little man struck Mourning right in the face before he went falling into the rift the thunderbolt had opened. For an officious little prick like him, though, Trickster hell might feel like Heaven.

Mourning managed to catch himself on the lip of the rift, holding himself between one world and the other with incredible, implacable strength. Unbelievably, he looked at Jude and smiled. "Out of all my names, you left out the most important one."

He folded his wings, seemed to relax, to accept his fate.

Jude tried not to listen, certain that this had to be one last trick, one last attempt to save himself or drag Jude down with him. Instead, he thrust the thunderbolt forward once more.

At the same moment, each Trickster spoke just one word.

Jude said the word that meant *close*, sealing the door to the other side and shutting Mourning away inside its awful gravity and rendering the thunderbolt an inert rod of cold metal.

Mourning said, "Father."

PART SEVEN

EPILOGUE

IT IS CARNIVAL, the day of the Bacchus Parade, and for New Orleans, it's very cold out. This past August made seven years since the storm, but no one, least of all Jude, is thinking about hurricanes, or failing federal levees, or loss. It is Carnival, and all is right with the world. Joy is a palpable sensation running through the streets, a drunken elation that's lasted almost two weeks straight. Right now, it seems like the celebration might last forever.

Jude stands on the neutral ground Uptown, his breath misting in the air, surrounded by roaring, chanting crowds screaming into the night, thinking about the seams he's been stitching together, about all the work he's still got ahead of him. The impact of bass drums shakes his bones, sets his blood throbbing in time with the beat called out by the throaty growl of brass horns. The parade rolls by: the marching bands in their proud uniforms and crested helmets; the dance squads marching in step, their tap shoes clacking in unison on the asphalt; the flambeaux with their long torches spinning above their heads, fueled by the propane tanks strapped to their backs; the revelers walking the route, costumed throngs with drinks in hand and bags of beads slung over their arms; the huge, brightly colored floats, like royal barges tugged down the river of St. Charles Avenue by rumbling, oil-reeking tractors; the floats, flickering lights and blaring music and masked riders; the floats, depicting scenes from myth and legend and cultures ancient and modern; the floats, casting off masses of beads and stuffed animals and trinkets into the oak branches and the waiting arms of the crowds below, worthless save for the connection, the celebration, that they inspire.

Jude leans against his staff—a long, slender stave of oak—that holds some of the magic of Grand Bois, the loa Cross had sealed inside an oak back when Jude had fought the three of them in Audubon Park. Jude had siphoned some of Grand Bois's power as payment for releasing the loa from the prison of the oak tree, opening the way out that Cross had closed. Bois was not the first lost thing he found and made right in the months since he'd become the Luck of New Orleans, nor the last.

Sipping an Abita from a plastic cup, Jude watches the King's float roll by, some celebrity actor dressed in red and silver and white getting to pretend to be King for a day, even though Jude knows the city's been ruled by a Queen for the better part of a year.

Though Jude has come only to watch, he raises his arm and shouts at the float. The comedian King throws two fistfuls of doubloons, glittering and ringing against each other over the noise of the revelers, into the air above the crowd. Jude snags one out of the air and glances at it—stamped with the god of wine who gives the parade its name on one side, the actor's face on the other—grateful that it doesn't bear the image of his own heart. Beside him, a familiar voice says, "Nice catch."

"Just lucky," Jude says, without turning, playing it cool.

"You wanna get lucky?" Barren asks, suddenly all sweetness and enthusiasm. "Honey, all you had to do was ask."

Jude can't help himself then, grinning and glancing over. His shock at what he sees must show on his face, because it makes his visitors laugh. Barren has painted himself a metallic silver and inserted glowing red orbs into the sockets of his eyes, a perfect depiction of one of the killer robots from the *Terminator* movies. Renai is wearing a form-fitting blue jumpsuit with yellow numbers on her breast, a bulky technological contraption strapped to her wrist. Sal, in his dog's shape, is wearing a red bandanna and some kind of armored harness.

"I get Barren's costume," he says, "but what are you two supposed to be?"

"I'm a vault dweller," Renai says, excited until she sees that Jude still doesn't get the reference. "Don't tell me gods don't play video games. They love *Fallout* down in the Underworld."

"I just watch," Sal said, holding up a paw. "No thumbs."

Jude shrugs, snatches a handful of beads arcing overhead, and hands them to a passing child. "Funny running into y'all like this."

All three of them seemed to want to say something, but Barren spoke first. "Jude, we need to talk to you. You've been unusually hard to find."

"Yeah," Jude said. "I've been dodging your calls."

"Why?"

"Just fucking with you, I guess." Jude bobs his head to the beat of a passing marching band, the trumpets blowing loud and clear, ignoring the shock and then anger that rolls across Barren's skull-face. "You know how we Tricksters are," he says, when the young musicians move on.

Barren sighs. "This is important, Jude."

"It's Papa Legba," Renai says. Jude softens a little at the concern in her voice, which is, no doubt, why Barren brought her along. "He's losing control more and more lately. Cross has gotten stronger somehow."

Jude finishes his beer and throws the plastic cup into a nearby garbage barrel. He blows warm air, tinged with just a bit of flame, into the cupped bowl of his numb hands. He misses—for the first time since he lost them somewhere—his old leather gloves. "And? What would you like me to do about it?" Jude's stomach rumbles. One of the downsides of being a Trickster. He's always hungry, now.

"Your goddamn job, maybe," Sal grumbles.

Renai puts a calming hand on Sal's head. "You have to help him, Jude. He's your father."

Jude lets out a sharp bark of a laugh, unable to stop himself. "Sure he is. Sure. Mourning tried that one on me too, at the end. Bet if I had them in a corner, Dodge or the angel or Thoth or even the vampire would claim to be dear ol' dad if they thought it would jam me up. Thing is, I don't care who my father is, not anymore. I know who I am." He waves a hand at them, stilling the arguments rising to all three of their tongues. "I tell you what, I'll look into it. For old time's sake. Because of all the shit we went through." He looks out over the crowd, the laughing, screaming mass of happiness that was Carnival, and smiles. "You ask me though, I'd put my money on Mourning. These days? Only the son of the devil could be such a busy man."

Renai, at least, gets the reference, but before she can say anything, Jude is already gone.

Jude enters what had once been Mourning's waiting room without bothering with the elevator. His satchel, his bag of tricks, slaps at his side as he moves behind the desk, to where the diminutive secretary's sad, wilting potted plant is all that remains of the imp. Jude taps it with the end of his staff, reaches out with his Trickster magic, and *changes*, letting his portion of Grand Bois's essence slip from the oak of his stave into the . . . whatever kind of tiny tree this is. The new little life stretches and preens, not yet fully conscious, but growing.

Management has been complaining about needing a receptionist for weeks, now.

Jude steps through into what was once Mourning's office, its only brightness the sunlight shining in through the huge window that takes up the back wall. Everything that made this Mourning's place got sucked into the void with him, except for the checkerboard marble floor, and that has now been largely covered up by the warm reds and oranges and browns of a huge Persian rug. A new desk stands where Mourning's once did—an edifice of mahogany, covered with papers and books and the various tools of the magician's trade. At the very edge, a nameplate in black and white reads R. CONSTANT, MANAGEMENT. The door, as it always has, disappears behind him when he walks through it.

She has her back to him, staring out over the New Orleans skyline, dressed in a woolen gray business suit, a scarlet belt around her waist. Regal Sloan—Constant, now—his best friend and partner in a world he'd tried, and failed, to leave behind. "So tell me," she says over her shoulder, "what kind of an ass-clown works during Carnival?"

Jude grins and crosses the room to stand beside her. "The kind that would be friends with a backstabbing, foulmouthed—"

"Okay, okay, I get it. What's new?"

"Voodoo folks are getting nervous about Legba. Something is pissing him off but good. And you don't want Legba angry. You—"

"Wouldn't like him when he's angry, I know. I'll get into it. And you got another request for a sit-down from the dhampir that Scarpelli sent to us. He's requesting that you reconsider your position."

"The hell would I do that?"

"A couple of dozen people vanished from the city along with Scarpelli when you banished him. Not nobodies either; some real movers and shakers. You'd be surprised how many bankers and real estate developers—"

"Are vampires? No, I really wouldn't." He sighs. "I'll sit and listen, if he buys me dinner. Food, not blood."

She chuckles, and they share a companionable silence. There's still a tension between them, Jude knows—betrayal and suspicion and jealousy and loss don't just go away overnight, but they're working through it. They won't be the same as they were before, just like the city can never again be what it was. But they're alive, and they're together, and they're doing their best, and to him, that's about all anyone can ask.

"I should be going," he says. "Check the front when I go; I left you a little present."

Regal nods, and then thinks of something. "Oh, right, the door," she says, realizing the far wall of the office was still solid. "Let me get that for you. You know Mourning controlled this thing the whole time? Just made it seem random?"

"He was good at that," Jude says. "But don't worry about the door." He leans out, through the window that just a second before had held a giant pane of glass, and would again once he was gone, stepping out into empty space, as if off the edge of a cliff.

"I make my own path now."

Later, in the short walk off the parade route to the house he lived in before the storm, Jude thinks about all the gods that have claimed to be his father, and in a way, it makes perfect sense. Every Trickster is a little bit of a bastard.

Jude can sense the loss surrounding him even now: a young woman gleefully losing her virginity in the back room of her parents' house; an old man losing the memory of his childhood home; a child losing his innocence, as he sees his father lying to his mother about another woman. He can see the glow of good fortune and the twists of bad luck awaiting everyone he meets.

But he can feel other things now, too, mysterious and potent and beautiful. Presences that are newly born. Nascent gods of drink and revelry, of lust and danger, gods of Carnival and Mardi Gras Indians and crawfish boils, of jazz bands and second lines, the minor pantheon of the reborn New Orleans. Others are older gods with new faces and new names, crab-shaped or pelican-headed, formed of Carnival floats and magnolia trees and Uptown mansions — gods of other lands and other times, shifting forms and acclimating to their new home, as Dodge had, and Barren. A few kept their old names, ancient, protean river gods and entrancing voodoo loa, all mingling and living with relative harmony. Within them all, Jude can feel a piece of Leon Carter, of his magic, his music, giving voice to New Orleans and her song — sugary, dark, and seductive as a good rum.

Jude thinks of all of this and holds all of it in his heart, this secret world that is his to protect, to make better. He lifts his fingers to the *X* spray-painted on the door, the symbol of all that was lost in the storm, all that still searches for a place to belong. He opens himself to his magic, to the possibility of change, to the hope that that which has been lost might be found.

He accepts it all.

In the end, the World Tree Yggdrasil will burn, and a giant wolf will eat the sun and the moon. Or seven seals will be broken, seven trumpets will sound, and a great Beast will have dominion over the Earth. Or the Fifth Sun will turn black, and the ravenous women who are the stars will descend upon the Earth to devour mankind. Or a great deluge will drown the world, leaving only an immense and empty ocean. Or Apep will succeed in his attempts to overcome the principle of ma'at, and the world will devolve into chaos. Or the Earth will start to shake and never cease, tearing great rents in the surface, casting man into the depths. Or a plague, or a great war, or a famine, or a horde of the undead will cover the planet, destroying mankind. Or a giant rock will fall from the sky and a cloud of ash will blot out the sun. Or the universe will cease its growth and begin shrinking, falling in on itself, tightening into a single, lifeless dot. Or the walls that were built to hold back the waters will break, and the deluge will rush into—and drown—streets and homes and lives.

In the end—and there is always an end—there will be those who are lost and those who mourn.

And yet. There are always those who refuse to let the end be the end. The man and the woman who cling to the highest branches of the World Tree and escape the flames, who return and rebuild a new world out of the one that burned to ash. Or the man, who goes by many names, who builds a massive vessel and rides on the waves of the great ocean until the flood has passed. Or the one who will sacrifice himself upon the bonfire and becomes the next Sun, dying so that the world might live. Or there are the faithful who live forever after evil has been cast into oblivion, the vigilant who survive the plague or the war and who create a world where such things do not happen. There are those who are lucky enough to return to their homes after the storm and the flood has passed, to rebuild, to remember. There is magic in all things, in songs and in fire, in the night sky and in the storm on the horizon, in voices raised high and secrets hidden deep, in stories and in change and in hope.

There is magic in beginnings, this is true, but there is also magic —such great and beautiful and powerful magic—in refusing to let something end.

This is not the book I set out to write. The ingredients are the same: New Orleans and syncretic myths and Tricksters and a murder mystery; and the seed crystal—that scene of a poker game full of gods—remains largely the same as when I first wrote it as a writing exercise in Bev Marshall's undergraduate fiction class at Southeastern. The novel it became, though, is profoundly different than the one I first envisioned.

After the writing exercise, our assignment was to turn our scene into a short story. I knew, even as I started writing it, that this thing growing inside me was novel-sized, but I believed I could put together something short story–shaped that I could build on later. I had a weekend to write it. My family and I had to stay with my aunt in Florida for a few days, so I brought my laptop with me, a clunky old Dell that overheated and died every few hours.

I began that other novel—the one that this one isn't—hunched over that overheating beast in the back seat of my parents' car on August 28, 2005 . . . a day before the federal levees failed and destroyed the city I was writing about.

Not that I really knew *that* New Orleans. Growing up on the other side of Lake Pontchartrain, across from the city, New Orleans was close enough to visit, but far enough away to still be something of a mystery. It was Oz, glimmering on the horizon. Just as fantastic, just as fictional, just as much a symbol of hope.

And from the safety of a living room in Florida, I watched it drown.

The thing you have to understand, if you've never lived along the Gulf of Mexico, is that this kind of thing didn't happen. You planned for it, you prepared for it—but no one ever really *believed* it could happen. My entire life, evacuations were weekends away from home.

Not months.

Not lifetimes.

There's far more to the story of this book, of course: years of writing and rewriting, the guidance of my MFA committee— Amanda Boyden, Joseph Boyden, and Jim Grimsley—the lessons I learned at Clarion West, a decade of living *in* (not simply *near* this great city), but truthfully, the biggest change occurred in those days and nights right after the storm. Watching the news, cut off from just about everyone I knew, feeling guilty and sad and fortunate all at once. My family escaped and had a home to return to, while far too many others did not.

If Jude and I share anything, it's an overabundance of good luck.

This isn't the book I set out to write. It'll never make up for the lives and the houses and the futures that were lost; no book could. Nor is this a requiem for the Oz that was gone before it ever existed. I'm certainly no authority on New Orleans, and wouldn't dare to speak for those who survived the storm itself. Those are not my stories to tell.

If my luck holds, though, this book might be worthy of my New Orleans, the home I've come to love.

ACKNOWLEDGMENTS

I have much to be grateful for, and the following is an incomplete list of those to whom I owe unrepayable debts of gratitude:

To my editor, John Joseph Adams, for his brilliant, enthusiastic guidance. Turning a manuscript into a novel is a lot of hard work, and John makes it look easy.

To my copy editor, Erin DeWitt, my cover artist, Will Staehle, and to Tim Mudie, Bruce Nichols, Hannah Harlow, Erika West, Larry Cooper, David Futato, and everyone else at HMH, for managing the magic trick of turning a bunch of words in a .doc file into a work of art.

To my agent, Seth Fishman, for taking a chance on me even after I vanished for a year's worth of revision.

To his assistant, Jack Gernert, for coming up with the title. To Will Roberts, Rebecca Gardner, Ellen Coughtrey, and everyone else at Gernert, for supporting and guiding this debut author through the gauntlet of modern publishing.

To Michelle and Bryan Camp Sr., for life, for the gifts of my youth, for the lessons of my adulthood. To Rose Camp, to Bryndon Camp, to Bryttany and Keith Wogan, for helping me become the man that I am. To Gerri and Ed Merida, to Abigail and Michael Labit, for welcoming a book nerd into your home, into your family.

To Becky Merida, for hugging the Hulk out whenever I need it.

To Hal Harries, for teaching me compassion.

To my writing teachers: Bev Marshall, who was the first to tell me my writing had potential; to my MFA thesis committee: Amanda Boyden, Joseph Boyden, and Jim Grimsley, who were the first to hold my writing to professional standards; to my Clarion West instructors: Mary Rosenblum, Stephen Graham Jones, Connie Willis, George R. R. Martin, Gavin Grant, Kelly Link, and Chuck Palahniuk, who are the luminaries I strive to emulate.

To my life teachers, otherwise known as friends: Les Howle, Neile Graham, Tracie Tate, Greg Herren, Nick Mainieri, Henry Griffin, Bill Lavender, Nancy Dixon, Candice Huber, Casey Lefante, Wayne Rupp, Niko Tesvich, Bill Loefehlm, Tawni Waters, Lish McBride, Alex Jennings, Alys Arden, and everyone in the UNO MFA program and the New Orleans literary community. Even something as wonderful as publishing a first novel would be a hollow accomplishment without great friends to share it with.

To the seventeen magical beings who are friends and family and inspiration all at once: Alyc Helms, Blythe Woolston, Brenta Blevins, Carlie St. George, Cory Skerry, Georgina Kamsika, Greg Friis West, Helen Marshall, Henry Lien, Indrapramit Das, James Harper, James Herndon, Kim Neville, Laura Friis West, Huw Evans, Nick Houser, and Sarah Brooks. To the Clarion West class of 2012, I don't think I could have done this without all of you, and I'm sure glad you're all in my life.

To Michael Thomas, you've earned my gratitude in many different ways over the years: roommate, best friend, best man, first reader. It's been just shy of twenty years of conversations, commiseration, dreaming up big projects, and inappropriate humor. Another twenty won't be nearly enough.

Finally and most importantly, to my lovely and loving wife, Beth Anne. The accomplishments I'm most proud of—the MFA, Clarion West, this book—I've done because the man, the husband, the writer who could do them, that's the one that you deserve. I haven't yet found the words to thank you for all that you do and for all that you are, but I promise to keep trying for as long as there's breath in me.